Dragonfly Ashes

Editing by Deb Hall at TheWriteInsight.com.

OTHER WORKS BY C.C. WARRENS

Holly Novels

Criss Cross

Winter Memorial (A Short Story)

Cross Fire

Crossed Off

Cross the Line

Crossroads

Seeking Justice Novels

Injustice for All

Holly Jolly Christmas

Imperfect Justice

Cherry Creek Mysteries

Firefly Diaries

Dragonfly Ashes

Mysteries, Mischief, and Marshmallows

Beneath the Watcher Tree

Secrets in the Attic

A special thank-you to my local fire department for answering my many questions. Any details that don't perfectly line up with procedure are due to creative license.

Thank you to my proofreaders, Elizabeth Olmedo and Erin Laramore, for helping catch those pesky errors that manage to survive the editing process with the sneaky resilience of cockroaches.

Dragonfly Ashes

This book is lovingly dedicated to:

Glenda Hofacre
The math teacher every kid deserves.

Hofie, you were a bright spot in the black hole of decimals and fractions. Patient, kind-hearted, and fun. Thank you for being you, and thank you for all the pencils you lent me in class. I was so bad at math that my pencils ran out of eraser before they ran out of graphite. That was by no means a result of your teaching ability. My brain simply wasn't hardwired for math; it was hardwired for stories.

You left this world the day this book published, so I'm glad I had a chance to tell you beforehand that I named a character after you. You are loved and remembered,

Hofie 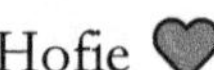

CHAPTER *One*

A shrill sound pierced the night, sweeping through the house like the unearthly wail of a banshee.

Noelle snapped upright in bed, heart in her throat, and stared into the shifting shadows of her bedroom. It took her sleep-muddled mind a moment to process the sound that had cut through the rattle of loose windowpanes and creaking boards.

A child's scream.

Tay, her son. He must've had a bad dream or—

Reality punched into her thoughts, sending fresh grief throbbing through her. No, it hadn't been Tay's cry. Her baby boy was gone, killed in a car accident more than a year and a half ago. That meant . . .

"Skyler," escaped beneath her breath.

She flung aside the blankets and leaped from bed, the coldness of the floorboards beneath her bare feet sending a shiver from her toes to the base of her neck. But there was no time to find her robe and slippers.

No time—because something was gravely wrong.

Skyler was the eleven-year-old girl she'd adopted, and in the months she'd lived with Noelle, she had never screamed like that. Not even when she had nightmares about the murder of her mother.

Noelle shoved her glasses on her face, but they did nothing to help her see the pile of clothes she'd stripped out of in a sleepy daze last night. She tripped, knocking a stack of books to the floor as she clutched at the nightstand for balance, and then staggered out of the bedroom.

"I'm coming, sweetheart!"

Fractured moonlight poured through the foyer windows below, lighting the staircase as Noelle hurried down it.

As her foot landed on the last step, the closet door in the foyer yawned open with a spine-tingling creak. She froze, one hand gripping the railing, and visually scanned the darkness for movement.

"Walt?"

The former resident, an old man who haunted the property like a ghost, hadn't been inside when she locked up for the night. No one but Noelle and Skyler had been in the house.

It's just the crooked foundation, Noelle told herself. It was hardly the first time a door had popped open unexpectedly in this house. They opened and closed at odd hours on their own. If she believed in ghosts, she would wonder if the house was haunted.

Four people had been murdered here over the years, three of those deaths so savage that Noelle had to rip the blood-stained wallpaper off the walls and paint over the spatter on the ceiling.

Death was in the bones of this house.

There's no such thing as ghosts, she reminded herself, refusing to let the superstitious whisperings of the village residents infect her thinking.

Still, goose bumps crawled along her skin as she turned her back on the open closet and rushed down the hall to Skyler's room.

She came nose to nose with the colorful firefly drawing taped to the bedroom door that read "Firefly's Palace." Cold air seeped beneath and around the unlatched door, whispering across her toes.

No.

She thrust open the door.

Her gaze landed on the empty bed and then bounced to the open window, the sheer curtains fluttering in the icy breeze. She gripped the door frame as the world seemed to tilt around her.

That window was supposed to be shut, with a hunk of wood jammed diagonally over the top pane to reinforce the flimsy lock.

"Skyler?" Noelle rushed forward, stepping over the hunk of wood on the floor, and bent down to peer through the screenless opening.

The moonlight that had lit her path down the staircase had slipped behind the clouds. Everything beyond the edge of the wraparound porch was doused in darkness, as if she could step off the edge into nothingness.

Had Skyler crawled out the window?

No, she wouldn't do that.

But she must've done that, because the alternative was terrifying. Not everyone from Skyler's dark past had been apprehended by the police. The leader of the crime ring had disappeared, and who knew how many others had slipped through the legal cracks?

God, if they took her, I'll never see her again. That world will swallow her up, and she'll be . . .

"Don't go there," she said aloud, cutting off her spiraling thoughts before they could thrust her into a panic she couldn't pull herself out of.

It had been months since the crime ring was fully disbanded. If someone wanted to come after Skyler, surely they would've done it by now.

Noelle closed the window and relocked it before turning back toward the bedroom, clutching desperately at the hope that Skyler was still here.

"Sweetheart, if you're hiding, I need you to call out, okay?"

She listened for the faintest shuffle or whimper, but the only sound was the squeak of the metal wheel in the mouse cage on top of the dresser. Ben and Jerry were running a marathon.

As she stared at the mice, a distant memory drifted through her mind: *Quiet as a mouse with a cat in the house.* That was the motto Skyler had lived by before coming to stay with Noelle—the motto her mother had taught her for her own protection. If someone dangerous was nearby, she would make herself as silent and invisible as a mouse.

The nook!

Noelle slipped back into the hall, scrutinizing every shadow. Anyone could've crawled through the bedroom window into the house. The village of Cherry Creek might be quaint, but it wasn't exempt from crime.

She flipped on the kitchen light and opened the door to the storage closet. The small space was empty but for a few jackets and pairs of rain boots. She wrapped a finger around the coat hook on the rear wall and tugged. It didn't move.

Thank you, Jesus.

The door masquerading as a closet wall had been locked from the inside, securing its occupant in one of the house's many hidden spaces. Courtesy of the paranoid man who built the house in the 1800s.

Noelle sank to her knees and pressed a hand to the paneled wall. "Skyler, honey, it's Noelle."

Silence stretched.

Noelle tried again, using the nickname Skyler's biological mother had given her. "Firefly?"

A frightened voice whispered through the wall. "Shh, we have to be quiet. There's a monster outside."

The hairs on the back of Noelle's neck lifted, and she twisted to see the window above the sink. The glass reflected the kitchen's interior, blinding her to anyone or anything outside. What exactly did Skyler mean by "monster"?

"Are you sure it's not Mr. Walt?"

"I thought it was him, so I opened my window to say hi, but then it wasn't him. It was a scary face," Skyler said, struggling to pronounce her *R*s.

Something thumped outside, and Noelle's spine snapped straight in alarm. She should've grabbed her loaded revolver from the safe in her room—or at the very least her phone on the nightstand—but it was too late now. If someone was here to hurt them, she would have to defend them with whatever she could find.

She reached out of the closet and switched off the kitchen light, making it harder for an intruder to see inside. "You stay right here while I go make sure everything is safe."

"No!" Skyler's desperate plea froze Noelle in place. "If you go outside, the monster will get you, and I'll be all alone again."

Pain pierced Noelle's heart. "You won't be alone, sweetheart. Never again. There are too many people who love you to ever let that happen. And I'm coming back after I make sure it's safe."

Skyler's tearful reply came a moment later. "Promise?"

"I promise. Keep the door locked and stay quiet." Noelle crept over to the counter and unsheathed a knife from the butcher block.

At the unmistakable thud and scrape of boots across the porch, she dropped low against the bottom cupboards, out of view of the window, and squeezed the knife between her knees to keep it from trembling.

CHAPTER Two

The knob rattled so hard Noelle could feel it in her bones, but the door remained shut. She eyed the two locks she'd installed after the last break-in.

There was still a dent in the plaster from where the force of the man's kick had slammed the door into the wall.

A series of violent thumps made her muscles twitch, and her gaze swung in the direction of the living room. If she could make it back down the hall before he kicked in the door, she might be able to reach the landline.

"Open up!"

The bellow cut through her fear as the voice, reminiscent of gravel in a wood chipper, registered as *familiar* and *safe* in the back of her mind.

Gripping the edge of the counter, Noelle pulled herself up and released the series of locks to open the door.

Walter Bechtel stood on the porch. Scarcely more than skin and bones, with a straw hat and a brown coat, and a rifle slung over one shoulder, he was every bit the scarecrow rumored to haunt these grounds.

"I heard a scream," he said.

Noelle set the butcher knife on the counter beside her and folded her arms against the cold air whipping through her thin T-shirt and sweatpants. "You heard it from your camper?"

"Pine trees out front."

Frustration nipped at her already frazzled nerves. Walt's camper was in a clearing on the other side of the woods, beyond the edge of her property. Unfortunately, he couldn't seem to break the habit of sitting outside and watching over the property that once belonged to his family. "We talked about this, Walt. It's not healthy for you to—"

"Where's Sky?"

Noelle bit the inside of her cheek as she clamped her teeth together. The lecture would fall on deaf ears anyway. She gestured to the storage closet Skyler had nicknamed the nook. "She said she saw a monster outside her window."

Walt's wrinkles folded into a frown. "I didn't see anyone. Must've come through the back woods."

Noelle looked past him, searching the blackness where the yard met the trees. There was an alternate explanation for why neither she nor Walt had seen this "monster."

Skyler's mother had been murdered in this house by a very human monster last October. It would only be reasonable for her to have nightmares.

"Did he get inside?" Walt demanded.

"Sky's window was open, but I haven't had a chance to check if—"

"I'll do it." He brushed past her, tracking mud across the linoleum with every stomp of his boots.

Noelle's eyes rolled heavenward, but by some miracle, she kept the bite of irritation from her tone. "Search away. And then maybe, instead of freezing outside, you could sleep in the room we set up for you." She shut the door and muttered beneath her breath, "Like a normal person."

Except the man was anything but normal.

"I'm fine outside," he grumbled, his skeletal frame disappearing down one of the two hallways.

Noelle sagged against the counter with a sigh. She never imagined when she purchased this fixer-upper through an auction that one of the previous residents would come with it.

It was like having a night watchman, a perpetually grouchy neighbor, and a relative who overstayed his welcome all rolled into one. He had watching posts hidden all throughout the property so he could monitor who came and went.

Though his habit of spying on the house from the shadows occasionally creeped her out, she understood his reasoning. This house was all that remained to connect him with his family, and he wanted to protect it as well as the little girl who had managed to thaw his frosty heart.

As floorboards creaked and doors opened and closed throughout the house, Noelle funneled her anxious energy into one of the few activities that calmed her nerves—brewing tea. She could open a tea shop with all the flavors she had stuffed in the cupboard.

The old man stalked back into the room fifteen minutes later, his expression sour as ever. "Nobody in the house."

Noelle suspected as much, but his confirmation soothed some of her nerves. "Thank you for checking."

"I saw you turned my grandfather's room into a cluttered mess."

"That cluttered mess would be my writing room."

"He would've approved. He liked books."

Noelle felt her eyebrows inch upward. That might be the closest he had ever come to saying something kind to her.

"I'm going to check the property," he said.

"If you find someone, ask questions first." Noelle nodded pointedly to his rifle. "Halloween is around the corner, and we've already had kids snooping around the property."

Although the house had been occupied for a year, the story surrounding it made it a magnet for the bored and curious youth of Cherry Creek. It was a testament to their courage if they could sneak into the haunted house and escape with a trophy.

"I know what I'm doing. I've been keeping troublemakers away from my family's house for decades. Never put anybody in the hospital or the ground. I don't need your advice," Walt snapped.

"You're crankier than usual tonight. Did you miss dinner?" He generally walked to the local diner for a free meal in the evenings, but it was several miles.

"That's nobody's business but mine."

That would be a yes then. She grabbed a muffin from the refrigerator and handed it to him. "At least have a muffin."

He gave the pastry a sniff and grimaced. "This is one of them gritty muffins with seeds and roots in it."

"Also known as whole grains."

He stared at it, deciding whether or not he wanted it, then asked, "Got any more honey?"

Noelle handed him the squirt bottle shaped like a bear. "Enjoy."

"I won't. But I'll eat it so I don't hurt your womanly feelings." He stuffed the items into a pocket of his filthy coat. "Tell Sky I'll keep watch. She don't need to worry about monsters."

She closed the door and locked it after he left, releasing a sigh of relief and exhaustion. She glanced at the digital numbers on the stove—two in the morning. She needed to get Skyler back to bed.

She returned to the storage closet and knocked on the back wall. "No monsters inside, and Mr. Walt's keeping watch outside. Why don't you open the door and have some tea with me?"

Skyler must've been weighing whether or not she wanted to leave the safe space, because seconds ticked by before the locks clicked on the inside.

The wall crept open to reveal a little girl with porcelain skin and corn-silk-blond hair. She couldn't have looked more different from Noelle, who had warm brown skin and hair as black as the night.

Skyler squeezed her stuffed firefly, Twinkle, to her chest, her blue eyes shimmering with tears. "Can we sleep in here tonight?"

Noelle considered the cramped space. She wasn't claustrophobic, but she also wasn't a contortionist. "I'm not sure it's big enough, sweetheart. It's not meant for sleeping."

"No, it's big enough." Skyler scooted over until she was against the wall and patted the blankets on the floor. "We can snuggle, like Mommy and I used to do before . . ." One of the tears spilled onto her cheek as she trailed off, and she smeared it away with her sleeve, her bottom lip quivering.

Noelle swallowed against the tightness of tears in her own throat. "Okay. We'll see if we can make it work." Leaving the tea behind in the kitchen, she crawled into the nook.

After some awkward shuffling, Noelle curled against the wall with one arm for a pillow. Skyler cuddled up against her like a little spoon and hugged Twinkle to her chest.

Noelle had no illusions about being able to sleep tonight, but to comfort Skyler, that was a sacrifice she was willing to make.

CHAPTER Three

Walt's boots crunched over dead leaves as he searched the property, listening more than watching for signs of someone who shouldn't be there.

With the moon trapped behind the clouds, he could barely see the tip of his rifle, but he didn't need to see. He'd lived on this land his entire life, and he could navigate every rise and dip in his sleep. No tree root or gopher hole would trip him up.

It was too bad he couldn't snare trespassers in his animal traps anymore, but he had to remove them all for Skyler's sake. The child bounced around the yard without a care for where she put her feet.

"Who's out here?" Walt called out, the wind snatching at his voice. "This is private property!"

Something heavy stirred the leaves to his right, and he snapped his rifle in that direction as he stepped around a towering oak.

"If you're here for the girl, you can't have her," he informed the darkness. Skyler was the first bit of sunshine in his life in over fifty years, and he wasn't about to let anyone hurt her or take her away again. "You can't have the woman neither."

He hadn't been able to protect Skyler's mother, who was barely more than a child herself when she was killed, but he wouldn't let her lose Noelle too.

"Show yourself!" He waited, but no one moved. "If I have to find you, it's going to make me mad, and I'll put more holes in you than a noodle strainer. Step out, and I'll only shoot you once. Nowhere vital."

But he would make sure the wound would remind the man to steer clear of this house and its residents in the future.

My heart pounded in my chest—so loud and sharp I expected it to lead the old man back to me.

I couldn't see him in the darkness, and I didn't dare move again. The leaves beneath my boots and the bark on the tree at my back had nearly given me away. There was no way to know how close he was, but I could feel him, like a prickle on the back of my neck.

I shifted my fingers around the knife in my hand, waiting.

A soft patter on the leaves overhead drew my gaze upward, and I squinted against the raindrops. It wasn't supposed to rain tonight. I had checked the weather before making my plans.

The crunch of leaves beneath the old man's boots grew fainter with every step, and my heartbeat slowed. He was walking away. I eased my grip on the knife, relieved that I wouldn't have to kill him. Tonight.

I peered around the tree at the house cloaked in shadows and fixed my attention on the girl's window. I couldn't tell from this distance if her bed was empty, but I suspected it was.

She would be curled up in Noelle's arms now.

The urge to be closer to the house, closer to her, was an ache in my soul, but thanks to the old man, I couldn't do anything to alleviate it. Frustrated, I waited for the crunch of his boots to fade away, then used the tree to push myself to my feet. I would have to come back another time.

Morning light streamed through the upstairs window, highlighting the dust particles in the air before splashing over the maps on the walls and the precariously stacked books on the desk in the corner.

Noelle's writing room wasn't tidy and organized with cute stationery and matching paper clips. It was an outward display of her inner Mad Hatter. Resource books stuffed with anything she could use as page markers, yesterday's tea cups, granola bar wrappers, notebooks filled with scribblings of ideas that never fully formed into anything useful.

One notebook was reserved for death facts. If anyone ever peeled back the cover of that notebook to peek inside, they would add her to the community watch list for disturbed individuals to avoid at all costs.

That woman in the Bechtel house has notes about how long it takes a human body to decay in humid weather. She's as crazy as that place is haunted.

The superstitious members of the village already gave her strange looks and a wide berth in public, as if the dark history of her house were a living thing that might reach through her and latch onto them.

It was absurd.

Rubbing absently at her neck and shoulders, which after last night's sleeping arrangements felt as kinked up as an old slinky, she stared at the nearly blank whiteboard in front of her.

She breathed in the scent of vanilla and peppermint tea rising from the mug she held and released the breath one disappointed moment later. Her "thinking brew" usually stimulated her creativity, but there was no flood of ideas this morning—or any of the mornings in the past four months.

Maybe it was the lack of caffeine.

She *was* out of coffee. A devastating realization after a cramped and restless night with an eleven-year-old who flailed like an overturned turtle in her sleep. Oh, how she missed the city with its convenient cafés on every corner. The only place to grab a cup of coffee around here was at the diner, which was a fifteen-minute drive through the country.

Swirling the tea in her mug, she stared at the two nameless, faceless heads she'd drawn on the whiteboard—the main characters she was hoping to meet before she sprouted another gray hair.

"Who are you, and what's your story?"

The only detail that came to mind was that the male character had a dent in the side of his head. Dropped-as-a-baby dent? Work accident? Trauma while chasing down nefarious villains?

"Terrible drawing skills," Noelle added out loud. She grabbed the dry erase marker and bit the cap, pulling it free. She rounded out the man's head and then stepped back.

She wasn't going to be able to see the characters until she knew some of the story. She glanced at the smudges of dry erase marker from every pitiful idea she'd wiped away.

What she needed was a real event to base her plot around. Something dark and mysterious. She'd put the task to her readers months ago, hoping they might dredge up an interesting event she'd overlooked, but none of their recommendations inspired her.

Sinking onto the stool in the center of the room, she glanced at the wooden cube on her desk with the words "Writer's Block" stamped on it. Trudy, one of the only women in town she'd managed to strike up a friendship with, had gotten it for her as a gag gift last spring.

Noelle simultaneously loved it and wanted to hurl it out the window. Unfortunately, only one of the two windows opened, and doing so would destroy the home of her writing room companion.

She turned her attention to the small spider on the glittering web in the corner of the window facing the backyard. Before having her son, she would've squealed and swatted the spider to death with a towel, but his love for naming them and treating them like friends had forever changed her.

"How are you on this dewy fall morning, Webster? Enjoying the sunshine?" She took a drink of her tea, grimacing. Peppermint tea went from delicious to unpalatable as it cooled. "I could use a brainstorming partner this morning. Any book ideas you'd like to throw out? Something to do with a *web*site? A man who gets wrapped up in a sticky situation and needs rescuing?"

She could imagine the spider giving her a you-can't-be-serious-with-those-embarrassing-puns stare.

"No, you're right. Those are terrible. I bet *you* could spin a few murder-y tales for me, considering how many flies you slaughter."

She lifted the mug to her lips on reflex, but tinkling laughter drew her from the stool and over to the window before she could take another regrettable drink.

Set against a backdrop of jewel-colored leaves and leafless bushes, Skyler twirled through the grass with a stick, streamers of ribbon, shoelaces, and strips of torn fabric chasing her every movement.

Walt had scrounged the materials to make her wand of streamers for her, and even though it was simple, the love he put into it made it one of her favorite toys. She twirled and leaped, all of the fear and stress from last night forgotten.

At least one of them had put the situation in the past. Noelle couldn't shake the whisper of unease still clinging to her nerves. As much as she wanted to dismiss the "monster" as a bad dream, she couldn't be certain that's all it was.

Noelle wasn't the only one still ill at ease. Walt slumped on a nearby stump, rifle in his lap, and watched over Skyler like it was his personal mission.

The old man's countenance was usually grim and guarded, but this morning, the hard lines of his face were softer, and even the corners of his mouth had a gentle lift.

It wasn't the warm sunlight spilling between the trees that eased the loneliness and grief he'd been carrying since he lost his family; it was the little girl who sprinkled sunshine and joy around her like handfuls of glitter.

Noelle squinted. Was that a flower tucked into the buttonhole of his shirt?

Another familiar figure came into view, no doubt pulled around the house by the sound of laughter, and warmth flooded Noelle's chest. He was tall and broad-shouldered, with sandy blond hair and a beard that hugged his lower jaw.

Derek Dempsey. The man she'd been dating for the past ten months.

She hadn't expected to meet someone so soon after her husband left her for another woman. Truthfully, she hadn't expected to meet someone new . . . ever. She'd been hanging onto life by her fingernails when she moved to Cherry Creek last fall, and Derek had offered her friendship. By winter they were both flirting with the idea of dating.

When Skyler spotted Derek, she dropped her ribbon wand and surged toward him, throwing her arms around his waist with a squeal of delight that made him laugh.

"Hey there, Mischief." He scooped her up so he could hug her back, revealing her filthy bare feet. Noelle shook her head in weary amusement. Skyler preferred to frolic barefoot through life.

She was ten years old the first time she tried on shoes, and she immediately dubbed them "toe pinchers" and kicked them off. Every time they left the house was a battle.

"How are you this morning?" Derek asked, his deep but gentle voice carrying across the yard.

"I'm good. Noelle says I have school at nine, so I'm getting all my playing in now."

"Sounds like a plan to me. Where is Noelle?"

"Upstairs with Webster."

Derek's head tilted. "Who's Webster?"

"Our writing room spider."

"Ah, so she's in her writing room. I should've known."

"Yes, you should have."

Derek grinned. "Thank you, smarty-pants." He lowered her to the ground. "Go play."

She started to race off, then stopped, turning back. "Can I have another hug before you go?"

"I'll come see you before I leave."

"Okay!" She cartwheeled through the grass, tumbled into a roll, and popped to her feet with her ribbons on a stick.

As Derek started for the porch, Noelle looked down at her oversize, stained sweatshirt and ratty sweatpants with patches of threadbare fabric. She hadn't expected him to drop by before work, and she was dressed like a teenage boy on a shower strike.

A door opened and closed downstairs.

No time to do anything about her appearance now. Unless she dashed into the bathroom and locked the door like an overly dramatic teenager, forcing him to wait while she pulled herself together.

She shrugged off the ridiculous notion. Tyrese, her ex-husband, would've been disgusted by the sight of her, but the first time she met Derek, she'd been wearing sweatpants and an oversize sweatshirt, and it hadn't scared him away.

She caught a glimpse of her hair in the small mirror on the writing room wall and smoothed her hands over the defiant pieces that stuck out around her face. They popped back up like baby cornstalks, and it made her think of Grammy, who taught her to love her hair from root to tip.

"Sometimes a black woman's beautiful hair is determined to throw up its hands and praise Jesus. Nothing will stand in its way," Grammy used to say, when Noelle's textured locks refused to be styled. And her hair was worshipping *hard* today.

Derek appeared at Noelle's open door with a tray of take-out cups in one hand. Bless him, he'd brought coffee. She'd used the last of her grounds yesterday and hadn't made it to the store.th

Affection softened his features when he looked at her, melting away all of her concerns about her appearance. "Morning."

"Hey. This is a pleasant surprise."

"I know we're seeing each other tonight, but I didn't feel like waiting that long." He nodded to the whiteboard. "Nothing yet?"

She set her peppermint tea on the cluttered desk and offered the whiteboard a disgruntled frown. "No. It should be filled with ideas by now."

"You just released your eleventh book, and you have a book signing tonight. I think you've earned a bit of a break."

She finished her eleventh book four months ago, and apart from a few social media announcements, the book coasted to its publication day. She should be plot-twist deep into a new book by now.

Derek handed her one of the mugs, a twinkle of amusement in his hazel eyes. "Cup of creamer, drop of coffee."

The corners of her lips curled up. He knew how she liked it. "Thank you for thinking of me."

He nodded to her hand. "Nice ring."

She flexed her finger to showcase the ring Skyler had made for her using braided twine. "Thanks, I'm partial to simple designs like this. Nothing gaudy that gets caught on everything." She glanced at him to see if the hint landed, but his expression betrayed nothing. "As far as this goes"—she gestured to the whiteboard— "I feel like I'm out of ideas."

"That beautiful head of yours is full of ideas." He set aside the tray and wrapped an arm around her waist, pulling her back against him so he could plant a kiss on her temple. "Something just needs to unlock them."

Something like a crow bar, she thought.

"If you're short on inspiration, drop by the diner and listen in for a while. That place is a hub for the interesting and insane."

Noelle laughed. "I don't think your sister would appreciate that comment."

Trudy, his youngest sister, owned and operated the local diner, and while she was barely taller than the mop she cleaned the floor with at the end of the night, she was spunky.

"We're not going to tell her I said that."

"Oh, you're scared now," Noelle teased.

"My hindsight is kicking in, and I'm realizing the mistake of insulting the person who makes my coffee every morning."

"Trudy would forgive you."

"*After* she punished me. Knowing her, she would invite Janet Robinson to the diner to have breakfast with me so she could watch me squirm."

Janet was the older, single woman who had set her sights on Derek years ago, and she never missed the opportunity to flirt with him at church. Noelle may as well be invisible by his side.

"I think if she could get away with it, that woman would kidnap you so she could have you all to yourself," Noelle said, only half teasing.

"That is a disturbing thought." His beard tickled the side of her face as he pulled her closer. "If you don't want to go to the diner for research, I could always offer some ideas."

"Oh no, I don't think I need any more of your *ideas*."

"I have great book ideas. Like a band of drunk, blind pirates staggering off their ship to rob banks, only to be thwarted by a well-armed captain of the sheriff's department."

She crooked her neck to look at him. "Drunk *and* blind? That would be something to witness."

"They're stealthier than you might think."

"Uh-huh."

"And . . ." He released her and walked to the whiteboard, using a marker to scribble around the male character's jaw. "The well-armed captain has a beard." He added facial features a kindergartener could've drawn. "Some hazel eyes."

"Those are eyes?"

His expression of feigned offense almost made her laugh. He snapped the cap back on the marker. "I think we can all agree that Skyler is the artist."

"True enough."

He handed the marker to her. "For the flood of ideas my suggestions will no doubt spark."

"Yes, such inspiring suggestions."

"I should go before I'm late for work."

Noelle nodded but asked, "Have you checked into Skyler's trafficking case recently?"

"It's not my investigation, but I keep tabs on it." Derek studied her. "What's got you thinking about that?"

Noelle hesitated before explaining, "Skyler said she saw someone outside her window last night."

"'Said she saw.' Meaning you doubt someone was actually there?"

"I didn't see anyone. Neither did Walt. And she said it was a monster."

"Given everything she's been through and everything she's witnessed, it's not really a surprise she's dreaming about monsters."

The therapist had warned Noelle that Skyler's trauma could manifest in different ways: emotional outbursts, attachment struggles, even nightmares, but she never said anything about sleep-window-opening.

"I'm not convinced she was asleep. She removed the security bar and opened her bedroom window," Noelle said.

Creases of thought formed around Derek's eyes. "If she *did* see someone, it could've been a kid in a mask gearing up for Halloween. Or one of the locals creeping around, trying to spook people."

"You don't think it could be . . . someone involved in the trafficking ring? Someone who slipped through the cracks?"

Derek shook his head. "Sky can't identify the leader of the ring or the remaining clients. She never met them. There's no reason to expose themselves by coming after her."

Noelle forced her fingers to relax around the paper take-out mug in her hand. "Right. I know you've said that before. I guess I just needed to hear it again."

"Skyler is the safest she's ever been, and I'll remind you of that as often as you need. If it'll give you some peace of mind, I'll check around for any reports involving masked trespassers."

"It would."

"Call me if something like this happens again. It doesn't matter what time it is. I'll come over and take a look around, okay?"

"Okay."

He checked his watch. "I need to go, or I'll be late. I'll see you at the book signing tonight." He brushed a featherlight kiss across her lips. "Enjoy your cup of creamer." He grabbed his coffee from the tray and left her to her creative process.

She turned back to the whiteboard. The intimidating blankness glared back at her, making her question whether or not she would ever have another worthwhile idea.

She drew her thoughts back from that rabbit hole of pessimism before she could tip over the edge and fall in. Unlike Alice, she wouldn't hit bottom in a wonderful land filled with inspiration; she would hit the bottom of a Ben & Jerry's ice cream container after stress-eating her way through it, and that wouldn't help her creativity or her thighs.

It was time for a break.

CHAPTER *Five*

The staircase banister wobbled beneath Noelle's hand as she made her way back to the first floor, and she made a mental note to reinforce the weak screws with more superglue.

The entire railing needed to be replaced. It was somewhere on her list of unaffordable repairs and renovations, and that list rivaled the length of a drugstore receipt.

All the major repairs had been done months ago so she could pass the state-required home inspection for adoption: replacing the windows and doors, laying a new roof, restoring the floors, updating the plumbing and electric.

Preparing her home and herself for adopting a child had eaten through most of her savings. It had been an eleven-month battle of prayer and patience, but it was worth every stress line and penny.

Even if the two of them had to scrape by on the royalties from Noelle's first ten books until the eleventh one gained traction, Skyler had a stable home.

Something clattered to the floor, and Noelle looked down in time to see a screw from the banister disappear into the gap between floorboards.

Well . . . maybe *stable* wasn't the best word to describe it. But at least they weren't racing around with pots and pans to catch raindrops leaking through the ceiling anymore. They could deal with the draft breathing through the house in the colder months, the wobbly fixtures, and the ever-moving doors.

Noelle's fitness band vibrated with an alarm. It was time for Skyler to get ready for her Friday morning lessons. Padding into the kitchen, she opened the back door. "Sky, honey, it's time to come in and get cleaned up for school."

Skyler swirled her homemade baton in excitement. "Yes! I get to feed Periwinkle today!"

Periwinkle was a parrot with a potty mouth. Glenda, one of Skyler's co-op teachers, had rescued him from a neglectful environment, and whoever owned him before must've spoken entirely in expletives. The first time Noelle met the bird, he cussed her up and down.

"Remember," Noelle said, as Skyler paused by the doormat, "if Peri tries to teach you new and inappropriate words . . ."

"Leave the parroting to the parrot. I remember. I get to feed him 'cause I had the funniest joke last Friday, and that was the challenge."

"What was your joke?"

"I told Ms. Glenda that Peri can't help the bad words he says, 'cause he's *fowl*-mouthed. Get it? Fowl . . . 'cause he's a bird."

"I do get it. Nice play on words."

Skyler scratched at a crust of mud on her bare calf, her face turning pensive. "Do you think Peri misses his family from before?"

Noelle opened her mouth to admit that she had no idea whether or not parrots could miss people, but Skyler asked another question before she could.

"They weren't the best family, and maybe they did bad things, but . . . would it be okay if he missed them sometimes?"

Noelle closed her mouth, taking a second to reevaluate her answer, because there was a deeper issue embedded in the question—one that had nothing to do with the bird.

"Peri spent most of his life with his original family, and he loved them very much. So it's absolutely okay for him to miss them. Normal even," Noelle said.

Skyler's eyes drifted to the side as she silently mulled over Noelle's answer, no doubt applying it to her own family situation.

Skyler's mother had done everything in her limited power to protect her, and some of her actions had had tragic repercussions for other young women.

Skyler's mother had been everything to her, but to the surviving victims of the trafficking ring, Natalie Jones had been one of the villains.

For the past year, Skyler had been struggling to reconcile the mother she remembered and loved with the woman who lured other girls into that house of horrors, including her friend, Maddie. The unquestioning love she once felt for her was now muddled with anger, hurt, and confusion.

"It's okay to be upset with someone and still love and miss them, sweetheart," Noelle added, wanting more than anything to help her through these big emotions.

Skyler scratched at the dirt patch on her leg again. "I should go get ready for school now."

"Make sure you wash your feet and put on some shoes."

Skyler made a face, like she'd been asked to pick up mouse poop with her bare hands. "Do I have to wear shoes?"

"You know the answer to that."

Skyler crossed her arms and lifted her chin. "Frodo didn't have to wear shoes, and he traveled all the way to Mordor, so I think I should be able to go to school without shoes. That's not even as far."

Ha! Now she was dragging literary figures into her shoe rebellion. Noelle couldn't even be frustrated with the smooth tactic. "Frodo was a hobbit with hairy, rough feet, not a little girl. It's very different."

"Trudy says I can be anything I want. Maybe I want to be a hobbit."

"Nice try. Shoes."

Skyler sighed and hung her head as she stalked down the hall toward her bedroom. "I hate toe pinchers."

Noelle smiled. She'd won this battle, but the war would rage on. She stepped out onto the porch in her slippers. Morning air, with more than a bite of winter chill, whipped through her clothes and raised goose bumps on her skin.

Walt pushed up from his stump in the yard, his usual scowl firmly in place, and stomped toward the porch. "I took another look around the property after the sun came up. Still no sign of who was here last night."

"Thanks for checking."

Walt scratched at his palms like he was trying to dig his way to the veins, and Noelle noticed the spots on his skin. She lifted her gaze to his face. There was a glaze over his bloodshot eyes, like he hadn't slept in days, and his cheeks were flushed.

"Do your feet itch?" Noelle asked.

"Maybe."

"How does your throat feel?"

"Scratchy." He cleared it and grimaced. "Must've swallowed a bug in my sleep."

"You look like you might have a fever." She reached forward to press her hand to his forehead, but he stepped back like he was evading an attack.

"What are you trying to do?"

"Check your temperature. I have a thermometer in the bathroom if you'd prefer I—"

"I'd prefer not to be treated like a child."

Noelle dropped her arm. "Then try not acting like one."

"I don't need mothering. I've taken care of myself for longer than you've been alive. I don't need you or anyone else taking care of me."

"You have hand-foot-and-mouth."

He stepped away from her. "Why are you listing off my body parts like a butcher planning to sell me by the piece?"

"No self-respecting butcher would sell your body parts. You're nothing but leather and gristle. Hand-foot-and-mouth is a virus that usually only hits kids. My son had it twice. I would guess Skyler brought it home to you."

Maybe the virus confused his emotional maturity level for his physical age. Twelve-year-olds were still susceptible.

"It won't kill you, but you'll be miserable for a week. I'm taking Skyler to school, and then I'm heading into town," she said. "The house will be quiet if you want to come in out of the cold. There's juice in the refrigerator and acetaminophen in the kitchen cabinet. It'll help with any fever and pain."

He rolled his shoulders back. "I'll take the juice because I'm thirsty, but you can keep your drugs."

"It's Tylenol, not a heroin stash."

"All the same." He kicked the mud from his boots before going inside, ignoring the no-shoes-in-the-house rule. Typical.

Noelle rubbed at her arms as she looked over the backyard: the thick patch of woods, the sagging shed that might not survive the next gust of wind, the pet cemetery cluttered with miniature gravestones and fallen leaves.

There was no one out there—she was almost certain of that now—but the feeling of someone watching her crawled the length of her back and sank its claws into her spine.

The typewriter-shaped bauble dangling from the rearview mirror swayed like a pendulum as Noelle navigated the winding back roads.

I only murder fictional people.

The glittery pink statement stamped across the typewriter brought a smile to her lips every time it caught her eye.

In a video interview she gave during the summer, the interviewer had asked Noelle how she felt when faced with the decision to kill off a character in her books.

"Some fictional people are harder to *off* than others. Because you do get attached," she had explained. "But the reality is that sometimes a character has to die to propel the plot forward."

When Derek watched her interview, he added this mirror bauble to her collection of cheesy author-themed décor, most of which were bumper stickers.

She laughed when she pulled it from the gift box. Not a cutesy laugh either, but a full-on donkey guffaw she wished she could erase from both their memories. How did her vocal cords even make that hideously embarrassing sound? It had to be the cold she had at the time.

A giggle drew Noelle's gaze to the backseat, where her daughter sat.

My daughter. The thought was still surreal. The adoption was finalized a month ago, and the child she'd been caring for all this time was now officially her daughter. There were no more hoops to jump through and no more fear that someone would swoop in and take away the little girl she loved.

Skyler's pale eyebrows bobbed and dipped with emotion as she devoured the book in her lap on the way to her teacher's house.

While in captivity, digital books had been her window into the world, and the characters she went on adventures with had been her only friends. Her affinity for books stayed with her as she moved into her new life, but it was their first trip to the library that awakened her love of paperbacks.

The moment they stepped foot in the library, Skyler had gasped, her wide eyes drinking in the endless shelves of books.

"These are for anyone?" she'd asked, doubting she would be allowed to pick any book she wanted and take it home.

"Yep, and you can borrow a book for two weeks, but then you have to bring it back."

"Two weeks? I'll read it in a day."

"Then I guess you better borrow ten."

Skyler had gasped again. "I can do that?"

"You can."

"Wow." She had taken a moment to rein in her excitement, and then said, "I need a shopping cart 'cause my arms are too little for ten books."

"How about a basket?"

"That'll work."

Noelle smiled at the memory. Skyler had experienced so many things for the first time this past year: playing outside, interacting with other children, chasing fireflies. Derek had shown her how to catch a firefly in a jar, a summer pastime for local children.

Skyler had stared at the captured creature with tears in her eyes, and then she lifted the lid from the jar and watched it launch back into the darkening sky.

"He's a firefly like me, and I don't want him to be trapped like I was. He should be able to shine wherever he wants to shine, like I get to do now."

Noelle's heart had cracked at her daughter's words, and her throat was so tight with her own tears that she barely managed to say, "You're right. All fireflies should be free."

From that point on, they watched the beautiful bugs twinkle in the trees and over the fields, but they never again tried to capture them.

Integrating Skyler into the world was an adventure. At times heartwarming, and at other times challenging. Her lack of education was one of those challenges.

What little she knew had come from her mother, whose education ended at twelve years old. She excelled at reading and writing, thanks to the Kindle her captors had provided to keep her quiet and compliant, but her understanding of math and science were closer to a first grade level.

She had no idea how to learn in a classroom.

Noelle was grateful for the retired teachers and stay-at-home moms in town who banded together to create a homeschooling co-op. They took turns teaching different subjects on different days, and the setup afforded each child the attention they needed.

Noelle pulled her eyes from the rearview mirror and back to the road, heart jumping at the sight of a dark human shape standing at the edge of the blacktop.

She sucked in a breath and swerved to avoid clipping him with the side of her car.

Pulse pounding in her temples, she glanced back. The man's black cloak whipped in the downdraft of her passing car, and the hood over his head billowed outward to reveal a disturbing mask—like an enormous insect had grabbed ahold of his face, leaving only slivers of skin visible.

What was wrong with people this time of year? They used Halloween as an excuse to don costumes and behave recklessly, sometimes criminally. If this was a Halloween prank to scare motorists, it was dangerous.

A quick look at Skyler revealed she was still engrossed in her book, unaware Noelle had come within inches of vehicular manslaughter.

Noelle pressed the brake to slow her Volkswagen behind a horse-drawn buggy inching up the hill in front of her at speeds a turtle could outcreep. She leaned over to see around them, but the rise of the hill obscured her line of sight. If she tried to go around them, she might collide with an oncoming vehicle.

Something stirred in the trees on her left, and she caught a glimmer of black. Was that . . .

She strained to see over her shoulder where she'd swerved to avoid the costumed man, but the roadside was empty. She turned her gaze back to the trees, and her grip on the steering wheel tightened.

He stepped into view about twenty feet back from the road, and even though his eyes were shadowed by the hood he wore, she could feel his attention. When he took a step forward, and then another, his speed picking up, fear darted through her.

He was coming straight for her car.

Noelle whipped the wheel to the right and stepped on the gas, launching out and around the buggy.

Please, God, don't let the horse panic.

The last thing she wanted to do was injure the family in the buggy. The young horse neighed and jerked in surprise, but the older man pulled back on the reins to control her.

"Look, a horse!" Skyler exclaimed. "Do you think we could stop and pet it?"

"Not a good time, sweetheart."

"Hey, that man gave us the bad finger."

Can't really blame him, Noelle thought. She had scared his horse, putting him at risk, and she could hardly stop and explain why.

She crested the hill in the wrong lane, praying there wouldn't be a car coming from the opposite direction, and then slid into position well ahead of the horse.

She checked the rearview mirror.

The masked figure was nowhere to be seen. Even a quick scan of the trees revealed nothing amiss. One moment he was charging toward her vehicle, and the next he was gone.

Her heartbeat slowed, and she relaxed her grip on the steering wheel. She made a mental note of the location and time so she could report the incident once they made it to their destination. If he planned to menace other drivers, someone was going to end up seriously injured. Or dead.

They pulled into Glenda Hofie's driveway ten minutes later.

The older woman stood on the lawn in cutoff jeans, rubber waders that reached above her knees, a rainbow poncho, and a straw hat. A ferret dangled from one hand, and a handicapped pig with a wheelchair under his rump scooted around the yard.

"Watch out for tree roots, Bacon," she called out.

Noelle almost laughed. The woman had named her pig Bacon. What had she named the chicken strutting circles around her ankles—Drumstick? Rotisserie?

Skyler dove out of the car, leaving Noelle to catch up. She dropped to her knees beside the rooster and petted his feathers. "He's such a pretty boy. What's his name?"

Glenda bent down. "His name is Winnie. I picked him up yesterday from a farm outside town."

"Why does he keep walking in circles?"

"The old couple said something was wrong with him when he was born, and even though he's mostly better, he still walks in circles like he did when he was a chick."

Noelle joined them in the yard and passed Skyler's lunch bag to her teacher to be refrigerated. "Morning, Glenda."

"Noelle. How are you on this fine day?"

"Caffeinated. So at least I have that going for me. How are you?"

"Living the dream."

Noelle's dream life was vastly different than the older woman's, but she was glad Glenda had managed to build a life she loved. Not many people could say that.

"The other kids should be here soon, and then we'll start in on our lessons for the day. You're welcome to stay," Glenda said.

After the monster scare last night, Noelle was tempted to accept the invitation, but she didn't want to hover. "Thank you, but I have some household chores to tackle."

"Do I still get to feed Peri?" Skyler asked.

"Of course. A promise is a promise."

Skyler wrapped her arms around Noelle's waist. "Love you, but I have to go now. I have important stuff to do."

Noelle hugged her back. "Love you too. Have fun and learn lots of interesting things."

"I will."

Glenda grabbed the pig. "Fetch Winnie and bring him inside. He'll get lonely out here by himself."

Skyler grunted as she scooped up the rooster, and then she was up the steps and running into her teacher's house.

Noelle dialed the nonemergency number for the sheriff's department and leaned against the side of her car as she waited to report the masked man menacing drivers.

CHAPTER Six

It was a calm morning at the Wade County Sheriff's Department, the quiet broken only by the hum of voices and intermittent nonemergency calls.

Judging by the stack of incident reports on Derek's desk, however, last night had been a different story. He looked from the mountain of files and then to the swallow of coffee remaining in his take-out cup.

He needed more fuel to tackle that mess.

He detoured to the break room.

Rusty, his oldest deputy, stood in front of the dual coffee maker, filling his personal mug from the pot no one in the department ever used. It had sat empty for so long it was practically for decoration.

"Morning, boss," Rusty said.

"When did you start drinking decaf?"

"When my doctor said I have hypertension. I told her I'm not hyper or tense, but she didn't find that too funny."

Rusty was the most laid-back person Derek had ever met. Even his speech was relaxed and slow, like he was in no hurry to get the words out. Heaven help him if he ever had to chase down a criminal.

"Other than that, you're in good health?" Derek asked.

"Fit as a fiddle." Rusty stepped aside, blowing across the surface of his coffee. "How's your sweet lady this morning?"

Derek regarded him curiously as he reached for the pot of regular coffee. "How do you always know when I've stopped by to see Noelle before work? I'm starting to think I should investigate you for stalking."

Rusty chuckled. "You always look and sound more relaxed after you see her. A good woman can do that to a man. Steal away all his troubles for a while."

There was some truth to that.

No matter how Derek's day started or ended, seeing Noelle lightened the weight on his shoulders. And Skyler . . . she reminded him what it felt like to be carefree and full of wonder—something he hadn't experienced much of, becoming the man of the house at eight years old.

"Also, there's a unicorn sticker between your shoulder blades," Rusty said with a lilt of amusement in his tone.

Derek laughed. "Why doesn't that surprise me?" Skyler had played him with that second hug before he left, patting his back and snickering. Derek returned the pot of coffee to the warmer and reached behind him—first over and then under—but the sticker was in that narrow space he couldn't reach from either direction. "You mind getting that for me?"

Rusty peeled the sticker from his back and held it out on the tip of one finger. "Want to keep it?"

He kind of did. He took the sticker from Rusty's finger and smoothed it onto the side of his coffee mug. "Noelle's doing all right," he said, in answer to the older man's question about his *lady*. "As all right as an author can be while trying to plan out a book. I never realized how stressful the writing process could be."

Rusty grunted. "Take it from a man who passed English by the skin of his teeth. Writing is easy. Writing something that makes sense and doesn't bore everyone to snot and tears is a whole different level of ability."

"I'm doing my best to help, but truthfully, I wouldn't know where to start with the whole writing thing."

"The alphabet."

Derek grinned. "Thanks."

"Sixty years of wisdom just like that up here." Rusty tapped his temple. "Always happy to share."

"If I can alleviate some of her worry, maybe she'll be able to concentrate better." Derek leaned against the counter. "Have you heard any chatter about trespassers or prowlers in Cherry Creek lately? Something that didn't make it into a report?"

Rusty's bushy gray brows pinched in thought. "Raina Miller called me the other night after seeing someone or something around their property."

Derek's shoulders stiffened. Raina Miller had been his wife's best friend from high school until the day she died. Why hadn't she called *him* if there was a problem? He would've driven over to check things out.

"I went over and took a look around, discreet as I could be. I didn't want Earl to feel bad that his wife needed to call another man to check things out," Rusty said.

Two years ago, Earl had an accident in the field when a bale of hay fell on top of him. Those hay bales weighed thousands of pounds, and it was a miracle he survived. The accident paralyzed him, and he struggled with the new reality that he couldn't physically provide for or protect his wife and home. Even though his presence and love were enough for Raina, it wasn't enough for Earl.

"Was everything all right?" Derek asked.

"As far as I could see at midnight. I asked Raina the next day if anything was missing, but she said she didn't think so. It was probably a coyote or fox trying to get to their chickens."

"Let's hope so." Derek would follow up with her later. Lacey was gone, but that didn't mean he no longer cared about the people who'd enriched her life—and his—while she was alive. Raina had been an amazing friend to her, and by extension, to him.

Rusty sipped his coffee. "Why the sudden concern about trespassers and prowlers? Someone bothering the girls?"

"I'm not sure."

Rusty's gaze caught on something through the break room window. Derek followed his attention to the wisp of a woman in her sixties, who drifted around the office with a tray of homemade muffins, delivering one to everyone in uniform. Carol—the widow of a former deputy.

Derek looked back at Rusty, who was still watching the sweet woman with longing. "In my experience, women aren't particularly fond of being stared at. You'll make a better impression if you go out there and talk to her."

Rusty pulled his gaze away from her. "A woman like her wouldn't want anything to do with an old toad like me."

"You're one of the best men I know."

"That may be, but Carol is practically an angel."

"A lonely angel since her husband passed. Most people thank her for the baked goods, but they don't take time to chat, and I think it would do her some good."

Rusty thought about it, then shook his head. "I wouldn't even know what to say. Did it hurt when you fell from heaven?"

"Maybe not that."

"I haven't really talked to a woman since my wife died. I don't know how to do it anymore."

"With words," Derek said, smiling as he lifted his coffee to his mouth.

"Funny, boss."

Carol floated into the room with her tray of muffins. "I hope I'm not interrupting, but I thought I would leave the rest of these muffins in here by the coffee."

Rusty removed his deputy hat and held it against his chest in a gentlemanly gesture that died out decades ago. "Good morning, Carol." It took him a moment to squeeze out anything more than a greeting. "You look real nice today."

Carol touched her short curls, and if not for the makeup covering her cheeks, Derek suspected a blush might've been visible. "That's nice of you to say, Rusty. Would you like a muffin?"

"I love muffins." Rusty set his hat on the counter to free up a hand.

"Would you like blueberry or chocolate?"

"Well, now that's a tough choice. What's your favorite?"

Derek took that as his cue to leave. He usually left the matchmaking to Trudy, but Rusty and Carol had both been alone long enough.

He closed his office door and sank into his chair behind the stack of reports. Wade County encompassed three villages and twelve cities. The villages were generally quieter than the cities, resulting in fewer visits from his officers.

He opened the first report.

A woman was arrested for attacking her husband in public. Again. Bridget Morrison's name crossed his desk several times a year. Her husband was a big man, but he was soft-spoken and gentle natured, and he never used his strength to defend himself when she flew into an abusive rage.

Derek shook his head as he signed the report, fully aware that nothing would come of the arrest. Tony Morrison would refuse to cooperate, the DA's office would decline to prosecute without a complainant, and the cycle of abuse would continue.

It was only a matter of time before Bridget killed her husband during one of her violent outbursts, but there was nothing anyone could do if Tony wasn't willing to accept help.

Derek moved on to the next report: a disgruntled customer at an Amish store who took her anger out on the merchandise. Apparently, the eggs had gone up in price, so she decided to break them all in protest.

Some adults threw worse temper tantrums than toddlers, and that was saying something considering toddlers flung themselves to the floor in the middle of a store and screamed bloody murder until their faces were coated in snot and tears.

Derek's phone dinged with an incoming recorded message from his baby sister. This was bound to be interesting.

He hit the play button, and Trudy's voice—still tinged with a Tennessee accent from her years down south—came through his phone speaker.

"So I was thinking."

About his love life, no doubt.

"It's been, what, ten months since you and Noelle started dating? That's long enough to grow and pop out a baby—I should know—so don't you think that's long enough to grow a relationship and pop the question?"

Derek released a sigh. His baby sister was lecturing him, and she wasn't even in the room. And ten months wasn't that long in the span of a lifetime. It took him ten years to finally ask Lacey to marry him.

His gaze slid to the cluster of framed photographs on his desk and the few personal items he kept in his office and settled on the photo of his late wife. It was the last picture taken of her before cancer consumed her body.

To the right was a candid photo of Noelle, her bright smile lighting up her entire face.

The two women couldn't be more physically different, but they were both strong, intelligent, beautiful ladies he could spend a lifetime laughing with.

"Okay?" Trudy said, and he realized he missed part of her message. He dragged his finger across the voice message to rewind it. "You deserve to be happy, and so does she. So let's talk when you have time, okay?"

As if she were giving him a choice. She would show up at his house in the middle of the night if he didn't make time to see her. He adored Trudy, but sometimes her meddling in his love life drove him to the brink.

He started to type out a response, when his desk phone rang. He grabbed it, cradling it between his ear and shoulder, as he finished his text to Trudy.

"Captain Dempsey."

"Hey, Captain, it's Bo Dellbright."

The name caught his full attention. Bo was a parole officer who monitored several of the ex-cons in the area, and if he was calling, it meant trouble. "What can I do for you, Bo?"

"You asked me to call you personally if a certain one of my parolees stepped out of line or failed to show up for his appointment."

Derek leaned back in his seat. "Nick Nelson."

Nick was a registered sex offender. He was put away for assaulting two teenage girls, but he was released early due to overcrowding. When he paid too much attention to Trudy, who was petite and blond like his first two victims, Derek decided to keep a closer eye on him.

"What did he do?"

"He missed his nine a.m. appointment. I tried calling, but he's not answering," Bo explained. "It's possible he overslept or is too sick to pick up the phone."

"Or he's doing things he shouldn't be doing." Derek had expected this to happen eventually. The man was a weasel, and he'd been pushing the limits of his probation since he was released. "Other than home or his job, do you know where he might go?"

"I don't know any of the places he hangs out. I contacted his counselor, who is court-ordered to divulge any relevant information concerning Nelson's treatment."

"What did he have to say?"

"They discussed the usual subjects Thursday morning, but he said Nelson seemed antsy. Excited and secretive."

"Excited and secretive. Are we thinking he's set his sights on a victim?"

"Hard to say. He could be hyped about a new video game coming out."

"I'll have someone track him down."

"If he's not unconscious in his trailer or in the hospital in critical condition, call me back. I'll violate his parole and have him tossed back in prison."

"I'll keep you apprised." Derek disconnected and called his brother-in-law. Trudy was older than Nelson's last two victims, but that didn't mean she was safe if he was ready to reoffend.

"Yeah," Brian said by way of greeting, and the sound of metal spatulas clanking on the flat grill filled the background.

"It's Derek. Have you seen Nick Nelson anywhere near the diner in the past few days?"

The clanking stopped. "That pervert who used to creep on Trudy? He's not suicidal enough to come back now that I'm here with her."

Brian had been one of Derek's deputies up until last year, when he was let go for conduct unbecoming an officer of the law, and he worked full-time at the diner now.

Utensils clanked in the background again as Brian tended to the food on the grill. "Why are you asking about the perv?"

"He missed his parole appointment."

"Can't say I'm surprised. I always knew the guy was a ticking time bomb, but I figured he would go off long before now."

"We don't know that he has."

"Don't play the diplomatic card. You wouldn't be calling except you're thinking the same thing as me. He's got a thing for blondes."

"Yes, he does. Keep an eye on Trudy."

Brian snorted. "You don't need to tell me to look after my own wife."

There was a time when Derek *did* have to tell Brian that, back when he gave more time and attention to his addictions than his wife, but Brian had grown a lot over the past year. "Fair enough. Call me if you see him. Do *not* break his bones."

"I didn't catch that last part. You're cutting out."

"Brian, I mean it. I know you hate the guy for creeping on Trudy, but do not confront him if he shows up at the diner."

"What . . . say? Can't . . ."

The call disconnected. Derek shook his head at his brother-in-law's antics and hoped he had the sense to mind his temper. He didn't want to have to lock him up for assault.

He tapped an extension into his desk phone and hit the speaker button. "Rusty, I need you in my office."

If it was possible to track down Nick Nelson, Rusty would. Derek hoped the man was simply passed out in his trailer, even if it was from a night of too much drinking, because if he was in the wind, any of the young women in the vicinity could be his next victim.

It was like a bug hugged his face.

The description Noelle had given of the masked menace made her cringe inwardly with embarrassment. That one was going to haunt her in the wee hours of the morning for weeks.

She was an author, a supposed weaver of words, and yet that was the only description of the man's mask she could cobble together. To make matters worse, the deputy on the other end of the line had choked on his drink, and some of that "choking" sounded suspiciously like laughter.

He recovered enough to assure her the department would send someone out to the road to look around. When he asked for her name, she decided anonymity would be less humiliating. But it was now her personal mission to find that exact mask, if only to make herself feel better.

She unlocked her front door and stepped into her unusually chilly house. Walt must've opened the window in his room. He had no concept of what it cost to heat a house this size.

She released a sigh and let her frustration go with it. Stressing about it wouldn't fix it. A warm sweater and a hot matcha latte, however, could fix almost anything.

Shrugging on her fluffy cardigan, she prepared her latte and settled at the dining room table with her laptop.

"Bug costume masks," she said, typing the words into the internet browser.

She scrolled through the results as she sipped her earthy tea. Lady bugs, bumblebees, a duck—because that made sense—praying mantis. In hundreds of results, nothing even remotely resembled what she'd seen.

It was possible the mask was homemade or commissioned, in which case, she wouldn't find a listing or photograph online. But why would someone go to that much trouble and expense for a mask?

She sat back in her chair and cradled her latte in both hands as she pondered that question.

Haunted house workers took great pride in their custom outfits, but they didn't put themselves at risk by standing on the side of the road or charging at vehicles. Especially in this part of the United States, where most citizens legally carried guns.

The clown-chase trend a few years back revealed the dangers of dressing up in a costume and chasing people in public for video views. That insanity screeched to a halt after a citizen with coulrophobia put two bullets in Pogo the Clown.

Some people found fear thrilling, but most people didn't, and they reacted defensively. If Noelle and Skyler had been on foot when the masked man charged toward them, she would've drawn her weapon.

Children in masks was one thing, but there was something unsettling about adults hiding their faces. It masked their features but also their intentions.

What were Bug Face's intentions this morning?

If Noelle hadn't pulled out and around the buggy to escape him, would he have collided with the side of her car? Would he have tried to get in the backseat with her daughter? Or was there someone else in the trees recording his antics for social media?

Unfortunately, she had no way to answer that question.

She stared at the less-than-helpful mask results on her computer, and then her gaze slid past the screen to the colored pencils and art paper Skyler had left on the table. Noelle wasn't an artist by any stretch of the imagination, but she could try her hand at sketching. How badly could it turn out?

Leaning forward, she grabbed the sketch pad and colored pencils and set to work creating the image in her mind.

"Hmm. A bit of green," she thought out loud. The mask had an iridescent quality unlike the plastic and felt ones that dominated her search results.

She added a touch of dark green and then lighter green.

Leaning back in her chair, she studied the final product. Not bad. If he had a head shaped like a gourd. "Here, Deputy, this is the green-and-black mask the man was wearing when he came running at my car this morning. Arrest him. He was clearly up to no gourd."

Nope. She did have *some* dignity, and the face-hugging-bug description was less embarrassing than this. She set down the colored pencil and closed her laptop.

The authorities would find the troublemaker . . . or they wouldn't. She had more important things to focus on. Like reinforcing the staircase banister before it caused a household accident.

In the kitchen, she rummaged through the junk drawer, only to find the super glue bottle was empty and half the items in the drawer were permanently fused together.

A sigh escaped. "Skyler."

How many times had she told her not to mess with the super glue? Apparently, accidentally gluing her fingers together hadn't been a strong enough lesson.

She tossed the empty container and the misshapen blob of pens and dry erase markers into the trash. Duct tape it was.

As she headed to the foyer, she used her teeth to rip off enough tape to securely bind a sumo wrestler—which of course she would only ever do in a book. She wrapped the loose piece of banister and then gave it a few tugs. It moved, but it was secure enough for now.

Her phone made an unusual ringing sound. Curious, she pulled it from her pocket and found her mother's face. *Oh no.* Mom had figured out how to use the social media video chat. This was the beginning of an endless stream of video calls involving wallpaper samples and sofa fabric choices.

She tapped the accept button. "Hey, Mom."

Mom looked back over her shoulder and called out, "It worked, Charlie!"

"Of course it worked!" Dad shouted back. "A bunch of know-it-all, baby-faced geeks get paid more than we do to make sure it works." The end of his sentence was punctuated by the pop of a nail gun.

Mom turned back to the phone, her face beaming. "Are you excited about tonight? I wish we could be there with you."

"To be honest, I'm sort of nervous."

"You've done this before. It'll be like riding a bike."

Considering she hadn't been on a bike since she wrecked hers into a tree and broke her clavicle at thirteen, that wasn't the best analogy.

"That bookstore will be packed with readers," Mom said.

"Of course it will." Dad appeared behind Mom, white dust mingling with the sweat on his forehead, and a protective mask dangling around his neck. "Our daughter is famous, after all."

"Not even close, Dad."

"I'm your father, which means I'm automatically right." He winked before his expression turned serious. He leaned closer to the phone, squinting. "What is that on the banister behind you? Is that duct tape?"

"Umm . . ." Noelle sidestepped to put the evidence of her crime behind her. "I don't see any duct tape."

"That is not how the Emory family fixes houses, young lady. We do not cut corners with super glue, hot glue, or that abominable substance known as duct tape."

Her parents had encountered every bizarre and destructive DIY "fix" known to man during their house-flipping career, and Noelle had committed a cardinal sin. At least she didn't glue the showerhead and door hinges on like the family whose house they purchased when she was fifteen.

There was so much glue holding that house together, Dad nicknamed it the Elmer's Estate.

Mom angled her face toward him. "Abominable is a bit strong, don't you think? At least it's gray duct tape instead of those blinding neon options they have nowadays. I can work the décor around gray, but there's nothing to be done for neon orange. Looks like a traffic cone."

"Aesthetics aren't really the priority, Abigail. One sneeze, and that railing will snap off and take whoever is leaning on it with it."

Mom opened her mouth to reply, but Noelle cut in. "It was either reinforce it with tape or risk your granddaughter falling over the side of the staircase and getting hurt."

The moment of silence that followed Noelle's statement made her stomach cramp. Losing their only grandchild had devastated them, and while they exchanged pleasantries with Skyler over the phone and requested pictures of her, there was a reluctance to their acceptance of her.

It wasn't that they disliked her; it was the uncertainty of the adoption process. They didn't want to fall in love with another grandchild and then lose her too.

"She's mine. Everything is official," Noelle reassured them.

"You're sure?" Dad asked. "You said her mother was in the system, and she's got no extended family, but what about her father? Did you do any digging into him?"

"Whoever her father is . . . he's a predator."

Natalie was pregnant when she ran away from her foster home at twelve years old, and her psychiatric evaluation suggested she sought approval and acceptance from older males. One of those older males—be it a teacher, a foster dad, or a sports coach—was likely the man who got her pregnant.

"He took advantage of a twelve-year-old girl," Noelle said, and even the thought of that made her queasy. "If he comes forward to claim Skyler as his daughter, his life will implode. He'll go to prison."

Dad grimaced. "I don't miss dealing with lowlifes like that from my time as a cop."

Mom reached back to place her fingers over Dad's hand on her shoulder. "Enough about that darkness. Any progress in the *mom* department?"

Noelle tried to hide her disappointment and hurt. "No. She still calls me Noelle."

Compassion softened her mother's voice. "Our granddaughter has had quite a rough life. I think as she continues to settle in, she'll come to accept you as her mother."

Noelle could only hope.

"I should really go. I have a lot to get done before the book signing," she said.

"Oh!" Mom exclaimed. "I mailed out Skyler's costume. It should arrive in a few days. I'll send you the tracking number so you can snag it as soon as it's delivered. I don't want it stolen by those fiendish porch pirates."

Noelle bit back a smile. Mom was paranoid about porch pirates.

The area of Seattle where her parents lived was brimming with thieves. Packages were still warm from the mailman's hands when they were snatched off doorsteps. Mom and Dad had had a number of items disappear, including the first printed copy of her book she sent them four months ago.

"I'll make sure Sky gets her package," Noelle assured her mother.

"Call us after the event tonight," Dad said. "I want to hear all about it."

His words warmed her. Dad had always been her biggest fan—even more so than Mom. He was an avid reader, and in between putting up drywall and fixing the messes left behind by previous home owners, he enjoyed reading her books.

Noelle told them she loved them before ending the video call.

She glanced back at the layers of duct tape around the spindles. Hopefully Dad didn't come to visit anytime soon, because *that* was just the tip of the gray, sticky iceberg.

Tossing the duct tape back beneath the sink, she decided to tackle the ever-growing laundry pile. Skyler was a fairy child. She was always outside, dancing through the mud and playing in the woods, and her clothes took a beating. Noelle picked up the dirty clothes piled beside the window and found one of Skyler's drawings on the floor.

She placed it on her dresser in case she wanted to pin it to her wall with the other miscellaneous things she'd printed or colored.

It was a cluttered collage of things and people she loved. Pictures of Skyler and Derek building a snowman, Skyler sitting on the porch steps beside Walt as she read him a book. The old man almost looked . . . happy. If such a word could be used to describe him. There were even a few selfies of Skyler and Noelle sprinkled throughout.

There was only one person missing: Skyler's mother.

Noelle opened the top drawer of the dresser and moved the socks and underwear to find the black-and-white sketch of Natalie. Skyler had no pictures of her, so the deputy who sketched her mother in an effort to identify her gifted her this one.

Noelle laminated it and taped it to the center of the collage, but Skyler pulled it down and stuffed it into the drawer where she wouldn't have to see it. She wouldn't even go visit her mother's grave at the local cemetery. Every time Noelle offered to take her, Skyler's eyes welled with tears, and she stomped out of the room.

It would take time for the rift to heal between Skyler and her mother, but one day she would be grateful she had this picture to remember her by.

Noelle sighed and closed the drawer.

Floorboards creaked, and she looked up to find Walt standing in the doorway to Skyler's room. Lines from his pillowcase creased one side of his face, and his eyelids drooped from sleepiness.

"You look like you got some rest."

Walt held up her questionable artwork. "Who drew this?"

Noelle tossed Skyler's dirty clothes into a basket as she debated whether or not she wanted to take credit for gourd man. "I did."

"Why?"

"Because I saw him on the side of the road when I was taking Skyler to school, and he . . . creeped me out."

"Did he see you?"

Noelle frowned at the odd question. "Yes."

Walt shifted nervously in the doorway and turned the drawing toward him, studying it for a long second. "Where is Sky?"

His nervousness was contagious, and Noelle tried not to let it fuel her own worry about her daughter. "Still at school. Why?"

"Did he see her?"

"I don't know. She had her head down because she was reading a book in the backseat. Why do you keep asking if he saw us?"

Walt flipped the picture back toward her. "Because this is the Dragonfly."

Noelle scrutinized her own artwork. "That looks nothing like a dragonfly to me."

"Not *a* dragonfly. *The* Dragonfly, and he's been dead for almost fifty years."

"Then that isn't who I saw, because this man was very much alive."

"Are you sure? Did you hear his footsteps? Did you see where he went?"

Noelle thought back. No, she hadn't heard the crunch of twigs and leaves beneath the man's feet as he rushed toward her car, but she hadn't been listening for it either. As for where he went . . .

It was almost as if he disappeared.

That wasn't possible. He must've ducked behind a tree or into a ditch to make it appear as though he'd vanished. Magicians performed illusions like that, and unobservant audiences were easily fooled.

Walt stepped into the room, and there was a sparkle of fear in his eyes that Noelle had never seen before. "Plenty of people have seen the Dragonfly's ghost over the years. But if he sees you, if he focuses on you . . . you die."

CHAPTER Eight

Walt's description of the Dragonfly swirled through Noelle's mind as she prepared for her book signing that started in two hours. She had never been one to believe in the spooky myths and legends that quickened other people's heartbeats.

A story about the dark side of human nature, however, was enough to make her draw her curtains and triple-check the locks on her doors.

This Dragonfly was nothing more than a campfire tale meant to instill fear. Much like the whisperings about her house. It was neither cursed nor haunted, but it *was* a place that had been struck by true evil more than once.

When she moved in a year ago, she could almost feel the people who once lived here. It was like stepping into someone else's interrupted story—an ordinary chapter cut short by tragedy. Apart from some looting, every room had been left as it was that night, providing a clear picture of the lives and deaths of the previous residents.

A veritable murder museum.

The house had sat abandoned for decades, falling into disrepair and local legend: the Bechtel house, haunted by the victims murdered within its walls and guarded by an evil spirit that took the shape of a scarecrow.

The legend was born of pure imagination and superstition. Much like the story about a dragonfly ghost and his stare of death. And it was not the kind of story she wanted relayed to her daughter, whose fear of monsters had sent her into hiding last night.

Noelle had crumpled up the mask drawing and requested that Walt keep his superstitions to himself. For Skyler's sake.

She pressed the back piece onto her earring, pinning the little book to her earlobe. The set was a gift from one of her readers a few years back. She'd received sporadic, surprise gifts over the years, some of them more unusual than others, but this was one of her favorites.

She considered her reflection in the cracked and chipped mirror of the upstairs bathroom, studying the wisps of gray around her temples and the deepening lines around her mouth.

Maybe it was just her inner critic, but the woman staring back at her looked much older than thirty four. Like she had aged a decade in the past five years.

Yes, well . . . a cheating spouse, the death of a child, and a brutal divorce will do that to a person, she reminded herself as she dabbed more shimmer onto her cheekbones.

She might struggle with the woman she saw in the mirror, but Derek didn't seem to mind her gray hairs, wrinkles, or thick curves. He still called her beautiful.

Setting aside the makeup brush, she checked one last time to make sure she'd gotten off all the green wax she applied to remove the peach fuzz from her chin. The last time she waxed, she missed a sliver, and she spent their entire date with a green string hanging from her chin.

When Derek pulled it off with a puzzled expression, she'd been mortified. There wasn't a corner dark enough to hide in.

She slid on her red-framed glasses, wrestling with whether or not to wear them. She had contacts, but sometimes they irritated her eyes. She slid the glasses back off and then on again.

"As good as it gets," she muttered to her reflection before turning away. She opened the bathroom door to find Skyler waiting in the hallway.

"What's as good as it gets?"

A dart of shame hit Noelle. She had a daughter now, and the way she spoke about herself would impact how Skyler thought of *her*self. She needed to be careful with her words. "Nothing. How do I look?"

Skyler looked over the blue sweater and dark jeans, and then gave a nod of approval. "Beautiful."

"Almost as beautiful as you."

Skyler grinned. "Yeah, I'm pretty cute. All the grown-ups say so. Can I have a snack? I'm starving to death."

"Death? Well, we can't have that. There are cheese sticks in the refrigerator." Skyler was off and running before Noelle could add, "And don't share them with Ben and Jerry!"

Skyler had a habit of sneaking treats to her mice, and they were nearly as round as the wheel they ran on.

Noelle descended the steps and padded into the living room cluttered with boxes of books and decorations. She had two hundred copies of her latest book. Surely that would be enough.

In the past, her publisher had organized these events and provided the supplies, but they had chosen not to publish her latest book. "Christian audiences aren't comfortable reading about human trafficking. Consider rethinking the plot," they had suggested in the rejection email.

Noelle had nearly slammed her laptop shut on the ridiculous feedback, but she couldn't afford to replace the computer if she cracked the screen. Super glue and duct tape wouldn't fix that.

Human trafficking *was* a difficult topic, and it wasn't for the easily ruffled, but it affected people from every walk of life, including Christians. Like most people, Noelle hadn't given it much thought until it affected *her* life. It crashed into her world last fall in the form of a terrified and orphaned ten-year-old girl who was desperate not to be dragged back into that nightmare.

There was no walking away.

There was no ignoring the *uncomfortable* truth.

Noelle picked up one of the two hundred copies and turned it over in her hands. *Stolen* was a work of fiction, but it was also a plea for people to open their eyes and see what was happening in the shadows of their own neighborhoods.

They could help save another Skyler.

She stared at the spine of her book. It was strange without the logo of her publisher. Their rejection forced her to navigate the unfamiliar avenue of self-publishing, where every step of the process was her responsibility. That included organizing tonight's event.

What if her mother was wrong and no one showed up? What if she spent four hours staring at the unmoving book shop door while listening to crickets serenade the death of her career?

She couldn't imagine people would want to travel for hours, only to wait in line for her signature. It wasn't like she was a celebrity. She was a woman who spent her days around the house, wearing sweatpants, sipping tea, and glaring at a blinking cursor on her laptop until she wanted to pull her own hair out in frustration.

Of course, if she ever bumped into Jaime Jo Wright—another Christian author whose books littered her e-reader—she would ask for an autograph. In the most awkward way possible, no doubt.

She hefted the first box of books and carried it out to the car. Ominous clouds crowded the fall sky, stretching well beyond the distant treetops, and Noelle eyed them as she popped her trunk.

"Don't you dare," she said.

Styling her hair for the book signing had taken a great deal of time, and if the sky opened up and released even so much as a sprinkle, her hair would resume the worship position.

Skyler carried out a box of decorations. "The boxes of books are too heavy, so I brought these."

"Thank you for the help."

"You're welcome." Skyler set the box on the ground and smacked her hands together to brush away imaginary dust. "Are you sure I can't come? I promise I won't wander around the bookstore *too* much. I could pass you books to sign and hand out bookmarks. I'm a good helper."

Unfortunately, bringing her would expose her to scrutiny and questions she wasn't old enough or emotionally prepared to handle:

Who's the girl?
Did you adopt her?
Are you fostering her?
Where did she come from?
What happened to her biological family?
Does she have anything to do with your latest book on human trafficking?

Noelle couldn't let that happen.

And then there was the risk to Skyler's safety to consider. Derek was confident none of the human traffickers or their clientele would target her again, but considering some of them were still out there, Noelle would rather not draw their attention. There would be pictures taken tonight, and she didn't want someone to capture Skyler in the background and splash her face across social media.

"You're an *amazing* helper, and when you're older, you can come with me."

Skyler squinted. “How much older? Are we talking months or years?”

Noelle almost choked with laughter at her choice of words as she returned to the house for another box. “Are we talking” was one of Derek’s more common phrases. “We’re talking years.”

Skyler sighed and stomped up the steps behind her. “Fine, but two at the most. I’ll be thirteen then, practically an adult.”

“Practically not.” Noelle picked up another box of books and hauled it out to the car. “You’ll be an adult when you’re eighteen.”

Skyler trailed behind her. “So I can come to your book stuff when I’m eighteen?”

“If you still want to, yes.” Noelle deposited the books into the trunk and went back for more.

What she wouldn’t give to have Derek around for this part. He was strong enough to carry two or three boxes at one time.

“I have time to take you to the diner, if you want to spend the evening with Trudy and Brian. They love having you there with them.”

“I’m going to hang out with Mr. Walt.” Skyler waited for Noelle to set the box in the trunk, and then added the five books she’d carried out with her.

Noelle still had some reservations about this babysitting arrangement. Walt would protect Skyler with his life, but beyond that, he had no sense of responsibility.

Movement in the corner of Noelle’s vision drew her attention to the porch. Walt stood by the railing, surveying the property like a sentinel as he puffed on his cigarette.

Where did he even get those? He didn't have an income to purchase them from the store, yet the man-made alcove inside the ancient pine trees was littered with as many cigarette butts as pine needles.

"Do you steal those cigarettes from the store?" Noelle asked. Because the church soup kitchen certainly wasn't catering to his addiction.

Smoke streamed from his nostrils like one of those angry cartoon bulls. "No need to steal them when people leave unfinished butts all over town."

He couldn't mean . . .

"Those are *used* cigarettes?"

He took a deep drag. "Barely."

The mental image of him scavenging used cigarettes from the ground and popping them between his lips nearly tripped her gag reflex. She should've known better than to ask.

"I don't want you smoking those around Skyler or in the house. That smoke is poison," Noelle said.

Skyler gasped. "But poison kills people." She whirled on Walt. "I don't want you to die, Mr. Walt. You can't smoke anymore."

"Now look what you've done." Walt grimaced and flicked away the smoldering nub.

Did he expect her to feel regret?

Skyler had so few loved ones in her life, and if he didn't prioritize his health, she would experience loss again sooner rather than later. Noelle wanted to avoid that at all costs.

"I would recommend you stay inside this evening. It's going to be bitterly cold, and considering you're already fighting a virus, it would be best to avoid taxing your body," she said, though she doubted Walt would heed her advice.

He would probably plop himself down in the wet grass for the entire evening out of sheer defiance.

"I'll call partway through the evening to check in. Please answer the landline," Noelle said. "And don't give Skyler a bunch of sugar like last time. There's leftover chicken casserole in the refrigerator."

"I looked after Sky before the two of you even met. I don't need you to tell me how to take care of her now," Walt replied, his lower lip stubbornly smashed against his upper lip.

Noelle rubbed at the twinge morphing into a headache above her left eye. *It's okay. It'll be all right. Everything will be . . . all right.*

Skyler hugged Noelle's waist and tipped her head back to look up at her. "I won't let him get into any trouble. I promise."

Noelle sighed. It was Walt's responsibility to take care of Skyler, not the other way around, but there was nothing she could do about that tonight. She climbed into the car and, reservations about this babysitting arrangement still gnawing at her, backed out of the driveway.

CHAPTER Nine

Concern spread through Derek as he leaned back in his chair, fingers gripping the edge of his desk. "You can't find him anywhere?"

Rusty shook his head, his expression grim. "I went to Nelson's trailer, but he wasn't there. As you can imagine, his neighbors weren't too forthcoming with information. All I could get out of them is that he didn't come home last night."

The trailer park outside the village used to be a family community, but over the years, families moved out and drug addicts and ex-cons moved in. None of the current residents were keen on cooperating with law enforcement.

"I called the paper factory in Cherry Creek, his place of employment, and his supervisor said he was a no-call, no-show for his shift today," Rusty continued. "First time since he hired him."

"So what happened that inspired him to risk his job and his freedom?"

"Rand, the bartender at the Copper Penny, said Nelson came in last night, already a few drinks in. He paid up and left around eleven. But that's not the troubling part."

"I'm not going to like this, am I?"

Rusty shook his head. "A teenage girl came into the bar at a quarter 'til. She tried to buy a drink. When Rand demanded to see her ID, she claimed she left it at home. Rand refused to serve her and told her to leave. When she argued with him, he threatened to call an officer to escort her from the bar. She left then, and not two minutes later, Nelson paid for his drink and left too."

Derek's gut churned. "Tell me she wasn't blond."

"And pretty, according to Rand."

Derek scrubbed his hands over his face, pausing with his fingers steepled in front of his mouth. "I've been through the incident reports from last night. There were no sexual assaults reported in that area."

"Maybe nothing happened."

"*Something* happened, or Nelson wouldn't be missing. We need to find out who that girl is and make sure she's all right."

"The bar cameras aren't hooked up—I asked—and she could've come from anywhere in the county. Rand isn't going to tell me the names of the customers there last night so I can interview them. He doesn't want law enforcement putting a dent in his paycheck."

"I would bet she's local to Cherry Creek. The Copper Penny is the only bar for fifteen miles. No one who isn't from the area goes there. Not when there are plenty of places to drink here in Weston."

"Assuming she's not homeschooled, she probably attends Cherry Creek High." Rusty checked his watch and grimaced. "The schools are closed now, but I can call on Monday, see if any female students didn't show up this morning. If he attacked someone last night, I seriously doubt she would've gone to school as usual."

Derek hated to wait until Monday. "Find out who the high school secretary is and see if he or she is willing to go back in and get that information for you. Tell them it involves a student's safety."

"And what about Nelson?"

"I'll call his parole officer. If he decides Nelson's actions violated his parole, we can put out a BOLO for him and his vehicle."

The car would be easy to spot. It was like one of the patchwork quilts Derek's mother used to make—unmatched pieces thrown together to make a whole.

"I assume you checked the surrounding hospitals to make sure he didn't end up there?" Derek asked.

"Sure did. I asked for him by name as well as any male patients who may have come in unidentified. The hospital in Morrville has an elderly John Doe, about forty years too old to be Nelson."

"Okay, let's focus on the girl Nelson followed out of the bar. Once we identify her and make sure she's all right, hopefully she can point us in his direction."

"I hate to be the one to ask this, boss, but what if there's no assault report because things went really, *really* south outside the bar?"

Meaning the girl was dead or missing and unable to report the incident.

Derek grimaced. "Let's hope that isn't the case. Keep me apprised of what you find out."

"Will do."

"Thanks, Russ." Derek waited for Rusty to step out before calling Nelson's parole officer back and giving him an update.

By this evening, every officer in the area would be on the lookout for the ex-con, and hopefully someone would come forward with information.

Is it wrong that I'm hoping he's dead in a ditch somewhere? He sent the silent question heavenward, but he already knew the answer.

God loved the Nick Nelsons of the world, too, something Derek would never be able to wrap his mind around. The man had wrecked the lives of two teenage girls. They would live the rest of their lives with the memories and pain, while their attacker was free and unrepentant. Finding Nelson dead in a ditch was preferable to him assaulting another girl.

Derek pushed up from his desk to change out of his uniform and into something more appropriate for Noelle's book signing.

He grabbed his duffel bag, but before he could heft it onto his shoulder, Rusty knocked and opened his door. "Thought you might want to know. We've got another fire."

Fires weren't unusual, especially this time of year. Bonfires easily spread to the dry leaves littering the ground. "Are we talking an out-of-control bonfire, house fire . . ."

"Barn. Raina and Earl Miller's. They were coming back from Earl's physical therapy appointment and found the structure engulfed in flames."

Internal alarms went off. "You were just over there, checking the property for a trespasser."

"Safe to say it wasn't a coyote or fox. And there's something else." Rusty paused before adding, "There's someone inside the barn. And he's on fire."

She was so beautiful—from the way her smooth black hair shimmered under the fluorescent lights to the sparkle in her eyes as she smiled. Even her red-framed glasses added a note of cuteness to her features.

With a graceful sweep of her pen, Noelle signed the book in front of her, closed the cover, and passed it back to the old woman in front of the table. "Thanks so much for coming."

"I wouldn't have missed it for the world. You're my favorite author, and I've been hoping you would have a book signing close enough for me to drive to."

"I'm glad this worked out."

"Me too. I did have a question about . . ."

The woman's voice faded to an annoying buzz in my ears, and the mental image of swatting her down like a fly flickered through my thoughts. She was soaking up Noelle's time like she was someone special, but there was nothing special about her. She was as plain as the beige wallpaper on the back wall of the bookstore.

When the self-important woman finally moved along, the line shifted forward, scarcely a scoot of my foot across the worn carpet. The line wrapped around the shelves and into every corner and crevice, but thankfully, I was only three people back from the table now.

I would've been at the front, but work kept me later than I expected.

My pulse picked up every time I inched forward. The old man with the rifle had kept me away from the house—away from her—last night, but he wasn't here to stand between us now.

"I know it's probably too soon to ask, since you just published this book, but when's the next one?" The woman in front of me asked.

Noelle laughed graciously. "A year or so."

"Well, I'll try to savor this one."

Good luck, *I thought. I tried to savor it too, but I had already devoured it ten times over. Even the acknowledgments, in which Noelle thanked her readers for all the prayers, well wishes, and patience during her time of grief.*

The last remaining obstacle between me and Noelle slid out of line and made her way toward the door. Sweat beaded across my palms, and my heart drummed in my chest as I stepped forward.

Noelle smiled at me, her eyes seeming to truly see me. "Hi there. Did you bring a book with you or would you like to purchase one? I have plenty."

I forced my fingers to release the book I held, no doubt leaving sweaty fingerprints all over the cover, and offered it to her. "I brought one."

Noelle took it from me and opened it, and two vertical lines appeared between her eyebrows as she looked up at me. "I have free bookmarks if you'd like some."

She didn't approve of me bending the pages. I should've thought to bring a pristine copy. "I know bending the pages is taboo, but there are so many things I want to mark that I would need a hundred bookmarks."

My explanation smoothed the skin between her eyebrows. "I'm glad you find value in it. Who would you like it autographed to?"

I gave her my name, a thrill shooting through me as I leaned forward to watch her write it. She signed her maiden name at the bottom—Noelle Emory—and looped the end of the Y *into a heart.*

I was glad she didn't change her author name when she married her ex-husband, Tyrese McKenzie. That sleaze didn't deserve her, and I was glad he was gone from her life.

Noelle lifted her pen from the page and closed the book as she looked up. The stiff and guarded shift in her posture made me self-conscious. Had I done something to upset her? Or . . . did she recognize me?

The screen of her phone lit up, and she glanced at it before saying to me, "It was very nice to meet you, and I hope you enjoy the rest of your evening."

She slid my book back to me.

There were so many things I wanted to say, but all my tongue managed to push through my lips was, "Thanks."

I caught a glimpse of her phone screen before she tilted it toward her, and my molars involuntarily ground together behind my smile when I caught the name of the sender: Derek. The new boyfriend.

I didn't have a chance to read the message he sent, but it was clear it relayed bad news. As Noelle silently read, she sank lower in her chair, and the sparkle of joy in her eyes flickered and died.

Flames licked at the evening sky, refusing to be extinguished as firefighters fought to control them before they could leap to the surrounding trees.

The old barn, filled with bales of hay and beds of straw, fed the flames faster than the water from the hoses could reach them. It was like battling a monster that refused to die.

Even from a safe distance, Derek could feel the heat of the fire stinging his cheeks. It was too hot and too unstable for the firefighters to enter, which meant the man inside would remain there until the fire was subdued.

There was no saving him.

There was no saving the barn.

Both would be burned beyond recognition before the last ember cooled. If there was anything to be grateful for, it was that the smoke inhalation likely would've killed the man before he ever felt the flames.

"This makes me sick," Rusty admitted, tipping his hat back so he could wipe his sweaty forehead with the handkerchief he kept in his pocket. It came away colored by the ash and smoke that thickened the air.

"Me too," Derek admitted.

First Raina had lost her best friend to cancer, then her husband had suffered a paralyzing accident, and now this.

"Why do terrible things always happen to good people?" Rusty muttered.

"Terrible things happen to everyone, Russ. It just feels worse when they happen to people we think don't deserve it."

He squinted against the curtain of smoke in the air to see the devastated couple. Tear tracks streaked their cheeks as they clung to each other, and Raina's chest heaved with grief.

The damage to their livelihood was immeasurable, and to make matters worse, someone had died in the destruction—a sight Raina would never be able to purge from her mind.

"Let's talk to Raina and Earl, see if they have any more information for us," Derek suggested.

Rusty sighed and fell in step beside him as they crossed the grass. "I can't help but feel like I missed something the other night. If I had searched more thoroughly, I might've seen something that could've prevented this."

"You do everything thoroughly, Russ. It's your only setting. If there was nothing to find, there was nothing to find."

Rusty shook his head. "I would bet my badge someone was casing this place, and they couldn't have gotten far before I arrived to check things out. I missed them."

"You're being too hard on yourself."

"Maybe so," he agreed, but his tone suggested he still had doubts. This situation had shaken his faith in himself. "Who's going to be working this investigation?"

"Raina was my late wife's best friend. I need my best deputy on this, and that's you."

Rusty opened his mouth to object, then closed it with a nod. "If you want me on this, who's picking up the search for Nick Nelson?"

"I'll put Jimenez on it."

Rusty looked at him like his brain was as fried as the barn. "Is that a good idea, boss?"

"Why wouldn't it be?"

"Nelson preys on women, and maybe you haven't noticed, but Jimenez is a woman. A small one at that. Isn't that . . . risky?"

The barest hint of amusement curled Derek's lips, and he looked at his deputy from a different era. "Jimenez can take care of herself. And if she finds out you think otherwise, she'll tie you to the back of a tractor and plow the field with you."

"That's a colorful image."

"I'm dating an author. She's rubbing off on me."

When Raina saw them approaching, she wiped the tears from her face and tried to straighten her shoulders.

"Derek." She embraced him, squeezing tightly. "It's been a long time."

Too long. He should've reached out over the years, but Lacey had been the connection between them, and it felt strange without her. "I'm so sorry this happened, Raina."

She sniffled and drew back. "Life certainly does seem to be kicking us a lot lately." She reached out and squeezed Rusty's hand. "It's good to see you again."

"How do you all know each other?" Derek asked.

Earl spoke up. "Rusty leads the men's group at our church."

Derek's eyebrows lifted, and Rusty adjusted the belt on his hips uncomfortably. "I might be quiet about my faith at work, but that doesn't mean I don't have any."

Raina's gaze trailed back to the barn, and fresh tears shimmered on her cheeks. "Cherry Creek has been my home since I was five. Who would do this to us?"

"Is there any chance it was accidental?" Derek asked. "Faulty wiring or combustible materials like wet hay?"

Earl shook his head. "We always make sure the hay is dry before storing it in the barn, and there's no electricity. We run an extension cord for fans in the summer, and we have portable lights for after dark. And before you ask, no, we don't use space heaters in the barn. The horses are fine with straw and blankets."

"Have you had any problems with anyone lately? For any reason, even something that seems insignificant?"

"Not that I recall. We get along well with everyone at church, and we don't go too many places outside of that and my physical therapy appointments."

"Have you seen anyone around the property lately who doesn't belong here?"

Raina shared a look with Rusty. She didn't want to mention his visit or the possible trespasser in front of her husband. "I—"

"A week ago," Earl said, "after Raina left for the store, I saw a man at the edge of our cornfield. He must've thought no one was home, because he was walking around the barn right out in the open. With his beard, his hat, and his clothes, he could've passed for one of the Yoders next door, but I didn't recognize him."

Raina looked down at him in surprise. "Why didn't you tell me?"

"I know you're always worried. About the finances, my health, the farm. I wasn't going to add to it. Besides, I handled it."

"What do you mean you handled it?"

Earl crossed his arms. "The way a man handles things out here in the sticks. I threw open the back door, pointed my gun at him, and told him to leave."

"Earl! He could've been armed too. And then what would you have done?"

"There was no way for him to know I don't have enough strength in my fingers to open a bottle of ketchup, let alone pull a trigger. He tore off through the field, and that was the end of it."

Raina looked like she wanted to throttle her husband for how he'd handled the situation, but she only said, "If you had told me, I might've been able to pass that information along to the sheriff's department when I saw someone sneaking around the barn Wednesday night."

Earl's head jerked up. "What?"

"Oh, should I have told you?"

Derek cleared his throat to interrupt their argument. They were both dealing with strong emotions, and someone was going to say something they shouldn't. "The sheriff's department has a forensic artist. Could you describe the man you saw last week?"

"Absolutely," Earl said.

"I'll have Deputy Grisham call this evening and schedule a time to meet with you. I know you have a lot going on, but sooner rather than later would be best."

Shouting voices drew every eye to the barn, and firefighters backed up, urging others to do the same. The roof buckled under the flames and crashed down, sending a plume of sparks and ash into the air.

Raina gasped and pressed a hand to her mouth. "That poor man. They'll never get him out."

"Any idea who he might be?" Rusty asked.

"No. No one should've been in there, and there was so much smoke, and the flames surrounding him . . ." Raina pressed a wadded up tissue to her lips. "All I could tell was that he was male."

"What about that Amish boy you hired to help out last year? Would he have any reason to be in the barn?" Rusty asked.

"Micah Yoder, one of the teenage boys from next door," Earl clarified. "He works in the mornings. The horses were fed, and there wasn't any field work planned for this evening."

Next door could be half a mile down the road in the country. Could Micah have spotted the smoke, rushed in to save the horses, only to get caught up in the flames himself?

"How is your relationship with Micah?" Derek asked.

"Good. He's a wonderful boy. A hard worker. And he loves our horses as if they were his own," Raina explained, and then a look of horror crossed her face, and she turned toward the barn. "You don't think . . ."

"We're only asking questions," Rusty said. "We don't want to jump to any conclusions."

"Good, because Micah would never set our barn on fire," Earl informed them. "He's not like those kids who caused all those problems a few years back."

Four years ago, a group of teenagers began setting fire to sheds and fences around Halloween for fun. Unfortunately, their fun came to a quick and deadly end when the youngest of the group stood too close to a shed when the flames ignited the flammable materials inside.

Micah might not participate in something like that, but that didn't mean other kids in the community wouldn't jump on a barn-lighting trend. There had already been one barn fire this month; two fires in two weeks was suspicious.

"Mr. and Mrs. Miller!" a male voice called out, and everyone turned to see a teenage Amish boy barreling toward them.

"Oh, Micah!" Raina swept the boy into a hug. "I'm so glad you're safe. We were worried you might've been in the barn when this happened."

"No, we were visiting family."

Derek and Rusty exchanged a look. If Micah was safe, then whose body was buried beneath all that scorched debris?

"How long until we can get in there and remove the body?" Rusty asked.

"One of the firefighters said it could be hours before the last of the flames go out, but no one moves the body until the medical examiner does a cursory inspection and photographs are taken."

"That's going to make for a long night."

Yes it would.

CHAPTER Ten

Icy wind nipped at Noelle's skin as she stepped out of the brick bookstore into the poorly lit parking lot, and she shivered.

Crisp fall leaves whispered across the blacktop like they were sharing secrets, and there was a faint whistle on the air as wind curled around naked tree branches.

Disappointment and a sliver of hurt cut through her as she surveyed the empty parking lot.

Even though Derek said he would be late tonight, he'd missed the book signing entirely. She hoped he might pull into the parking lot at the last minute and ask her how the night went while escorting her to her car—which sat in a pool of darkness left by burned-out lamps.

Perfect place to be jumped by a murderer and stuffed in your own trunk, her imagination offered up.

Another internal voice, one that sounded suspiciously like her ex-husband, scoffed inside her head. *You're being paranoid, and it's embarrassing.*

The words were so clear and sharp that he could've been standing in front of her, spitting them into her face.

One of the few things she'd excelled at during her marriage was embarrassing her husband. He was a partner at a prestigious law firm, and she was a woman who "never outgrew her childish fondness for made-up stories."

He would've mocked her for scheduling this book signing, and even though it was a success, he would've found a way to diminish it.

"Get out of my head," she muttered, shoving away the hurtful memories. Tyrese was no longer a part of her life, and he didn't deserve space in her thoughts.

Shifting the box of books and decorations to one arm, she dug around in her purse for her keys. Her hand cramped as she closed her fingers over the key ring. She must've autographed two hundred books tonight. Her hand wasn't the only thing that was tired. If she subjected her cheek muscles to one more smile, they might spasm in protest.

Despite the tiredness stretching from her brain to her fingertips, the night had been enjoyable. Her readers—the most eclectic and wonderful people—had poured in from all over, allaying her earlier fears.

Some had brought their own books to be signed, but many purchased the copies she'd brought with her, and she was grateful she only had the one box to haul back to the car. The extra cash would help too. Skyler needed some new clothes.

The thought of her little girl brought a smile to her lips. When Noelle called the house halfway through the book signing, Skyler had answered—breathless and giddy from dancing around the house to music still blaring in the background.

The snap of a lock behind her made her flinch, and she glanced back at the shop, catching a glimpse of the shopkeeper as he turned out the interior lights. The patio light overhead winked out next.

Right then. Time to go.

Another gust of cold air scraped along Noelle's exposed skin as she crossed the dark parking lot. What she wouldn't give for a remote car starter so she could sink into a preheated vehicle.

Bracing the box on her thigh, she popped open the trunk. She was about to drop the armload inside when a reverberating bang made her jump. Her grip slipped, and everything crashed to the pavement, scattering around her feet.

Heart pounding in her throat, she hunkered behind her open trunk lid and scanned the darkness for the source of the bang. Was it a gunshot? She'd grown up in Seattle, where gunshots were common at all hours.

Another bang drew her gaze to the alley.

She half expected a dark figure to flee from the opening, but all she saw was a metal dumpster, the lid trembling against the wind holding it to the side of the neighboring building. When the gust of wind moved on, the lid dropped back down onto the dumpster with a crash.

The tension left Noelle's body on a laugh. She'd been ready to crawl into her trunk to hide from a dumpster drive-by. "Oh, I'm glad no one saw that."

Sometimes she forgot that the city of Weston wasn't like the area of Seattle where she lived before.

Shootings were so rare, they still made front-page news in the local papers.

She crouched to gather up her belongings.

"I was beginning to think you wouldn't come out."

Her attention snapped toward the unexpected voice, the hairs on her arms and neck rising in alarm.

A man emerged from the shadows, his outdated wide-bottom jeans swishing like bells around his feet as he moved. The lamplight caught the glossy cover of Noelle's latest book, *Stolen*, clutched in his hands, but even without it, she would've recognized him.

The way he leaned over the table while she autographed his book this evening had made her uncomfortable. She didn't have an unreasonably large personal bubble, but if she could feel a stranger's breath on her skin, they were too close.

Not trusting him to be any more respectful of her personal space now, she stood and searched her brain for a polite response. "If I didn't say it earlier, thank you for coming to the book signing. I appreciate the support."

He lowered his eyes and clutched his book to his chest. "An autographed copy will be a perfect addition to my collection."

She forced a smile despite her nerves. "I'm happy I could sign the book for you. I hope you have a good night."

He took another step forward. "I've been waiting for you since the bookstore closed thirty minutes ago."

The admission sent her pulse racing, and she assessed him, trying to decide whether he was a threat or just socially clueless.

Maybe he doesn't know that waiting to catch a woman alone in a dark parking lot is a social faux pas, she thought, but her inner critic scoffed in response. *Of course he knows. He's dangerous.*

"The car I drove isn't too far. We could go get some coffee together and talk," he suggested.

He couldn't seriously expect her to say yes to that invitation. "It's pretty late for coffee. Besides, I really need to—"

"Tea," he hurried to say, like he was trying to stave off her refusal. "I know you really like hot tea."

His eager steps brought him far too close, and Noelle stumbled over her belongings on the ground as she backed beyond his reach. "Whoa. Look, um . . ."

His eyebrows dipped when she hesitated on his name. "Zac. You wrote it in my book."

Right. Zac with only a C.

"Yes. I remember." She glanced down at her belongings. Where had her phone and gun landed? Were they still in her toppled purse, or had they slid under the car? "Tea is a thoughtful invitation, but I need to get home. If you have any questions or ideas you'd like to share, send me an email, and I'll get back to you as soon as I can, okay?"

"But I made the drive from Columbus."

"And I truly do appreciate that, but . . ."

"You said you wanted to see me."

She blinked. "What?"

"I commented on your social media post about this book signing and said I would be here. You said, 'I look forward to seeing you there.'"

A chill that had nothing to do with the dropping temperature wrapped around Noelle's spine, and she floundered for a response. Most of her readers would've recognized that as an invitation to the event, not an invitation into her personal life.

"I think you misunderstood," she finally managed.

"You're saying you didn't want me to come?"

"No, that's not what I'm saying. It's just that . . . this isn't really the appropriate setting for a conversation. It's . . . making me a little uncomfortable."

"You think I'm a creep, and you want me gone," he said, and the way his voice and expression dropped flat made her heart skip.

That wasn't normal.

"I'm not a disgusting pervert."

"I didn't say you were," Noelle managed, and she could almost hear her father's voice in her head: *That's my girl. Defuse the situation if you can. If you can't, fight with anything you can get your hands on.*

Zac's hardened features relaxed. "Good. Because it's not true. After you get to know me better, you'll realize that."

Noelle shifted her key ring in her grip, the cool metal of her car key slipping between her middle and index finger. "It's been a long day, and I'm exhausted, so I'm going to call it a night."

She stepped away from the car, hoping she could dash around to the driver's side and lock herself in before this situation spun completely out of control.

"You can't leave." Zac grabbed her arm, snatching her out of motion. "I have to tell you something."

Noelle's heart pounded in her temples as she prepared to slam her key into his throat and start a fight she wasn't sure she could win. But then a light flicked on behind her, and the door to the bookstore opened.

The kind voice of the old bookshop owner called out. "Ms. McKenzie, is everything all right?"

Thank you, God.

Noelle's fingers remained tight on her keys as she regarded Zac like a rabid animal that might attack at any moment. "Thank you for checking, Mr. O'rello. I think I'd like to come inside and make a call."

"Come on then. I was about to head out, but I forgot my cell phone by the register. Else I wouldn't have realized you were still here. I can wait with you for a few minutes."

Noelle jerked her arm free of Zac's grip and backed toward the building. The flat expression on his face as he watched her retreat chilled her. She stepped into the safety of the bookstore and accepted the old man's phone.

With shaking fingers, she punched in Derek's number.

CHAPTER Eleven

The scent of smoke clung to Derek as he stripped out of his jacket and hung it on one of the wall hooks inside his office. He lifted the hat from his head, brushing at the ash speckling the brim, and a breath laden with exhaustion and grief escaped his chest.

This was the second barn fire in two weeks, but this one did more than destroy the family's equipment and supplies vital to their livelihood; it ended a life.

The victim, a man whose identity remained a mystery, had been found slumped against one of the barn's thick support beams, his wrists together in his lap. The body position was unnatural for someone trying to escape a fire. Even an unconscious man wouldn't fall into that position.

The medical examiner would give his determination tomorrow, but Derek suspected Abbott would rule the death a homicide.

Elsa, his white Labrador retriever, wagged her tail as she came over to greet him. He patted her head with one hand and rubbed at his dry, bloodshot eyes with the other.

It had only been a year since the last Cherry Creek homicide, and news of another murder would hit the community hard.

A part of Derek's job was keeping the community informed about criminal events and safety hazards in the area. If he didn't get ahead of this, fear would spread through the small village as quickly as the flames across the straw-covered floor of the barn.

He would wait for the autopsy results before he buckled down on what to tell the public. Right now, all he wanted to do was wash away the scent of smoke and death, change into clean clothes, and head over to the bookstore to see Noelle.

He glanced at his watch and then dropped his chin to his chest with a groan. The book signing ended almost twenty minutes ago. He'd missed it entirely.

Nicely done, he silently scolded himself.

Noelle's ex-husband never supported her writing career, and it had taken a lot of courage for her to invite Derek into that part of her life. He had rewarded that courage by becoming so immersed in his work that he lost track of time and left her waiting and wondering.

He had never been good at balancing his job and personal life. Lacey was the one person who had helped him regulate his tendency to fixate on work.

"You okay, Cap?"

Derek peeled open his irritated eyes to see Deputy Jimenez, one of the few female officers in the department. "I told you to quit calling me Cap. I'm not Steve Rogers."

"Maybe if you lost the beard there would be less confusion."

"The beard stays."

She shrugged. "Weren't you supposed to be somewhere important this evening?"

"Noelle's author event. Unfortunately, I missed it."

Jimenez hissed in a breath between her teeth. "You want me to grab a blanket from the supply room so you don't freeze in the dog house tonight?"

"Your thoughtfulness is touching. But Noelle doesn't solve problems by shutting people out or giving them the silent treatment."

Jimenez propped her hands on her belt. "My family doesn't do the silent treatment either. Mamá starts screaming in Spanish, grabs the wooden spoon, and starts swinging it around like it's a maraca."

"Don't ever invite me to one of your family get-togethers. I have a feeling I'll have to arrest someone."

"You should take flowers when you apologize. All women like flowers."

"Even you?"

"Roses. I love how they're beautiful but they also stab people."

Derek was too tired to smile at her amusing antics. "Sometimes I wonder how you passed your psych evaluation, Jimenez."

"A secret I will never share." She zipped her lips with her fingers and winked. "Anything you need from me before I go?"

"Why are you even here this late?"

"I had to put a pervy grandfather in lockup and fill out the paperwork. Glad to pass that one off to the DA and wash my hands of it. Literally. I felt so dirty after touching him, I had to scrub my hands twice."

Derek grimaced. He hated cases like that. "I'm sorry to do this to you, but I need you to look into the whereabouts of Nick Nelson. I'm concerned he might be active again."

She offered him a flat stare that might've frightened a smaller man. "I finish with one perv, and you hand me another."

"You intimidate them with that homicidal stare of yours."

She lifted her chin. "You bet I do. I will happily wreck that man's day. First thing tomorrow. Night, Cap, and good luck with your lady."

Derek glanced at the bundle of flowers lying on his desk. He'd picked them up on his lunch to give to Noelle as a congratulations bouquet. Now they would be apology flowers.

He grabbed his phone from his pocket to call her, but before he could unlock the screen, an unknown number popped up.

He tapped the green button to answer. "Derek Dempsey."

"Derek."

The terrified voice shot adrenaline into his heart. "Noelle? What's wrong?"

Derek's fingers gripped the steering wheel too tightly as he turned his cruiser into the parking lot of the bookstore—a red brick building that stood tall between a closed thrift store and a cornfield.

His headlights washed away the shadows left by burned-out lamps, but the assailant was nowhere in sight. When Noelle called, the man was still on the premises, rummaging through her belongings on the ground. The darkness was too thick for her to identify what, if anything, the man picked up before he abandoned her things and rounded the building.

Derek's primary concern was her gun. If the man was as unstable as Noelle described, and he had her revolver, he might do something impulsive.

Derek drew his sidearm as he climbed from his vehicle, keeping it angled toward the ground. He scanned his surroundings, his gaze sliding over the dark shop windows, Noelle's pink Volkswagen, and landing on the cornfield.

The field stretched as far as he could see, the tall, golden stalks offering cover for anyone who hunkered down.

Derek knew he should wait for the Weston police unit wailing ever closer—inside city limits was their jurisdiction—but he couldn't wait around for backup if the woman he loved was in danger.

God, if he's got Noelle's gun, please help me to see him before he sees me.

He inched toward Noelle's car. His first priority was to recover her gun, if it was still there, and then he would check the grounds to make sure the man was gone.

He grabbed his flashlight from his belt and clicked it on as he crouched by the trunk, visually sifting through the items scattered on the ground. He found her phone, but no gun. He bent lower to illuminate the undercarriage of the car, and the beam of light caught the barrel of a silver revolver.

"Thank you," fell beneath his breath.

Noelle didn't think the man came here with the intention of hurting her, which meant he might not have brought a weapon. Even so, that didn't mean he was harmless.

Derek retrieved the gun and cell phone, tucking them securely into the pockets of his uniform.

A clanking sound from the back of the building grabbed his attention, and he rose, squinting in that direction. He didn't want to go down that unlit alley between the bookstore and the cornfield, but he needed to.

Steeling himself, he rounded the corner.

The dried leaves of the cornstalks rustled and flapped in the breeze, adding to his already taut nerves. Derek was born and raised in the country, and few things about the area truly rattled him, but fields of corn were at the top of that list. People wandered into mazes of corn in the fall for fun. After his childhood experience, he would have to be hog-tied and dragged.

He swept his flashlight over the rows as he moved and then over the side of the building to check the integrity of the windows. None had been broken into.

A rusted truck was parked by the back door under a security light—the owner's, most likely. The clanking sound came again, and he snapped his flashlight toward movement. A soup can, caught by the wind, rolled along the pavement as a hungry raccoon chased after it. Poor guy probably fished it out of the dumpster for dinner, only to have the wind snatch it away.

The wail of sirens cut out.

Backup had arrived. They could finish searching the surrounding area for a threat while Derek checked on Noelle. He returned his flashlight to his belt and tugged on the lever of the metal door at the back of the building. Locked.

He pounded the side of his fist on the door and shouted, "Noelle! It's Derek."

A minute later, the bolt on the inside slid sideways, and the door screeched open. Noelle appeared in the doorway, lines of worry creasing her forehead.

Derek holstered his sidearm. "He's gone."

She surged forward and threw her arms around his neck. "I'm glad you're here."

He held her and released a breath of relief into her hair, grateful she was safe. The situation could've taken any number of awful turns. "Are you sure you're okay?"

She buried her face in his neck. "I'm sure."

"He didn't hurt you when he grabbed you?"

"He surprised me more than anything."

He tightened his arms around her, wishing he had never responded to that barn fire. Rusty could've handled it, and his presence had done little to comfort Raina and her husband. "I'm sorry I wasn't here. I should've been."

Her breathing hitched the way it always did when she was about to cry. He hated it when she was hurting. It was even worse when he was the source of that pain.

"You smell like smoke," she finally said, her voice thick with restrained tears. "Was there a fire?"

"Yeah."

"Is everyone okay?"

He hesitated. "The property owners are fine, but someone died in the fire. It looks intentional."

Noelle drew back in surprise. "Murder?"

He nodded and changed the subject. She didn't need death and grief added to the stress she was carrying tonight. "Why don't we get you home? We can worry about filing a report and identifying him tomorrow."

She swiped at the moisture beneath her eyelashes with her fingertips. "I don't think there's much point in filing a report. I'm sure I blew the whole situation out of proportion."

Derek bit back his anger—not at her, but at her ex-husband, who had never missed an opportunity to make her doubt herself. It was a wound she still struggled with. "Please don't do that."

Confusion etched those adorable quotation marks between her eyebrows. "Do what?"

"Dismiss your instincts and doubt your perceptions. Those instincts are there for self-preservation, and you're an intelligent woman who knows what she sees. I don't doubt you, and you shouldn't either."

He'd seen plenty of women downplay dangerous situations because they were afraid of being labeled as hysterical or paranoid, and it usually put them in even more danger.

Noelle averted her eyes as she processed his words, and when she looked back at him, she said, "Thank you."

Derek kissed her forehead. "There's nothing to thank me for."

An officer appeared at the edge of the building on Derek's right and paused, appraising the two of them. Satisfied that neither of them matched the description of the man they were looking for, he relaxed. "You Captain Dempsey?"

Derek nodded once.

"I watch your community update videos on Facebook." The officer looked from him to Noelle. "Dispatch sent us here for a potentially armed prowler, dressed like he walked out of the 1970s. Have you seen him?"

"I think he left before I arrived," Derek said.

A female officer crept out of the alley between the two businesses, spotted her partner, and shook her head. The man wasn't hiding in there either.

All eyes turned toward the swaying stalks of corn. If he was out there in the field, no one was going to find him.

CHAPTER Twelve

Treetops bowed and whipped in the storm sweeping through Wade County, pelting the roof of Noelle's Volkswagen with twigs and acorns as she navigated the back road. Dead leaves clung to the wipers, smearing raindrops across the windshield with every lazy swipe.

She glanced at the twin beams in the rearview mirror. Derek had insisted on escorting her home to make sure no one else followed her.

Before tonight, she wouldn't have believed any of her readers capable of something so intrusive and unsettling. She'd received an unusual gift or message here and there over the years, but nothing that made her fear for her safety. The bulk of her readers were amazing, *normal* people.

"I am not going to let one slightly off-balance man spook me," she muttered, straightening her back in determination.

Besides, he hadn't actively tried to harm her. He could simply be . . . socially dysfunctional.

Put it behind you, she thought.

As she turned into her driveway, her headlights brightened the faded and scarred structure that hid from the road behind trees even older than it was. The house's appearance and history might make it a magnet for bored village kids and sensational stories, but it was home.

Noelle parked her Volkswagen about ten feet from the porch, leaned back against the headrest, and released a few deep breaths, determined to expel every molecule of anxiety from her body. She didn't want to carry it inside to her daughter.

Derek opened her driver's door and offered her a hand out. She slid her fingers into his as she climbed into the chilly drizzle.

Her gaze reluctantly trailed to the quiet back road as he shut the door. "You're sure he didn't follow us?"

"I'm sure."

"He could've driven with his lights off."

"Light still catches on a vehicle. I watched every time a car drove past in the opposite direction. He wasn't behind me."

"Maybe he stayed really far back or—"

"Hey." He threaded his fingers through hers, squeezing gently. "I promise you he was not behind me. You've got nothing to worry about." He lifted their intertwined hands to his lips and planted a warm kiss on her knuckles. "Okay?"

At his certainty, another sliver of her anxiety slid away, and she nodded, even as her inner voice criticized, *So much for not letting the creepy man spook you.*

Unlike Derek, who had chosen a career in law enforcement, she wasn't built to deal with unhinged individuals. She preferred they stay trapped within the pages of her stories, where she could close the cover and walk away when things became too intense.

Her phone vibrated in her purse, triggering the fitness band on her wrist to do the same. She slid up her jacket sleeve to see the notification: "Call from Dad."

She paused partway up the front porch steps. "My dad is calling."

Derek noticed her hesitation. "Do you not want to talk to him?"

"He'll figure out something went wrong tonight, and he can be . . . overprotective." Like "jump on a plane and appear on her doorstep in twelve hours" kind of overprotective.

"It's good to have a dad who wants to keep you safe. It means he loves you." The glint of sadness in his eyes tugged at her heart.

Derek had been eight years old when his father died, and the burden of protecting his sisters and mother had fallen on his small shoulders. For that little boy, an overprotective father would've been welcome.

"I'll give you two a minute." He squeezed her hand before letting go and putting space between them.

Noelle answered the call. "Hey, Dad."

"Hi, pumpkin. How was the book signing?"

She rubbed at her forehead and stared at the flickering sconce beside the door, considering how to word her response. "A lot of people showed up, which was a nice surprise."

"Hardly a surprise."

"Honey, would you send me a picture of you and your handsome man friend so I can hang it on the wall in the dining room?" Mom called out. "Wear something blue to complement the yellow wallpaper I put up."

A frown slid into Dad's voice. "Man friend? What is that?"

"He's in his thirties. He's not a boy. And they're not engaged yet, so I can't call him her fiancé. What am I supposed to call him? Her lover?"

Dad choked. "Don't say that. I don't . . . I don't want to hear that word."

"There's nothing wrong with the word *lover.* Unless your mind is in the sewer."

"It's *gutter*, Abigail. If your mind is in the gutter, which it isn't. And for the record, *I* put up that wallpaper while you looked online for curtain fabric. Because apparently none of the fifty sets of curtains we own match."

Noelle massaged her forehead as she listened to the lighthearted bickering about their latest renovations. Mom and Dad could argue over whether it was five thirty or half past five. It was never mean-spirited, and it usually amused her, but she didn't have the patience or the energy for it tonight.

"I appreciate you guys calling to hear how the event went, but it's been a long night, and—"

"What happened?" Dad asked.

Noelle rolled her lips between her teeth and stared at the door in front of her. How did he always know when something was bothering her?

"I know you, Ellie. Something happened. I can hear it in your voice," he said.

With a sigh of resignation, she filled him in on the evening's events. "It really wasn't that big of a deal. You don't need to worry."

"I'm your father. You don't get to tell me not to worry about your safety. I'm catching the next flight to Ohio."

Noelle bit back her frustration. That was precisely what she didn't want. As much as she would love to see her parents, she didn't want the visit to revolve around protecting her.

"It was a freak incident, Dad. There's nothing you can do by coming here."

"It doesn't sound like a freak incident to me. It sounds like a disturbed man obsessed with my baby girl, and I would like to set him straight."

"We don't even know who he is."

"Put that man of yours on the phone."

"Dad—"

"If he has any kind of backbone, he's standing next to you right now to make sure that mental case didn't follow you home."

Derek crouched at the far end of the porch, examining a wobbly railing spindle with a carpenter's eye, no doubt working out what he needed to do to fix it.

Her unsuspecting, kindhearted boyfriend had never even spoken to her father before, and this was not how she hoped their first conversation would go.

"Derek, my dad . . . would like to speak with you."

Derek rose and approached, taking the phone from her hand without hesitation. "Mr. Emory. Derek Dempsey."

"Take me off speakerphone," Dad demanded, and Noelle sighed. She had hoped to slip that detail past him and listen in on the conversation.

"Yes, sir." Derek offered her an apologetic smile and switched the phone off speaker, pressing it to his ear. "Yes, sir, I have noticed she has a habit of eavesdropping."

Noelle's mouth fell open, and she whispered defensively, "I'm an author. It's a research tactic. The things people say when they're out in public is practically gold."

Derek's grin broadened for an instant before he turned serious. "No, sir, we don't know who the man is outside of the first name he gave. I have every intention of looking into him and his whereabouts."

A sharp crack echoed through the darkness, and Noelle flinched closer to the door, cold fingers plunging into her purse to grab the handle of her gun. A freshly snapped branch crashed down in the driveway.

Derek covered the mouthpiece of the phone and whispered, "This storm is getting worse. I'll be in shortly if you want to go in."

Jittery from the fresh jolt of adrenaline, she fumbled to unlock the dead bolt and twist the knob. She retreated into the house and closed the door against the wind.

"What happened?"

She jumped at the unexpected voice.

Walt hovered by the foyer window with his rifle. "Why is Deedee here this late, and why did he drive his cop car?"

Noelle rested her head back against the door and willed her pulse to slow before she had a heart attack from all the stress. "There was an . . . incident at the book signing. Derek escorted me home."

Walt scrutinized her. "Was it the Dragonfly?"

Not the dragonfly nonsense again. Noelle dropped her purse on the entryway table. "No, it was a reader. An ordinary, very much alive man."

Walt gave a skeptical grunt.

"How did things go here?" she asked.

"Fine. We played board games and ate gummy worms and cookies for dinner."

"Gum . . ." Noelle pinched her lips shut and tried to rein in her frustration. "I asked you not to give her a bunch of sugar. There were leftovers in the refrigerator."

"She wanted gummy worms."

"Of course she did. She's eleven," she snapped. Why couldn't he follow that one simple instruction?

She blew a calming breath through her lips and decided to let it go. Scolding him wouldn't fix the problem; it would only make him combative.

"Thank you for spending the evening with her," she forced out.

"Didn't do it for you, but I suppose you're welcome just the same. We saved you some gummy worms."

With that, Walt stalked through the house and out the kitchen door.

Noelle massaged from her temple to her eyebrow. The man was going to give her an eye twitch from all the unnecessary stress. People would think she was winking at them.

She hung her jacket on the coat rack and unzipped and stripped off her boots. She preferred no shoes in the house, but the crusty dirt clumps on the floor from the treads of a man's boots were just one more indication of Walt's disregard for her rules.

God had to be testing her patience.

There was no other explanation for this living arrangement that made her want to write the man into a book and commit literary homicide.

Dodging the dirt clumps in her socks, she found her sweet girl asleep on the living room couch, one hand clutching a bag of candy, and one sockless foot dangling over the edge of a cushion.

In an instant, Noelle's anger gave way to love. She bent down to pick up the sock, wiggling it back onto the little foot.

The front door opened and closed again, and Derek appeared in the doorway. He tapped her phone against his palm. "So . . . your dad's intense."

Noelle removed the bag of candy from Skyler's hand and twisted the open end shut. "He used to be a cop. It's been decades since he left the force, but that cop still comes out when he's feeling suspicious or protective."

"I noticed. I've never been on the opposite end of an interrogation before, but I think your father now knows enough about my personal and professional life to write my biography."

Noelle winced. "Sorry."

"It's understandable. You're his daughter, and in his absence, he wants to make sure the man watching over you is competent and trustworthy."

"And what was the verdict?"

He handed her phone back to her. "He agreed not to jump on a plane tonight so long as I keep him updated."

"That's high praise."

Derek leaned his head against the doorway, his gaze falling on Skyler. "Seeing her stretched out on the couch like that makes me realize how much she's grown this past year."

Skyler had been severely malnourished and all but starved when she came into their lives, leaving her small for her age. Now that she had plenty of food, her body was sprouting upward like a bamboo tree. Evidenced by the jeans that were a couple of inches too short.

"Want me to carry her to bed?" Derek offered.

"No, I don't want to wake her. She can sleep out here tonight." Noelle unfolded the blanket from the back of the couch and draped it over her. "Do you want to stay for a cup of tea?"

"Do you ever drink water?"

"There's water in my tea."

He huffed a laugh. "I guess that's true. But I should get home. I need to feed Elsa and try to wash off some of this smoke and ash before I go to bed. Are you going to be okay tonight?"

She nodded even though she doubted she would be. Despite his assurances, she couldn't shake the fear that the man might've followed them here.

Derek pushed away from the wall and cupped Noelle's face in both hands, his thumbs caressing her cheeks. "Good night, Noelle McKenzie."

He kissed her, and when he pulled away, everything in her ached for more. *Ask him to stay*, she thought, but as tempting as that was, she couldn't suggest it.

Her faith was much stronger now than it had been when she was dating her ex-husband, and for this relationship, she wanted to do things in the order God intended. Marriage *before* physical intimacy.

The last time she was intimate with a man while dating, she became pregnant with her son, and the marriage of obligation that followed left her miserable and her husband resentful. That wasn't a chance she wanted to take with Derek.

Against every instinct in her body, she said, "Good night."

His hands fell away from her face. "I'll see you tomorrow."

She walked him to the door and stood on the porch as he climbed into his cruiser and backed out of the driveway.

Saying good-bye at night and watching him drive away was getting harder. Crawling into bed with only blankets to wrap around her at the end of a difficult day was no longer enough. She wanted more, but after how terrible her last marriage was, *more* might not be possible.

CHAPTER Thirteen

Noelle stared out her bedroom window at the fallen leaves dusted with snow as she tugged a sweatshirt over her thermal top. At some point during the night, the temperature had dropped low enough to freeze the icy rain into flurries.

The cold seeping through the thin windowpane left a permanent chill in the room, and Noelle was tempted to curl back up beneath the mound of rumpled blankets on her bed. They would still be warm, and she could burrow under them and hide from what happened yesterday.

But even if she could make the conscious decision to avoid thinking about it, her unconscious mind had its own method of dealing with things.

She had tangled herself in the sheets last night as she tried to escape the man from the parking lot. Everywhere she turned, he stood there with that disturbing blank look on his face—the kind serial killers wore in murder documentaries. She'd woken up damp with sweat and twisted like a hot pretzel in her bedding.

It was a wonder she slept long enough to have nightmares. With her anxiety heightened, every crack, groan, and whisper of sound during the storm sounded like someone breaking in. She didn't remember retrieving her gun from the safe, but she woke to it resting on the nightstand.

It was ridiculous. She'd been grabbed, not *attacked*, but the fear of what might've happened if the bookshop keeper hadn't interrupted was still alive in the back of her mind. So was the fear of what *might* happen if last night was only the beginning.

Her fingers found the pendant at her chest, and she slid it back and forth along the chain as her gaze moved to the laptop charging on the dresser.

She needed to know more about this Zac.

If he was truly a threat, there should be some indication beyond last night. Some outward sign of emotional instability.

She crawled back into bed with her laptop and settled against a mound of pillows for some old-fashioned social media stalking. She brought up her author page on Facebook and scrolled through the posts until she found the one about the book signing.

There were hundreds of comments, and she scanned them until she found a man named Zac Inman. His profile photo was a stick figure holding a computer, which would make it harder to identify him, but how many readers could she have with that name?

"I'm glad this book signing is closer to home. I'll be there," she mumbled, reading his comment aloud.

Nothing unusual about that.

She clicked on his profile. It was set to private, so all she could see were the few posts and pictures he shared with the public—like the picture of his autographed book he uploaded last night, accompanied by a brief description: "Can you believe it? I have a signed book."

The photo caption was surprisingly normal. Had Noelle checked his socials before the book signing, none of what he posted would've made her question her safety in his presence. Maybe he *was* just a socially clueless man and her anxiety was exaggerating the situation.

That little voice inside her head telling her she wasn't safe must be wrong. Even if Zac was a little off, Derek was certain they hadn't been followed last night. She was safe here in her home.

And happy, she told herself firmly. She was not going to let her daughter know something was bothering her.

Closing her laptop, she stared at the painted walls of her bedroom, and the dismal shade of watered-down dirt stared back. She'd gotten the paint at a steep discount because a dissatisfied customer had exchanged it.

Can't imagine why.

She had never liked it, but it masked the blood stains that had seeped between the panels of wallpaper she ripped down. Maybe it was time for something different. A color that walked the line between cheerful and relaxing.

She added *browse paint colors* to her mental to-do list as she dragged herself off the mattress and made her bed. She settled Tay's stuffed spider between the two front pillows, its bean-filled legs stretched out in all directions.

Skyler wasn't the only one who slept with a stuffed animal. On rough nights, like last night, Noelle wrapped her arms around the velvety spider that reminded her of her little boy and hugged it tightly. It brought her a small measure of comfort.

She lifted her eyes toward heaven and said, "Good morning, little man. Mommy loves you." She blew a kiss at the ceiling, hoping Tay might catch it on the far side of heaven.

Now it was time to be a functional adult.

Skyler needed a breakfast more nutritious than Cheerios with sweet peanut butter milk. It was something Noelle had eaten regularly as a kid—milk for calcium, peanut butter for protein, and sugar for taste. Eggs and meat had been scarce in her family.

She grabbed her doorknob and twisted, but nothing happened. She twisted it the other way, feeling the internal pieces shift, but not enough to release the latch.

"Oh, come on. Don't do this again. Not this morning."

The hardware was old, and if it wasn't sticking in place, it was so loose the knob jiggled in her hand, threatening to fall off. She wrenched the glass knob left and then right to no avail.

"Why?" She thumped her head against the door.

Why did things always go sideways when she was already having a difficult morning?

Releasing a measured breath, she lifted her forehead from the door and twisted the knob with a sharp tug. The latch released and the door jerked inward, smashing into her big toe. Pain triggered a rapid-fire release of curse words in Noelle's brain, but by the time they made it through her Jesus filter *and* her mom filter, all that came out of her mouth was a whimpered, "Ow."

Her toe throbbed, but kicking the door in revenge wouldn't make it any better.

She cast the glass knob a vengeful look. "Get your act together or I'm replacing you. Original to the house or not."

Limping out of the room, the clanking and scraping of dishes drifted up from the kitchen below.

Oh no.

She'd stayed in her room too long, and Skyler was trying to make breakfast by herself. Her sweet girl was great at many things, but using a gas stove to make scrambled eggs with cheese wasn't one of them.

Noelle hurried down the steps, hoping to prevent a fire and screaming smoke alarms, when Skyler announced, "No, it has to be chocolate chips."

Skyler's tone suggested this argument had been going on for too long. But who was she arguing *with*?

The familiar and comforting tenor of Derek's voice replied, "Blueberries are good in pumpkin pancakes. Especially the dehydrated ones."

Visions of flames devouring the walls and ceiling faded from Noelle's mind, and she found herself smiling as she padded down the hall toward the kitchen.

"I'm allergic to blueberries," Skyler said.

"How do you know that?"

"They turn my mouth purple."

Derek laughed. “Nice try, but blueberries turn everybody’s mouth purple.”

“Do they make everybody’s mouth feel weird and itchy?” Skyler challenged.

“Are you trying to scam your way into chocolate for breakfast?”

Noelle stepped into the kitchen as Skyler planted her hands on her little hips and offered Derek a look of indignation. “Would I do something so criminal?”

“She *is* actually allergic to blueberries,” Noelle informed him.

Derek turned toward her with the bag of dehydrated blueberries in his hand. “How did I not know that?”

“It’s a recent development. She was fine eating a few every now and then, but then she ate a whole container in one sitting and her lips swelled up.”

“Chocolate chips it is then.” Derek swapped the bag of dried berries for the bag of chocolate chips. He squinted at Skyler as he poured some into the bowl. “This doesn’t mean you won.”

“With chocolate chips in our pancakes, everybody wins.” She dug her spoon into the batter and mixed.

Noelle grabbed a mug from the cupboard and reached for the coffee pot. “I didn’t know you were coming by this morning.”

“I wanted to add some much-needed brightness to your day. I do have to go in and work on a few things, but the department will survive if I’m a couple of hours late on what’s supposed to be my day off.”

Gratitude welled within her.

He was always thinking of her, and even after ten months together, moments like this still surprised her. He was so different from her ex-husband that sometimes it was hard to believe they were the same species.

She lifted her mug toward him. "Thank you for refreshing the coffee supplies. I still haven't been to the store."

"I grabbed some when I picked up the breakfast ingredients. It's Trudy's recipe, so the pancakes should turn out well."

Trudy had a recipe for everything. If she took the time to build a recipe book and sell it, she could make quite a bit of money. Women would buy a copy even if they didn't have the culinary skills to boil a potato. It was the dream of being a good cook.

"I should've gotten the recipe from her. Skyler has wanted pumpkin pancakes for weeks, and I've been trying, but none of them have turned out well," Noelle said.

Skyler paused in her mixing of the batter. "Those last ones were like snot cakes. I bet they would've stuck to the wall."

"That's not an experiment I wanted to clean up."

"But it would've been fun."

Derek ruffled her hair. "Go clear the table while Noelle and I finish preparing breakfast."

"Okay." Skyler abandoned her station and skipped into the dining room.

Derek scooped pancake batter into the skillet and then leaned back against the counter, hands gripping the edges. "Rough night?"

"I wish I could say no." Noelle dressed up her coffee with pumpkin spice creamer. "I feel ridiculous for being so rattled."

The incident with Zac didn't hold a candle to the traumatic situations she put her characters through. She might need to be more merciful in her next book.

"You're not ridiculous. You were scared and threatened, and there was no way to know whether or not he would take things to a violent level. It's okay to feel how you feel," Derek said.

She drew in his words along with a deep breath, and then exhaled. "I suppose you're right. I've never been in a situation like that before, so it hit me pretty hard."

"Have you given any thought to pressing charges? Grabbing you the way he did is considered assault."

Noelle squirmed at the thought of paperwork, interviews, and possible court proceedings over something so mundane. "No, I don't want to deal with all that. I wasn't hurt, and when I looked him up on social media this morning, I didn't see any red flags." She caught the subtle thinning of Derek's lips even though he said nothing. "You disagree."

"It's your decision. I do think it's important to have a record of the encounter, even if you don't want to pursue charges."

"I'll think about it."

Derek flipped one of the pancakes. "I'll check into him when I get to work. But if he has a history of violence or stalking—"

"Then I'll press charges. Unless you find something concerning, though, I'd rather put it from my mind. I don't want that one bad interaction to color my memory of an otherwise wonderful evening."

Of course the evening would've been better had he showed up like he promised. She cringed inwardly at the selfish thought. Someone's property had been destroyed, and another person had lost their life. Helping them was infinitely more important than attending her book signing.

"I know I said it yesterday, but I'm sorry for not being there last night," Derek said.

Noelle offered a halfhearted smile. "Always with the mind reading."

"I know how hard it's been for you to invite me into your world of writing, and I don't want my broken promise to change that or make you doubt that I care."

Noelle stared into her mug as she wrestled with whether or not to voice the question that had been nagging at her since she learned about the fire. "You have at least eight deputies per shift. I guess I don't understand why you couldn't let them respond to the emergency call instead."

She braced herself for his defensive reaction, but then she remembered he was nothing like Tyrese. He wouldn't shout and fling accusations at her to deflect attention from his own actions.

"Raina Miller, the woman who owns the barn that was set on fire, was a friend of mine," he explained.

"Past tense?"

He nodded, lips tight. "She was Lacey's best friend, and even though my wife was the bond between us, we spent a lot of time together in school and during my twenties. We were permanent fixtures in each other's lives. And then Lacey died and . . ."

"You lost touch."

"We were both grieving, and for me . . . Raina reminded me that Lacey was gone. I couldn't be around her without focusing on the unfillable void between us. I think I unconsciously put distance between us."

"It sounds like you did what you needed to do to heal."

"I did, but in doing what was best for me, Raina lost two friends. That was my fault. When that call came in, I knew I had to help her, but I hate that it means I broke a promise to you."

Noelle set down her coffee and crossed the kitchen to take his hands. "If you had explained everything to me last night, I would've told you to go help her. She was in the middle of a crisis, and even though it's been . . . six years or so . . . she needed a friend."

He squeezed her fingers. "Thank you for understanding."

Noelle paused as an idea occurred to her. "Why don't we invite them to dinner sometime?"

Derek blinked in surprise. "Are you sure?"

"I don't know them, obviously, and there's no guarantee they'll like me, but they're important to you. A connection you lost. If I can help you rebuild that relationship . . . I want to do that."

Derek's eyes glistened as he stared at her, and then he wrapped his arms around her, pulling her into a hug. "What did I do to deserve you?"

"Don't be too grateful. I'm only offering because I want Raina to tell me all the embarrassing stories about teenage Derek."

He laughed and released her. "If that's the cost, I'm still grateful. But I will have to build a ramp. Or at least find one. Earl is in a wheelchair from a farming accident."

"I'm sure you can work that out."

He scooped pancakes from the skillet onto a platter. "Sky, you got that table cleared off?"

Skyler's voice came back from the dining room. "Sorry, I got distracted by our sign. I'll do it now!"

Noelle cast him a quizzical look as she grabbed butter and syrup from the refrigerator. "Sign?"

"Skyler and I talked about her monster, and I explained that it was most likely someone in a mask trying to spook people. So we're making a No Trespassing sign. I put the wood pieces together this morning, and now we're working on the letters. Come take a look."

She followed him into the dining room. Walt sat in one of the chairs with his rifle, looking as glassy-eyed as he had yesterday.

Skyler shoved her hands toward the wooden sign lying across two chairs while the painted letters dried. "Isn't it amazing?"

Noelle tilted her head to read it. "Trespassers will be hunted."

"Oh no!" Skyler gasped. "It's supposed to say *haunted*, not hunted!"

"I like it the way it is," Walt grumbled.

"I'm sure you do," Noelle said. "But if we're posting that out by the road, it needs to be slightly less homicidal."

Skyler looked between them. "How do we fix it? There's no room for an *a* before the *u*."

"I can fix it." Derek set the platter of pancakes on the table and grabbed one of the paint markers. He drew an arrow pointing between the *h* and *u*, and then wrote the letter *a*. "There."

Skyler scrunched her face. "Your letter *a* looks like the number two. Now people are going to read it like ha-two-unted. And that sounds like a sneeze."

Derek laughed. "I think they'll understand. We'll weatherproof it before I go to work and after it dries, Walt can help you put it out by the road."

"Sky, would you mind grabbing plates and silverware from the kitchen?" Noelle asked.

"I'm on it." Skyler dashed from the room.

Noelle and Derek looked at each other in confusion, and Noelle asked, "Where did that expression come from?"

"Sounds like something Brian would say. We'll blame him."

Skyler returned with plates and forks. "Mr. Walt, you can sit by me. And Derek too. Noelle can sit on the other side of the table."

"All by myself," Noelle mumbled in Derek's direction. "I swear this child has favorites, and I'm not on the list."

He grinned. "Parents usually aren't."

They all gathered around the dining room table, and Skyler said the breakfast prayer, thanking God for everything—from books to best friends. The only thing she forgot to thank Him for was the food.

CHAPTER Fourteen

Derek studied the face on his computer screen, memorizing the man's features in case he made another unwelcome appearance. There was nothing unique about him, except the oversize prescription glasses fifty years out of date.

Zac Inman was thirty-eight years old, five foot nine, and 160 pounds. He had a driver's license but no vehicle registered to his name.

Based on the last ticket he received for a traffic violation, the car he drove belonged to his mother—Lorna Inman. They shared an address in Columbus, Ohio. Apart from that traffic violation, Zac had no known criminal history.

That didn't mean he *had* no criminal history, only that he hadn't been linked to any crimes yet.

The tap of a shoe against the door frame drew Derek's attention. His brother-in-law stood there with a take-out food bag and a cup of coffee.

Brian was a stocky man with rough and slightly crooked facial features, like someone who got into parking lot brawls on a regular basis.

"Hey." Derek minimized the tabs with Zac's personal information on them. "What are you doing here?"

Brian lifted the bag and mug at the same time. "Running my wife's errands. Trudy made you lunch."

Derek checked his watch. "It's only ten thirty."

"I don't ask questions. The answers usually leave me more confused." He strode in and set the items on Derek's desk.

"How did either of you know I would be here on my day off?"

"Raina Miller's barn burned last night. You two were friends for a long time. We both knew you would be here, working on the case."

He supposed he was predictable in that regard. "Jared's working the grill this morning?"

"Yep." Brian dropped into one of the guest chairs in front of the desk and scanned the people on the other side of the window, some of whom regarded him with disdain. "I see it's as cold inside as it is outside."

Derek rose from his chair and pulled the string attached to the blinds, closing the slats. "You didn't leave on the best of terms. There's bound to be some hard feelings."

Brian had been terminated a year ago—quietly—for conduct unbecoming an officer.

Brian's lips puckered and then thinned. "That's fair, I guess."

"How are things going as a volunteer fireman?"

"Pretty good. I wasn't on call last night, but I hear the Miller fire was a bad one. Someone died?"

"Yeah." Derek dropped back into his chair with a sigh. "I'm still working on my statement for the public."

At this stage of the investigation, there were more questions than answers, so the most he could do was encourage the residents of Cherry Creek to be vigilant—for themselves and for their neighbors.

"I'm sure you'll find the right thing to say. You usually do." Brian's gaze dropped to Derek's chest, and the skin above the bridge of his nose puckered. "You're still wearing Lacey's rings."

Derek pressed a hand over the wedding band and engagement ring he usually kept hidden on a chain beneath his clothes. Lacey had been on his mind more than usual today, and he had pulled them out to see them again.

Cooking breakfast for the woman he loved was something he used to do for his wife. She would lean against the counter beside him, sipping coffee and soaking up the moment the way Noelle had done this morning.

And making the pancake mix with Skyler . . . it was a moment he and Lacey had dreamed of having with their child. But she died before they could ever fulfill that dream.

Derek savored every second he spent with Skyler and Noelle—he loved them both beyond measure—but with his memories of Lacey so close to the surface, it left his emotions tangled.

He returned the rings to their usual place beneath his uniform. "Yeah, I still wear them."

"You don't think that might bother Noelle?"

It was a question Derek had silently wrestled with for months. The last thing he wanted to do was hurt Noelle, but he couldn't bring himself to put the rings in a box on a shelf. Not yet.

"Honestly, I don't know. She knows I wear them, and she knows they were Lacey's, but we really haven't discussed them. I try to keep them out of sight."

"Obviously I'm not an expert on relationships—I'm just trying not to destroy mine—but I've always heard that women get pretty sensitive about a guy holding on to things from a previous relationship."

Derek had heard that, too, but Noelle hadn't said anything about the rings bothering her. Maybe she was choosing not to for his sake. She was selfless that way.

"You're doing better with your marriage than you were last year," Derek said, shifting the subject away from his relationships. "Trudy's happier. I can see it."

"Yeah well, considering how bad things were, *better* isn't exactly hard to accomplish." Brian looked down at the floor. "I'm trying to make her happy. To give her the husband she deserves, as you put it."

Brian had been so drunk during that conversation last year, it was a wonder he remembered it.

"Thank you. For trying," Derek said. "I know it's not easy."

Brian bobbed his head. "I should let you get back to work. You've got a lot on your plate."

"If you don't mind, there's one more person I'd like you to keep an eye out for."

"What am I, the neighborhood watch?"

Derek picked up on the amusement in his voice. "Right now, pretty much." He brought up Zac's photo in the BMV—Bureau of Motor Vehicles—database and turned the monitor toward Brian. "This guy was at the book signing last night, one of Noelle's readers, and he cornered her in the parking lot afterward."

"Because nothing says I'm your biggest fan like waiting for you in the shadows like a serial killer." Brian leaned closer to capture every detail of his face. "By the looks of this guy, the books he reads have sturdier spines than he does. He actually confronted her?"

"Tried to convince her to go with him. *For tea.*" Derek doubted very much the guy was interested in sipping tea together. "He got upset and grabbed her when she tried to leave."

Brian straightened. "Is she okay?"

"She was shaken up last night, but not hurt."

"I assume you're showing me this because you think the little weasel might pop up again."

"I'm hoping it was an isolated incident. He doesn't have a record. But if he does come to town looking for her, there's a good chance he'll ask around at the diner. I know you and Noelle got off to a rocky start last year, but I—"

"That was my fault, not hers."

Derek liked this new path his brother-in-law was on: taking responsibility for his mistakes and trying to make amends. It was too bad it took almost dying for him to recognize the need for change.

"I don't have any hard feelings toward Noelle. Not anymore. If this guy comes around looking for her, I'll set him straight," Brian assured him.

Derek's phone rang, and Rusty's name popped up on the screen. He thumbed the answer button and pressed the phone to his ear. "Hey, Russ."

"Hey, boss!" Rusty shouted.

Derek jerked the phone away from his ear. Rusty must be using the speakerphone setting. Derek could never make him understand that he didn't have to raise his voice.

Tentatively returning the phone to his ear, he said, "Yeah, Russ, what's up?"

"Autopsy's done. You want to come with me to the ME's office or should I fill you in afterward?"

"I can meet you there."

He needed to be an active part of this investigation for Raina. Not that he didn't trust Rusty, but this was the least he could do for the woman who had been his friend.

"All righty. See you soon, boss."

Derek disconnected and set down his phone before turning his focus back to his brother-in-law. "I appreciate you looking out for Noelle."

"Whatever you need, *boss*." Brian grinned on the last word.

Derek shook his head. "You can go now. And try not to make any enemies on the way out of the building."

Brian pushed up from the chair. "Everyone here already hates mc. Give me an actual challenge like . . . don't stop at the vending machine and buy a Snickers."

"What's wrong with a Snickers?"

"I'm not gambling and I'm not drinking, so I landed on sugar as my new vice. Now I'm getting cavities. If not for the rigorous fire department training, I would be fat."

Ah. It wasn't enough to simply stop the addictive behaviors. They left a void that needed to be filled, and Brian was reluctant to fill that void with what he called "religion." He was bouncing from one physical addiction to another.

Derek grabbed his sidearm from the desk drawer, palmed his keys, and snagged his fresh coffee before looking at his brother-in-law. "Let's go."

"Go where?"

"I'm heading to the medical examiner's office to meet Rusty, and I'm going to walk you past the vending machine freshly stocked with candy and out the front door."

"What, are you my sweet-tooth sponsor now? Can I call you at three in the morning when I'm craving a Snickers?"

"I don't care what addiction you're struggling with at three in the morning. You can call me. Now get out of my office." Derek gave Brian a light shove between the shoulder blades. "I have a murder to investigate."

Noelle set a basket of laundry on her bed, vowing to fold the clothes and put them away later. Of course, later might be tonight or next week. She wasn't adding any time stipulations to that vow.

Wrinkles were trendy, right?

She rubbed at the ache in her lower back from hauling laundry up two flights of steps—a reminder that she was thirty-three going on 205. In ten years, she was really going to regret buying a house with three levels and a spider-filled crawl space that served as attic storage.

Fat chance she was ever going in there.

She wasn't even sure her hips would fit through the miniscule opening. She would end up wedged tighter than a cork in a wine bottle. And all those little spiders would creep through her hair and weave their sticky webs.

The mental image made her shudder.

She left the laundry for later and wandered down the hall to her writing room. She hadn't tortured herself by staring at her whiteboard of undefined characters and invisible ideas yet today.

The door drifted away from her fingertips, and she stepped into her space of comfortable chaos. As she moved through her routine—switching on the electric kettle for tea and plugging in the twinkling lights for ambiance—she mentally sifted through criminal cases and articles she'd read over the years, hoping something would click.

Where was her scrapbook?

She riffled through the research books on her desk until she found it. She opened the cover and flipped through the newspaper clippings and printouts of murders, unsolved mysteries, serial predators, and bizarre accidents.

Okay, so it wasn't exactly a *normal* scrapbook with picture cutouts and adorable 3-D stickers. It was more of a murder-and-mayhem file. Some of the articles dated back decades.

"Serial killer exacts revenge for death of wife and unborn child. Family stalker. Well of bodies discovered." She bypassed each clipping. "Ghost slays family during their sleep. Kansas Carver."

She paused on that one, skimming the article to refresh her memory. The man had murdered fifty-one people, six of whom lived not too far from the home she shared with Tyrese. She remembered the shock she felt as she watched the news broadcast.

Since losing her baby boy, she couldn't bring herself to write about any villain who murdered children, and the Kansas Carver spared no one.

She continued flipping through the book, her frustration growing. There were plenty of dark and twisted possibilities to draw from, but nothing sparked. With a sigh, she tossed the scrapbook back onto the pile of books.

She prepared her peppermint tea, drawing in the invigorating aroma as she waited for the tea to steep. She needed something she could connect with. Something . . .

Her gaze snagged on a dark shape near the tree line at the side of the house, and her fingers tightened around the mug she held.

It couldn't be.

Her feet carried her to the window, mindless of the voice in the back of her mind warning her to retreat. A man hovered by the edge of the trees, black cloak stirring around his feet in the breeze.

Noelle's heartbeat picked up. It was him, the lunatic who charged at her car. How was he here? She had taken a different route home yesterday to avoid a second encounter. He couldn't have followed her.

Except he somehow did.

He tilted his head, the angle suggesting he was staring directly at her. Walt's warning from yesterday came back to her: *Plenty of people have seen his ghost, but if he focuses on you . . . you die.*

Walt would have her believe this was an evil spirit come back from the grave, but she knew better. There was a living, breathing person under that cloak and mask, and evil intentions or not, he was trespassing on the property where her daughter played.

She could go down there and order him to leave, but she had no way of knowing how dangerous he was. She set aside her mug of tea and pulled her cell phone from the pouch of her sweatshirt, calling up the nonemergency number for the sheriff's department.

Not that her first phone call had resolved anything. If the sheriff's department had caught him menacing vehicles, they must've let him off with a warning.

The writing room door creaked open as Noelle's thumb hovered over the call button, and she turned to find Skyler in the opening.

She darkened her screen and tucked away her phone. "Hey, sweetheart."

With Skyler having nightmares about monsters, the last thing she wanted to do was feed that fear by reporting a masked trespasser in front of her. Her daughter needed to feel safe in their home.

Skyler raised the bottle cap of water she held between both hands. "This is for Webster."

"I'm sure he'll appreciate that."

As Skyler tiptoed across the room, Noelle turned back to the side window. The figure was gone. She searched the trees for any sign of him, but there was nothing. Not even a flicker of black from the wind snatching at his cloak. How was that possible?

He's been dead for almost fifty years. Walt's words skittered through her mind and across her nerve-endings. *Plenty of people have seen his ghost.*

Goose bumps crawled up her arms.

Get a grip, Noelle. She would sooner believe she was hallucinating from too little sleep and too much anxiety than believe the spirit of a dead man had crawled out of Hell to come after her.

She dropped the blinds over the window.

Skyler set the bottle cap on the adjacent windowsill beneath the glittering web and bent down to see their friendly writing room spider. "Hi, Webster. I brought you some water. In case you're thirsty."

Spiders got most of their liquid from what they ate—a fact Noelle only knew because of her son's spider obsession—but Skyler's gesture was sweet.

"Have you seen Walt since breakfast, Sky?"

Skyler blew Webster a kiss and told him to "be happy" before she straightened. "He was really tired, so he sat down on the couch to rest for a minute and fell asleep."

The HFM virus didn't usually hit people so hard, but the old man was chronically underweight, exposed to the elements, and smoking used cigarettes by the pocketful. It was a wonder some other illness hadn't dragged him into the grave before now.

"Noelle." Skyler plunked on the arm of the upholstered writing chair. "Can a kid have two moms?"

Noelle's brain stalled at the unexpected question—a question that, in modern American culture, was the equivalent of a land mine. What in the world had inspired it? "What makes you ask that?"

"Sami said kids can only have one mom."

Ah, Sami. The know-it-all in Skyler's homeschool group. Noelle had met the girl's mother, and it was clear the child's rudeness was learned.

Skyler scowled. "I asked her how she knew that, and she said, 'Everyone with a brain knows that. That's why you don't know.'"

Sami was a brat, but Noelle kept that thought to herself as she sat down in the oversize chair. She patted the open space beside her. "Do you remember our last conversation about Sami, when she was making fun of the way you speak?"

Skyler slid off the arm of the chair and into the space beside Noelle. "You said people who choose a spirit of meanness can't be trusted to tell the truth and aren't worth listening to."

"That's right. No matter what she said, there's nothing wrong with your brain, and there's nothing wrong with asking questions when you don't know the answer."

Skyler looked up at her. "But what *is* the answer?"

Noelle wished she could've been a fly on the wall to catch the context of the conversation that had sparked Skyler's concern about mothers, but she was going to have to answer blindly. "Sometimes a child has a birth mom and a stepmom. And sometimes she has a birth mom and an adoptive mom. There are even people who have foster moms or women they look up to *like* a mom."

Skyler rubbed at a stain on the arm of the chair. "So it's okay if I have two moms? My mom . . . she wouldn't be mad at me?"

Noelle's heart flooded with hope. Skyler was wrestling with whether or not it was okay to call her mom. "You were the most important person in the world to your mom, and she wanted you to have a life full of love. And even though she's not here anymore, she would still want you to have a family."

Noelle wanted her to have a family too—more than just her and some long-distance grandparents. Skyler deserved aunts, uncles, cousins, and especially . . . a dad.

Derek had yet to broach the subject of marriage, and every time she thought about mentioning it, anxiety and uncertainty strangled the words before they could leave her throat. But that was a concern for another day. Skyler deserved her undivided attention.

Noelle wrapped an arm around her daughter's shoulders. "Even though I'm your adoptive mom, I want you to know you don't have to call me Mom if you don't want to, okay?"

As much as she longed for it, she would never force that on her. If Skyler ever called her Mom, it would be her decision and her timing.

"Okay." Skyler continued rubbing at the stain on the chair. "Do you think maybe someday you'll have another baby?"

Yet another unexpected question.

"Would it bother you if I did?" Noelle asked.

Skyler shook her head. "It would be cool to have another brother."

Another brother. This was the first time Skyler had ever mentioned a sibling. "You have a brother?"

"Mom had another baby, but . . . he died."

The sadness in Skyler's voice was so tangible it pressed against Noelle's chest. To an isolated child with no friends and no one to talk with other than her mother, that baby brother had represented hope—another connection in a disconnected life.

"Losing him must've been really hard," Noelle said.

"Mom cried a lot after the bad man took him away. He said it was for the best 'cause the house wasn't a nursery, and nobody wanted to hear a baby crying all the time."

Noelle's instincts stirred as she turned over Skyler's words. Something in her phrasing was . . . off. "Did your baby brother stop crying *before* or *after* the bad man took him away?"

"After."

The answer didn't come as a surprise, but shock still squeezed the breath from Noelle's lungs. Natalie's baby was alive when he was ripped from her arms.

"Mom didn't name him, but I did. I called him Row 'cause he was always moving his arms in Mom's belly like he was rowing a boat."

Noelle smiled, even as she fought back the urge to expel what was left of the pancakes in her stomach. That horrid man had murdered a baby. "That was a good choice for a name."

"Do you think Row has a grave?"

God, how do I answer that?

Despite all the books she'd read on raising a traumatized child, these were the kinds of questions she wasn't prepared for, the ones so tangled up in years of hurt that she feared making the wound deeper with her answers.

Lord, I feel ill equipped. I don't know what to tell her.

Not the truth. She couldn't tell her the truth.

Human traffickers didn't see people; they saw merchandise, and to them, that baby's life wouldn't have mattered any more than the paper cup their coffee was served in.

Noelle cleared her tight throat as she stared into her daughter's innocent, hope-filled eyes. "I think that . . . even if he does have a grave . . . it would be really hard for us to find. So the best thing for us to do would be to . . . make him a new one in the backyard cemetery."

Granted, it was a pet cemetery, and Walt was protective of the ground that memorialized the animals his family had lost, but he wouldn't deny Skyler a plot for her baby brother.

Skyler brightened at the prospect. "Yeah, and then I can plant flowers on it. And we can make a cross and something with his name on it."

Noelle blinked at the pressure of tears behind her eyes. "That sounds like a plan." She drew in a breath, paused, and then asked the question she was already certain she knew the answer to. "Speaking of graves, how would you feel about visiting your mom tomorrow?"

Skyler mulled over the suggestion, then shook her head. "She hurt my friend."

"Sweetheart—"

"I don't want to talk to her yet."

Noelle smoothed a hand over Skyler's hair, tucking a few wild strands behind her ear. "Okay. We'll go when you're ready."

She pushed up from the chair. "I'm going to go play now."

"Do me a favor and stay inside for a bit."

With Walt asleep on the couch and this supposed dragonfly phantom lurking around, she didn't want Skyler outside alone.

"I'll draw a picture for Maddie at the table. We still get to go see her, right?"

"In about an hour."

Maddie was the friend her mother had hurt. Natalie lured the girl into human trafficking so she could steal her car and escape with Skyler. She did it to protect her daughter, but the damage to Maddie's life was irreversible.

Noelle watched her daughter flit from the room, then grabbed her laptop off the side table where she'd left it to charge before the book signing.

She opened an internet browser, rested her fingertips on the keys for an indecisive moment, and then typed her query into the search bar: "who is the dragonfly?"

CHAPTER Fifteen

The stench of burnt human flesh scraped along Derek's airway, triggering his gag reflex and threatening to bring up the coffee in his stomach.

He waffled on the threshold of the medical examiner's office, tempted to retreat back into the hall where the smell didn't cling to every air molecule.

Releasing a breath through his nose, he stepped into the room and let the door swing shut behind him. He had a case to solve, and lingering in the hallway with his nose pinched between two fingers wasn't going to make that happen.

He was acquainted with the scent of death and decomposing corpses, but burnt human remains was quite possibly the worst thing he had ever smelled.

He paused by the nearby shelf to grab the Vix Vaporub that Abbot kept stocked for law enforcement visitors. He dabbed it liberally beneath his nose. It didn't eliminate the stench permeating the room, but it softened the impact.

Abbott, the medical examiner, stood beside the arson victim's remains on the metal slab, scribbling notes onto a clipboard. "You shouldn't be surprised, you know, given your life choices," he informed the victim.

Derek stopped a few feet from the table and cleared his throat. "Ab . . ." He cleared his throat again to dislodge the bile and phlegm strangling his voice. "Abbott."

The doctor straightened and looked toward Derek, his pale complexion and gaunt, sharp features making him the perfect candidate for a vampire movie role. "Captain. Take off your shoes before coming any further into the room please."

"My shoes?"

Abbott waved his pen at Derek's feet like it was a magic wand. "During the last case, the detective tracked dog feces all over the floor. I had to stop my work and scrub the floor from corner to corner. I would rather not have a repeat incident."

Derek suppressed an eye roll at the man's eccentricities and bent to untie his shoes. "Where's Rusty? I thought he was going to be here for this."

"Deputy Ramone was feeling a bit queasy. I sent him out for some fresh air before he could add his stomach contents to the olfactory atmosphere."

As if summoned by his name, Rusty stepped through the door. He hit the invisible wall, swallowed twice, and then started forward again in blue crime scene booties. "Sorry, boss. I needed a minute to . . ."

"I get it. You good now?"

Rusty released a breath and then nodded.

Derek rested his hands on his belt as he stared at the unrecognizable remains. "You told the victim he shouldn't be surprised by this, given his life choices. I take it that means you have an ID?"

Abbott set down his clipboard and passed a file folder to Derek. "The rapid DNA test results came back with a match."

Derek flipped open the folder. "That's unexpected."

Rusty leaned closer to peer at the contents. "I guess you can cancel that BOLO you put out for him."

Nick Nelson, their missing sex offender, was present and accounted for.

"Not that I'm sad he's dead, but why would someone murder him?" Rusty asked.

"Anyone who ever met the man would be tempted to murder him," Derek said. "What I'm curious about is why they chose this gruesome method when a gun or a knife would've done the job."

"He upset someone."

That would be a large pool of suspects.

Derek closed the folder. "What can you tell us about the condition of his remains?"

Abbott pointed to the wrists. "There are impressions around his wrists consistent with rope. The killer also secured him to the barn beam by coiling rope around his upper body. There are grooves around his biceps from how tight the binding was. I sent fiber samples to the lab for analysis."

Derek approached the metal slab. "Have you determined cause of death?"

Abbott turned Nelson's head to the side, and the crisp sound of the tissue sent Derek's stomach rolling again. "There's a laceration on the back of his head. He was struck with a blunt object, and the impact was hard enough to split the skin and crack the skull."

"Is that what killed him?" Rusty asked.

"No. The resultant bleeding on the brain likely would've killed him over the next couple of days, but he expired before that could happen."

"So the fire killed him."

"No, there was no smoke in his lungs."

Rusty released an exasperated breath through his nose. "Then what did he die of, Doc?"

"That's the question."

Rusty frowned. "Surely you have some idea what led him to kick the bucket. Was he hit by a car? Did he fall down some steps? Drown in the crick?"

Abbott's thin eyebrows inched upward. "I assume you mean *creek*, and no, there's nothing to support any of those scenarios. I did find some surface irritation to the back of the sinuses and throat. Considering he was dead before the fire, the irritation wasn't caused by smoke."

"What might've caused it?" Derek asked.

"A number of things. Post nasal drip, a rhinovirus, inhaling some kind of chemical. I'm leaning toward the latter given the visible damage to his liver. I sent tissue and blood samples to the lab. We should have something by Sunday."

"Anything that might help us while we wait for those results?" Derek asked.

"His stomach was empty, which means he didn't eat or drink anything within five hours of his death."

"No trace of alcohol either?" Rusty asked.

"It might register in the blood test, but his digestive tract was clear." Abbott handed Derek another folder. "Close-up photos of the head wound. Hopefully it will help if you find a weapon to compare it to."

Derek opened the folder to study the wound. It could've been caused by anything with a rounded edge. "Thank you."

"There's one last thing you might find interesting." Abbott picked up a glass jar with something long and black in it. "I found this in the left corner of his mouth."

"*In* the left corner?" Rusty repeated.

"This thread was pulled through three holes around his lips before the excess was stuffed into his mouth."

Disgust rippled across Rusty's face. "What's the purpose of that?"

Abbott set the jar back on his tool cart. "It appears someone attempted to sew his mouth shut but gave up. Not surprising. It would've been a disturbing process."

Derek stared at the thread in the jar. What did Nelson say that was so offensive someone would want to stitch his mouth shut before setting him on fire?

"I know it will be a while for your official report, but let me know if you discover anything more," Derek said.

"I'll send over my report when it's finished."

"If you don't mind—"

"With the medical jargon broken down into layman's terms, yes," Abbott said. "I'll have my assistant add a note that strips it down to the basics for you."

"Appreciate it."

Derek hated medical jargon. Having to define every other word in the report in an effort to make sense of it was not only irritating; it was a poor use of time during a busy investigation.

Rusty stripped off his blue booties while Derek pulled on his shoes. "What are the chances Nelson wasn't drinking the afternoon before he died?"

"Slim to none."

"So either he died after a five-hour nap, he decided to quit drinking, or whoever killed him abducted him well before his death and withheld food and water."

"The only thing we can say for sure at the moment is that this wasn't an impulsive murder. There are several easier and quicker ways to kill someone than to abduct them, tie them up in a stranger's barn, and set it on fire." Derek's phone rang as he finished lacing up his shoes, and he answered, "Captain Dempsey."

"It's Jimenez. Two kids spotted and called in Nick Nelson's car out by the old mill. There's blood on and in the trunk, and his phone was inside. It was dead, but I'm charging it with my emergency charger, and you're going to want to see what's on it."

Myths and legends rustled through Noelle's brain, twisting and turning like the leaves on the trees around her, as she drove toward town.

Her research this morning had offered up a wide array of dragonfly stories, which were popular across many cultures, but nothing about a man who went by that moniker.

The beautiful winged insects spanned the spectrum of ill will and good fortune, but it was the darker stories that stuck with her.

One of the common American myths surrounding the insects was that they fluttered in through a window at night and stitched together the mouths, eyes, or ears of those who misbehaved.

Nothing disturbing about that.

Another myth suggested dragonflies were originally shapeshifting dragons, tricked by Coyote into transforming into an insect, and they were never able to regain their original form.

That explained the disappointing lack of fire-breathing dragons hoarding piles of treasure in dark caves. They all shrank into insects.

According to a myth stemming from Swedish culture, a dragonfly would circle the head of a person and weigh their soul, deciding whether they were good or evil.

Nothing matched with what Walt had described. With some delicate weaving of myths one and three, and the determination to find a pattern, she could see a connection between judgment and punishment, but nothing more.

Noelle turned into the parking lot of Trudy's diner and slid her pink Volkswagen into the last vacant spot at the far end.

Skyler twisted against her seat belt as she inspected the vehicles, and then pointed to a car parked behind them. "They're here!"

Noelle barely had a chance to turn off the engine before Skyler flung aside her seatbelt and lunged for the door handle. She threw open the door and took off for the entrance, her tiny sneakers slapping the pavement. She muscled open the heavy glass door with a grunt and disappeared inside.

Her excitement was precious. Having a friend meant so much to Skyler, and having to wait a month in between visits was tantamount to torture.

Grabbing her purse, Noelle climbed from her car and took in the picture windows across the front of the diner.

Trudy had asked Skyler to create a mural for fall, and her window artwork inspired a festive cheer in anyone passing by. The scene boasted a cornfield, a barn, and an orange pumpkin with a winking face and buck teeth.

Skyler insisted it wasn't finished, but Noelle couldn't imagine what else she might add.

A man leaving the diner held open the door for Noelle as she stepped onto the sidewalk. She started to offer her thanks, but the way he stared at her made the words catch in her throat.

His irises were too small for his eyes, like egg yolks surrounded by white on all sides, and they appraised her as she approached. Was he undressing her with his imagination or contemplating her murder? It was hard to tell from the hard expression on his face.

"Thank you for holding the door," she managed, turning to avoid touching him as she slipped through the opening.

He let the door fall shut behind her, but he lingered on the sidewalk for another moment, studying her like she was an animal at the zoo.

She tried not to stare back, but she caught his departure out of the corner of her eye. That man had missed his calling as a chainsaw killer in a horror film.

She filed the uncomfortable encounter away in the corner of her brain and took in the diner. It had a charming atmosphere with upholstered booths, photos of locals on the walls, and beeswax candles flickering in Mason jars on the tables. In honor of the season, brightly colored leaves had been wrapped around the jars with twine, and strings of warm yellow lights hung from hooks along the walls.

This was the kind of place where Noelle could set up her laptop, sip endless refills of coffee, and disappear into the novel she was writing.

The sugary aroma of cherry cobbler rushed forward to overwhelm her senses. It hung so thickly in the air, she could practically taste the ingredients on her tongue: tart cherries, a squeeze of lemon, heaps of white sugar, and a buttery biscuit layer.

Her mouth watered.

You are not hungry. Don't do it.

In all honesty, though, did a person *need* to be hungry to indulge in cobbler?

"If it isn't one of my favorite people," a chipper voice with a Tennessee lilt called out.

Trudy Mason, who might be five feet tall if she stretched onto her tiptoes, padded toward Noelle in worn sneakers and a stained apron. Her hazel eyes usually twinkled with an optimism and alertness that Noelle could only achieve with an adrenaline shot to the heart, but a haze of tiredness hung over her today.

Before Noelle could mention it, Trudy hugged her and said, "Your munchkin blew through here and out the back door like the blizzard of '78."

Noelle puzzled over the odd expression as her gaze slipped past Trudy to the metal door at the rear of the kitchen. "I take it Maddie needed some air?"

Trudy angled her head toward the booth where Maddie's parents sat and whispered, "More like she needed space."

Beverly Wingate's blond hair was tucked into a bun as tight as her expression, and her wedding ring clinked a nervous rhythm against the coffee mug between her hands. Her husband, Gary, glanced at her from behind the local newspaper and then whispered something.

A hushed argument ensued, and Beverly started to rise, but her husband laid a gentle hand on her forearm.

"Tragedy affects everyone in the family, not just the victim," Trudy said, her tone compassionate. She shook off the dismal moment and asked, "How is it that you always look so gorgeous?"

Noelle looked down at her jeans and oversize sweatshirt. "How long has it been since the baby let you sleep? I think the hallucinations have started."

"For your information, I got four whole hours last night, and just to spice things up, I decided to spread those four hours out as much as possible."

"*You* decided, huh?"

"Well, it might've been Logan who made that decision. Unilaterally. Without consideration for anyone else. He's a bit of a baby boss that way." She wrestled a stray blond hair back into her wild bun. "I don't know what's got him so out of sorts, but he's been fitful for a week."

"Is Brian taking some night shifts with him?"

"He's a really solid sleeper, so he doesn't usually wake up when Logan cries, and I don't see the point in both us having a bad night's sleep."

"Trudy . . ."

Trudy glanced around and then lowered her voice. "He has a really hard time fighting his addictions, and I don't want sleepless nights to wear him down. We can't afford for him to relapse. *Literally* can't afford it. We'll lose the diner, and since he was let go from the sheriff's department, it's all we have."

Noelle pressed her lips together, wishing there was something she could do to lessen the burden on her friend's shoulders. "Why don't I take your shift waiting tables after church tomorrow? I'm sure Brian and I can handle things, and Skyler can finish her artwork on the window."

"What about your writing?"

"Maybe I'll overhear something here that sparks an idea for a book." Noelle shrugged. "Inspiration can come from anywhere."

"If you're sure, I won't say no to a day off. I'll take the baby to visit his grandmother. She's been begging me to keep him overnight."

"On the subject of writing"—*sort of*—"do you know anything about someone called the Dragonfly?"

Trudy's forehead creased. "Of course. He was Cherry Creek's one and only serial killer. He murdered five people."

That was not the answer Noelle expected. "Why couldn't I find anything online about him?"

"You might be able to find a few sparse details, but it happened in the 1970s. There was no worldwide web to splash it across, and from what I understand, the local paper didn't call him the Dragonfly. That was more word of mouth."

"What happened to him?"

"He was committed to the local asylum in 1972. He escaped two years later and disappeared. Now he's a spooky story people whisper around the campfire to scare each other," Trudy said.

"Why do people call him the Dragonfly?"

"When they caught him, he was wearing this hood and a really bizarre mask that looked like a dragonfly. The four wings folded around the eyes."

The description matched the mask Noelle had tried to draw, and anxiety unfurled in her chest, causing her heart to flutter. "Is it possible he's still alive?"

"That depends on who you ask. His body was never found."

"Do you know his real name?"

"Peter Ashton, if I remember correctly."

"Excuse me, we would like to order a couple of salads," Mr. Wingate said.

"I'll be right with you," Trudy said, before turning her attention back to Noelle. "I assume you're heading out back to check on the girls. I could bring you some cherry cobbler. It's still warm from the oven."

Oh, that was tempting.

If she kept indulging in Trudy's baked treats, though, she wasn't going to be able to button her jeans. Of course, there was always the hairband trick she learned as a kid, when buying new clothes wasn't in the budget—loop it through the buttonhole and then hook it around the button. It always gave her an extra half inch of wiggle room.

"Another time. I'm trying to be more health conscious with my eating," Noelle said.

"So . . . cobbler but no ice cream?"

"Trudy."

"I'm kidding." She grinned, the expression equal parts cute and mischievous. "I'll come see you before you go." Trudy left to tend to her customers.

Noelle nodded to Maddie's parents before weaving through the kitchen and out the back door.

There was a bench a few feet from the rear of the building, and two figures sat facing the creek, the water still murky and bustling from the storm last night.

The metal door squeaked as it closed, and a slender girl with ash-brown hair styled in a pixie cut stiffened as she turned, wariness shadowing her delicate features.

Noelle offered a reassuring smile. "Hey, Maddie."

The tension eased from the teenage girl's shoulders, but the wariness remained. "Hey, Noelle."

"You got a new hairstyle, I see."

Maddie self-consciously swept a finger behind her ear, as though to tuck away strands of hair that were no longer there. "I needed a change."

She needed to look less like the girl who had been abducted and trafficked, Noelle suspected. She'd thought about changing her appearance after the divorce so that she no longer looked like the woman who had been betrayed and abandoned by her husband, but it wouldn't have healed the wounds.

"It's a beautiful day for some fresh air," Noelle said.

"I'm not out here for the sunshine. I needed a break from my mom."

Noelle thought about the jittery woman who tried to march this way before her husband stopped her. "She's worried about you."

"I know, but she's trying to make everything perfect and safe, and I feel like I can't breathe. How am I supposed to move forward when she's treating me like I'm as fragile as cracked china? She never treated me that way before."

Noelle sat beside her. "Protecting your kids while letting them grow and take risks is always a challenge. And when you've seen them hurt, it's even harder."

"I need time with my friends." Maddie glanced at Skyler, who glowed with joy at being called a friend. "I need to be able to leave the house on my own without being shadowed."

"Give her time. She needs to find her balance again too."

Maddie stared out at the creek. "I don't know if she will. She's anxious and angry and . . . we had a fight this morning. She thinks these visits are unhealthy and counterproductive to my healing."

That was absurd. Maddie and Skyler had both experienced something most people couldn't understand,

and despite their age difference, they shared an unbreakable bond.

"Where is that idea coming from?" Noelle asked.

Maddie fidgeted with the rubber band around her wrist. "She found out Skyler's mom is the person who pretended to be my friend so she could lure me to the house. I think she must've read my diary."

Skyler's shoulders drooped. "Now she thinks I'm bad like my mom, doesn't she? She doesn't want us to be friends anymore."

Noelle's heart pinched at the shame pressing her daughter lower on the bench. Before she could soothe her, Maddie said, "My mom can think what she wants, but she's wrong. You are not bad, and neither was your mom."

"But you were hurt really bad, and it was all 'cause she tricked you."

"Your mom didn't choose to be there. Those people took her when she was a little girl about your age, and they made her do those things. I don't blame her for that."

Skyler's eyes widened. "You don't?"

"No. Not anymore. Your mom . . . she was only five years older than me. She was a scared girl trying to survive while protecting the only person she loved."

"You mean me?"

"Of course I mean you. You were her whole world, and she was yours. I can't be angry with her for doing what she did to protect you from the horrors the rest of us girls went through."

Skyler lowered her head. "It made her cry. She didn't want to hurt people."

"No, she didn't. And I think, if she'd had more time, she would've found a way to save the rest of us too."

That brought Skyler's head back up, and her chin quivered. "But Mister killed her, and she didn't get to save anybody."

"She saved *you.* She brought you here, to this place that's now your home, and you saved the rest of us."

Skyler swiped at a fat tear on her cheek. "I did?"

"If your mom hadn't brought you here, to Noelle, to Derek, if you hadn't told them about the house and drawn the picture that led them to us, they would never have found us."

Skyler's eyebrows knitted as she thought about that.

"Even though your mom did some bad things, Sky, God brought good things out of it. Like our friendship."

"Yeah, that's a pretty good thing."

"Your mom had a good heart. She deserves forgiveness and grace for the decisions she had to make." Maddie paused before adding, "I know it can be hard, but I also know it's possible because Jesus forgives us when we make mistakes or bad decisions. Sometimes the things we say and do really break His heart, but He gives us grace because He understands our struggles. Do you think you can understand your mom's struggles?"

Skyler nodded. "She did the best she could in a bad place, surrounded by bad people. I think . . . maybe I can give her grace."

Maddie wrapped an arm around Skyler and pulled her close. "You have a good heart just like your mom, and I'm glad I have you as a friend."

Skyler snuggled into the embrace. "Me too."

Noelle caught Maddie's eye and mouthed, "Thank you."

This young woman's forgiveness and grace carried more weight than anything Noelle could ever say. Maybe now Skyler would be able to let go of the hurt and anger she felt every time she thought of her mother.

CHAPTER Seventeen

Leaning against the desk in his office, Derek scrolled through the photos on Nick Nelson's phone. There were about twenty candid shots of a petite blond girl. Sixteen or seventeen, and completely unaware she was being photographed.

"You think that's our teenage girl from the bar?" Rusty asked.

Derek called up the info for the latest photo. "This one's from two nights ago, when Rand said Nelson was at the bar. Look at the angle of the shot."

It was taken from an upward angle, like Nelson had his camera at his side and was trying to catch as much of the girl's body as possible while she stood nearby.

"The pictures before that are from another night. Looks like a Cherry Creek football game." Derek checked the date those images were taken. "A week before."

"He went to a high school football game, even though he's not supposed to be within two hundred yards of any school, and took pictures of this girl," Rusty said.

"That explains his excitement during therapy Thursday morning. He spent the entire week fantasizing about this girl, and then she walks into the bar—or he follows her in—on Thursday night. He follows her out, disappears, and his car shows up at the old mill with blood in the trunk."

"And then somehow he ends up human kindling in a fire twelve miles away the following night," Rusty said. "And what about the girl he was taking pictures of?"

"There was a lot of blood in the trunk. Could be hers," Jimenez said.

If the girl was the victim bleeding in the trunk, and Nelson drove her out to the mill to follow through with his perverse intentions and then dump her body, why abandon his car out in the open with blood smears on the trunk? Did his killer grab him from the mill?

"Do we have an identity for this girl?" Derek asked.

Jimenez referred to her notes. "The teenage girl at the scene with her boyfriend, the ones who called it in, said the girl's name is Zoe. No last name. They're both cheerleaders from different schools, but at one of the basketball games, our witness found Zoe crying over boyfriend problems and tried to comfort her."

"What school does she attend?"

"Cherry Creek High."

"Hang on a minute," Rusty said. He left Derek's office and returned with a sheet of paper. "The secretary for Cherry Creek High School agreed to go in and check the absences list for me. She emailed the names a couple of hours ago." He ran a finger down the list and tapped one. "Zoe Quenton, a senior, did not show up to school on Friday."

"Track her down." Derek handed the phone back to Jimenez. "Find out if she's safe and accounted for. If we have a missing kid, I don't want to lose any more time. You two are working together on this now. I want Nelson's car torn apart. If there's a dust particle in there that can help us piece this mess together, I want it found and analyzed."

"Sure thing, boss," Rusty said.

"Yes, sir."

Jimenez ducked out of his office, but Rusty paused to let a tall woman with a smattering of dark freckles enter before he left.

Deputy Kara Grisham hovered by the doorway. "Sir, I have that sketch for you. The one for the man Earl Miller saw lurking around their barn a week before the fire."

He took the folder she offered. "Did he look familiar to you?"

"No, and Mr. Miller saw the man from quite a distance, enough so that it would blur the finer details of the man's face. I'm not sure how helpful it will be."

Derek opened the folder to view the sketch, and despite her warning, disappointment swept through him. This could've been a sketch of almost any married man in the Amish community—a long, scraggly beard, no mustache, an average nose, and a wide brim hat.

He couldn't share this with the public in conjunction with details about a murder and not one but two fires. It would throw suspicion on the entire Amish community, and that would only amp up the tension and fear in Cherry Creek.

Derek closed the folder. "Do you still have connections to the Amish community?"

Grisham shifted uncomfortably. "My grandparents refuse to acknowledge me, since they shunned my mother when she left the community and married an Englishman, but I've built cordial relationships with some of my cousins."

"I need someone to show this sketch around and see if anyone recognizes him, but I don't want to put you in a position that makes you feel uncomfortable. If you're not up for it—"

"I can handle it. I'll do that now and let you know what I find out tomorrow. Or should I wait until Monday so you can enjoy a day off?"

"I doubt I'll have a full day off for a few days." He passed the sketch back to her.

"Grisham!" someone called from outside his office, and another deputy appeared in the doorway. A baby-faced young man named Kemper. He was the newest member of the department. "Two girls ran away from the group home on Arbaugh road again. I was going to respond, but . . . I don't really know how to handle teenage girls. Do you think you could . . ."

Grisham sighed. "I'll come with you."

Alone in his office, Derek dropped behind his desk to work through the information he wanted to include about the arson and murder in the video on the sheriff's department social media page.

There was a time when press conferences were the primary method of informing and reassuring the public, but times had changed. Social media had a much further reach.

Derek barely had a chance to refocus before a man stepped into the doorway. Forties with a thick patch of premature gray hair and a mustache to match.

"Captain Dempsey?"

"Guilty. And you are?"

"Deputy Fire Marshal, Andy Bradshaw."

Derek rose from his chair to shake the man's hand. "Good to meet you. I heard you would be dropping by after a walk-through of yesterday's scene. Have a seat."

Bradshaw squeezed into one of the guest chairs, his bulky frame more muscle than fat. "I agree with the assessment that the Miller fire was arson. It appears gasoline was placed around the perimeter of the barn to accelerate the flames."

"Any accelerant around the victim?"

"No. The fire started outside and worked its way inward and upward. Due to how hot and fast the barn burned, the flames did eventually reach the victim, but that begs the question. If the intention was murder, and they immobilized the victim beforehand, why not douse him directly?"

"The victim was dead before the fire started. We're waiting on the lab for more details."

"It's possible the fire was set to destroy any evidence the attacker may have left behind. It wouldn't be the first time that happened."

"Still, dousing the victim to ensure the evidence was destroyed rather than leaving it to chance would make more sense." Derek propped his elbows on his desk and interlocked his fingers in thought. "The arsonist could be squeamish. Watching another human being burn, whether you feel they deserve it or not, would be hard to stomach."

"And he released the horses first."

Which indicated the arsonist wasn't a psychopath. He cared about the welfare of the animals, even if he could rationalize murder.

"You had another barn fire a week ago that was ruled arson by one of my colleagues. Gasoline around the perimeter," Bradshaw said.

"The Kirby barn, yes. They were away when it happened, and they came home to find their goats wandering loose in the field when they should've been penned up. But there was no body found."

"Could've been a test run. Someone perfecting his methods before delving into murder. Did you notice anything unusual at the scene?"

Derek thought back to the report. "I didn't directly respond to that scene, but nothing stood out in the paperwork or photographs."

Bradshaw tapped his phone screen and then set the device on the desk in front of Derek. "My colleague took this at the Kirby scene the following morning. He wasn't sure it was relevant."

Derek squinted at the charred tree. "Is that bits of blue spray paint on the bark, or is the light playing tricks?"

"It's paint. When I arrived at the Miller scene this morning, one of your deputies was studying this." He reached forward and flicked the screen.

Derek found himself staring at a strange design spray-painted on the trunk of a tree in blue paint. "How did we miss this last night?"

"It's a dark shade of blue that wouldn't stand out at night. Anyone could've missed it."

Derek swiped back and forth between the pictures. "It's the same shade."

Bradshaw dipped his chin in confirmation. "To the naked eye. We'll have both samples analyzed and compared. At the first fire, the paint was found on the side of the tree facing the barn. If there was more to the symbol, the flames destroyed it. At the second fire, the arsonist placed the signature on the far side, away from the flames."

"To make sure it survived the heat." Derek scrubbed his hands over his face and sat back in his chair.

Two fires, a signature present at both scenes, and a murder. Their arsonist escalated between fires one and two, and he wanted to be recognized for his work, which meant . . . he was just getting started.

CHAPTER Eighteen

Decorating for fall on a shoestring budget required hours of scrolling through Pinterest and a smidgen of creativity with nature.

Skyler stretched onto her tiptoes on a chair and held up one end of the festive garland they had glued together from acorns found in the woods. "Is this a good spot?"

"Looks good to me." Noelle passed her a few pieces of clear tape to secure it. It hung over the kitchen window at a slightly uneven angle, but that was part of its charm.

Skyler hopped down and dusted off her hands. "Perfect. Although . . . the squirrels will be sad we took their food."

"They have plenty." Noelle handed her a homemade pumpkin latte with whipped cream and cinnamon on top. "I think you'll like this even more than hot chocolate."

"I don't think that's possible." Skyler tipped the mug to her lips and took a sip. Her eyes widened with appreciation, and her small sip turned into a gulp and then another. She finally came up for air with a gasp. "Wow. That's the best fall drink I ever tasted."

"Even better than apple cider?"

Skyler scrunched her face. "That was the *worst* fall drink I ever tasted."

Apple cider had been relegated to the "hate" list with shoes, baked beans, pears, and sweet potato fries.

Skyler gulped down the rest of her latte, set the mug on the counter, and smeared away the leftover from her lips with her shirt sleeve. "I could drink that every day of my life."

"Maybe once a week until Thanksgiving."

"Can I go collect some leaf branches for the vase on the table now?"

Noelle pulled her lips between her teeth as she debated her answer. It was something they planned to do, but that was before all of this nonsense with the Dragonfly.

Don't be a helicopter mom, she told herself.

She grabbed the clippers from the junk drawer and held them out. "Stay where I can see you from the back porch. If you see anyone in the woods, come straight back to the house. Don't talk to them."

"Promise." She snatched the clippers and dashed out the kitchen door.

"Shoes, Sky."

Skyler skidded to a halt at the bottom of the steps, stomped back onto the porch to slide her bare feet into her rain boots, and then took off again.

Noelle followed her outside and brushed away the leaves from one of the rockers she'd found at an estate sale. Everything in this house was cobbled together from thrift stores, auctions, and items she found on the side of the road.

A part of her wished she could give Skyler more, but the joy radiating from her daughter as she hunted for the brightest branches to cut for the vase reminded her that life isn't about material things; it's about meaningful moments.

Skyler's life here was rich with simple but love-filled moments she would carry with her for the rest of her life.

As Noelle sat down, a gust of wind unleashed a shower of colorful leaves, thickening the layer that already covered the yard. At some point, she was going to have to rake the leaves out to the roadside for collection, but the prospect was daunting.

When she bought this place, she hadn't considered the amount of yard work country living entailed. It was enough to make her miss her apartment in Seattle, with its cement "yard."

Noelle took a sip of her own pumpkin latte, savoring the blend of sweet honey and spicy nutmeg and cinnamon.

Walt climbed down from his tree house in the woods, rifle strap slung over his shoulder, and joined Skyler in her efforts to grab branches.

Noelle opened her Facebook page to scan for updates. Derek had uploaded a community update video to the sheriff's department's page.

She pressed play and sipped her latte as she watched. Derek's posture was stiff, and the cadence of his voice was stilted as he addressed the public. The poor man was so uncomfortable behind a camera that it made her uncomfortable on his behalf.

"Last night, the fire department and sheriff's department responded to a barn fire on Ely Road. While the property owners were unharmed, there was one fatality. The victim has been identified, and steps are being taken to notify next of kin."

He didn't name the victim, which was a respect afforded to the deceased's family, but Noelle had her suspicions about who the victim might be.

"The investigation into the fire is still ongoing, but we have determined that an accelerant was used," Derek continued. "At this stage of the investigation, we do not have any suspects, but we do believe the arsonist may have visited the property within days of setting the fire. If you have any information regarding the Ely Road fire or the ongoing investigation into the Tuttle Road barn fire, please contact the sheriff's department."

Noelle frowned. There had been *two* barn fires? What were the chances they *weren't* connected?

"If you notice or have noticed anyone suspicious around your property or around the property of a neighbor, please contact the sheriff's department immediately," Derek said. "Updates will be posted here as the investigation continues."

That second-to-last sentence piqued Noelle's curiosity. He didn't say it outright, probably to prevent a panic, but his carefully chosen words suggested he thought the someone might be prowling the village in search of another barn to light up.

The video already had several comments, and Noelle expanded the comment section. Two people thanked the sheriff's and fire departments for protecting and serving the community, but the third comment—left by an AJ Conroy—was more antagonistic.

"Tell the public what's really happening. The Dragonfly is back, and he won't stop until he's caught."

Trudy said the Dragonfly was a serial killer, but she hadn't mentioned he was an arsonist.

A knock came from the front of the house. Noelle glanced at Skyler—she was safe with Walt, who was pulling higher limbs down into her arm range—and then set down her latte and strode through the house to the front door.

She peered through the foyer window to identify her guest. A trim man, about five foot nine, with a thick beard and mustache stood at the top of the steps with a massive bouquet of flowers.

Was he lost?

Maybe the woman he was here to pick up for a date brushed him off by giving him the wrong address.

Poor guy.

Noelle opened the door, and the man's wandering gaze returned to focus on her. "Can I help you?"

He cleared his throat before speaking, but his voice was still raspy, like he was struggling with a cold. "These are for the lady of the house."

"I think you might have the wrong house," Noelle said gently. Derek brought her flowers from time to time, but no one had ever paid to have them delivered. "Who are you looking for?"

"Noelle . . ." The delivery man cleared his throat again. "Sorry if I'm hard to hear. My voice does this every time the season changes. These are for Noelle McKenzie."

Surprise washed over her. "Really?" She accepted the bouquet. "Who are they from?"

"Not sure. I'm just the delivery driver."

"Do I owe you anything for the delivery?"

"No, everything is taken care of. Have a nice day, Ms. McKenzie."

"You too. And thank you." She closed the door and breathed in the eclectic scent of the bouquet. She pulled the card from the holder tucked in with the stems, and a smile bloomed on her lips as she read the message:

I'm sorry about last night.

You deserve better.

Derek was the sweetest man. He knew how much she loved pink roses, and the bouquet was peppered with them. She carried them into the kitchen and deposited them in a vase that didn't do them justice.

The smell of fall permeated the house, from the branches of colored leaves in a vase on the dining room table to the pine boughs draped over the doorways.

Skyler sat at the dining room table, stringing beads onto fishing line to drape over the grave marker they planned to make for her baby brother, Row. As she worked, Skyler regaled Walt with an overview of the book she was reading.

Noelle wasn't sure if it was disinterest or fever that glazed the old man's eyes, but he was struggling to focus.

"She climbed onto the horse, and then the horse neighed and flew into the air," Skyler explained.

Walt blinked a few times before saying, "Horses can't fly."

Skyler heaved a sigh as though having to explain a flying horse were a burden. "It's a fiction book, Mr. Walt. Anything can happen in a fiction book."

Noelle placed a mug of tea on the table in front of Walt. She had prepared three mugs of honey chamomile and added vanilla, cinnamon, milk, and extra honey to Walt's.

He eyed the offering with suspicion. "What's this for?"

"Generally people drink it, but I suppose you could try to intimidate it with your stare instead. Though something tells me you'll blink first."

"It's good for sore throats," Skyler said. "You should try it."

Walt picked up the mug and sniffed the contents. His eyes widened in surprise before slipping shut. All at once, he was both an old man and a boy, savoring the sweet aroma of the warm tea his mother used to make for him. His eyes moved behind his lids, like he was walking through memories, and longing softened his hard features.

When he opened his eyes, he said, "This is my mother's tea. She . . . used to make it for me when I had a bad dream that made it hard to go back to sleep." He looked at Noelle. "How did you do this?"

"I met an elderly woman at church who used to visit your mom for tea on Sunday afternoons, and she got the recipe from your mom. She copied it down for me."

"Why?"

Noelle shrugged and lifted her own mug of tea to her lips. "Because I wanted to."

Because he needed it. He had been without his family for so long, the memory of them no doubt fading day by day. Scent is one of the strongest senses tied to memory, and she hoped the tea would bring his family back to life in his mind, if only for a little while.

He drew in another breath of the fragrant steam and blinked away the growing sheen in his eyes. "Are you trying to make me like you?"

"I know better than to waste my energy," Noelle said.

Walt grunted. "You're not *entirely* unlikable."

Noelle opened her mouth to respond, paused, and then said, "Thank you . . . I think."

Derek's telltale knock on the front door pulled Noelle away from the dining room. She set aside her tea and opened the door to find him standing there in jeans and a flannel, with two boxes of pizza. Elsa squeezed past his legs into the house, gave Noelle's hand a sloppy kiss, and then trotted down the hall in the direction of Skyler's voice.

Derek stepped inside. "Hey."

"You didn't have to bring pizza. I have a frozen one I could've warmed in the oven."

"Pizza does not come frozen. That's a flattened hot pocket." He slid the pizzas onto the entryway table so he could strip off his jacket and boots. "The decorations look nice."

"Thanks. Next on the list is going to the pumpkin farm to pick out some pumpkins for Skyler to paint."

Derek's eyebrows lifted. "Traditionally pumpkins are carved."

Noelle spread her hands wide. "The miniature artist has spoken."

"Derek!" Skyler squealed. She raced down the hall toward him and hopped into his arms.

He caught her. "There's my other girl." He hugged her tightly and kissed the side of her face. "Did you see any monsters today?"

Skyler shook her head. "Nope. The sign is working perfect. I think they're scared of being hunted *and* haunted."

"Good. They should be." He lowered her to the floor and rested a hand on top of her head. "Did you grow since this morning? I swear you're taller."

"Noelle says I'm growing by leaps and bounds." Skyler leaped across the foyer like a gazelle and then teetered on her toes with a puzzled expression. "What's the difference between a leap and bound?"

"Uh . . ." Derek looked at Noelle. "Maybe we should ask the author."

Noelle smiled. "They're synonyms. But I always think of leaping as a jump from where you're standing, and bounding is a jump with a running start."

Skyler took that as her cue to run through the living room, jumping as she went. "Bounding makes you go a lot farther."

"It does. Bound your way to the bathroom and wash up for dinner. Derek brought pizza."

Skyler bounced down the hallway like she was a hurdle jumper, all the while chanting, "Leaps and bounds. Leaps . . . and bounds."

Derek shook his head as he scooped up the pizzas. "I wish I had half that energy. I can barely walk from my house to my car some days, let alone get a running start."

"She's been going nonstop all day." Noelle hooked an arm through his, leaning against him as they walked down the hall. "How was your not-day-off?"

"Busier than I expected."

"I saw your community update."

"Did it leave you feeling reassured?"

"It left me curious. How bad is it really?" She asked. When he paused for too long, she said, "Sorry, I know you can't share the details of an ongoing investigation."

The mystery writer in her wanted to collect all the information so she could piece it together, but she wouldn't compromise his job to sate her curiosity.

"I can tell you that, given the information we have, this place shouldn't be at risk. You and Sky are safe," he said.

"Because the serial arsonist is targeting old barns, not old houses."

Derek cast her a concerned glance. "I don't recall saying anything about a serial arsonist."

"I read between the lines. The first and second fire are most likely connected, given the type of structure and time frame, and your comment about watching for suspicious people on or around properties in the village suggests you think he'll strike again, which would make him a serial offender."

Amusement tilted Derek's mouth as he slid the pizzas onto the kitchen counter. "Would you like a job with the sheriff's department?"

"Sorry, I have a full-time job staring at a blank whiteboard and snapping the cap on and off my dry erase marker."

"Still no ideas?"

"Plenty of ideas, but none that I'm excited about." She pulled napkins and silverware from a drawer. "The victim in the fire—was it the sex offender you guys were looking for?"

Derek paused. "How did you figure that one out? I haven't released that information yet."

"Yesterday evening, you put up a post on the sheriff's department's social media page requesting information about a missing sex offender from the area, and this afternoon, that post was updated to say the matter had been resolved. It's a small town. One person goes missing, an unidentified body turns up, and then the missing person situation is suddenly 'resolved.' No point in wasting resources looking for someone you know is dead."

He grunted. "I suppose that was more obvious than I intended. I wanted to inform his next of kin before we make his murder public."

Noelle grabbed a bottle of Coke from the refrigerator to pair with the pizza. "I saw the comment on your video about the Dragonfly."

Derek grimaced. "People like that make our jobs harder. We need real information to solve crimes, not conspiracy theories and superstition."

"You don't think the Dragonfly could be behind the fires?"

"To my knowledge, ghosts can't light a match."

"I was under the impression he's still alive and in hiding somewhere."

"That's the impression a lot of people have, but no, Peter Ashton, the inspiration for the Dragonfly legend, is dead. He died in 1974."

Noelle frowned as she looked out the kitchen window into the backyard. If the Dragonfly was dead, then who was running around in his costume?

Assuming Walt was right about the mask. She needed to see a picture or artistic rendering of the Dragonfly mask to confirm that for herself.

Derek noticed the paint color cards on the counter. "What are you thinking about painting?"

"The main bedroom. The current color is too depressing. What color do you think would look nice?"

"That sounds like a question for your mother. Isn't she an interior designer?"

"She is, and she would pick a color that's trendy right now. Like asparagus-vomit green. But she doesn't have to stare at those walls every night before bed. I would like a different opinion. What color would you choose if it were your bedroom?"

He hesitated. "I probably shouldn't admit this to the daughter of two people who flip and style houses, but I don't care what color the walls are. No color is fine."

"Insane-asylum white." She bit back a sigh. "Safe choice."

Truthfully, she couldn't care less about choosing a new paint color right now. She had hoped the question would serve as a segue into a deeper conversation about marriage and building a life together in this house, where the paint colors would be relevant to him as well.

Unfortunately, Derek wasn't picking up on her subtle hints.

"Nice flowers," he said.

Noelle followed his focus to the bouquet he'd sent earlier. "Thanks. Some thoughtful person sent them to me."

"Pink roses. Someone knows you well."

"Yes, he does."

Derek's eyebrows lifted as he grabbed plates from the cupboard. "He, huh? Do I know this thoughtful guy?"

"I think you're acquainted." Amusement quirked up one side of Noelle's lips. "He's very sweet. Funny. And even though I never thought myself a beard person, his beard unexpectedly works for me."

An odd expression crossed his face as he set the plates on the counter. "Are you talking about me?"

Noelle wrapped her arms around his waist from the side. "It wasn't obvious?" Maybe she needed to work on her flirting skills. Add that to her list of things to research.

"I didn't send those."

"Funny."

"I'm not joking. I picked up flowers for you yesterday on my lunch break, but with everything that happened, I forgot them on the desk and they were already wilting by the time I made it into the office this morning."

She pulled back and looked up at him. "But there's a card apologizing for what happened last night. I thought you sent them because you didn't show up." At his serious expression, unease fluttered through her. "You really didn't send them?"

"No, I didn't. There's no name on the card?"

"Only the message."

"Could your parents have sent them?"

"No, they wouldn't leave them anonymous, and Mom would've texted me immediately to let me know they were here. She's paranoid about things being stolen."

Derek rounded the counter and removed the card from the holder, touching only the thin edges. He turned it over. "There's no business imprint. Do you know who delivered these?"

Unease churned in Noelle's stomach, smothering what little appetite she had. "I didn't get his name. He was an average guy with a beard. He was polite and professional like every other delivery person."

"Did you notice any logos on his clothes?"

"I didn't look."

Why hadn't she looked? She'd been so dazzled by the beautiful bouquet that she hadn't been able to see anything else.

"It's possible he was a random person paid to deliver them," Derek said. "There are a lot of people trying to make ends meet by picking up orders from restaurants and stores and dropping them off. Someone could've given him this bouquet and an address and paid him to deliver them."

"Who would've done that?"

"One name comes to mind. This could be Zac Inman's way of apologizing for the way he behaved last night."

Noelle hugged herself for comfort. "That means he knows where I live."

And that was a chilling thought. She had never met someone whose mood could shift from happy to anger and back to happy again in the space of a resting heartbeat. The man wasn't stable.

Something clicked in the back of Noelle's mind. "My driver's license. When he was digging through my stuff on the ground, and I couldn't see what he took, what if he didn't take anything? What if he wanted my address?"

"That's possible. Give me a plastic bag. I'll have this card tested for prints."

Noelle fetched a Ziploc bag from the drawer and passed it to him. "What good will that do? Sending someone flowers isn't a crime."

"It is if it becomes a pattern of harassment and stalking." He slipped the card into the bag. "Honestly, I doubt we'll get anything from it, but it's worth a try. And if we do get something, it'll be good to have it on file."

"What if he shows up here?"

Derek smoothed his fingers over the seal of the plastic bag as he thought. "I'm sure Walt can keep an eye on the back of the property. Elsa and I can sleep on your couch to keep an eye on the front. If that's all right."

Noelle shifted uncomfortably at the idea of him spending the night even if it was in the living room. She didn't trust herself to not make the same mistake she'd made with Tyrese. "I don't know. That couch is really uncomfortable and . . . what would we tell Skyler?"

"I have a pop-up camping tent in the back of my truck. We can set it up in the living room and have an indoor camping night. She'll love it, and it'll feel like a special occasion."

Her concern dwindled. If Skyler slept in the living room with him, it would make things easier. "Okay, that should work."

Derek wrapped his arms loosely around her waist. "I'm not going to let anything happen to you or Skyler.

No one's getting past me." He kissed her forehead and then slid his arms the rest of the way around her, wrapping her in safety.

"What's taking so long with the pizza?" Skyler shouted from the dining room. "Some of us are starving! Isn't that right, Mr. Walt?" A pause. "Mr. Walt said he's starving too; only he said it with a grunt. He's so hungry, he can't even speak!"

Noelle laughed against Derek's chest. "She certainly has a gift for hyperbole."

"We should feed her before she starts eating the furniture." He stepped back and picked up the pizza.

Noelle grabbed the plates and napkins and followed him into the dining room for what she hoped would be a relaxing family dinner.

CHAPTER Nineteen

Noelle curled up beneath a blanket in the oversize living room chair, a book open in her lap. Her eyes retraced the same sentence for the fifth time before she tucked the bookmark between the pages and closed the cover.

She couldn't focus on her suspense novel when her life was actively turning into one. Dead men in cloaks and masks, an unbalanced man cornering her in a parking lot and then sending her flowers.

What next? Would he break in and scrawl a deranged love note across her bathroom mirror with her favorite tube of lipstick?

She slid from the chair and returned the book to the bookshelf Derek was building along one wall of the living room. He said it should be finished and painted by Christmas, and then he would wrap it in a bow for her.

Tugging the blanket around her shoulders, she strode to the window and parted the drapes to see out. A deputy cruiser sat in the driveway behind Derek's truck, and the two men stood on the porch, talking in quiet voices.

Derek handed the enormous deputy the Ziploc bag containing the card, as well as the flower vase wrapped in plastic. "I want these dusted for prints and analyzed. Results come directly to me."

"Yes, sir. I'll get on that now." The deputy turned and tromped down the steps.

As the cruiser backed out of the driveway, Derek opened the front door and stepped inside. Cold air swirled through the room, sending the flames in the fireplace dancing.

Derek leaned a folded tent against the wall and closed the door. "The temperature is dropping fast."

"Well, we are in the *'ber* months."

With the exception of September, the remaining *'ber* months fluctuated between lukewarm and might-lose-my-toes-to-frostbite.

"True enough." Derek bent down to untie his boots, and the rings dangling on a chain around his neck slipped free of his T-shirt. He swept them back beneath his clothes, casting her an apologetic glance. "Sorry."

Noelle had seen the necklace before, and she'd felt the rings beneath her fingers on several occasions when she pressed a hand to his chest, but they had never really discussed them.

"You don't talk about her," Noelle said.

Derek arranged his shoes beneath the entryway table, taking longer than necessary. "I've told you about Lacey."

"A little. Before we started dating."

He straightened and met her eyes. "I've always heard that it's . . . insensitive to discuss a past relationship with the woman you're currently seeing."

"She's not an ex-girlfriend who might pop back into the picture. Lacey was your wife, a huge part of your life and your identity. You can talk about her with me."

He considered that for a moment before speaking. "I was afraid that might hurt you. With the way your ex-husband treated you, giving attention to other women over you . . ."

"You thought I might feel like you were doing the same by talking about Lacey while you're in a relationship with me."

"Judging by this conversation, I'm guessing I missed the mark on that one."

"Lacey is a part of your story, and you may not have noticed, but I love stories."

One side of his mouth quirked up, and he glanced at the unfinished bookshelf. "I've seen a sign or two to support that. Is there anything in particular you want to know?"

"Tell me . . . about a time Lacey surprised you or made you laugh so hard you could hardly breathe."

Noelle walked back into the living room and sat down on the lumpy couch, leaving room for him on either side.

He dropped down on her left. "It would have to be the lobsters."

"I'm already intrigued."

He told her about the time they were dining in a seafood restaurant, and Lacey learned that the lobsters were alive when placed into the boiling water. She dashed through the kitchen, rescuing the creatures while belting out, "Not Sebastian!"

Noelle laughed. "Sebastian, the lobster from *The Little Mermaid*?"

"It was her favorite Disney movie. In her defense, she was only seventeen at the time."

"And what were you doing while she was freeing the seafood?"

He grinned. "Regretting that I didn't take her to Burger King."

Noelle propped an elbow on the back of the couch and rested her head in her hand, a smile on her lips. "She sounds delightful."

"She was. Lacey was passionate about everything she did. She was a wild spirit with a good heart. We dated on and off in high school, but after that, we settled into friendship. When we were twenty seven, she *finally* agreed to marry me." He grinned. "Even then, she responded to my marriage proposal with, 'Sure, sounds like an adventure.'"

Noelle pulled her lips between her teeth to keep her smile from growing. Lacey sounded both hilarious and unpredictable, and Noelle would've liked to have known her under different circumstances.

"That's an interesting way to accept a proposal. I think I would stick with the traditional yes."

The slap of bare feet on the wood floor announced Skyler's approach before she rounded the corner into the living room in her pajamas, freshly washed hair spilling down her back.

She planted her hands on her little hips and declared, "Let's get this party started, kids."

Noelle choked back a laugh, but Derek didn't try to restrain his. It washed over the room as he stood and grabbed the rolled-up tent from beside the door.

"This tent is pretty easy to put together. We slide the poles into the sleeves and connect them, and it will stand on its own," he said.

Skyler plopped to her knees in the empty space they had made in the middle of the room after dinner. "Are there directions?"

"I've done it enough times. I'll show you how to do it."

Noelle watched from the couch as the two of them set up the tent and arranged the bedding inside. Derek encouraged Skyler every step of the way, praising her successes and helping her through the steps she struggled with.

She bloomed under his attention, soaking up the affection and quality time. Noelle's heart longed for this to be permanent—this little family.

Was it foolish to wish for that when her last marriage ended in disaster eighteen months ago? How soon was too soon to build on to her life?

Her therapist advised her not to rush into another marriage, to give herself time to heal from the thousand cuts to her heart. But in the most unexpected way, Derek's tenderness and dependability were helping those wounds heal.

And yet, despite how close the two of them had grown over the past year, neither of them had broached the subject of marriage. Was she the only one longing for it? Maybe it was too soon for him to consider marrying another woman after losing his wife.

Or maybe he doesn't want to marry you. The cruel inner voice cut through her, bringing to mind the argument she had with her ex-husband when she confronted him about one of his many affairs.

Look at yourself, Noelle. Overweight, graying hair, you waste hours a day focused on a world that only exists in your head. I look forward to the day I'm no longer stuck with you.

The searing pain she felt that day echoed through her, body and soul. What if the reason Derek hadn't broached the subject of marriage was because there was something about her that *he* didn't want to be "stuck with?"

Derek grabbed the pack of UNO cards from the bookshelf and opened the box. "Noelle, you want to join us in the tent for a game?"

When he looked at her, the slight upward tilt to his mouth flattened with concern.

Noelle turned her face away and leaned down to stroke Elsa's head. "I think I'll take Elsa outside for some fresh air. I'm sure she needs to go to the bathroom anyway."

Elsa's head lifted at the word *outside*, and she scrambled to her feet with excitement.

"I'll come with you," Derek said.

"But what about the card game?" Skyler protested.

"I'll be back in a few minutes. Give them a good shuffle, and I'll deal them out when I come back inside." Derek handed her the box of cards before getting to his feet.

"Okay." Skyler slid the cards from the box. "Noelle, can we go visit my mom tomorrow?"

The request caught Noelle so off guard that she froze, half bent over as she hooked the leash onto Elsa's collar. "Sure. We'll go before my shift at the diner." She exchanged a pleased glance with Derek as they led Elsa toward the front door.

Noelle bundled up for the frigid temperature, but the icy draft that slapped her in the face when she opened the door still raised goose bumps on her skin. Elsa led the way out the door and down the porch steps into the grass.

———

Derek stuffed his hands into his jacket pockets as he walked beside Noelle. Something was on her mind tonight, something that made her look away from him in the living room, but he didn't dare hazard a guess as to what.

Despite growing up in a household of all women, he had never perfected the skill of reading a woman's thoughts.

"Where did Walt disappear to tonight?" he asked.

"The tree house, I think. It's far too cold to sleep outside, but he says he can't see threats coming from his room inside the house." Noelle gave a subtle disapproving shake of her head. "I fixed him a thermos of coffee, some muffins, and gave him an extra sleeping bag for the night."

She said that like it was nothing special, when in truth, it was an act of love. Walt was a difficult man to tolerate, but she went out of her way to take care of him anyway.

"I'm sure deep, deep, *deep* down beneath his snarky attitude and hatred for life, he appreciates that kindness," Derek said.

"I won't hold my breath for a thank-you."

Derek drew in a lungful of cold air and released it before asking, "You want to tell me what you had on your mind in the living room?"

She kept her focus on the ground, watching their feet in the leaves. "Nothing that's important right now."

Derek's eyes narrowed. "Did you just lie to me? I feel like you just lied to me."

"No, I didn't say it's *not* important, only that it's not important for us to talk about it right now. At nine o'clock at night, while we're walking the dog and freezing our toes off."

"My toes are toasty."

"Thank you, Mr. two layers of wool socks."

Amusement tugged at him. "It's not my fault you slipped on shoes with holes in them. Why *are* you wearing Crocs when it's thirty-three degrees?"

"Because they're quick and easy to slip on." She shot him a stern look. "Don't judge me."

He held up both hands. "Wouldn't dream of it."

Elsa stopped to sniff around in the leaves, and Noelle bounced on her frozen toes for warmth as they waited. Elsa turned up her nose and resumed walking without doing her business.

"Your dog is very particular."

Derek couldn't disagree. "She's a bit of a queen."

Noelle huffed in amusement. "Well, maybe you can convince Queen Elsa to find a spot and *let it go* before we freeze to death."

"It's a bit of a waiting game with her."

Wind blew through the trees, and Noelle tugged her pink beanie lower over her ears. "Can I get your opinion on something I've been wrestling with lately?"

Derek braced himself. Hopefully she was going to share whatever had left the wounded expression on her face in the living room. He wanted to fix it, but he couldn't do that unless she confided in him.

"I have more opinions than I know what to do with," he said. "What's on your mind?"

"One of the girls in Skyler's Friday class likes to tease her about the way she says the letter *r* like it's a *w*, and it makes her self-conscious around other kids. I'm considering putting her in speech therapy, but . . . I don't want her to think there's something wrong with the way she speaks. Her peers have instilled that fear in her, and if I send her to speech therapy, I'm afraid it will confirm it in her mind."

Derek pondered the situation as they walked. Skyler's speech impediment didn't bother him—more often than not, he found it adorable—but future employers might be reluctant to hire someone whose speech made them harder to understand.

"I think she's old enough that you could ask her if she would like to go to a speech therapist," he said. "If it's something *she* wants to change about herself. Even actors and actresses use vocal coaches to help them speak differently. It's nothing to be ashamed of."

Elsa stilled, head cocked toward the trees ahead. Her nose worked as she scented the air, and a soft rumble escaped her chest.

Derek eased up his coat and rested his hand on his sidearm. "What is it, girl?"

He visually searched the trees, but the moonlight scarcely illuminated the branches. Something in their depths had ruffled Elsa, and she was singularly focused on the possible threat.

Derek looked over at Noelle. "Stay here for a second."

She nodded stiffly, both hands gripping Elsa's leash.

Derek crept toward the trees ahead, leaves and twigs crunching beneath his boots. He should've brought his flashlight with him, but it was still in his truck. "If you're not supposed to be here, now is the time to leave," he called out.

Something stirred, and Elsa let out another rumble. A creature darted out of the trees, around Derek's feet, and across the yard, white stripes glowing in the moonlight.

Derek released his gun. "Nice, Elsa. You nearly got me sprayed."

Elsa chuffed at his reproach. She had a hate-hate relationship with skunks ever since one sprayed her, resulting in tomato baths for a week. The critters were now number one on her enemy list.

Noelle released an audible breath. "Well, that near scare warmed me up." She let Elsa pull her forward as the search for a bathroom spot resumed. It took her another moment of sniffing about to find the perfect patch of leaves.

Business finished, she looked up at them to make sure they understood that she was done and ready for a dog biscuit and cuddles.

"Finally," Noelle breathed. "Now, if we could backtrack and find my toes that froze off, we can go in."

Derek laughed and wrapped an arm around her. "I'll lend you a pair of my wool socks and make you some more hot weed broth while you thaw under a blanket."

"Dandelions are not weeds; they're flowers."

"They're weeds masquerading as flowers, and they're an invasive nuisance that overtake my yard every summer."

"I think they're beautiful."

She leaned into him, making their attempts to climb the steps onto the porch awkward and unbalanced, but neither of them made any move to pull away.

———

The anger smoldering in my chest was the only thing keeping me warm as I watched Noelle retreat into the warmth of the house . . . with her boyfriend.

Derek Dempsey.

Captain *Derek Dempsey.*

Like he was something special. He was no better than her lawyer ex-husband, choosing his job over the woman he was supposed to put first. He was supposed to love and support her, but he was across town watching a barn burn when he should've been by her side.

I had seen the hurt in her eyes when she received his text message full of excuses. I didn't know exactly what he said, but it hardly mattered.

I knew the kind of man she was looking for—the kind she wrote about in her books—and he wasn't it. He didn't deserve the affection or tears she wasted on him. And he certainly didn't deserve to spend the night at her house.

Why couldn't she see that?

Pain splintered through my temples, and I forced my jaws to relax. Mind your temper, or you'll end up with a migraine.

Dempsey crossed in front of the living room window and closed the curtains. Despite the urge to grind my molars until they turned to sand in my mouth, I exhaled slowly, my breath forming a cloud in the cold air. If Noelle couldn't see that history was about to repeat itself, I had no choice but to step in.

CHAPTER *Twenty*

Something snapped Derek out of a dead sleep, and he blinked at the upholstery in front of his face.

He was stretched out on a couch, but the dark fabric sprinkled with flowers wasn't his. It took his drowsy brain a second to register where he was—Noelle's living room.

Movements thick and slow with sleep, he propped himself up on an elbow and hooked a finger around the edge of a drape to pull it aside. Not a trace of morning light disturbed the darkness.

He glanced at the tent in the middle of the living room, the sides incandescent from the battery-operated strand of lights taped to the inside.

Skyler was still asleep, curled around Elsa, who had taken to the girl the first day they met.

Derek listened for the sound of footsteps overhead to indicate that Noelle was awake and restless, but the house was quiet.

What had woken him?

A soft thud against the outside of the house drew him upright on the couch. That didn't sound like the rest of the creaks and groans he'd come to associate with this house.

Another thud shattered the possibility that the disturbance was naturally occurring. Someone or something was outside, and it wasn't a skunk this time.

Dragging his phone from his pocket as he climbed off the couch, he checked the time: a little after one in the morning.

As quietly as he could, he grabbed his gun and flashlight from the side table, shoved his feet into his boots, and opened the front door. The sconce with faulty wiring flickered and buzzed beside his head as he stepped out onto the porch, its intermittent light more of a distraction than a help.

He closed the door behind him to protect Skyler from the chilly air and clicked on his flashlight.

Something struck the house mere inches from him, and his pulse jumped. He flicked the beam of light toward the point of impact, following the glistening substance down the side of the house to the porch floor.

It wasn't a bullet.

The golden yolk of an egg was splattered across the board among shell fragments, and as he swept the beam of light down the length of the porch, he found more white shells.

The next egg hit Derek in the chest, splattering down the only pair of clothes he had with him, and the cackling laughter of teenage boys filled the night.

Derek caught them with his flashlight beam as they ducked behind the pine trees. "Okay, you've had your fun! Go home."

One of the boys popped back into view and hurled another egg. Derek sidestepped it, and it cracked against the door.

Derek shook his head as he started down the steps. Egging houses was nothing new; he'd done it when he was a teenage boy, but he had the sense to run when the homeowner emerged.

It was self-preservation.

He crunched through the leaves toward the pine trees, and the hushed voices of the boys grew more frantic.

"Dude, he's coming. We gotta go."

"Man, he's huge. We're so dead."

Derek approached slowly. "If you're still here by the time I reach those trees, I'm arresting you for trespassing and having a long, detailed conversation with your parents when they come to pick you up from the sheriff's department."

One of the boys let out a curse. "He's a cop. You egged a cop!"

"I didn't know! He's not in his uniform!"

The boys, who couldn't be more than fifteen, scrambled for the bikes they had left lying in the grass. Their legs pumped frantically in their efforts to escape, and Derek watched them go.

Kids.

He started to turn back toward the house, when something smashed into the side of his head. The impact knocked him off his feet, and he landed facedown in the damp leaves.

Pain split through his head, shrouding his thoughts in fog, and he fought through the confusion to make sense of what had happened.

Someone had hit him.

He wrapped his fingers around the handle of his gun, which had landed a few inches away, when a gunshot cracked through the air. Derek braced himself for searing pain, but none came.

A thick branch hit the ground beside him, and footsteps tore through the leaves as someone fled toward the road.

Derek rolled onto his back with his gun and snapped the barrel up to aim at the figure approaching from the darkness. "Don't move."

"Relax, Deedee." Walt stepped forward, rifle gripped in both hands. "I just saved your life."

Derek lowered his gun and dropped his aching head back into the grass, a breath of relief escaping his lungs.

Noelle handed Derek a wrapped ice pack before folding a leg beneath her and sinking onto the couch beside him.

Her insides still trembled at the realization that he could've been gravely injured or killed tonight. Whoever struck him did so with the intention of serious harm.

The gunshot had woken her from a fitful sleep, and when she rushed downstairs with her revolver, only to find the couch empty and Derek sprawled motionless in the grass . . .

"I thought you were dead when I saw you lying there," she admitted.

He pressed the ice pack to his head and winced. "When I heard the gunshot, I thought I was too."

"Walt to the rescue."

"He'll never let me forget it. 'Remember that time I saved your life, Deedee?'" Derek said, mimicking the old man's grouchy drawl. He grimaced at the pain in his head. "I've never been taken out by a tree branch before."

"I think the tree branch had some help."

"I was so focused on making sure the kids left that I didn't notice anyone coming up behind me. You'd think it was my first day on the force and not my eighteenth year."

"You had no reason to think anyone else would be out there."

"The whole reason I'm here tonight is to make sure no one else, like Zac Inman, might be out there. I should've kept my guard up."

Noelle handed him two capsules of Tylenol. "Give yourself some grace."

"I can't promise that, but I'll try." He tossed the pills back with a swig of water.

"Do you think . . . could this have been Zac targeting you for some reason?"

"I looked into him earlier today. Or . . . yesterday. He doesn't have a criminal record, and there's no known history of violence or stalking."

"No *known* history."

He nodded and then winced again. "Everyone starts somewhere. But there's no way to know if it was him. I didn't see who hit me, and all Walt could tell me was that the guy was dressed in dark clothing."

"And preparing to bash you over the head a second time. *After* you were already on the ground. That wasn't a teenager afraid of being caught for hurling eggs or someone hoping to break in. This attack was personal."

"As far as I know, I haven't made anyone angry lately. I suppose it could be someone who read between the lines of my community update like you did. They may think I know more than I do."

Noelle rested a hand on her foot, toying with a string from the seam of her sock. "What do we do now?"

"Try to get some sleep."

She offered him an incredulous look. "You think either of us is going to be able to go back to sleep after that?"

"Probably not." He slouched against the couch cushions and stared at the tent. "If only we could sleep like a child. Deep and carefree."

"*That* child could sleep in the middle of a battlefield."

Gunshots, doors opening and closing, cold air sweeping through the house. Nothing disturbed Skyler's heavy sleep tonight. Her soft snores filled the quiet between their whispered words.

"If we're going to be awake all night, we can at least get comfortable." Derek stretched out an arm, inviting her to slide over. "Try to avoid the egg slime."

Noelle suppressed a laugh and readjusted so she could curl up against him. The feeling of his arm around her soothed what remained of her fear. He would have an intense headache for a few days, but at least he was safe.

CHAPTER Twenty-one

Morning light pierced Derek's eye sockets like miniature knives, and the lump on his head throbbed in rhythm with his heart.

He'd managed to doze off despite the pain, and when he woke a little after dawn, Noelle was gone. She had slipped away without disturbing him.

He followed her soft voice to the front porch, but paused with his fingers on the knob when she said, "I don't know, Trudy. Maybe it's me. Maybe I did something."

Derek frowned at the pain in her voice.

What did she think she had done? Did she think she was responsible for what happened to him last night? Even if the person who attacked him was Zac Inman, she wasn't to blame.

She must be on the phone, because he didn't hear his sister respond before Noelle said with a sigh, "No, you're right. It's hard not to let those thoughts run wild in my head, but I'm trying to ignore them."

Derek backed away from the door to give her privacy during her call and made his way into the kitchen to put on some coffee and down some Tylenol.

He pulled two mugs from the cupboard while the coffee brewed. The first one read, "I kill people for a living," and the second one read, "Tears of my readers."

The second mug, if he remembered correctly, had been a gift from a reader. Noelle always spoke about her readers with such fondness. The connection she had with them was unique, and they enjoyed surprising her with special gifts as much as she enjoyed surprising them with her stories.

God, please don't let Zac Inman ruin that for her, Derek prayed.

She had already lost so much in the past couple of years—her marriage, her child, her home—and he wanted to safeguard this author-reader connection she cherished. Somehow, he needed to protect it.

When he carried two coffees back toward the front door, Noelle's voice had been replaced by the whisper of bristles.

He squinted as he opened the door, wishing he had sunglasses to dampen the morning rays. "Coffee delivery."

She paused in her scrubbing and sat back on her legs. "Thanks. I didn't want to wake you by filling the house with the aroma of coffee."

"That definitely would've woken me." He handed her the readers' tears mug. "I remember you telling me about this mug. It was from a reader, wasn't it?"

Her smile was so faint it could hardly be considered a smile. "Yeah, she sent it along with a box of tissues. It was a pretty fantastic surprise."

"What's the weirdest gift you've gotten from a reader?"

That question lifted the corners of her lips a little higher. "A pair of socks with crime scene tape on them and a set of handcuffs."

Derek blinked. "Someone sent you handcuffs?"

She shrugged. "You asked for weird."

"What did you do with them?"

"I would like to say I used them to wrangle bad guys in my neighborhood, but I hung them on my writing room wall beneath a sign that said, 'Sorry I'm late. I was kidnapped by a book.'"

"Sounds like something you would have on your wall."

"Most of the gifts were normal. Bookmarks, funny socks, even the occasional book. After Tay died, someone sent me a book on grief, and there was a handwritten note inside that said . . ." Her voice trailed off, and her mouth parted in surprise. "It said, 'I'm sorry about what happened to your son. You deserve better.'"

Derek's law enforcement brain kicked into gear despite minimal sleep. The message on the flower card had said, "I'm sorry about last night. You deserve better."

Derek crouched in the doorway. "Those exact words were written in the book? 'I'm sorry about . . . you deserve better'?"

Noelle nodded. "I'd forgotten all about it."

"Do you remember anything else about it?"

"There was no return address, and none of my readers took credit for it, but I knew it must've been one of them."

"There would've been a post office origin if you looked up the tracking number on the package."

She shook her head. "I was so mired in grief, I didn't even think about that."

"That's okay. Do you still have the book?"

She stared into the distance as she searched her memories. "No. Tyrese won the court case for the house and most of the contents, and he only gave me a day to get out. I left a lot of stuff behind. The last time I saw that book, it was still on our bookshelf in the living room."

The muscles in Derek's jaw tightened, which only made his head throb harder. "I sincerely hope I never meet your ex-husband."

"Afraid you won't like him?"

"Afraid I'll end up in jail." The way the man treated Noelle disgusted him, and Derek wasn't entirely certain he would be able to avoid knocking some sense into him.

"Have you heard back about the vase or the card?" Noelle asked.

"There was a text on my phone when I woke up this morning. No prints on the vase, and only a partial on the card. Not enough to run a search. Unfortunately, until we have another sample of handwriting to compare it to, the message on the card doesn't tell us much."

"Sorry. It didn't even occur to me to grab that book when I left. I could text Tyrese, but even on the off chance he didn't toss the rest of my things in the trash, I doubt he would be considerate enough to take a picture of the message and send it."

"You have nothing to be sorry for, and I will never ask you to reach out to that man. He doesn't deserve to be a part of your life in any way, shape, or form."

A smile curled her lips. "The phrase 'in any way' encompasses all possibilities, including *shape* and *form*. You don't need to add them."

He slid to a seated position against the door frame. "It's an expression I was raised with. Don't knock it."

"Just trying to be helpful." She dunked her scrub brush in soapy water and resumed scrubbing at the egg residue on the porch.

"I can grab another brush so we can knock this out before church," he offered, even though the last thing he wanted to do was get on his hands and knees to clean. The pressure in his head might make his skull split apart.

"You shouldn't be doing anything but resting today. Besides, I need to do this. It's one thing I can control right now."

Her comment told him she was feeling anxious this morning. When her anxiety began to sweep over her, she tried to focus on one thing she could control in that moment. It helped keep her afloat until it passed.

"Did you get any sleep last night?" Derek asked.

"Not much. You're not the most comfortable pillow."

He tipped his head. "I'm not sure if that's an insult or a compliment."

She grinned. "I wouldn't worry about it too much." She paused her scrubbing. "Something's been bothering me since we talked about Peter Ashton last night."

"Okay."

"You told me he's dead, but Trudy said he disappeared, and the man who commented on your community update video believes he's still alive. Is he presumed dead because he disappeared, or was his body found?"

"The case is well before my time, so I don't know much about it, but I don't believe a body was found. My understanding is that the fire was so hot it destroyed his remains. If there was anything left to find, it was impossible to separate from the debris." He took a swallow of his coffee. "What's got you thinking about that this morning?"

"What if you're right and your community update upset the person who's setting these fires? He could be upset that you didn't give him credit or worried you might piece things together. You were attacked less than six hours after you posted that video."

"It's possible. But if I did upset someone, it wasn't Peter Ashton."

Noelle made a thoughtful noise. "I'm sure I can find a few details by scouring the internet, but is there anyone living from that time who might be able to tell me more about him?"

"Your best bet would be Rosie Duhan. She worked at the institution while Peter Ashton was a patient there."

"Did she know him well?"

"From what I understand, yes."

"How do I get a hold of her number?"

"No need." Derek checked the time. "We're going to see her in about two hours."

Rosie Duhan was the elderly woman who stood by the church doors and wished everyone a blessed week as they left the building. She was a stout woman with a halo of curly white hair and a sweet demeanor.

Derek kept a gentle grip on Noelle's hand, and she held onto Skyler's, forming a chain as he cut into the crowd streaming toward the double doors where the woman stood.

Bright tangerine flashed through the corner of Noelle's vision.

Oh no.

Janet Robinson swooped left and right through the crowd like a vulture homing in on a fresh carcass. Her tangerine lips were pressed tight, and her heavily lined eyes were focused, as she made her way to her target.

The forty-something woman, whose dress was tighter than a corset and bright enough to put a highlighter to shame, twined her arms around Derek's. "Hey there, Captain. Almost missed you this morning."

Derek slid his arm free from her tentacles with some effort. "Good morning, Ms. Robinson."

"I told you, call me Janet." She kept pace with them. "I was thinking about bringing some food to the department later. I'm sure you're all working tirelessly to get this arson mess resolved, and it could be a real morale boost. Will you be at the department? We could . . . catch up over my homemade lasagna."

Noelle choked at her brazenness, and Derek and Janet both looked her way.

Janet offered her a saccharine smile. "Noelle, I didn't see you there."

"Really? Must be because I blend into the crowd so well."

Derek tried to restrain a laugh.

Janet shifted uncomfortably. "I . . . that's not . . . of course I didn't mean . . ."

"Enjoy the rest of your week, Ms. Robinson," Derek said.

Janet's eyelashes fluttered, like her brain was struggling to comprehend the fact that she'd been dismissed. "Oh. Yes. Of course. You too." She remained where she was as the three of them continued walking.

"That woman does not like me," Noelle said, keeping her voice soft so no one could overhear.

"That's because you're ten times prettier than she is, and the only way she can make herself feel like she has a chance is to pretend you don't exist."

"I doubt that, and I'm hardly ten times prettier than her."

"No, you're right. I meant eleven."

Warmth infused Noelle's cheeks.

Skyler poked her head forward. "How pretty am I?"

"There aren't enough words in the English language," Derek said, reaching over to tousle her hair.

As they approached the exit doors, old Rosie Duhan came into view.

"Do you mind taking Skyler to the car while I talk with Rosie for a few minutes?" Noelle asked.

"Not at all." Derek took Skyler's hand when Noelle released it and walked with her out of the church.

His subdued exit was a testament to how badly his head must be hurting. He usually challenged Skyler to race him to the car, and she never turned down a chance to run.

Noelle approached the elderly woman. "Rosie? I'm—"

"Noelle." Rosie reached out to take her hand. "I remember you. We bumped elbows at the café one morning. I believe there was a maple donut up for grabs."

Noelle laughed. "Yes, we decided to split it. I was wondering if I could have a few minutes of your time to discuss something I may someday consider writing a book about."

"Sounds exciting."

Noelle gestured to the metal chairs and café style tables under the patio in front of the building. "Would you join me?"

Rosie grabbed her claw-foot cane from its resting place against the building and inched her way down the ramp. She eased into the nearest chair. "What can this old gal help you with?"

Noelle took the seat across from her and pulled a notepad and pen from her purse. "I understand that you worked at the local asylum in the seventies."

"Yes indeedy. But we didn't call it an asylum. There was such a stigma surrounding that title, and most of our patients were severely mentally delayed rather than mentally ill."

Noelle nodded and made a note of that. "Is that why it was called the Developmental Center?"

"I thought so, but I never asked for the origin of the name."

"Most of the patients were mentally delayed, but there were some who were mentally ill?"

"We had a few schizophrenic patients, and a few with unknown mental illnesses at the time. And then of course there was that one patient who wasn't like the others. I assume he's the reason we're having this chat."

Noelle offered her a sheepish look. "Am I that transparent?"

Rosie rested both hands on the top of her cane. "You're hardly the first to ask about him."

Given that Peter Ashton was a legend in the area, that wasn't surprising.

"My understanding is that Peter murdered several people. What qualified him to be placed in a mental institution rather than a prison?" Noelle asked.

Rosie grunted. "I asked that very question and nearly lost my job. Peter Ashton was the son of the local preacher and his wife. The judge who presided over the case should've recused himself. He attended Pastor Ashton's church. The pastor and his wife pleaded for their son to be placed in the local institution where he could be helped and monitored. They claimed his beliefs were caused by mental illness and that he had a mental deficit that made it hard for him to understand right and wrong."

"He was a psychopath?"

Rosie tilted her head. "He could distinguish between right and wrong, but the standard by which he judged right and wrong was his own, and that superseded the law. He believed the people he killed were evil and the world would be better without them."

That was both fascinating and disturbing.

"What exactly were his beliefs," Noelle asked.

"He believed he was a dragonfly reincarnated and, for that reason, he had the right to weigh a man's soul and exact judgment."

Like the myths Noelle had read about. "Please tell me he didn't stitch his victims' mouths shut."

"The police and sheriff's department did their best to keep many of the details quiet, to prevent a panic, but there was a rumor that he stitched the mouths and eyes of his victims shut while they were still alive."

Noelle's stomach cramped in revulsion. "How long was he a patient at the asylum?"

"Nearly two years. But then the fire started." Sadness touched her sweet features. "September sixth,

1974. A day none of us who worked there could ever forget."

"Do you know how the fire started?"

"I wasn't at work that night, so I'm not sure how everything happened. We assume Peter faked a medical emergency to draw the night attendant into his cell and then killed him for his keys and set the fire."

"If he had the keys, he could've escaped without drawing any more attention to himself. Why start a fire that would attract the authorities and first responders?"

Rosie was quiet for a moment as she considered the question. "I suppose he judged us for imprisoning and medicating him, and he decided everyone in that building deserved to die."

A shiver crawled down Noelle's spine. Peter Ashton would've been a terrifying person to know. "What do you think happened to him that night?"

"I know the authorities never found his body, but I firmly believe he died in that fire. That kind of evil doesn't stop of its own accord, and that day was the last day anyone died at the hands of the Dragonfly."

Noelle had read about incidents where people mysteriously disappeared with no possible exit or were presumed dead without remains, but with the scientific means that existed nowadays, it was hard to accept that such things could happen.

"Is there anyone else alive who worked there during that time that I could speak with?"

"Joseph passed away from cancer not too long ago, but he had a lot of thoughts on Peter. Morton moved away. Herby Conroy died in the fire that night."

Conroy.

That was the surname of the man who commented on Derek's video. Were the two men related? In such a small village, it seemed likely.

"Herby has a grandson here in town. Allen Junior. I'm not sure what he may know beyond that silly legend," Rosie said.

"You don't believe the stories?"

"I don't believe in ghosts. That said, I do believe evil spirits exist and that they can take a number of shapes to deceive and torment the living."

The haunting figure in the mask and cloak flashed through Noelle's mind. There was certainly something about him that felt evil.

Noelle closed her notebook. "Thank you so much for your time, Rosie."

"Anytime, dear. At my age, reminiscing keeps the memories from slipping away."

If Noelle were in her position, she doubted those were memories she would want to hang on to. She would be grateful if they slipped away.

She made her way to her car. Derek was on the phone, his expression serious, and Skyler was in the backseat with her nose in a book.

"I'll be there in twenty minutes." Derek disconnected and pocketed his phone. "What did Rosie have to say?"

"She gave me some backstory on Peter Ashton and the name of another person I can speak with. Is everything okay? That phone call sounded serious."

"I have to go to the department for a few hours."

"But what about your head?"

"I'll take it easy. You two are going to the cemetery?"

"To visit her mom. Then home to change for my shift at the diner. We need to be there around noon to start prepping for lunch."

The diner was only open from one to seven on Sundays so Trudy could sleep in and then attend the second church service.

"Brian will be there with you, and he knows to keep an eye out for Zac." He ran his hands down her arms and gripped her hands, worry clouding his hazel eyes. "The cemetery is relatively isolated. Be careful up there."

"I have my revolver."

Derek lifted her hands and kissed her knuckles. "I'll see you this evening."

He climbed into his truck in the neighboring space. They had driven separately in case his arson investigation pulled him away. Noelle watched his taillights disappear from the lot and then looked at her daughter.

Time to go mend the fracture between Skyler and her mother.

CHAPTER Twenty-two

This place had soaked up centuries of tears, witnessed partings both apathetic and soul crushing, and yet it was somehow peaceful. More peaceful than a cemetery had any right to be.

Sunlight speckled the various styles of gravestones, and a cool breeze whipped through the trees, unleashing a shower of fall leaves.

Ordinarily, Skyler would spread her arms and twirl under the deluge of orange and yellow, but today she was somber. She held Noelle's hand as they crunched up the gravel path weaving around and through the cemetery.

"There's so many graves," Skyler said, her voice barely more than a whisper. "I don't know how to find my mom."

"I'll show you."

Suppressing her own discomfort at being in a cemetery, Noelle led her toward the far end. A meager slab, provided by the state, marked the resting place of Natalie Jones.

The poor young woman had lived half her life as a slave to twisted human beings, only to be murdered hours after she finally breathed freedom. The fear and shame she must've lived with . . .

She deserved a new beginning, not a cruel ending.

Skyler clung to Noelle's side as she stared at the headstone. "What do I say?"

"Whatever's on your heart."

After another moment of hesitation, Skyler released Noelle's hand and walked forward. "Hi, Mom." She fidgeted with the bundle of droopy flowers she held. "I'm sorry I didn't come visit sooner. I was sort of mad at you for a while, 'cause you did bad things, but . . . Maddie said she forgives you 'cause you did them to protect me. And she says I should forgive you too." She swiped a sleeve across her face to catch her tears. "I'm not mad anymore, and I really miss you."

Noelle wrestled with the need to step forward and wrap her arm around Skyler and offer her comfort, but she didn't need comfort. She needed to feel the grief and loss that she'd been trying to avoid for the past year.

"I tried not to when I was mad, but I couldn't help it. I miss your hugs and cuddles and all the times we used to talk about stuff." Skyler drew in a shuddering breath and blew it out, calming herself. "You always said you like yellow flowers, so I brought some." She placed the flowers in front of the stone. "I grew these all by myself. I'm really good at it. I like all the colorful flowers, but I don't like the prickly weeds. Noelle calls them thistles, and they do their very best to poke me."

Thistles were no joke. They grew as hardily as poison ivy around here. With every step through the countryside, a person risked being attacked by various poisonous plants or miniature cactus daggers. But she would take those over stepping around drug addicts sprawled on the sidewalk and dodging wet cement that reeked of urine.

"I got to pet a chicken. His name is Winnie, and he's really soft," Skyler continued, filling her mom in on her new life.

Noelle let her gaze wander over their quiet surroundings. Every time she saw a cemetery, her memories tried to yank her back to the day she buried her son.

As if the sky were weeping with her, rain had pattered across the tops of the umbrellas around her. She didn't have the strength to hold an umbrella above her head for the service—she barely had the strength to stand—so the rain trickled down her face to mingle with her tears. That day, she thought her knees might give out and send her toppling into the open grave along with her son's casket.

A woman she didn't even know had stepped close to her, sharing her umbrella, and offered her a tissue. "He lives on as a part of your story." The words had been so different from everyone else's platitudes that they stuck with her.

Tay might no longer walk this earth, but as long as she remembered him, he would live on. The same could be said of Natalie.

A prickle of unease brought Noelle's mind back to the present, and she shook off the tendrils of grief that tried to cling to her. Her gaze slid over grave markers and trees, searching for anything unusual.

A man stood by a grave a few rows back, head bowed, his ball cap obscuring his face. Was he watching them? Listening in on Skyler's one-sided conversation with her mother?

To what end? her inner voice challenged. There was nothing to be gained by eavesdropping on their visit. But something about his presence and body posture didn't sit well with her. *You can't assume that any man alone at a cemetery is up to something.*

Her attention moved to an older woman five plots to their right. A bandana was tied over her gray hair, the way women used to wear it to protect their hair from turning into a windblown rat's nest in a convertible.

Was it just Noelle's troubled thoughts putting her on edge? Given the events of the past few days, it wouldn't be hard to believe.

Small fingers slid into Noelle's palm as Skyler took her hand and drew her forward.

"Mom, this is Noelle. You didn't get to meet her 'cause she showed up after . . . after you went away. She kept me safe from Mister, and she said I could live with her." Skyler looked up at Noelle for reassurance before turning her attention back to the grave. "She's my second mom, but she's not replacing you. I'm allowed to have a mom and an adoptive mom. And don't worry, she takes real good care of me, even if she makes me wear shoes."

Noelle's throat tightened with emotion. It had been almost two years since anyone had called her Mom, and even though it reminded her that she would never hear Tay's voice call out to her again, it was more sweet than bitter. She had been praying for this moment for months, because it meant Skyler had fully accepted her—not as a temporary caretaker or an adult friend but as family.

Derek tried to focus on his deputy's forensic breakdown of Nick Nelson's car, but the construction crew hammering away inside his skull made it difficult.

"The blood in the trunk and on the rear of the vehicle are a match to Nelson. Judging by the blood placement, his abductor propped him in a seated position against the back of the car while he unlocked the trunk. There are blood smear zigzags, like he had some trouble lifting Nelson into the trunk," Jimenez explained.

There was something significant about that, but his brain took an extra beat to make the connection. "Nelson couldn't have been more than a hundred seventy pounds. Easy enough for a grown man to lift."

"Dead weight is heavy, but even I could lift him up and dump him in a trunk, and I'm six inches shorter and fifty pounds lighter than he is . . . was. It's a matter of technique. I would guess his killer was trying to lift his limp body up by the armpits."

"Good way to throw out your back."

"Amateurs," she muttered. "But it's safe to say his killer is the one who drove the car to the mill and dumped it."

"Any helpful prints on or inside the car?"

"There are prints all over that thing. I don't think the guy washed his car in the past decade. It will take a while to lift them all and run them."

Derek wouldn't hold his breath. Even novice criminals knew to wear gloves nowadays.

"If the killer dumped the car at the mill, then someone picked him up to bring him back to civilization. A taxi, an Uber, an unsuspecting driver. We need to find that person," Derek said.

"I'll reach out to the Weston cab companies as well as Uber, see if any of them had a fare pickup in that area."

"Good. I'll put out a public request for information in case he hitchhiked." Derek jotted down a note to remind himself to make that social media post.

"There was a long strand of hair recovered from the trunk too. Do we think it's possible that he went after that blond girl at the bar, and she turned the tables on him and decided to roast him?"

Derek made a noise of skepticism in the back of his throat, but he didn't outright dismiss the possibility. From what Rusty had relayed over the phone this morning, Zoe Quenton was five feet tall and under 115 pounds. Her size *would* explain the difficulty getting the man into the trunk, but he couldn't see an eighteen-year-old girl hauling around a body and then setting a barn on fire.

"If he attacked her Thursday evening, it's most likely transfer. Her hair got on him during the struggle and that hair ended up in the trunk with him. Rusty's bringing her in for a conversation, so we'll know more soon," Derek said.

"I heard he tracked her down alive and well."

"She's alive, but 'well' remains to be seen." The girl had burst into tears over the phone when Rusty mentioned the Copper Penny bar, and it took some convincing to get her to come to the station for a face-to-face conversation.

Derek spotted the petite blond girl maneuvering around desks as she made her way toward his office, Rusty by her side. She was legally an adult, but she looked no older than fifteen.

"Thanks, Jimenez. Keep me updated on anything else you discover," Derek said, dismissing her.

Zoe shuffled into the office, arms hidden inside the oversize sleeves of her sweatshirt, long blond hair mounded on her head in a messy bun like the one Trudy wore. She fit Nelson's type to a T.

Rusty closed the door to give them privacy. "Zoe, this is Captain Dempsey. You might recognize him from the sheriff's department's social media sites."

Zoe sank into one of the chairs. "I remember you from when you came to our school and taught the active shooter training. I thought you were pretty cute." Her cheeks flamed, and she ducked her head. "Sorry, I shouldn't have said that."

Derek let the comment roll off him. "I appreciate you coming in."

"Yeah, well . . . your deputy kept calling my cell phone, and I was afraid that if I didn't answer, he might call my dad. He's traveling for work, and he doesn't know what happened. I didn't want him to come home and put his job at risk. It's the only income we have since . . . my mom died a few years ago."

"Would you mind telling us what happened Thursday night?" Derek asked.

Zoe lifted her head to look at Derek, her eyes shining with anxiety and embarrassment. "Like all of it?"

Derek leaned forward and rested his arms on the desk. "I know it's hard, but it would be helpful if you can tell us everything you remember."

Zoe's attention bounced between Rusty and Derek. "I'm not in trouble for not reporting what happened, am I? Because I thought that was supposed to be my choice."

"No, you're not in trouble," Derek assured her. "We just need to know what you remember about Thursday night."

She fidgeted with her sleeves and looked down at her lap. "It sort of started *before* Thursday night. Last Sunday at the football game, my boyfriend was being a jerk. He was flirting with other girls, and it made me so mad. This older guy . . . he started talking to me, and I noticed my boyfriend was watching, so I flirted to make him jealous."

Derek slid a photo of Nick Nelson across the desk for her to identify. "And this is the guy?"

Tears spilled down her face as she nodded. "I swear I didn't know what kind of person he was. I didn't know what . . . what he did to those other girls. I only wanted to make Kyle pay attention to me."

That flirtatious interaction must've been enough to set off Nelson's twisted urges. He would've spent the entire week fantasizing about his next move.

"And Thursday?" Derek asked.

She blew out a long breath and rubbed at the brace on her left knee. "I twisted my knee during cheerleading practice a few weeks ago, so I've been on the sidelines while it's healing. I was still supposed to show up to practice and watch the routines, but Kyle sent me a text. He broke up with me over a text message." She swiped a tear from her cheek. "I um . . . I smoked some weed and then drove to the Copper Penny." She looked between Derek and Rusty. "I swear, I was barely buzzed. I only smoke on occasion, when I'm stressed."

"We're not interested in penalizing you for smoking weed before driving," Rusty said. "Though keep in mind for the future, that is illegal."

She nodded. "I went into the bar, but of course they carded me. So I went back out to the parking lot to smoke some more. I didn't realize he'd followed me out of the bar until . . ." She raised a hand toward her mouth. "He grabbed me from behind and covered my mouth. I couldn't scream. He dragged be around to the side of the building and down to the ground."

Derek tensed—he didn't want to hear the details likely to come next—but he didn't interject. He wouldn't let his discomfort silence her.

"And then this guy came out of nowhere and hit him across the back of the head," Zoe said.

It took a second for her unexpected words to click into place in Derek's aching head. "Someone intervened?"

"I don't know who, but he saved me. I got up, ran to my car, and drove home. I thought I was going to wreck from shaking so hard."

"Do you remember anything about the person who saved you?" Rusty asked.

Zoe squinted as she searched her memories. "He was about your height." She looked at Rusty, who was about five foot nine. "It was so dark, all I could see was a long beard and a hood."

"It's possible your rescuer came from inside the bar," Derek said. "When you were inside, did you notice anyone with a hood and beard?"

"Um . . ." She stretched and twisted the sleeves of her sweatshirt. "Yeah, actually. There was this one guy at one of the tables. He had a hood and a long beard."

"What made you notice him?" Derek asked.

"There was something weird about the way he looked. I can't really say what it was, but there was . . . something. And he had this sort of . . . tremor, I guess you would call it? Like he had the shakes or something. And he kept staring at me."

"Were you standing beside Nelson at the time?" Rusty asked.

"Yeah. I guess the old guy could've been staring at him."

Considering Nelson was the victim, it was a safe assumption he was the center of the man's focus and not the girl.

"Did you see anything that might help us identify that man?" Derek asked.

Zoe sighed and shook her head. "No, I'm sorry."

"Why not report the attack?" Rusty asked.

"Are you kidding me? I'm underage. I was at a bar that I drove to while high on weed. I didn't want to get arrested. I didn't want my dad to know how badly I screwed up," she admitted, wiping away fresh tears with the sleeve of her sweatshirt.

"What did you screw up?"

"Everything. I stupidly flirted with a perv at least fifteen years older than me, and then I went to a bar and almost got myself . . ." She trailed off, swallowing hard.

"Listen to me," Derek began. "Driving while under the influence of marijuana was stupid, but you're not going to do that again, right?" When she nodded, he continued. "Good. Everything else that happened was not your fault. Nick Nelson was a disturbed individual, and whether you flirted with him or simply walked past him, his mind would've gone to the same dark place. At the bar, he saw an opportunity, and he took it. He made that choice."

She relaxed a fraction in her chair.

"Would you mind describing the older man to a sketch artist?" Derek asked. "It would help our investigation."

"I guess I could try, but I need to be home by five. That's when Dad gets home from his weekend trip, and I don't want him to know anything about this. He'll be disappointed."

"You can choose not to tell your dad, but you should know that lies only serve to divide people. He might be upset for a while after you tell him the truth, but it's only because he loves you." Derek punched an extension into his desk phone to connect with one of his deputies. "Grisham."

"Yes, sir?"

"Would you come to my office, please? I have a young lady here who needs your help recreating the face of someone she saw Thursday night."

"On my way."

Grisham arrived a minute later and led Zoe away to a conference room. Rusty closed the door after she left. "Our arsonist and killer is an older man with a beard and some kind of shaking disorder."

That would account for his difficulty putting Nelson's body in the trunk, but they didn't have enough information to assume the old man and the mysterious hero were the same person. There were a lot of men with beards and hooded sweatshirts, especially this time of year.

Derek wrapped a hand over one fist in front of his mouth, thinking. "Talk to the bartender at the Copper Penny and find out what he remembers from Thursday night. He might recall whether or not someone left the bar shortly after Nelson."

"And if no one did?"

"Then our Good Samaritan was arriving rather than leaving the bar, which means no one will be able to help us identify him."

CHAPTER Twenty-three

Skyler worked diligently on her window mural at the diner, alternating between coloring and bites of leftover cherry cobbler with ice cream.

Noelle paused beside her, dirty dishes in hand, and studied the scarecrow that looked an awful lot like a certain grouchy old man. "Is that Walt?"

"Yeah. In his scarecrow costume."

Walt didn't need a costume to pull off that role. His everyday attire and permanent menacing scowl were enough to project the image. "It's very nice." Noelle gestured to the scene with the stack of plates in her hands. "Why the red truck?"

"It's a really pretty shade of red, and plus it's right there." Skyler pointed through the window to a red truck in the parking lot.

Noelle leaned left to get a better angle of the vehicle. Sure enough, there was a red truck. And it had a silhouette of a stripper on the side window.

How tasteful, she thought with a grimace. Hopefully, Skyler left that detail out of her window mural.

"Maybe we can convince Walt to come here and eat with us sometime so he can see your beautiful artwork."

Skyler's shoulders drooped. "He won't come. He doesn't like all the people staring at him."

Noelle pulled her phone from her apron. "Why don't I take a picture of it then, and we can show him that?"

Skyler popped to her feet with a happy grin. "Can I take the picture?"

"Of course you can." Noelle handed her the phone. She noticed one of her customers staring at his roast and potatoes like there was something wrong with it. She stepped closer to his table. "Sir, is everything all right?"

He looked up, scratching at his short beard that was more salt than pepper. "Sorry?"

"Is everything all right with your meal?"

"Fine. The food is fine. Just a lot on my mind." He paused before asking, "Have you ever been in a situation where you wondered if you made a huge mistake?"

Noelle hesitated as she thought back to her first marriage, but she wasn't going to share that with this man. "Everyone makes mistakes."

"But what if it's one you can't fix?"

"Then I guess you move on. If your mistake hurt anyone, ask forgiveness and try to mend what's broken."

He grunted in thought and then readjusted in his seat to face her, his overly tan skin creasing like leather as he considered her. "You're dating the captain of the sheriff's department, aren't you?"

Noelle shifted uneasily with the plates she held. "And if I am?"

"Has he told you anything about the arson cases he's heading up?"

Suspicion threaded through Noelle. "What are you, a reporter?"

"A curious and concerned citizen. There's a rumor that this latest fire matches the Dragonfly's MO. Victim bound and burned in a barn he had no business being in."

"I recommend not giving too much attention to rumors. And even if Captain Dempsey *had* told me anything, I wouldn't share it. I suggest you move on to a different story. No one here is going to answer your questions."

Another man in his seventies grumbled around a mouthful of stew, "Man's got a right to say what we're all thinking."

The reporter turned in his seat to home in on the slightly older man. "What do you know?"

"I was here when the Dragonfly made his first appearance. It was quite a dramatic affair for a small village with little more than family drama to keep law enforcement from falling asleep at their desks. He was caught before he got to finish his act. Now he's back for act two. More people are going to burn."

"Stop." Noelle sent the man a hard look. "Whether the arsonist is or isn't this *Dragonfly*, my child is sitting right here, listening to every word. She doesn't need to hear this."

The man paused with his spoonful of stew halfway to his mouth and twisted to see Skyler sitting on the windowsill. He snorted. "Unless your ovaries ran out of ink, that white girl ain't your child."

Noelle flinched inwardly at the crass comment. How dare he say something like that to her? Let alone in front of Skyler.

"You know what *has* run out?" Noelle grabbed the bowl of stew from in front of him and added it to the stack of dishes in her arms. "Your time in this diner. Get out."

"You can't take my dinner."

"You haven't paid for it, so you have no right to it. Find your dinner elsewhere."

The man dropped the spoon, letting the contents splatter across the table and wall as he stood. "You got no right to . . ." His gaze trailed past her shoulder, and he swallowed the remainder of his protest. "I can find better stew from a can anyway."

The older man grabbed his coat and stormed out.

As the door drifted shut behind him, Noelle clutched at the top of the booth bench to steady herself. She loathed confrontation, but she couldn't let her daughter think that man's behavior was acceptable.

She glanced behind her to see Brian, a furious expression on his face. He shifted his jaw and turned back toward the kitchen.

Noelle's gaze swept over the embarrassed and surprised faces of the remaining customers. Even the reporter had the decency to look uncomfortable with the older man's behavior. He sank back down in his booth and tried to disappear.

Skyler held out Noelle's phone. "I'm all done taking pictures."

Noelle cleared her throat and tried to regain her balance after that tense situation. "Did you get some good ones?" She checked the photo gallery on her phone, scrolling through endless still shots of the window. "I said *a* picture. Not sixty."

"I only took thirty. But we have to preserve it, 'cause after Thanksgiving, Trudy said I could do a Christmas one."

"We'll save a couple of the best ones." Noelle dropped her phone back into her apron. "I know you heard what that man said, but he's wrong. Skin color has nothing to do with what makes people family."

"I know." Skyler's face turned serious. "I guess nobody told him about foster moms and adoptive moms and stepmoms. He's old, but he doesn't know anything more about moms than Sami, and she's twelve."

Noelle smiled and kissed the top of Skyler's head. "I love you, my sweet Firefly."

"I know that too."

Noelle started for the kitchen with her armload of dirty dishes. She needed to set them down before her arm broke off from holding the weight for so long.

A woman reached out from one of the booths and grazed her elbow. "Excuse me. Sorry. Could I get some of that cobbler the little one's eating?"

Noelle looked down at the forty-something woman with blond Shirley Temple curls. "I'll see if we have any left."

"Thank you." The woman turned in her seat to see Skyler. "That's a very nice drawing. You're quite the artist."

"I'm going to be a painter someday. Or maybe a writer. Or maybe I'll become an archaeologist. They find cool stuff and get to tell stories about it."

"Those all sound like wonderful options."

"What do you do for a job, Miss . . ." Skyler squinted. "What's your name?"

"Sally, and I sell homeowners insurance."

Skyler tilted her head, clearly trying to make sense of the answer. "What's homeowners insurance?"

"Something that's necessary but unfortunately dull."

Noelle slipped into the kitchen past Brian, who was cooking a steak on the grill. He turned to her and whispered, "I see Sky's making a friend."

Noelle grunted in amusement. "Kids her own age, she struggles to befriend. But adults? She wraps their heartstrings around her little fingers."

"I know. I'm one of them."

The first time Brian saw Skyler, she was being kidnapped, and he nearly died trying to stop it from happening. After that, their bond only grew.

"Sorry I cost you a customer tonight. I'll pay for his meal so it doesn't come out of your budget," Noelle said.

"I don't want customers like that. And you're not paying for his meal. Just toss it and be done with it."

Noelle nodded and carried the dishes to the sink. Scraping away the leftovers, she stacked them in the dishwasher tray and pushed it through.

When she returned to the dining room with the blond woman's cherry cobbler, Brian was delivering meals to two gentlemen at a small corner table.

The oldest of the two men, whose bald head gleamed under the glow of the overhead light fixture, tipped his face up to get a better look at Brian. "I got twenty bucks riding on OSU winning the game tonight. Ralph has twenty on Michigan. You in?"

Brian stilled at the question, his hand trapped beneath the plate he'd been sliding onto the table in front of the man. He swallowed and pulled his hand free. "I don't gamble."

Ralph, eyebrows thick enough to qualify as shrubs, leaned forward and pinned Brian with a look. "Since when?"

"Since I promised my wife no more gambling."

"Trudy? She wouldn't mind you placing a wager on a sporting event. Ain't like it's a poker game," the bald man said.

"Even if she does care, she'll never know," Ralph added. "It's twenty bucks, not two hundred."

Brian's breathing grew shallow as he wrestled his greatest temptation. The twenty dollars wasn't the issue. It was the rush that came with giving in to an addiction. It was the compulsion to give in again and again.

"Brian." Noelle stepped into the dining room. "Could you help me with something in the kitchen?"

Brian stiffened, eyes wide, like a deer caught in the twin beams of a car. He stepped away from the table and followed her into the kitchen. "I wasn't going to do it."

"Really?" Noelle asked, her tone devoid of judgment. She already knew the truth; his startled reaction to her calling his name betrayed the direction of his thoughts.

He swallowed and averted his eyes. "Okay, yes, I was thinking about it. It's only twenty dollars."

"And then forty, and then four hundred, and then four thousand. It's a slippery slope, and you know it. The safest thing to do is avoid the slippery grass altogether."

"It's like an itch beneath my skin, and all I want to do is scratch it."

"Temptation is a part of life, and if it's an area you particularly struggle with, well, that's why you have friends." Noelle took his sweaty hand and squeezed it. "I've got your back."

Brian squeezed back before letting go. "Thank you. Did you actually need my help with something, or . . ."

"No. I thought that would be a less embarrassing approach than smacking you across the back of the head to jar your senses."

Brian grinned. "Thank you."

"I'm going to run out to my car and grab my lip balm. Watch Skyler and make sure she doesn't wander out the front door to chase butterflies or something."

"I can get it if you tell me where it is."

Noelle nodded at a burger sizzling on the grill. "You have an order to finish preparing, and it's fine. My car is right outside the back door. It'll take me less than sixty seconds."

Brian grabbed a spatula and flipped the patty before it could burn. He eyed the back door with indecision. "Keep your eyes open out there."

"I wasn't planning to walk with them shut." She flashed him a teasing smile and then made her way through the kitchen to the back door. It squealed open, cool, fresh air swirling around her.

The back of the parking lot was strictly for employee vehicles, and Noelle picked the area less than twelve feet from the door. She fished the keys from her apron as she crossed the well-lit lot to the driver's side of her car.

She couldn't believe she'd forgotten to bring in lip balm. She always kept one with her, but she'd given the one in her purse to Skyler, and now her lip-balm-loving world was out of balance.

She slid the key into the lock, but before she could twist it, she caught a reflection in the window of a man moving up behind her. Fear burned through her stomach like acid.

Zac Inman.

She whirled toward the man and reached for the gun at her back. Her fingers brushed across bare skin. *Crap.* She'd left her gun in her purse in the office so she didn't alarm any of the customers.

A satisfied smile stretched Zac's already too-wide mouth. "Found you."

Noelle's eyes flickered to the door of the diner and then back to Zac. "What are you doing here?"

"I'm here to see you. I drove by your house, but your car wasn't there, so I kept going until I spotted it. I passed this building three times before I noticed the bright pink Volkswagen back here."

Noelle's throat constricted. She'd been right. He did know where she lived. "Did you get my address from my license?"

"I figured out your address months ago, but I did double-check it against your license at the bookstore."

Months ago?

"I work with computers and data mining, and it's easy to track down personal information on the internet," he explained. "I would've come to see you yesterday, but . . . the way you reacted to me at the bookstore . . . I was upset," he continued.

Noelle glanced at the door again. "I really need to tend to my customers."

When she moved toward the diner, he blocked her path. "You can't leave. We need to talk."

Noelle visually searched for help, but the diner backed up to the creek. There was no one. Would Brian hear her call out over the din of the diner?

"You can't be here, Zac. You need to go," she said.

That eerie flatness crawled over his features again. "I don't like being told to go away."

She parted her lips to shout for Brian, but Zac's hand clamped over her mouth in the same instant he drove her up against the side of the car with his body. Her back smacked against the driver's door, the key ring attached to the lock punching into her spine.

A whimper of pain leaked through the fingers over her mouth.

"Don't scream. This is our moment to talk," Zac said, his face so close to hers that she could feel his breath with every adrenaline-laced pant.

Noelle thrust her knee into his groin, and he doubled over in pain. She darted for the diner. Before she could reach the door, it opened, and Brian leaned out.

"You said sixty seconds, not—" Brian's words cut off as she nearly plowed into him. He looked her over and then past her to the man struggling to stand up straight. He bit out a curse as the situation registered. "What happened?"

Noelle moved behind him. "He grabbed me."

Before Zac could fully uncurl from his pained position, Brian flung him to the ground and pressed a knee into his back. "You're under arrest."

Zac twisted and thrashed, trying to escape, and Brian pressed his knee deeper into the man's back as he forced his arms behind him.

"Noelle, grab the flex cuffs from my trunk." He wiggled his key ring from his pocket and tossed it to her.

She snagged it out of the air and rushed to his car beside hers, popping the trunk. She blinked at the bag of supplies—bolt cutters, zip ties, road flares, a first aid kit, duct tape, and a dozen other jumbled items.

"What is all this stuff?" she asked.

"First responder supplies. I might not be a deputy anymore, but I like to be prepared if I happen across an emergency."

Noelle grabbed the flex cuffs and closed the trunk. "Here."

Brian took them and fitted them around Zac's wrists. The man let out a whine. "That hurts."

"Let that be a reminder to keep your hands to yourself in the future." Brian wrestled his cell phone from the back pocket of his jeans and turned his attention to Noelle. "Derek said you didn't file a report the first time. We're filing one this time."

It wasn't a question, and Noelle didn't argue.

She hovered by the back bumper of her car, half dazed by what had just happened, while Brian called 911.

Derek popped a handful of quarters into the vending machine and selected a package of trail mix. The bag dropped down, and he bent to retrieve it as he turned over the information from the phone call he'd had with Rusty.

The bartender, Rand, recalled a man in his sixties—suffering from some kind of palsy—who ordered his beer by pointing, paid in cash, and then slipped out a few minutes after Nelson. It was possible he simply walked to his car and drove off, ignoring the sexual assault taking place along the side of the bar, but it seemed unlikely.

Shoes squeaked into the room behind him, and he turned to find Grisham. "How did things go with Zoe?"

"Good. She has a better memory than she thinks she does." Grisham handed over the sketch. Without a name to attach to the man, she paper-clipped a note to it that read Copper Penny Customer.

Derek studied the bearded man's face—faint creases around his eyes, wiry eyebrows, salt-and-pepper hair that grazed his ears, and a smudge on his cheek beneath his left eye. All but one of the details fit the bartender's description.

Derek pointed to the mark. "Is this an accidental smudge?"

"Zoe said it looked like a birthmark the man was trying to hide beneath concealer. But a shadow of it was still visible," Grisham explained.

"This does not look like the type of man who wears makeup."

"Unless he has good reason to hide it."

A facial birthmark was distinctive, and if he planned to dabble in illegal activities—little things like murder and arson—maybe he *was* trying to conceal it.

"Did you have a chance to ask your cousins about the Amish man lurking around the Miller barn?" Derek asked.

"I did. He's not Amish."

"How can you be sure?"

"For one, his beard's not right. The way Mr. Miller described it, the hair comes up higher than a traditional Amish beard. There shouldn't be any hair here." She traced her fingers over her cheeks and below her bottom lip. "It generally follows the line of the jaw."

"You didn't mention that yesterday."

"I thought he might've described it wrong. That's common for people who aren't members of the Amish community. I didn't want to put too much stock in that detail."

"But now you're certain that detail matters."

She nodded. "My cousin Mary works at one of the Amish stores where they sell handmade clothing and headwear. She said an older man came in to purchase one set of men's clothing, but he was dressed in khakis, a sweatshirt, and a baseball cap."

"Did he have a birthmark on his face?"

Grisham nodded. "And she said it looked like he was trying to hide it."

Derek's heart skipped at the connection. "Was there anything distinctive about his voice?"

"No, she said he didn't talk. Didn't even say hello. And he paid for the transaction in cash, so there's no credit card receipt we can check."

The Copper Penny customer and the man who purchased the clothing were clearly the same person, but . . .

"If he came in looking so different, how did she recognize him from the sketch you made of the Amish man? There's no facial birthmark on that one."

"Mary said it was his eyes."

Derek studied the sketch, but he didn't see anything unique about the man's eyes. They might be slightly farther apart than the average person's.

"Thank you, Grisham. This is great work."

Derek carried the sketch and his snack back to his office. He found a folder on his desk that hadn't been there ten minutes ago. It was the toxicology report for Nick Nelson.

Flipping it open, Derek found a handwritten note to break down the medical jargon for him.

> The irritation lining Nick Nelson's airway and lungs was caused by trichloromethane, more commonly known as chloroform. The drug was administered through inhalation, and toxic doses were found in the blood. This coincides with the damage to his liver. Cause of death: trichloromethane toxicity.

Nelson was bashed over the head and then chloroformed sometime before or after he was thrown into the trunk of his own car. The ingredients used to make chloroform weren't controlled, and it was easy enough to find a recipe online to make it homemade. Knowing how much to administer, however, was a bit harder to figure out.

No one *happened* to have a container of chloroform with them. Their arsonist and murderer had brought it with him to the bar with the intention of taking someone. The question was, was Nelson the intended target or a victim of opportunity?

A woman's voice came through the intercom on Derek's desk phone. "Sir, dispatch received a 911 call from Brian Mason. Police units are on their way to your sister's diner."

Derek's heart jolted. Noelle and Skyler were at the diner.

CHAPTER Twenty-three

Derek threw his truck into park in the diner parking lot and leaped out. His head pounded violently from his increased heart rate, but he didn't slow.

He wrenched open the glass door, sending the hanging sign flipping back and forth between open and closed.

Like the parking lot, the dining room was empty of customers. Skyler sat in one of the booths with a coloring book, her foot bopping back and forth to the soft music spilling from her headphones.

Noelle stood by one of the booths with a tray of dirty dishes in her hands. The relief that softened the worry lines on her face when she saw him matched the relief he felt.

She set down the tray as he crossed the room, and he swept her into a hug. She wrapped her arms around his neck with a trembling exhale.

Neither of them said anything for a beat.

Gratitude, anger, and fear warred for control inside Derek. He was grateful that Noelle was safe, but furious this had happened. Again.

This man had come after her twice, and both times the altercation turned physical. This time more aggressively than the first. What would he do if he caught her alone again?

"How are you?" he finally asked.

"Fine."

He leaned back and searched her face. "I think I deserve more than the autopilot answer you give everyone else, don't you?"

She dropped her forehead against his chest. "Rattled, stressed, about one more incident away from a fit of hysterical laughter."

"You are the only person I know who gets so stressed they laugh."

"It's either that or cry."

He tightened his arms around her again. "I need you to press charges. I know it's not a fun process, but I need you to do that for me."

He didn't want to get a phone call that she was missing or dead because this man couldn't accept that she didn't want a relationship with him.

"I gave my statement to the officers already."

Good, he thought. *Hopefully being arrested will put the fear of God into him.*

"None of this makes any sense," she muttered. "I'm not . . . the kind of woman stalkers are supposed to gravitate toward. I'm not a model or an actress. I'm not young and beautiful. I'm—"

"Excuse me?" Derek leaned back to see her face, offended by the way she was speaking about the woman he loved.

"You know what I mean. I don't turn heads. Most days I have a hard time reconciling the fact that *you* love me and want to be a part of my daily life. For another man to go out of his way to be in my life . . . it doesn't make sense."

"First of all, you *are* beautiful, and you're only thirty-four. Let's not start looking at retirement homes just yet. And stalkers choose who they choose. While it's *about* you, it's not *because* of you."

The rear door of the kitchen squeaked open, and Brian stepped inside, his expression grim. "Inman's in the back of the police cruiser if you want a word with him. He's been mirandized, but he didn't ask for a lawyer yet."

Derek released Noelle. "Has he said anything to explain his behavior?"

"He's refusing to speak with anyone but Noelle."

Derek caught the flicker of fear on Noelle's face and said, "That's not happening." He wasn't letting that man anywhere near her. "I'm going to take the girls home."

"I need to finish cleaning up. I don't want Trudy to have to deal with that in the morning."

"I'll take care of it," Brian said.

Noelle looked around at the mess. "Are you sure?"

"I'm sure."

Noelle tapped Skyler's shoulder to get her attention. "Come on, honey. It's time to go home."

Skyler turned off her music and bagged up her art supplies. "I have to give hugs first." She ran through the dining room and launched herself at Brian.

He caught her, hooking an arm under her legs to keep her from falling.

She wrapped her arms around his neck. "Good night. Love you a lot."

Brian kissed her forehead. "Love you too, Bug." He lowered her to the floor, and she sprinted back into the dining room to take Derek's hand.

She looked up at him, her face bright with joy, completely unaware of the danger this evening. If it was within Derek's power, he would shield her from danger for the rest of her life.

Chains creaked as Derek glided back and forth on the porch swing, savoring the chill of impending winter as he sipped his coffee.

Unlike the women in his life, who gravitated toward crackling fires and fuzzy blankets on top of sweatpants, he found the nip in the air both invigorating and relaxing.

Elsa let out a contented sigh at his feet. She didn't care for the rain, but cooler temperatures suited her. Come the first snow of the season, she would be romping through it and trying to bite snowflakes out of the sky.

Lacey had chosen her name well, even if the two of them had never met.

Headlights turned into the driveway, and Trudy's car puttered to a stop beside Noelle's Volkswagen.

Derek leaned forward, mug of coffee resting between his knees, and waited for his baby sister to join him. He'd known this visit was coming. Aside from the fact that he ignored her request to discuss his marital status, Brian would've told her about the incident at the diner.

Trudy climbed out from behind the wheel in baggy sweatpants and an oversize sweatshirt that made her look three feet tall. Of the four kids Mom gave birth to, Trudy was the runt of the litter.

She wrapped her arms around herself, like her multiple layers weren't enough defense against the cold, and scampered up the porch steps. "Only crazy people sit outside when it's thirty-seven degrees."

"You know I like the cold."

"It's like Mom gave birth to three kids and a polar bear."

He lifted the blanket he'd brought out for her. "I had a feeling you would need this."

"Oh, thank heavens." She shiver-hopped over to the swing and sat down, drawing her legs up and tenting the blanket around her until she was covered from chin to toes. "I didn't think I would need a coat."

"Looks like you were wrong."

"I was less right than I usually am."

"Also known as *wrong.*"

"I am hardly ever wrong."

"So you admit it happens."

She slanted a mock glare his way. "Are you trying to pick a fight? Because I can take you."

Derek snorted. "Prove it."

She stared at him like she was seriously considering it, then said, "It's too cold to leave my cozy cocoon. You get a pass this time."

He smiled and reached down to retrieve the insulated mug of decaf coffee with cream and sugar, offering it to her. "This is for you."

She poked a few fingers out of the blanket and took it from him. "You are my favorite brother." She uncapped the sip spout, then paused. "Wait a minute. You already had this prepared. How did you know I was coming?"

"Twenty-eight years of life experience."

"I am not that predictable."

"You are, but in a good way."

She gave a grunt of acceptance and sipped her coffee. "How's Noelle?"

"Shaken up. She's having a hard time wrapping her mind around the fact that she has a stalker and what it could possibly mean for her life."

"Brian said he came after her at the book signing, too, which everyone seemed to know about but me. It's not like I'm your sister and her best friend or anything."

Derek gave her a chiding look, reminding her without a word that it wasn't about her.

Trudy scowled. "I know it's not about me, and I'm not trying to make it about me, but she's my friend, and how can I know to be there for her if she doesn't confide in me about what's going on? Someone should've told me."

"She wanted to put it behind her."

Trudy inhaled a breath and released it before saying, "I can understand that. What happened at the bookstore?"

"He cornered her in the parking lot. He was gone by the time I got there. My guess is he took off into the cornfield."

"Oh," Trudy said, her tone carrying the weight of the story behind his cornfield aversion.

Derek scowled. "Don't say 'oh' like it holds some significance."

"It's okay that you're afraid of cornfields. You did almost die of hypothermia."

"I'm not afraid of them. I'm wary of them. And if I had seen him go in, I would've gone in after him." He might've needed to do some deep-breathing exercises during that pursuit, but he would've gone.

Almost dying in a cornfield when he was eleven had left him with some apprehension about entering one again.

He and his friends had snuck out one October night to visit the largest cornfield in the area, one that spanned four hundred acres. They wanted to see the ghost of the dead farmer rumored to walk between the rows on a full moon. Something moving between the stalks spooked them, and the boys scattered in fear. Derek ended up lost and alone in the cornfield with a twisted ankle. He hobbled for hours, searching for the edge of the field where their bikes were parked, but eventually his ankle gave out, and he curled up on the ground to wait for someone to find him.

"So this guy is an obsessed reader?" Trudy asked, drawing his thoughts back to the present.

Derek nodded. "He's behind bars right now, so she's safe for the night." He could go home and sleep in his comfortable bed without worrying about her safety, but he would never be able to rest knowing she was frightened.

"What happens tomorrow? What if he posts bail and comes after her while you're at work?" Trudy asked, voicing the fear that had been nagging at him for the past several hours.

He told Noelle everything would be fine before she retreated into the bathroom with a book and bottle of bubble bath, but he was worried. He couldn't stay here all day to protect her, and he couldn't ask Brian to step back from the diner to look after her until this stalker situation was sorted out. Trudy couldn't afford to pay someone to cover his shifts.

"I don't know," he admitted. "I'll save that worry for tomorrow. Today has given me enough to worry about."

"I take it you're spending the night again," Trudy said, a question lurking beneath her statement.

"On the couch," he clarified. "Noelle needs to rest, and if she knows I'm here, between her and any threat, I think she'll be able to let her guard down and get some sleep."

"You know you could marry her, and then you wouldn't have to sleep on that lumpy old couch."

"Trudy," he said on an exasperated sigh.

"Am I wrong?"

"We haven't even discussed marriage."

"Because every time she drops a hint, you step around it like it's a land mine."

"What hints are you talking about?"

"She asked your opinion on the paint color . . . for her bedroom, which would only be relevant to you if . . ." She waited for him to answer and then rolled her eyes. "If it was eventually going to be your bedroom too."

Was that what that conversation was about?

"I thought she just wanted a second opinion."

Trudy dropped her head against his shoulder with a groan. "You are such a guy."

"Oddly enough, I was born that way."

She lifted her head to look at him. "And what about the less than discreet comments she made about the type of ring she likes?"

He searched his memory. "I don't remember that conversation."

"How . . ." Trudy scrunched up one side of her face. "Never mind. What about all the times she's asked you for advice about Skyler?"

"What about those times?"

"You are a childless man, Derek. No woman is going to ask a childless man for parental advice, unless she wants *said* man to be a serious part of her child's life and future. Like, say . . . I don't know . . . a father." She stared at him like she was waiting for the dots to connect in his brain.

Was that really how women's minds worked?

"If she wants to talk about marriage, why not bring it up?" he asked.

"She's afraid of what you'll say."

Derek frowned. "What does that mean?"

"She's afraid you'll say that you don't want to marry her because she has too much baggage or because there's something wrong with her."

Frustration flooded him. "Why would she . . ." He trailed off as the answer to his own question slapped him in the face. Her ex-husband.

The man frequently pointed out her flaws and made her feel like there was something wrong with her. And then he cheated on her and left her because he didn't think she was worth being married to.

"Are you there yet?" Trudy asked.

He sighed. "I'm there. All this time, I thought her experiences made her uncomfortable with the idea of marriage, and that's why she never mentioned it. But really . . . she's been worried that my silence on the issue means I don't want to marry her."

"She knows you love her, but the insecurities he left her with are deep and hard to get past." She took another drink of her coffee and shivered from the cold. "Now that all that is cleared up, I think we should go ring shopping."

Derek reached into his pocket and pulled out a velvet box, popping the top to show her the ring. "I bought one three weeks ago."

Trudy gasped and grabbed the box, letting the blanket slide from her shoulders. "Oh my goodness. It's beautiful! She's going to love it." She turned the box left and right, the stones catching the light from the porch sconce. "Wait . . . three weeks?" She eyed him. "Why is it still in the box and not on her finger?"

"Because I still love her."

"And you say women are confusing."

"This entire conversation proves that point." He pulled the chain with the wedding band and engagement ring from beneath his shirt.

"Oh. You mean you still love . . . Lacey." Trudy closed the velvet box. "Well, of course you do."

"You say that like it's normal. She's been dead for six years, Tru, but I still feel her. I still miss her, and I think about her. I should've been able to let her go by now."

"So you're going to hold on to this ring until you can?"

"I keep waiting for it to happen."

"There's nothing wrong with you still loving Lacey and thinking about her. You were friends for half your life before she finally agreed to marry you. You had plans for a future together, and it was cut short."

Derek stared at the rings on the chain. How could he put into words what he'd been wrestling with for months? "Sometimes when I'm with Noelle, something we're doing reminds me of Lacey, and I find myself thinking about her and how much I wish she were still here. That's not fair to Noelle. She deserves more than some of my heart. She deserves all of it, and until I can give her that, it's better if the ring stays in the box."

Trudy was quiet for a moment, formulating her thoughts. "When Noelle lost her son, she never imagined having another child. And then along came Skyler. Noelle opened her heart to that little girl, but that doesn't mean she closed her heart to her son. Tay will always be a part of her. Her boy is gone from this world, but no matter how much time passes, she'll always miss him and think about him. That doesn't stop because Skyler is in her life now. I'm sure there are moments with Skyler that make Noelle think of Tay, but that doesn't make that moment with Skyler any less precious."

Derek remained silent as he absorbed her words.

"When you lost Lacey, you didn't think you would ever fall in love again. And then you met Noelle. Opening your heart to her doesn't mean closing your heart to Lacey. You will think of her, you will love her, and you will miss her because she is forever a part of you. But you need to remember that love is not finite. You can love the woman you lost with your whole heart, and you can love the woman in front of you with your whole heart."

Derek tried to clear the pressure of tears from his throat.

"I know you don't want Noelle to feel like she has to compete with Lacey for your love and attention, but . . . Noelle loves all of you. That includes the parts that Lacey helped shape. The parts of her that rubbed off on you over years of friendship. If anything, she'll want to know more about the woman who helped you become the man she loves."

"You're right about that last part," Derek said. "Noelle brought up Lacey last night. She wanted me to share some stories about her."

"I'm right about all the parts. Just so we're clear." Trudy handed him the velvet box. "Don't keep that ring in the box for too long. Noelle makes you happy, and you deserve to be happy. Not for a while, but for the rest of your life."

She burrowed back beneath her blanket and leaned her head on his shoulder.

Derek opened the box to study the ring and the future it promised. He had a few things to think about over the next few days. He lowered the lid back down. "Thanks, Tru."

"For what?"

He rested his head on top of hers. "For caring enough to meddle in my love life."

CHAPTER Twenty-four

Noelle padded down the steps in her slippers, squinting against the morning sunlight streaming through the foyer windows.

On her way to the kitchen, she dialed the number for Allen Conroy that she'd found online this morning. Rosie said he was the grandson of a doctor who died in the asylum fire. He could have more information on the Dragonfly.

"Yeah," a man answered.

"Hi, am I speaking with Mr. Conroy?"

"Depends on who's asking."

"My name is Noelle McKenzie, and I'm looking into the Dragonfly, Peter Ashton. I was hoping you might have some time for me to stop by and speak with you today."

There was a pause on the line. "I guess that's fine. I'll be home all morning until two. After that, I have to leave for work."

Noelle suppressed her excitement. Research was a part of the writing process she always enjoyed. Not that she was certain this research would result in a book. For now, it was simply answers for her own peace of mind.

"I can be there around ten," she said.

"That works." He gave her directions that meant absolutely nothing to her, but she wrote them down anyway.

Go southeast on Cable Road? He couldn't tell her to take a right after the gas station with cigarette poles out front? Or make a left at the boulder that looks like a troll? She had no idea which direction was southeast.

Satellite willing, her GPS would find it.

Voices carried through the back door into the kitchen as she hung up.

"What kind of stalker?" Walt asked.

"The kind that wants to be close to her," Derek replied, keeping his voice soft. "I doubt he'll cause any more problems after today, but keep an eye out anyway."

Noelle's stomach dropped at the implications of their conversation, and she opened the door to find the two of them standing on the porch. "Is he out?"

Derek turned toward her, his expression apologetic. "He had a court appointment first thing this morning, and he posted bail."

Noelle clutched at her necklace, squeezing the pendant against her palm. He was free, which meant she was no longer safe. "I should go get my gun."

Before she could turn to go back upstairs, Derek stepped forward and caught her arms in a gentle grip. "I know this is scary, but it's going to be all right. One of my deputies is tailing him now, and it looks like he's heading home to Columbus."

Maybe the knee to the groin had driven home her rejection, and he would stop obsessing.

"You said he has no criminal history. So this could've been a one-time thing," she said.

Derek offered her a sympathetic look. "I don't think you can consider two separate attacks a one-time thing."

Noelle dragged her pendant across the chain and then back. "Admittedly that wasn't my most sound logic."

"It looks like he's taking the threat of imprisonment seriously, but I would feel better if you keep your gun on you at all times and let me know where you're going and when until I'm sure he's no longer a threat."

"I can do that."

Thankfully, Skyler had a zoo field trip scheduled for today. She would be at least forty-five minutes away from danger and surrounded by other children and chaperones.

Noelle had hoped to be one of those chaperones, but Skyler asked her not to come. She wanted to try to make friends with the other kids, and she thought having her mom figure around would make that harder. Noelle was officially uncool.

Just as well. If Zac planned to come after her again, it would be best if she wasn't around children. She would use this time alone to do some in-person research into Peter Ashton.

Noelle rubbed at her knuckles after knocking on the rough door in front of her, the splintered wood and chips of paint a better deterrent for solicitors than a sign in the window.

Though there was one of those, too, warning trespassers of bodily harm: "Solicitors will be shot. Survivors will be shot again."

Apparently, Skyler and Derek's homemade sign declaring that trespassers would be "hunted" wasn't unusual for this area of the country.

Noelle's gaze dipped to the smashed doorbell and then back to the door. She decided to "knock" with the toe of her boot this time. "Mr. Conroy! It's Noelle McKenzie."

He knew she was coming, so why wasn't he answering the door?

She stepped to the right to peer through a window, but she couldn't make out much inside. Was he around back tending to the animals? She'd heard a variety of animal calls as she pulled up.

Descending the steps, she rounded the house. "Mr. Conroy?"

She searched in every direction as she stepped around goats and chickens, but there wasn't a soul in sight.

She brushed past a large truck parked behind the house, and the warmth radiating from the hood caught her attention. Conroy said he planned to be home all morning until two, but this truck was still warm from being driven.

She pressed a hand to the hood and jerked it back. Not warm, *hot.* Whoever was here had arrived shortly before she did.

But then why was no one answering?

Noelle started to turn back toward the house when she noticed the black sticker of a pole dancer on the side window of the vehicle.

This truck belonged to one of the three older men from the diner last night—the gamblers or the reporter?

She examined the license plate. Florida. The two gamblers lived here in town, and they were regulars at the diner, which meant this truck must belong to the reporter who was asking for information about the arson and murder. But why would a reporter come all the way from Florida for a story about two fires in a small town?

Something about that scenario didn't feel right.

She typed the license plate into her phone. If the man was up to something, Derek needed to know who he was and what his intentions were. Cherry Creek didn't need an outsider stirring up trouble.

Her gaze trailed to the shed in the backyard. The structure was at least as old as the house, and the sides were beginning to bow inward. Three padlocks and a chain hung from a door so old the hinges would pull free under a forceful gust of wind.

"That's not normal," she muttered. She approached the shed and peered through one of the grimy windows. The interior was dark, but she could make out a dirt floor, a walkie-talkie on a shelf, some basic gardening tools, and a bench.

There was nothing visible to justify the excessive locks. Her attention snagged on a fresh boot print in the dirt leading out and around the shed, and she started to follow it.

"I suggest you stay away from there."

Every nerve ending in her body jumped at the man's voice, and she whirled around to find the speaker standing in front of the woods, a rifle in one hand.

"That building is fit to collapse any day. It's a hazard," he said.

Noelle put some distance between her and the structure. "Sorry. I knocked on the front door, but there was no answer."

He raised the gun. "I spotted the coon that's been killing my baby chickens. I didn't want to miss the chance to get rid of him, but the slippery devil is faster than my bullets. Sorry I wasn't here when you knocked."

Noelle eyed the gun as she asked, "You're Allen Conroy?"

"AJ. My dad is the first Allen Conroy. Judging by the sound of your voice, you're the lady I spoke with on the phone. Noelle, is it?"

"Yes, that's me."

His eyes flickered over her, appraising. "You're prettier than I expected."

Noelle wasn't sure how to respond, so she decided to ignore it. "Why all the locks if the building is too unsafe to use?"

"We live in the United States of lawsuits. I don't want some dumb kid and his friends snooping around inside and getting hurt, only to have their money-grubbing parents sue me into destitution."

She supposed that made sense. She had heard of robbers winning lawsuits because they were injured while breaking into someone's house. The court system was absolute lunacy nowadays.

AJ nodded toward the house. "You're welcome to come in."

Noelle's feet remained planted in the grass as he rounded the house, and she glanced back at the woods. Where was the reporter?

Maybe he's dead and AJ left his body in the woods. Shooting at a raccoon could be his way of explaining away a gunshot.

"You don't need to be scared of me," AJ hollered. "I hunt pests that terrorize my animals, not people."

Noelle stiffened at his comment, which was uncomfortably in line with her thinking. She slid her hand into her purse and wrapped her fingers around the handle of her gun, the hard surface bolstering her courage.

She was armed, and she had texted Derek to let him know where she was going and whom she planned to meet.

"I appreciate you allowing me to visit," she said, joining him on the porch. "I'm sure you have other ways you prefer to spend your downtime than answering a bunch of questions."

He opened the door and gestured to the opening. "Ladies first and all that."

She stepped inside and moved to the left, putting the wall at her back. "I haven't seen you around town before."

"I'm pretty self-sufficient out here, but I've been to the diner a time or two. I've seen you there. With your cop boyfriend." AJ stowed his rifle in a gun cabinet.

"Make yourself comfortable on the couch. I'll be back in a minute."

He stalked down the hallway, and a moment later, a bathroom faucet turned on.

Noelle perused the interior of the house. It was packed with belongings from three generations—from one of those old wooden floor TVs with a turn dial to the plasma sitting on top of it. There was an old record player and a stereo.

"There's a lot of history in here," she called out.

"This was my granddad's place before it was Dad's. I like the history. It keeps me in touch with my granddad even though I never had the chance to meet him," AJ called back. He returned a moment later, rubbing his hands together. "Want a beer?"

"Um, no thanks. I'm not much of a drinker."

AJ detoured to the kitchen to grab himself a beer from the refrigerator and used a tool to snap the top off the bottle. "Sorry about the wood smoke smell in here. I have a fire pit in the backyard, and the smoke comes in through the open windows. Sticks around for a while."

"It's not a problem." She took a seat on the couch.

He dropped into the recliner across from her. "You said over the phone that you're looking into Peter Ashton. Are you some kind of crime blogger or investigative reporter?"

"Not exactly."

"Then what's your interest?"

What could she say? She didn't want to admit that she was seeing a figure everyone else believed to be the ghost of the Dragonfly. "I heard the legend, and as an author, I'm curious to know the real story."

"An author, huh?" He took a sip of his beer. "I've been interviewed by bloggers and investigative reporters before, but an author is a first."

She could only imagine how many curious people crawled out of the shadows, wanting interviews and details about the violent death that impacted his family decades ago. It would've been a sensational story.

"I understand your grandfather worked at the asylum during Ashton's commitment," she said.

"He was a shrink, or whatever the politically correct name for those people is nowadays. He worked nights at the asylum in case there was a crisis. His death really messed up my dad. He was seventeen when it happened."

Noelle released her gun in favor of her notepad and pen. "Did he ever talk to you about those days?"

AJ grunted. "That was *all* he talked about. My dad was obsessed with what happened."

"Obsessed in what way?"

"It bothered him that Ashton walked away from the fire that night. He spent most of my childhood following rumors about him, trying to track the man down. The whole situation made him furious. All anyone in the village talked about was Peter Ashton. His upbringing, his struggles, his crimes. He became a celebrity while the people he killed and the lives he ruined faded into the background."

That was the way of the world. People were fascinated by the dark and twisted, propelling killers to fame, when it was their victims who deserved remembrance.

"He did find out some interesting things while talking to people around the village. Granddad used to record observations about the patients. He wasn't supposed to, but I guess he was a bit of a rebel. His last tape got mixed up with another employee's personal effects. Dad recovered it."

He rose from the recliner and opened a drawer to fetch a cassette tape. From the stacks of clutter, he pulled out an old radio cassette player and plugged it in.

"It's strange hearing Granddad's voice on a tape. This, and the stories my dad told, are all I have to know him by." He inserted the tape, but he paused with his finger over the play button. "I assume, since you live in the old Bechtel house, you're not easily creeped out."

Noelle stiffened at his comment. She had never met the man before, and yet he knew where she lived?

Of course he knows. You're the only person in this town with a complexion darker than peach fuzz, her inner voice reminded her. *And rumors here move faster than the black plague through Europe.*

"You moved in last fall, if I remember correctly," he said.

Noelle squared her shoulders to project confidence. "Am I supposed to be rattled that you know the same information as everyone else around town?"

A slow smile crossed his lips. "Yeah, you can handle the tape." He pressed play and leaned back in his chair.

A man's voice came from the radio speakers. "This is September fifth, at zero one hundred hours. My request to have patient A reevaluated and potentially moved to a penitentiary was dismissed. I firmly believe patient A does not belong in this institution. I see none of the developmental delay that would qualify him to be here. What others call a mental deficiency, I can only describe as evil. I am not a superstitious man, but when I'm in the room with him, I can feel that evil, as if it is a sentient presence."

The man's description was chilling. Noelle couldn't fathom how anyone could work with murderous psychopaths.

"The patients were placed in the communal dayroom today, like every other day. There's nothing to do in that room. No games or activities. They're simply left to stew in madness," the voice on the tape explained.

Noelle frowned at the doctor's description of the dayroom. It sounded miserable. Thankfully, great strides had been made with regard to patient welfare over the past fifty years.

"Patient A left his mark on the wall in his own blood, from a cut on the tip of his finger," Doctor Conroy continued. "A dragonfly. The calling card of death he left at the scene of every brutal murder. I can't help but feel that symbol is a threat. I believe we're all in danger here."

Noelle recalled the date mentioned at the start of the recording: September 5. The asylum fire started on September 6. Doctor Conroy's assessment had been right. The symbol was a threat.

"Patient A's delusion of reincarnation is not harmless. It is a justification for violence, and I believe, based on what he's been chanting in his room these past several nights, that violence is what he intends. Listen."

Noelle cocked an ear toward the speakers, trying to make out the faint voice speaking in the background. It grew steadily louder, but she still had to strain to hear over the static of the old recording.

"I am the dragonfly. I decide who lives and dies. I am the dragonfly. I decide who lives and dies. And from the ashes they shan't rise. But first I stitch their lips and eyes."

Noelle's fingers tightened around her pen. There was something deeply wrong with that man, more than psychopathic tendencies.

All at once, the chanting stopped, and that same chilling voice said, "I see you, Dr. Conroy. I see you clearly."

The recording ended, and AJ turned off the tape. Noelle's insides felt cold as those final words reverberated through her. Walt had told her that if the Dragonfly sees a person, they die, and Dr. Conroy died the very next night.

"No one took my granddad's concerns seriously, and because of that, people died," AJ said. "The state should've given the families of the fire victims some kind of compensation, because they could've prevented it if they had listened. But they refused and claimed they had no knowledge."

"Have you shared this tape with anyone?"

"Only a few people. Dad shared it with some of the people in his conspiracy circles. It didn't change anything."

"Where's your dad now?"

He shrugged again. "No idea. He took off when I was fifteen. Said he couldn't stand this town anymore. Left me the house, his old truck, and wished me luck."

"He just left you? What about your mom?"

"She died when I was four."

"That's a lot for a child to handle. I'm sorry you had to do it alone."

"He was always more interested in finding his father's killer than being my dad. Peter Ashton destroyed my family. And the people of Cherry Creek . . . they couldn't care less about our suffering. My dad abandoned me when I was still a kid, and not a single person in this town noticed. I learned to fend for myself. Hunting, doing odd jobs for people in the community."

"I'm so sorry. No child should have to go through that."

He swirled the beer around the bottle. "Yeah, well, what happened, happened. Now I get to kick back and watch karma do its work."

"Karma?"

"Two barn fires, one person dead. It's obvious to anyone who's got two cents to rub together—the

Dragonfly is back, and this village is in for a rough season. I always figured he would come back to finish what he started. Not sure why he picked now, but I've got no complaints."

"What makes you think Peter Ashton is behind the fires?"

"Because I've seen him."

Noelle's breath caught. "You've actually seen Peter Ashton, the man no one has been able to find in the past forty-eight years?"

"Mask and all. But he wasn't looking for me."

"Who's he looking for?"

"Only the people he's chosen for death can tell you that. The way he stares at them, like he's reading their soul . . . there's no way they don't realize they're going to die."

Noelle's heartbeat quickened as she thought back to her two encounters with the Dragonfly. The way he seemed to stare at her from a distance. Was she on his list of potential victims?

AJ's beer swished in the bottle as he took a swig. "You look nervous. Something weighing on your soul, Ms. McKenzie?"

She snapped her gaze to his at his choice of words. "My soul is fine. No one, not even this supposed Dragonfly, has the right to judge it."

He grinned, amused that she'd caught his reference. "Any more questions I can answer for you?"

"Where's the reporter?"

He tilted his head. "Reporter?"

"His red truck is parked outside. It's still warm, so I know he hasn't been here long. Strangely, I haven't seen him."

"Not sure what you're talking about. That red truck is mine."

Noelle stiffened at the blatant lie. "With Florida plates?"

He shrugged. "I get around."

Noelle stared at him, but his bland expression remained firm. He wasn't going to flinch first and tell the truth.

Noelle stuffed her pen and notepad back in her purse and slung it over her shoulder as she stood. She needed to get out of this house. "Thank you for your time. I'll call if I have any more questions."

Because she certainly had no plans to come back.

As she pushed out onto the porch, her phone notified her of an incoming message. She dragged it from her sweatshirt pouch to check it. The message was under requests in her Instagram inbox.

She didn't recognize the username of the sender, but as she read the unsettling message, she knew who was hiding behind the cryptic name.

"You should've listened to me. Now bad things are going to happen."

CHAPTER Twenty-five

A witness had finally come forward, claiming that he picked up a man from the old mill out on Smithvail-Western Road at twelve thirty Friday morning.

After he described the man, Derek showed him the sketch of the Copper Penny customer, and he confirmed the likeness. Unfortunately, the passenger gave a false name on the Uber app and paid with a prepaid card.

To make matters worse, he'd been wearing gloves, which meant dusting the driver's rear doors and seating compartment for fingerprints would be a waste of resources.

The notable difference between this encounter and the previous two was that the man uttered a single, raspy sentence: "Copper Penny bar." The driver dropped his passenger at the bar, where he must've had his own vehicle.

"Knock, knock."

Derek pulled his attention from the computer screen, where he was creating a media post with the suspect sketch. His stress melted away the moment he saw his visitor. "This is a nice surprise."

"I'm not interrupting?" Noelle asked.

"Never. How did your interview go?"

She closed the door and sank into one of the guest chairs before answering. "It raised some concerns actually."

That wasn't what he expected to hear. She was interviewing the grandson of a man who was murdered forty-eight years ago, and the murderer was dead. It sounded safe enough. "What happened?"

"It might be nothing, but it didn't feel right, so I thought I should tell you."

Derek searched her face. If Conroy had crossed a line with her, he would pay the man a visit himself.

"At the diner I met a man, and I think he was a reporter. He didn't confirm it, but he was asking questions about the fires."

Derek bit back a sigh. He didn't care for reporters or journalists. They were nosy, inconsiderate, and out to twist the truth in whatever way would garner the most attention.

"Today I saw his truck at AJ's place. It was parked behind the house like he was trying to hide it from view. When I asked AJ about it, he lied and said the truck was his. It has Florida plates."

"Did you see the reporter at all while you were there?"

"No, and that's the disturbing thing. The hood of his truck was still scalding hot, so I knew he must be there somewhere, but he was nowhere. And then AJ stepped out of the woods with his rifle. He claims he was shooting at a raccoon."

Derek leaned forward. "You're worried he did something to the reporter."

"I'm *worried* he killed him, though I can't for the life of me imagine why."

"I can send someone over to do a wellness check. I don't suppose you got the license plate on that truck."

She pulled the notepad from her purse, tore off a sheet, and handed it to him. "I recorded it in my phone and then wrote it down. You said to trust my instincts, and my instincts are telling me something is suspicious."

Derek opened up the BMV database on his computer and typed in the plate number. "Hmm. Not a reporter. The truck belongs to Allen Conroy."

Those adorable quotation marks formed between her eyebrows. "Senior or junior?"

He checked the birth date. "Senior." He turned the screen toward her so she could see the driver's license photo.

"That's him. So much for AJ's dad moving away twenty something years ago and him not seeing him since. Why lie about that?"

"Some people are pathological liars." He straightened out the screen and stared at the photo. Allen Conroy senior was in his sixties.

According to his driver's license, he lived in Florida. Yet he was here in Cherry Creek. Was it a coincidence he dropped in during the same month the fires started?

"What exactly did he say about the fires?" Derek asked.

"He wanted to know if you had told me anything about the arson."

Was he trying to gauge the direction of the investigation because he was involved? If he was the arsonist, that would explain why he didn't want anyone to know he was here.

"Did AJ tell you anything else about his dad?" Derek asked.

"That he was obsessed with his father's murder. AJ has pretty hard feelings toward the village. He says the fires are karma."

"That's interesting. Did he say why he thinks that?"

"He and his father are both angry about the way the Ashton investigation was handled and about how people gave more attention to a killer than his victims."

Derek wasn't aware of any mishandling of the case, but sometimes families were unhappy with the legal system's decisions no matter the outcome.

"I know you said he's dead, but AJ said he's seen someone wearing the Dragonfly costume around the village, and he's convinced it's Peter Ashton," Noelle said.

Amusement curled the corners of Derek's mouth. "That masked figure gets around. An anonymous complaint from a motorist crossed my desk Saturday morning. She claims he charged at her car and then disappeared."

Noelle squirmed in her chair, then reluctantly admitted, "That was me."

The smile slid off his face. "You called in that report?"

"Yeah."

"Why didn't you give your name?"

"Because I knew it would cross your desk, and I didn't want you to think I was crazy or interpreting the situation wrong. I also didn't want you to worry."

He leaned forward and captured her eyes. "Being concerned with your safety comes naturally, but I would never assume you're crazy. You could tell me a flying saucer landed on the lawn, and I would believe you saw exactly that."

"While looking for a reason to explain how I saw that?"

He spread his hands. "Looking for the reason behind things is part of my job."

"Whoever is under that cloak . . . he charged at my car. I don't know what his intentions were, but I do know he's real. I saw him again near the house."

Derek tamped down the rush of worry and frustration. She should've told him she had not one, but two, encounters with the masked figure. "When did you see him near the house?"

"Late Saturday morning. I was in my writing room, and he was at the edge of the woods. I swear he was looking right at me. And then . . ."

When she didn't continue, Derek said, "He disappeared."

She inhaled and then paused before saying, "I don't believe in ghosts, so there's only one other explanation. Someone out there is dressing up like the Dragonfly and trying to frighten people."

Except there hadn't been any other reports.

"I know it's not my place to tell you what you can and can't do, but I've got to be honest—with everything that's going on, I don't love the idea of you interviewing people about Peter Ashton," Derek said.

If she stumbled across the actual perpetrator, it could put her life in danger.

"I think my interviews are over. I'll focus on online research for a bit. But . . ." She tucked her notepad back in her purse. "There is something I should tell you. I received an Instagram message from an account I'm not familiar with, but I'm almost certain it's from Zac."

His body immediately tensed. "What did it say?"

"'You should've listened to me. Now bad things are going to happen.' I can't decide if it was meant as a warning or a threat."

His hands fisted. It sounded like a threat to him. Her repeated rejection had hurt Zac's fragile ego, and his response was to lash out at her with a message that would instill fear.

"That's why I came here instead of going home. I was afraid he might show up at the house," Noelle admitted. "And with Walt not feeling well lately, he might be asleep, which would leave me on my own."

Derek rose from his chair and rounded the desk to take the chair beside her. She was doing her best to remain composed, but she was hugging her purse to her stomach like it might protect her. "I doubt he went to the house. He's probably afraid of getting arrested again. But to be on the safe side, I'm going to send a deputy home with you."

"Where are you going?"

"To Columbus to have a long conversation with Zac Inman. I want to make sure he understands exactly what he's in for if he continues down this path."

"Just a conversation?"

"Unless he escalates matters."

"But if he escalates things, you don't have any authority in Columbus. It's a different county," she pointed out.

"I'm not going to arrest him, but I will speak with the local police department and inform them that he's stalking the loved one of a law enforcement officer. They'll be sure to remind him regularly that his actions are being monitored."

She nodded stiffly.

"I'll have Grisham escort you home and park outside in her cruiser," he said. "You mind taking Elsa home with you?"

Elsa lifted her head from her dog pillow in the corner, ears listening for key words like *walk, treat,* or *let's go.*

"Skyler will be thrilled to have her. They'll be chasing each other around the house," Noelle said, pushing up from her chair. "Be cautious with Zac. There's no way to know what he's capable of. I don't want you getting hurt or . . . having to hurt someone again."

Derek's mind flinched away from the memory. Last year, he'd taken his first human life, and even though it was justified, even though it was to save a house full of trafficked girls, it left an ache in his soul.

"I promise I will take every precaution." He kissed the lines of concern etched between her eyebrows. "I'll see you tonight."

He called out to Grisham and explained the situation. Once he was certain Noelle was in good hands, he closed his office door and called his brother-in-law. One of the precautions he planned to take was backup.

Brian sounded tired when he answered. "Yeah."

"You working this evening?"

"No, Jared's on the grill tonight. Why?"

"I need your help. Bring your gun."

CHAPTER Twenty-six

Derek knocked on the door and then tucked his cold hands into his coat pockets. The wind whipped around him and stirred the metal bird chime.

His gaze drank in the details of the house—the cement stoop beneath his boots sloped as one end sank slowly into the ground, two of the steps had cracked apart from the shift, and one of the few remaining strips of siding tapped in the wind.

"Nice place," Brian muttered.

"From what I could gather about Abby Inman, she's on disability. The primary income is her son."

Brian glanced at the empty space beneath the awning that provided adjoined parking with the neighboring house. "Doesn't look like he's here."

Zac had left town in the direction of Columbus, but that didn't mean he didn't double back in the hope of catching Noelle alone.

"I never thanked you properly for looking out for Noelle last night," Derek said.

"Is that statement your idea of a proper thank-you?"

"Pretty much. Unless you want me to dig deep for something that will make us both uncomfortable."

"Nah, I'm good."

Derek pulled a hand from his pocket to knock again, but the door snapped inward before his knuckles could make contact.

An older woman's face hovered in the crack, her distrustful eyes assessing them. When she spoke, her voice creaked like she smoked a pack of cigarettes a day. "I don't need whatever you're selling."

"We're not selling anything," Derek said. "Are you Mrs. Inman?"

"*Ms.* Inman. Never saw much point in getting married, seeing as men aren't good for much more than knocking you up and leaving you to deal with the mess. What do you want?"

Derek did his best to appear disarming. "We'd like to speak with Zac, if he's here."

She pressed a cigarette to her lips, inhaled, and puffed smoke through the opening at him. "What did that perverted waste of flesh do now?"

The smoke burned down Derek's windpipe into his lungs, and he barely suppressed a cough. "We have a friend in common, and I was hoping we could talk."

Her lips twisted into a cruel smile. "Zac doesn't have friends. He has obsessions. You should see the woman he prattles on about now, like she hung the stars."

"Who might that be?"

Ms. Inman reached for something beyond their view. In Derek's peripheral vision, Brian shifted his right hand closer to the holster hidden beneath his jacket.

When her hand came back into view, she held a book. She tossed it to Derek so unexpectedly that he fumbled to catch it. "There's the porker on the back cover."

Derek turned the book over to find a picture of Noelle. Anger tightened the muscles of his jaw, but he bit back the words he wanted to snap at the woman. "I take it you don't like her writing."

"I don't have time for books. Zac bought it for me. He thought since *he* likes it, I would like it."

"So you don't know anything about the author?" Brian asked.

"I know I don't like her fat face. What is she, a size fourteen? No self-respecting woman allows herself to balloon out like the Pillsbury Doughboy."

The effort it took to withhold his anger was physically painful, and Derek worked to loosen his jaw. He couldn't upset this woman and risk shutting down the flow of information. Right now, Noelle's safety was more important than verbally defending her.

Ms. Inman turned her cold eyes on Brian. "I don't like your face either. Did your daddy smash it into a wall too many times when you were tottering around his ankles?"

"I've been in a few fights," Brian said.

"Lost them, I see." Ms. Inman snatched the book back from Derek. "I'm out of kindling for my evening fire. This will do."

Somehow, Derek wasn't surprised that she burned books. She would probably spit on a cop and stomp on the American flag too.

"Why do you think Zac is obsessed with her?" Derek asked.

"I have no idea. I would understand if she was a model, but she clearly isn't. I would know. I *was* one before that leech latched onto my uterus and wrecked my life. My body never went back to how it was before, and nobody wants a model with loose skin and stretch marks. Never mind the chronic pain he left me with."

"He never offered up any explanation for his fascination with her?" Derek asked, finding that hard to believe. People talked in detail about what they were passionate about, in some form or another.

"I doubt he even knows. Idiot boy wouldn't know what to do if he met a woman. He's never even had a full conversation with one."

In all his years with the sheriff's department, Derek had never heard a mother talk about her child with such hatred and disdain. If Noelle's safety weren't at risk, he would leave simply to avoid hearing her spew more cruelty.

"Is Zac home?" Brian asked.

Ms. Inman blew another stream of smoke in their faces. "Do you see a car in the driveway?"

"When was the last time you saw him?"

She considered Brian with renewed interest. "That sounds like a cop question. Are you a cop, Flat Face?"

"Fireman."

"I bedded a few cops in my day, but I never really cared for firemen. All that ash and smoke. Permeates everything it touches, and it was not touching me," she said, flicking ash from her cigarette onto the stoop. Her cold eyes swung back to Derek. "What about you?"

"I'm not here in an official capacity, but I work for the Wade County Sheriff's Department."

"What did that twisted little creep do?"

"He's stalking someone."

"What did I tell you? Obsessive," she said. "Did you come here with the intent to scare him?"

"We only came to speak with him. Do you have any idea when he'll be back?"

"I haven't seen him since yesterday afternoon, when he crawled out from under his rock to leave the house."

Derek caught Brian's eye. Zac had left the department in a taxi this morning, picked up his mother's car from the impound lot, and headed out of town toward Columbus. If he wasn't planning to come home, what was his destination?

"Any idea where he might go?" Brian asked.

"No. He hardly ever leaves that room."

If Derek lived in a house with this nightmare of a human being, he would hide in his room too.

"Does he keep a journal or a calendar?" Brian asked. "Something that might help us find him?"

"You can check for yourselves." She widened the door to let them in.

Derek looked around as he stepped into the foyer. The house was as worn down inside as it was outside, and it hadn't been updated since the seventies—paneled walls, laminate furniture, and brown shag carpet.

"Does anyone else live here?" he asked.

"My parents used to. Dad's in a home now, because I wasn't going to spend my days wiping drool off his double chin, and Mom's dead. I let Zac stay here so long as he brings in money."

"Where's his room?"

She jerked her chin toward the carpeted staircase. "The attic."

"Thank you."

"Don't expect me to bring up tea and cookies."

Derek led the way up the narrow staircase.

Brian whispered as he followed, "There's something wrong with that woman."

"I'm not sure she's any more stable than her son. *Disturbed* seems to run in this family."

Derek didn't want to feel sympathy for the man stalking Noelle, but growing up with a woman like this must've been traumatic. She could've given him up for adoption if she didn't want him, but she kept him so she would have a target for her anger and bitterness. Her son never had a chance at normalcy.

"I thought you were going to blow a fuse when she started badmouthing Noelle," Brian said.

"One more comment and I would've."

"If that were Trudy she was badmouthing, I would've helped her fall down the porch steps."

"No you wouldn't. You're not that kind of guy."

"Okay, sure, but I would've thought about it," Brian admitted.

A narrow, enclosed staircase led from the second floor to the attic. Derek opened the door at the top and scanned the room before entering.

One side of the attic was cluttered with dusty boxes, shirt sleeves and pant legs hanging out like someone had been digging through them. Judging by the patterns on the shirts, this was where Zac had found his seventies attire. The other side of the attic had a strand of lights strung between the exposed beams. A desk with computer monitors occupied one wall, and a twin-size bed and bookshelf occupied the other.

Brian turned in a circle. "Somehow I expected creepy stalker photos all over the walls."

Derek had expected that too.

He paused beside the bookshelf to examine the titles. Zac had every one of Noelle's books, in both paperback and hardcover. "He's definitely a fan."

He plucked each book from the shelf to check the title pages, but the only one signed was the copy of *Stolen* he'd taken to the book signing the other night.

Derek's gaze slid down the bookshelf. Zac had books from other authors, too, both paperback and hardcover. He was a reader but also a collector.

Brian toggled the mouse on the desk, and the computer screen brightened to display a password entry box. "What do you think the password is?"

"You could always try *password.* It's the most commonly used."

Brian pecked at the keyboard. "I guess Mr. Inman doesn't like to be common. I'm going to try Noelle's name." He typed it in, then grunted. "I really thought that would be it."

"Try something book related. His passion for reading goes beyond Noelle's books." Derek scanned the binders stacked on top of the bookshelf in alphabetical order. Each one was labeled with an author's surname.

He pulled the one labeled Emory.

He flipped it open and found a laminated picture of Noelle. It was the one on the back of all her books. He turned the page, and his gut clenched.

Noelle's biographical information filled the page, including the names of her parents, her divorce, the loss of her son, who she was dating now. The next page listed her books and their release dates as well as all of her public appearances. The page after that listed facts about her—her favorite color, the flavors of tea she liked, her aversion to jogging, the brand of clothing she wore most, her favorite season.

Derek's stomach soured with every new piece of information. These details would've been scattered throughout the internet, and it would've taken untold hours to gather it all.

"I'm in," Brian announced.

Derek returned the folder to the shelf and joined him by the desk. "What was his password?"

"His first and last name, no spaces." He pulled up the computer calendar, but it was blank. "Okay, let's see what sites he's visited recently." He checked the recent URLs. "Facebook, Instagram, some adult sites, a blog about being a better man, an online therapy site, Chatbee—"

"Chatbee?"

"It's a social platform where you can create groups and chat with like-minded people. Like Discord." Brian clicked the link to the site, but it prompted him to log in. "Dead end."

Derek spotted a notebook on the desk, half hidden beneath a wadded up T-shirt. He dragged it out. Several sentences were written across it and then scratched out.

> Hi, Noelle, my name is Zac.
>
> Noelle, I'm Zac, your biggest fan.
>
> Noelle, I love your books.
>
> Hey, Noelle. I came all the way from Columbus to see you, and I have something to tell you.

Brian winced as he read over Derek's shoulder. "He was rehearsing what to say when he met her? I can't help but feel a little sorry for the guy."

"Being nervous about meeting someone doesn't excuse the rest of his behavior." Derek pulled up the photo of the bouquet card on his phone and compared the handwriting to the list Zac had written.

"What are you doing?" Brian asked.

"Zac sent Noelle a bouquet of flowers Saturday with a note apologizing for what happened at the book signing."

"And then he proceeded to attack her at the diner on Sunday. I don't think the guy understands the concept of an apology."

Derek grimaced. "The handwriting's not a match."

"The few times I ordered flowers for Trudy, it was over the phone, and the employee fills out the card with whatever you want it to say. If that's the case, the handwriting won't match. What about prints?"

"A partial, but not enough to search." He found a loose sheet of paper from the same notepad on the desk, and he picked it up. "ForeverMineNE. What do you make of that?"

"Could be a username or a password for something else. Forever mine sounds stalkerish. What do you think the NE stands for?"

Derek felt his jaw tensing again, intensifying the headache that had been plaguing him for days. "My guess would be Noelle Emory."

"Emory?"

"It's Noelle's maiden name. And also the name she uses on her books." Derek set down the paper and used his phone to capture pictures of both the username and the practice greetings Zac had written out.

Brian's phone let out a beep. He pulled it from his coat pocket to check it. "I'm being called to a fire in Cherry Creek. It's another barn."

They were ninety minutes away.

Derek stuffed his phone in his pocket. "Let's go. If this fire is anything like the last two, it'll burn for hours."

CHAPTER Twenty-seven

Skyler placed a few mum cuttings on the grass inside the wrought iron fence and then sat back on her legs.

The pet cemetery in the backyard had a new grave marker—a cross bound together with twine and glue, and a bead necklace with three letters on it: Row.

There was no actual plot, because there was nothing to bury, and there was no birth and death date, because there was no way to find that information. But it was the symbolism that mattered.

"I love you, baby brother," Skyler said. "We would've been really good friends. I would've read you stories and everything."

Noelle sat beside her, giving her this moment to say good-bye to her brother. Walt stood on her other side in stoic silence. How long had it been since he visited the graves of his family? Had he *ever* visited?

"You would like our new mom," Skyler said. "She lets me be loud and dance to music. I don't have to be quiet anymore. She would've let you be loud, too, instead of taking you away."

Noelle rubbed her daughter's back. If only it were possible to go back in time and rescue her baby brother. Noelle would've opened her home to them both.

"Mr. Walt, how come there's no grave markers for *your* family?" Skyler asked.

"They're buried in the local cemetery," he said.

"Do you visit them?"

"I don't go to the cemetery."

"You used to not come in the house, but now you do 'cause of me." Skyler stood and tucked her hand into his. "You could go to the cemetery to visit your family if I go with you. I know you could."

The crackle of a radio drew everyone's attention to Deputy Kara Grisham, who had moved from her cruiser to the back porch to watch over them. They were too far from the house to catch the hushed words coming through the radio speaker, but when Kara stepped off the porch into the grass and looked into the distance, Noelle's stomach dropped.

Dark smoke stretched through the air above the trees. The arsonist was back.

Deputies were already at the fire scene when Derek arrived with Brian, who needed to make a quick stop at the fire station for his gear.

Brian leaped from the truck and dashed toward the raging fire without a second of hesitation. Seeing his dedicated and fearless response, Derek was certain the fire department was where his brother-in-law had belonged all along. Working as a deputy for the sheriff's department had never been his final destination.

Derek slid from the cab and homed in on Angel Jimenez, who had set up a perimeter around the scene.

"Hey, Cap," she said. "Nice flannel."

Derek ignored the commentary about his off-duty wardrobe. "Tell me there's no one inside that barn."

Jimenez grimaced. "Wish I could. We don't know the sex of the victim, but firefighters saw someone inside."

Derek scrubbed both hands over his face and turned toward the blaze. "Any witnesses?"

"No one saw the barn go up, but get this—dispatch received a call from a woman who nearly hit a person on this road around the time the neighbor called in the fire, which was about fifteen minutes after it started. This *person* was dressed in a black cloak with a mask."

Derek glanced at her to see if she was joking about that last detail, but her face was serious. The masked and cloaked figure that had twice taunted Noelle had just been spotted in the proximity of a barn fire.

"Captain?" Jimenez said when he didn't respond.

He stared at the fire that grew and thrashed against the water pouring down. "I want Allen Conroy senior and his son brought in for questioning first thing in the morning."

Whoever was running around the village, dressed as the Dragonfly, was doing a whole lot more than playing dress-up.

Allen Conroy Junior leaned back in the interrogation room chair, arms crossed, with one ankle resting over a knee.

Nothing about his posture suggested he was nervous or even upset about being dragged down to the department at eight in the morning.

"Do you know why you're here, AJ?" Derek asked from across the table.

"I assume because your lady friend implicated me in something. She was awful quick to leave my house after our chat."

"She did express concerns."

AJ shrugged. "I didn't do anything to be concerned about. If she's saying I did, you may want to look at the source. Someone with her job knows how to spin a tale."

"So you don't have hard feelings toward Cherry Creek?"

AJ puckered his lips and then made a smacking sound. "Not hard enough to put my freedom at risk by lighting up barns."

"And murdering people."

"I told Ms. McKenzie that I only kill wild animals, not people. It's not my fault if she walked away with a different idea."

Derek stared at him, and AJ stared back, unflinching. "Where were you last night around six o'clock?"

"Eating dinner in my living room. I like those Hungry Man microwavable meals. Mashed potatoes, ham, gravy."

"Anyone with you?"

"Just me, myself, and God."

Derek made a thoughtful noise in the back of his throat. "Your dad wasn't hungry enough to join you?"

AJ cocked his head. "I haven't seen dear old Dad in twenty-five years. It would be strange for him to pop by for dinner on a random Monday night."

Derek slid a picture across the table of a red Ford truck that matched the license plate Noelle provided. "Look familiar?"

AJ leaned forward to study the picture, then dropped back against his chair. "Lots of people have that model truck. Doesn't make it my dad's."

"I didn't say it was your dad's. How do you know this is what he drives if you haven't seen him in twenty five years?"

AJ paused, but only for a fraction of a second. "We were talking about my dad. I assumed you were showing me the picture because it's what he drives. Anyone would make that connection."

The man was a quick thinker. Tripping him up wouldn't be easy.

"This model truck with your father's license plate was spotted parked by your house," Derek explained.

"There's never been a truck like that on my property. And you can tell your lady that's the last time I help her with a story. First she snoops around, and then she spreads lies."

Derek doubted Noelle would be heartbroken about losing him as a future source of information. "She gave me the license plate. It's statistically impossible for her to have pulled the numbers and letters out of thin air. She saw them."

AJ parted his lips on one side and sucked in a breath through his teeth. "Don't know what to tell you."

"I assume your dad is staying somewhere else, since his truck wasn't at your house when my deputy came by this morning. Any idea where he might be staying?"

"Why all the interest in my old man?"

"He's been asking around town about the arson investigation, but he doesn't seem to want anyone to know he's here."

AJ leaned forward. "I see where you're going with this. You're angling for the easy route, hoping you can blame my dad for these fires. Here's a suggestion—why don't you do your job and find Peter Ashton this time? He's the one behind this."

"Peter Ashton died in the asylum fire."

"Check your facts, Barney Fife. His body wasn't recovered from the fire along with the others."

"Fire is capable of destroying human remains. And considering he was never seen or heard from again, that's the only plausible explanation."

AJ's eyebrows lifted. "You really think that fire was hot enough to reduce the Dragonfly to ashes while leaving the other bodies intact? You think his bones had a lower melting point?"

Derek brushed off the question he didn't have an answer to. "Why doesn't your dad want anyone to know he's back in town?"

"No idea. If he *is* back in town and you find him, tell him I still hate him."

Derek placed the sketch of the Copper Penny customer in front of him. "Do you recognize this man?"

Surprise flickered across AJ's face before giving way to satisfaction. "Everyone knows him. He's the man who started all this fifty years ago."

"You're saying this is Peter Ashton."

"Obviously fifty years changes a person, and this is a drawing, not a picture, but I recognize this birthmark on his face." AJ tapped the smudge on the sketch. "You're not looking for a copycat setting these fires. You're looking for the original Dragonfly."

Derek rummaged through the records room for the case files on Peter Ashton. The case was so old that the materials were never scanned into the electronic system.

He would make sure that oversight was fixed.

In a dark corner of the room, coated in decades of dust, he discovered the file box he was digging for. He dragged it to the center of the room and flipped off the lid.

The interior was bursting with folders and loose papers. Derek fingered through the folders, getting a feel for what the box contained—incident reports, investigation notes, and photos that spanned five homicides and the asylum fire.

"I heard you were down here in the tombs," Rusty said, and Derek looked up to see him in the doorway.

"I needed to look into the old Peter Ashton case, but none of the information was in the system."

"If I remember correctly, only cases going back forty years were scanned and entered, and it was a mountain of work." Rusty's eyebrows knitted as he took in the clutter. "You think these fires are connected to the ones in 1972?"

The skepticism in Rusty's voice matched the doubt Derek felt. "It's unlikely, but I want to make sure there's no connection. And I want to base that on actual case facts rather than the embellished stories floating around the village."

"I heard that someone spotted the Dragonfly near the second fire. The rumor that Peter Ashton is back is already spreading."

Great. Just what he needed to deal with.

"Some people really think he's still alive," Rusty said.

"It's always been my understanding that he died in the fire, and his remains were burned to ash."

"That's the widely held belief of most law enforcement. Psychopathic killers don't stop unless someone stops them. At least that's what experience has taught us."

That was Derek's understanding as well, though killers did differ in how long they waited between murders. Some stopped because they were arrested for another crime. Others stopped because watching law enforcement struggle to put the pieces together was as satisfying as the crime itself.

"Anything useful from the second autopsy?" Derek asked.

"We have an ID." Rusty held out a folder, and Derek took it from him.

He recognized the name of the victim: Bridget Morrison. She was released yesterday morning after her husband posted bail. "We have her prints on file, but not her DNA. How did Abbott get an ID so quickly?"

"She was in an accident when she was younger, and she had a titanium hip replacement with a serial number on it."

"Why these two victims?" Derek muttered, searching his mind for any connection between Nelson and Morrison that might've drawn the killer's attention.

"They're both criminals. Nelson was on the sex offender registry, *and* he was about to attack another girl. Bridget Morrison has attacked her husband multiple times."

"But she was never convicted."

"She's been plenty convicted in the court of public opinion. And when she was arrested the other day, she would've shown up on the criminal watch app."

The criminal watch app was a mobile app that tracked who was recently arrested and for what reason. There was a lawsuit pending to have the offenses removed for privacy purposes, but both pieces of information were a matter of public record.

Derek closed Bridget Morrison's folder. "So he's targeting people he thinks deserve to die?"

Rusty shrugged. "Unless there's another connection we're not seeing."

There were no doubt plenty of connections they weren't seeing.

"He's three for three on choosing barns that are unoccupied, which means he's taking the time to watch these people and learn their schedules. I can't believe none of them noticed someone hanging around outside in a vehicle," Derek said.

"It's an avenue to pursue."

"Anything else pertinent in the autopsy?"

"No contusion on the back of the head like there was with Nelson, and Bridget Morrison died of smoke inhalation," Rusty said.

"Chloroform?"

"Abbott said her throat was irritated and raw from breathing in the hot air and smoke, so any irritation from chloroform would be impossible to see. He sent samples to the lab."

"So he hits the male victim on the back of the head to subdue him, but doesn't use the same approach with the female victim. Witnesses put him around five foot eight, five foot nine, and Bridget Morrison is . . ."

"Five foot three and a hundred and ten pounds," Rusty provided. "Easy enough to subdue with chloroform, even if she did struggle."

"We need to find out where she was taken from. Our killer may have left evidence behind."

"I was going to head over and talk to her husband now. I'm not sure whether he'll be heartbroken or relieved. At least she won't be able to put him in the hospital again," Rusty said. "Oh, that black string Abbott pulled from Nelson's mouth . . . he called it twine . . . none of that was found on or in Bridget Morrison's body."

Derek handed the folder back to Rusty. "Appreciate the update."

"Oh, one more thing. Nelson's car. None of the fingerprints came back useful. They're mostly Nelson's. A few child prints on the sides. Kids like to touch everything. Leaves and dirt in the driver's floorboard and Nelson's blood on steering wheel and shifter. Looks like it was on the killer's gloves when he got behind the wheel."

Derek grimaced. "So nothing useful then."

"Doesn't appear to be."

"Thanks, Russ."

Rusty nodded and left him alone in the records room.

Derek opened the file on Peter Ashton. He sank onto the edge of the table in the center of the room as he stared at a picture of the seventeen-year-old arsonist. There, on his cheek, in the exact place recent sketches indicated, was a birthmark.

CHAPTER Twenty-nine

There weren't many things that scared Derek—losing the people he loved and getting trapped alone in a cornfield chief among them—but as he flipped through the old case file photos of Peter Ashton's victims, having his mouth and eyes sewn shut while alive made it onto that list.

According to the file, the fact that he stitched up the faces of his victims was withheld from the public. All of the funerals would've been closed casket, given the condition of the remains, but the families were informed.

Despite law enforcement withholding the detail about the stitches, the rumor still spread. That twisted detail was part of what made Ashton a legend.

Some effort was made to stitch Nelson's mouth shut, but then the killer gave up and shoved the rest of the twine into his mouth. There was no effort at all with Bridget Morrison.

Derek turned to another picture in the file and stilled. Someone had snapped a crime scene photo of a symbol spray-painted on the trunk of a tree near the smoldering ruins of a barn. Derek grabbed his cell and found the image the fire Marshal had sent him.

On the tree at the Miller barn, the blue symbol was difficult to make out, but in the photo from the first arson and murder fifty years ago, that same symbol was crisp and clear.

A dragonfly.

Derek set his phone beside the image, comparing the two crime scene photos. The most recent symbol looked like it was painted by an unsteady hand, but the loops of the wings and the thorax trailing down the tree trunk were comparable.

"Captain."

The baritone voice came from Deputy Fire Marshal Andy Bradshaw, whose broad frame barely fit in the doorway.

"Bradshaw, come in."

The big man lumbered to a chair. "I'm sure you've already guessed that fires two and three are connected. Victims were bound in the same way, gasoline around the barn, animals released prior to ignition. And the same symbol spray-painted on the closest tree."

"Anything on the paint analysis?"

"Paint from scenes one and two are a match to each other and to a brand of spray paint called Rust-Oleum Ford Blue. Scene three appears to be a match, but we'll test it to be positive."

"I'm sure our local hardware store carries it. We can speak with Toby, the owner, to see if—"

"That brand and color of paint was purchased six days ago at your local store." Bradshaw placed his phone on the desk and spun it to face Derek. "The shop owner let me view his security cam footage, and he emailed me this screenshot."

Derek leaned forward and pressed two fingers to the screen, widening them to zoom in. A bearded man with a baseball cap stood by the counter, only three quarters of his face visible. It certainly looked like the Copper Penny customer. "I'm surprised Toby remembered him."

"He didn't until we viewed the footage. He said the guy had been in twice. Once at the beginning of the month and then last week. Placed his paint and money on the counter without a word."

Derek squinted at the image. "You can't see the name or color on the can. It's too grainy."

"The shop has only sold three cans of that paint this month. One was a credit card transaction for Ben Brady, and the other two were cash transactions."

"And our silent guy paid cash."

"Correct."

"These symbols he's painting . . . they're similar to a previous series of fires." Derek picked up the folder and rotated it to face the fire marshal. He pointed to the picture of the symbol.

Bradshaw's prominent forehead seemed to fold down over his eyes as he studied it. "When was this?"

"1972. Peter Ashton was responsible for three barn fires and murders before he was caught."

"I've heard of him, but I've never looked into the case. These symbols are much neater than the recent ones. It could be a different hand at work, but if you're thinking it's the same man, his fine motor skills could've declined with age."

AJ's antagonistic voice echoed through Derek's mind: *You really think that fire was hot enough to reduce the Dragonfly to ashes while leaving the other bodies intact?*

"It's widely believed Peter Ashton died in the asylum fire, but his remains were never found. Is it possible the fire burned up his body?" Derek asked.

Bradshaw shook his head. "Even with the concentrated heat of fourteen to sixteen hundred degrees Fahrenheit used by crematoriums, bone fragments are still found. There's no chance a building fire broke down a human skeleton. If his body wasn't found, his remains were either illegally removed before the coroner arrived, or he didn't die in the fire."

Derek sat back in his chair as he absorbed that. Forty-eight years ago, law enforcement made an assumption that allowed a serial killer to go free. Peter Ashton could still be alive.

Noelle erased the nameless, undefined characters on her writing room whiteboard. As much as she wanted them to take on shape and personality, she couldn't force them.

It was hardly the first time her characters rebelled by remaining mysterious. They also had a tendency to evolve in directions she didn't intend when she first dreamed them up.

She might be the author, but more often than not, she felt like the scribe recording the events as they unfolded instead of guiding them.

In the place of her uncooperative characters, she taped up the printed photo of seventeen-year-old Peter Ashton she had downloaded from the internet.

She could only imagine what it must've been like to stand in the young man's presence. Even in her writing room, fifty years after the photo was taken, the evil staring out of his eyes made the hairs on the back of her neck prickle.

Her gaze trailed to the window facing the side woods. There was no one out there, but the memory of the Dragonfly standing among the trees, watching her from beneath his hood, was enough to make her close the blinds *and* the curtains.

She rubbed at the anxious flutter in her chest as she returned to her whiteboard. She would not be shaken off course by fear. If the Dragonfly's attention meant she'd been chosen as a victim, then he would come for her like he had the others.

And she wanted to know everything about the man beneath that mask when he did.

In her research into Peter Ashton, she had landed on a crime blog. It was a treasure trove of information about the murderer and his life. But it lacked the answer to the question everyone asked: Is the Dragonfly alive or dead?

Noelle taped up the sheriff's department's sketch of the arson suspect now circulating on social media.

Given the passage of time since Peter Ashton's disappearance, if he were alive, he would be sixty-seven years old—the approximate age of the man in the sketch.

Noelle studied the two images. She wasn't an expert at facial comparison, but there were some obvious similarities and differences.

The age was correct; the two men had the same birthmark. The nose was slightly different, but age and injury could account for why it looked softer and bulkier. The eyes were . . . off. That could easily be eyewitness error. Yet something about the man in the sketch was familiar.

The bearded man bore a greater resemblance to Peter's father, Ainsley Ashton, than he did to Peter. Obviously, Ainsley wasn't the arsonist. He would be in his nineties if he were alive.

Noelle taped a picture of Ainsley Ashton to the whiteboard and wrote beneath it: "Deceased, 1995, Parkinson's–related accident."

Noelle stared at her note, her memory churning. One of the side characters in her seventh book had Parkinson's disease. She didn't remember the exact number from her research, but there was a percentage of cases where the disease was hereditary.

If Peter Ashton was still alive, there was at least a small chance that he inherited his father's genetic predisposition for Parkinson's.

Uncapping her marker, Noelle wrote the word *Parkinson's* under Peter's name with a question mark. The condition was degenerative and debilitating. Surely, someone suffering from it couldn't be abducting people and setting them on fire.

She moved on to the aspects of Peter's crimes:

Victims bludgeoned and kidnapped
Wrists bound
Eyes and mouths sewn shut
Tied to a beam with rope
Barn drenched with gasoline
Fire set
Symbol painted on a nearby tree

Noelle taped up the grainy picture of the symbol left at each of the 1972 fire scenes, a dragonfly inside a circle. "The calling card of death," Doctor Conroy had called it. Peter Ashton's way of announcing to the world that he'd chosen this victim, judged his soul, and deemed him worthy of death.

Noelle picked up her mug of tea and took a long sip, as if it might cleanse her pallet of the bile this man's evil brought up her throat.

Along with the symbol of the dragonfly left at every scene, Peter Ashton wore his dragonfly mask while committing his crimes. A witness confirmed seeing him in full costume at the last 1972 barn fire. The sheriff's department collected the costume for evidence.

Clearly, someone had it recreated.

With enough time, she could find the mask maker, and that might lead her to the identity of the person who commissioned it. But that wouldn't happen before another person died.

Noelle bent down to fill out the timeline and the names of the victims before moving on to column two of the whiteboard.

If Peter Ashton was dead, then someone with an agenda was responsible for this latest string of fires. Someone who knew enough about the Dragonfly to make it appear that he was back.

The Conroys were her primary suspects.

Allen Conroy Senior supposedly moved away twenty some years ago, but he happened to drop in on Cherry Creek around the time of the recent barn fires and murders.

Noelle made bullet points of what she knew about the elusive Mr. Conroy:

Keeping to the shadows
Fishing for info on arson case
Fits age of suspect
Bitter toward Cherry Creek
Obsessed with Dragonfly
Struggling with consequences of a mistake he can't fix

Noelle was interested to know more about the mistake the older man had been referring to in the diner, but there was no way to find out. Even if she had another chance encounter with Conroy Senior, she doubted he would be forthcoming. She moved on to AJ:

Concealing his dad's presence

Bitter toward Cherry Creek
Thinks fires are karmic punishment
Claims to have seen the Dragonfly

Noelle capped the marker and stepped back to study the information. Conroy Senior looked like a pretty good suspect for the current arsonist.

He didn't resemble the sketch, but it wouldn't be the first time a killer used a disguise to hide his identity or steer an investigation in a certain direction. He could be portraying Peter Ashton, and his son could be dressing up in the Dragonfly costume.

Noelle twisted the marker between her fingers as she tried to break down the motive for that theory.

According to his son, Conroy was obsessed with the Dragonfly, which would make him an expert on the details. He was angry that the man who killed his father was never arrested. Could he be committing these murders to force the sheriff's department to take another look at the original crimes?

Noelle shook her head.

No sane person would murder innocent people in the pursuit of justice. It didn't make sense.

Maybe this was just someone trying to scare people by bringing a legend to life. There was enough information out there to imitate the Dragonfly. She added another vertical line, leaving the third column blank for the time being.

A gasp came from downstairs, and Noelle turned toward her writing room doorway. "Sky?"

Skyler bubbled up the steps into the room. "The mailman delivered a box! Can I bring it in?"

Noelle opened her mouth to say yes, then stopped. As far as she knew, she wasn't expecting any packages. What if it was another delivery from Zac—something more sinister than a bouquet?

"Let's get it together," Noelle suggested.

They went downstairs to the foyer, and Noelle rested a hand on the revolver holstered at her back as she unlocked and opened the front door. Her gaze swept over the property before dropping to the package on the doormat.

A note had been written in permanent marker on the outside, the lines perfectly spaced and justified.

Amusement lifted the edges of Noelle's lips. *Mom.* No doubt she slid a ruler across the flattened box as she wrote her message, aiming for the precision and tidiness reflected in all areas of her life.

That gene skipped a generation.

Noelle couldn't even get the blinds to hang straight in the windows. They always ended up sagging on one side. She picked up the big box and turned it to read the message.

"Dear porch pirates . . ."

Noelle snorted back a laugh. Mom had written a polite note to any potential thieves.

The remainder of the message read, "If you don't have a mom to buy you socks and underwear for Christmas and birthdays, help yourselves to this box."

"Nice, Mom."

No one wanted socks and underwear, especially someone else's.

Skyler gasped again and pointed. "It has my name on it!"

"Yes, it does. This is a gift from your grandma." Noelle had forgotten it was coming. Any minute now, her mother would . . .

Noelle's phone dinged with an incoming text message. Sure enough, it was her mother informing her the package was delivered and she should grab it before it gets stolen. Noelle texted back: "It's being delivered to your granddaughter's arms right now."

Noelle passed the box to Skyler. "Go ahead and open it."

Skyler dropped into one of the porch rocking chairs and worked at the tape with her stubby nails, so excited she vibrated in place. Noelle captured a few pictures to send to her mom.

Box ripped to shreds, Skyler pulled out the handmade firefly costume, complete with black wings, glow sticks for the back, and a headband with antennae.

"Oh my goodness! It's the most beautiful thing I ever saw!" Skyler shouted. She sprang from the rocker and twirled with her costume like a princess from a Disney movie. "I love it so much. I have the best grandparents ever!"

"Let's call your grandma so you can thank her."

Noelle video called her mother. Mom's face appeared on the screen a moment later, and she pulled down the protective mask she wore when they were in the demolition phase of renovating a house.

"Hey, Mom. Skyler would like to chat with you, if you have a few minutes."

"I always have time for my granddaughter."

Noelle handed the phone to Skyler. "Don't run and don't spin. Grandma gets motion sick from the wind blowing."

"Exaggerator," her mom muttered as the phone changed hands. When Skyler held up the phone in front of her face, Mom squealed, "Oh, there's my precious girl. How are you, sweetheart?"

"I'm great! Thank you for the present. I've never had a costume before." Skyler carried the phone with her as they chatted, taking careful steps so she didn't make her grandma sick.

Noelle was so grateful that, even though her parents had been reluctant to attach to Skyler, they never let her know it. All they ever showed her was love.

Derek climbed the rickety staircase to the second floor of the house, making his way toward the glow spilling from the open doorway ahead into the hallway.

After his day of stressful revelations, he needed a couple of hours to decompress with his two favorite people.

One of those favorite people was so engrossed in her adventure book that she barely took the time to let him in and hug him before flitting back into the living room with *his* dog. Elsa had chosen her soul mate—an eleven-year-old girl who snuck her extra treats and read her stories.

He couldn't blame Elsa for her choice.

He pushed the partially closed door the rest of the way open with his fingertips and found Noelle sitting on her stool in the middle of the room like the subject of an old oil painting—legs elevated on the rungs, one fist propping up her chin, and a distant, thoughtful expression.

"I feel like I should take a picture and label it 'Author in Her Natural Habitat,'" Derek said.

Noelle inhaled sharply and straightened, turning to see him. "I didn't hear you come in. And don't you dare take a picture. My hair is a mess, and this sweater has more holes in it than a target at the shooting range."

"That depends on who is doing the shooting. I hit my target every time." He stepped up behind her and wrapped his arms around her shoulders, planting a kiss on her cheek. "And you're always beautiful to me."

She reached up to rub at the arms holding her. "I'm glad you're here."

He looked at the organized chaos on her whiteboard. "I see I'm not the only one working this arsonist case."

He felt her shoulders rise and then fall with a sigh. "I feel like I've seen your arson suspect before. There's something familiar about his face."

"Maybe it'll come to you when you're not thinking about it."

"Hopefully. And then there's this masked Dragonfly who keeps popping up around the village like it's a terrifying game of whack-a-mole. I want to make sense of it."

Derek wanted to reassure her that it was nothing more than a prankster playing games, but after what he learned from the fire marshal, he wasn't so sure. "He was spotted near last night's fire."

"I heard. I think everyone has."

He skimmed the information she'd collected, his gaze snagging on the word *Parkinson's*. The witnesses said the bearded man, currently their primary suspect in this latest string of murders, had a tremor.

"Where did you find that detail about the Parkinson's?" he asked.

"A crime blog. It's my only source for that detail, but I'm sure people around the village could confirm it."

If Peter Ashton developed Parkinson's like his father, did he come home and resume killing simply to prove to himself that he was still capable? Were people dying because he received a bad diagnosis?

"This guy compiled so much information about Peter Ashton and his family that it's practically a Wikipedia page," Noelle continued.

He stiffened at the mention of a Wikipedia page. That was essentially what Zac Inman had created on Noelle; only it was in binder form rather than web-page form. The man had compiled everything there was to publicly know about her.

Derek hadn't told Noelle about the binder.

He wasn't sure whether or not he should. She had the right to know, but knowing wouldn't change the level of danger; it would only frighten her more. But he couldn't keep something like this from her. They might have the occasional miscommunication, but they didn't keep secrets from each other.

He drew in a breath, holding it as he fought to decide the right course of action. "When Brian and I went to speak with Zac, he wasn't there."

"You mentioned that last night." She studied his face. "Was there something you *didn't* mention last night?"

"He has several binders, one for each of his apparent favorite authors, and they include a lot of personal information. Dates, preferences, biographical info."

She stared straight ahead as she processed this new revelation. "I guess I shouldn't be surprised. It's a very . . . stalker thing to do. But it doesn't really change anything."

"I'm sorry I didn't tell you last night."

"I understand why you didn't," she said, but her tone contradicted her words. There was a hint of understanding, but also something else. Disappointment? Hurt?

"Why don't we go downstairs and find something more relaxing to do than staring at a murder board," he suggested.

"If you're ruffled by my murder board, I should show you my murder scrapbook."

"For deniability purposes, I probably shouldn't know about that."

She laughed as she slid off the stool. "It's a scrapbook of articles about murder that I look through for inspiration sometimes."

"Murder and inspiration don't fit in the same sentence."

"They do in my world."

She flipped off the light on her way into the hall. Derek caught her hand before she could reach the steps and tugged her back toward him. She gasped in surprise as their bodies collided.

"I thought you wanted to go downstairs."

He selected a slow song from his phone and tucked it into the back pocket of his jeans. "Then I realized . . . I was in the wrong when I withheld that information from you last night, which means we need to work it out."

"Do we? Because I thought we already talked it out."

"Mmm, no, you know how things work in my family. Issues are resolved over a slow dance." He placed her arms around his neck and rested his hands on her waist.

Her mouth curled up at the edges. "You're putting your toes at risk."

"You've stepped on them enough times, they're practically numb."

Her mouth dropped open in mock outrage. "Oh, really? Now you do owe me a dance, because that was a flagrant lie."

"Flagrant?" He moved their combined bodies into a gentle glide in the middle of the hallway. "That word's not in my personal dictionary."

"Outright offensive, bold-faced."

"Ah, in that case I accept those charges."

She shook her head in amusement as they danced, swaying left and right to the soft music. "Since we're supposed to be discussing your offenses, I appreciate you trying to protect me from what you learned about Zac, but after all the secretiveness and deception in my marriage with Tyrese, you know how I feel about withholding things from each other. Which is why I'm sorry that I didn't tell you about the masked man as soon as I saw him."

"See? Dancing fixes everything."

She tipped her head in partial agreement. "It certainly makes things harder to avoid. No more secrets, okay?"

He made a thoughtful noise in the back of his throat. "I can't agree to that just yet."

Anxiety sparkled in her midnight eyes, and the arms around his neck tensed. "Why not?"

"Because I do have one last secret to tell you, but I can't do it right now. Don't worry, though. I think you'll like it." He kissed the tip of her nose and let his hands drop from her waist. He nodded to the second-floor bathroom. "I need a minute, and then I'll see you downstairs."

Casting him curious looks over her shoulder, she headed down the stairs.

He stepped into the bathroom and closed the door. Reaching beneath his shirt, he drew out the chain holding Lacey's rings. He held them in his palm, remembering what it felt like to slide each one onto her delicate finger.

Trudy was right. He would always love Lacey, and she would always be alive in his thoughts. But he was ready for more in his life than remembering the past. He wanted to make new memories, to build a new family.

He kissed the rings and whispered, "I love you, Lacey." He tucked the necklace into his pocket and pulled out the velvet box with Noelle's engagement ring.

He popped it open.

The petite diamond was surrounded by embedded tourmaline stones. Noelle's birthday was in September, not October, but she had told him once that she wished she had been born in October because she loved the pink stone more than the sapphire.

He smoothed his thumb over the stones.

As much as he wanted to go downstairs and drop to one knee, he didn't want her memory of the proposal to be overshadowed by a stalker. As soon as he figured out how to permanently remove Zac Inman as a threat, then he could ask the question that would change both of their lives.

CHAPTER Thirty

The peace Derek felt yesterday evening as he curled up on the couch with the girls to watch a movie evaporated the moment he stepped foot in the department this morning and learned that a teenage boy had been shot last night.

Georgie Tucker, thirteen, had been out looking for a bit of mischief with his friends in Cherry Creek, and he caught a bullet because a frightened farmer thought he might be the arsonist looking for another barn or victim to burn.

Derek's initial concerns had been right—the first murder sparked fear among the village residents, and the second murder elevated that fear to panic. And now a child was fighting for his life.

Unfortunately, the sheriff's department was no closer to formally identifying or locating the arsonist. He may as well be the ghost many believed him to be.

He must've watched the families whose barns he burned, learning their schedules, because he knew when to bring his victim there. Yet no one saw a suspicious vehicle or lurker in the area. Except the Millers, and there wasn't enough information there to produce a lead.

He must've watched the victims for the perfect opportunity to grab them. No one saw him abduct Nick

Nelson or Bridget Morrison. Though taking Nelson from the bar parking lot had been risky.

Derek scrubbed his hands over his face and stared at Rusty's incident report on his desk. He'd gone to the Morrison home yesterday to interview Bridget's husband.

Tony Morrison had posted bail for his wife on Monday morning, and by Monday night she was dead. According to the report, Bridget's propensity for violence resurfaced after the couple arrived home Monday morning. She attacked her husband with a knife.

The defensive wound on his forearm was deep enough to need stitches, and he drove their only vehicle to the hospital.

When he returned home, Bridget was gone. There was no sign of a struggle beyond a shattered glass on the back porch. But there were tire tracks in the backyard that didn't match the Morrison's vehicle, and according to Tony, they weren't there when he left.

A partial print was lifted from a larger piece of broken glass, but it matched Bridget Morrison. By all appearances, she was startled, subdued—likely chloroformed—and then a vehicle was backed up to the rear porch so her unconscious body could be moved.

Ashton didn't chloroform his original victims. He bludgeoned them. But if this killer was almost seventy and wracked by tremors, he wouldn't be able to overpower or easily move his victims. Chloroform would give him the advantage he lost with age and illness. And backing the car up to the porch would've made it easier to move a body.

Where did he hold them after he abducted them? Nelson was held for around twenty-one hours, and Bridget would've been held for around eight.

Nelson wasn't kept in his car. Based on when he attacked Zoe, he was abducted from the bar around eleven thirty p.m., and the arsonist called for a pickup at the old mill at twelve thirty in the morning. That was, at most, a fifteen-minute drive, which left forty-five minutes unaccounted for. The arsonist transported Nelson somewhere first, then dumped his car and arranged a ride.

But where did he take him?

Derek shuffled through the files on his desk to find the forensic report on Nelson's car. There was blood, hair, and even vomit found in the trunk—a bad enough head injury could cause nausea—but no urine. Nelson wouldn't have been able to hold his bladder for twenty-one hours.

The killer was keeping his victims somewhere else. His residence? The woods? An abandoned property?

If this killer was impersonating the Dragonfly, or if . . . he *was* the Dragonfly, where would he stash his victims until he was ready to kill them?

Derek picked through his files again until he found the detailed report on Peter Ashton's crimes. He flipped through the documents, skimming for any mention of where he held his victims during the hours prior to their deaths.

Nothing was explicitly stated.

It might be a place that meant something to Ashton or one of his previous victims. They would need to pore over every page of the files for clues.

A knock on Derek's office door preceded the sheriff's appearance. He wasn't a big man. He had thin shoulders and a square chin, but he held himself with authority. "You ready?"

Derek glanced at the time on his computer, the muscles in the back of his neck tightening with apprehension.

The sheriff had arranged a Cherry Creek Town Hall meeting to dispel the fear sweeping through the community, but he had uncovered nothing to alleviate it.

"Sir, I can't promise the community that the person behind these fires is not Peter Ashton. The evidence points more toward him than anyone else, and according to the fire marshal, there is no possible way Ashton died in the asylum fire. He walked away that night."

Sheriff Malone looked around to see if anyone was listening and then closed the door. "Under no circumstances do you confirm the belief that a serial killer from the past is back for another sweep."

"Then what do I tell people?"

"Whatever is necessary to establish calm."

"I won't lie."

"I'm not telling you to lie, but be careful with the information you provide. If the fire marshal is right, and Peter Ashton walked away, then the sheriff's department of 1974 screwed up. The sheriff's department of *today* will be held accountable," Sheriff Malone said. "If you're wrestling with your moral compass about withholding information about a serial killer from the public, that thirteen-year-old boy who was shot because of this chaos, Georgie Tucker, died twenty minutes ago."

Derek closed his eyes and offered a silent prayer for the family of that boy and for the farmer who shot him.

I leaned against the back wall of the room, dressed as inconspicuously as possible, as I watched the town hall meeting. The sheriff spoke to the crowd first, but Derek Dempsey had my full attention.

He surveyed the people in the room like he was looking for someone. For me, most likely. But he would never recognize me beneath my disguise.

Anger smoldered in my chest as I watched him. I hated everything about him. The way he hurt Noelle, the arrogant way he carried himself, his propensity to put work before the woman he claimed to love.

He didn't love Noelle.

He didn't deserve *Noelle.*

The sheriff offered the crowd a few platitudes before introducing Dempsey. He stepped onto the platform behind the microphone and spewed much of the same useless rhetoric: "We'll get through this as a community," and "Let's pull together to protect our neighbors."

"This man has killed two people. How do we know he won't come after us next?" a woman demanded.

Before Dempsey could answer, a man asked, "Why is the sheriff's department ignoring the most likely suspect?!"

"Victims tied up and burned to death in barns. Peter Ashton is back. He's back to finish what he started fifty years ago, and you're not even looking for him!" another woman called out.

Fear flickered across Dempsey's face before he regained his neutral expression.

Oh, he didn't want anyone to know about Peter Ashton. He was afraid of the public's reaction, of the chaos such a comment might stir up.

The sheriff tried to silence the woman by telling her that spreading rumors would only harm the community. Like she was a hysterical child rather than an adult making logical connections. I couldn't let that happen.

I cupped my hands over my mouth and shouted, "It's not a rumor! I've seen him!"

Of course, I hadn't actually seen the man, but the fear that surged through the room at my comment was exhilarating.

"I saw him too! The sheriff's department never solved that case, and now more people are dead!" a woman shouted.

The sheriff whispered something to Dempsey and then abandoned ship like a coward. I lingered to watch Dempsey twist in the wind. He didn't belong in Noelle's story, but until I could permanently remove him, making his life difficult was the next best thing.

CHAPTER Thirty-one

Derek dropped his head back against the porch rocking chair and released a breath that dissipated into the cold night air.

Nothing about the town hall meeting had gone the way he hoped. The intention had been to quell community fears, but all he managed to do was give fear a platform to spread.

How many more innocents would die because people were panicked? It was nearly Halloween. Kids like Georgie Tucker weren't going to stay safely indoors, and it could cost them their lives.

Derek had failed his community this afternoon, and there was nothing he could do about it. Nothing except find the man responsible.

Noelle joined him on the porch and held out a mug. "Here, this will take your mind off things."

He doubted anything short of a coma would take his mind off his concerns, but he accepted the mug. Curiosity nudged his eyebrows closer to his hairline. "Why is it so green?"

"It's supposed to be."

Derek lifted the mug of green sludge to his lips, then paused. He had a feeling this stuff was going to coat his tongue like algae and hang around until he scrubbed it off with a wire brush.

Noelle lingered by his chair, waiting for his opinion. "You're stalling."

"How do you know I'm not savoring the aroma?" He breathed it in and immediately wished he hadn't. It even smelled like algae.

"You might like it."

Sure, and the stack of paperwork on his desk would sign and file itself. Bracing himself, he tipped the mug and took a sip. He nearly gagged as he swallowed. "That . . . is grass. You dumped grass clippings into the blender and then poured them into a mug, didn't you?"

Noelle laughed. "It's green tea."

"There's no denying the green part. *Tea* is questionable."

"I mean it's matcha green tea. It makes an earthy latte."

He shook his head. "No amount of cream, sugar, or fancy foam can make that palatable." He offered the mug to her. "Throw it back in the yard where it belongs."

She laughed again and handed him the mug she'd been hiding behind her back. "Don't worry, the latte is actually mine. This one's yours."

The aroma of peppermint hit his nose as he reached out to grab the handle. "That's a relief." He took a sip of the mint tea and swished it around in his mouth to dilute the lingering grass clippings.

"The community meeting wasn't as bad as you think," she said.

"You were there?"

"I watched it online."

He groaned. "Someone recorded it?"

"People record everything nowadays."

Derek dropped his head back against the rocker and watched Skyler romp through the leaves with Elsa while Walt stood guard. "Every time I thought people were calming down, someone from the back of the room would shout something that stirred them back up again."

"I'm sorry it didn't go the way you planned."

He rolled his head toward her without lifting it from the back of the rocker. "I'm worried about this village. The fear this arsonist is stirring up. A thirteen-year-old boy was shot and killed, and if we don't put an end to this soon, I doubt he'll be the last."

Noelle reached down and placed a hand on his shoulder. "That's not on you."

He pressed his head against her forearm, needing the comfort of her skin against his. "It feels like it is. That boy will never grow up, and the farmer who shot him will likely be prosecuted, but the emotional toll killing a kid will take on him is unimaginable."

"Fear makes people desperate and reckless. But this won't go on forever. You'll figure out who's doing this. Whether it's one of the Conroys, Peter Ashton, or even someone else who isn't on the radar yet, you'll catch him."

He wanted to kiss her in gratitude, but the only part of her within his reach was her lower arm and hand, so he lifted her hand from his shoulder and pressed his lips to it. "Thank you for always believing in me."

A drawn-out buzz came from somewhere deep in the house, and Noelle dropped her head forward with a groan. "The dryer beckons."

"If the clothes are dry, there's no rush."

"That's what I've always thought, but I can't keep sending Skyler out of the house with clothes that look like they've been wadded up in a trash bag for a month. And I hate ironing more than I hate folding. I don't even own an iron. That's how much I hate it."

Derek released her hand. "If you're not back in fifteen minutes, I'll come down and rescue you from that dungeon of a basement."

"By then the thousands of cob spiders will have woven me into a web." She shivered and turned to go inside.

Derek drank his tea and resisted the urge to torture himself by looking up the recording of the town hall meeting Noelle had watched. Nothing good would come of it.

Skyler bounded up the steps, cheeks flushed from all the excitement. "I love playing in the leaves. It's almost as fun as snow."

"No, nothing beats a snowball fight," he said.

She climbed into his lap, something she was quickly becoming too big to do, and sat sideways so she could face him. Intense thought churned behind her eyes as she considered him.

"What's on your mind, Mischief?"

"Can I call you Daddy?"

The question caught Derek by surprise.

Before he could think of a way to answer, she said, "Trudy said I can call her Aunt Trudy, and then there's Uncle Brian, and Noelle's my second mom. I never had a dad. I've read about them, and . . . I think I should have one 'cause . . . I want one."

She blinked big, hopeful eyes at him.

He set aside his mug of tea and wrapped both arms around her. "Tell you what, if Noelle says yes when I ask her to marry me, you can call me Daddy."

She gasped. "When are you going to ask her?"

"Soon, I hope."

"Are we talking hours or days?"

He grinned. "Probably a week or two."

Her shoulders sagged. "That's forever."

"It'll give you something to pray about."

"I'll pray like nobody's ever prayed before." She hopped down and took off back into the yard. A moment later, she shouted, "God, I'm praying extra loud so you hear me over everybody else, and so you know how much I want this!"

Derek snorted as she emphatically explained her wishes to God. Skyler never ceased to amuse and amaze him. If everything went the way he hoped, soon she wouldn't just be a little girl that he adored. She would be his daughter.

CHAPTER Thirty-two

The next couple of days passed by quietly. Fall festivities lifted the spirits of the village, and the haunting shadow of the Dragonfly faded to the backs of people's minds.

No one could completely forget about the looming danger, but bobbing for apples and visiting the festival food stands was a pleasant distraction.

The air was thick with the aroma of deep-fried food and sugar-sprinkled donuts, and the musical sound of games being played.

Carb-rich, spend-every-penny-in-your-pocket joy.

Skyler flitted about in her firefly outfit, inspecting everything without going too far. She looked adorable in her one-of-a-kind costume with green glitter on her cheeks, bright green nail polish, and an empty glow-in-the-dark pumpkin bucket clasped in both hands.

Noelle hooked her arm through Derek's and leaned against him as they trailed behind Skyler. "I know you've got a lot on your plate with the investigation, but I really appreciate you taking the evening off."

"There's nowhere else I would rather be."

Despite his words, she could see the stress lines creasing his forehead. With so many people gathered in town for the festival, there were bound to be barns left unattended.

"You're worried he might target another barn tonight," Noelle said, keeping her voice quiet.

"I am. He's probably already got a victim locked away somewhere. No one's been reported missing yet, but it's only a matter of time." Derek drew in a breath and released it. "Let's not talk about this tonight. We're here to relax and enjoy each other's company."

"Is it time for the corn maze yet?" Skyler asked with a bounce.

Noelle checked the time on her fitness band. "We have about twenty minutes before it starts."

"It's too bad they didn't stick with the setup they had last year. Trunk-or-treat in the park," Derek said.

"Don't care for mazes?"

"Mazes don't bother me. It's the cornfields."

That comment piqued Noelle's interest. "What's the backstory behind that?"

"I should've known better than to mention that to you," he said, but his tone was lighthearted. "When I was about Skyler's age, a few of my friends and I snuck out after dark to explore the biggest cornfield in the area. Rumored to be haunted."

She laughed. "Of course it was."

Cherry Creek and its superstitions.

Derek told her the story about how he ended up hypothermic and alone in the field until searchers found him shortly before dawn.

"I wouldn't have set foot in a cornfield after that either," Noelle said. "Did you and your friends ever find out what or who was in the field that night?"

"Nope, but looking back, I expect it was regularly haunted by hungry deer. Dozens of them. Every time I thought something was chasing me, it was actually a deer running away from the noise I was making. Bambi nearly killed me."

"Ah, so revenge is the reason you kill innocent animals," she teased.

"That's called hunting, and I've seen you eat meat."

"Chicken. But I buy that from the store."

Derek's eyebrows lifted. "And you think she died of natural causes on the way to the freezer section?"

Noelle huffed a laugh. "No, I don't. But it's easier when I don't have to think about how she got there."

"That's because you're softhearted. And that's one of the things I love most about you." He kissed her temple. "I think it's time for some cotton candy."

Noelle pinned him with a look of disapproval. "She's about to go through a maze and collect a bucket of candy, and you want to sugar her up *before* that?"

"I'll take responsibility for putting her to bed." He pulled money from his wallet and stepped over to a vendor to purchase two cotton candies. He handed one to Noelle. "Pink for the beautiful lady." He passed the blue one to Skyler. "And blue for the munchkin."

Skyler beamed up at him. "Blue is the best flavor."

"All the colors taste the same," Noelle pointed out.

"Only grown-ups with no imagination think that."

"No imagination," Noelle repeated, popping a sugary puff into her mouth. "Did you hear that? Me, the writer of books, has no imagination. Must've been the dust mites dreaming up those stories all these years. So kind of them to let me put my name on the cover."

"Those dust mites are *mite-y* good writers," Skyler announced.

Derek gave Skyler a fist bump. "Good one."

"Can we get cotton candy for Mr. Walt before we go home tonight?" Skyler asked. "He's still really itchy and tired, and it might make him feel better."

"I don't think a sugar cloud will help him, but maybe we can bring him some dinner," Noelle suggested.

Derek's phone dinged, and he pulled it from his pocket to read a text message. A parade of emotions crossed his features: surprise, anger, and then resignation.

"What's wrong?" Noelle asked.

"It's from Trudy. She and Brian had a fight when she overheard him placing a bet in the dining room."

Oh, Brian, she thought.

He had been doing so well.

Addiction was a lifelong battle, and there were bound to be missteps, but the strain a relapse would put on his and Trudy's marriage could break them apart. He should've considered the potential repercussions.

"How is Trudy doing?" she asked.

"Not good. She left him to close down the diner and went home. She wants to know if I can come over and talk." Derek looked at Skyler and then at Noelle, conflicted. "The three of us are supposed to spend the evening together."

"She's your sister, and she's in a bad place right now. You need to go comfort her."

He pressed his lips together and swept his thumbs across the screen to send a response. "As soon as I feel like Trudy is in a good place, I'll come rejoin you two."

"Promise?" Skyler asked.

"I promise." He scanned the surrounding faces for possible threats before saying softly, "You girls be careful."

Noelle's stalker was still unaccounted for, and the arsonist was lurking somewhere in the shadows of this village. But the weight of the revolver in the holster at the small of Noelle's back bolstered her confidence. "We'll be fine. Give Trudy a hug for me. And try not to be too hard on Brian."

Hardness glinted in Derek's eyes. "I can't believe he did this again."

"People make mistakes, Derek. You can talk to him about it, but I suggest waiting until tomorrow when you're less angry."

"If less angry is the requirement for talking to him, I might need a month." He leaned forward and kissed her cheek. "I'll see you two later. Have fun."

"Come look!" Skyler snagged Noelle's hand and pointed toward a fenced-in area with a sign that read

Fainting Goats. Noelle smiled as she thought back to one of her earliest conversations with Derek about fainting goats, and then let her daughter tug her toward the enclosure of animals.

Derek clenched the steering wheel of his truck as he turned onto the road where Trudy and Brian lived.

He hadn't been this furious with his brother-in-law in almost a year. Brian had become more than his sister's husband; he'd become a brother to Derek, and this gambling relapse felt like a betrayal.

If Brian was struggling with his addiction, why didn't he call? Derek couldn't have made it any clearer that he was here for him, anytime of the day or night.

He glanced at his phone in the cup holder. Everything in him wanted to snatch it up and call Brian so he could verbally shred him. But Noelle was right. He needed to wait for his anger, and even some of his hurt, to pass before he initiated that conversation.

Right now, he couldn't approach it from a place of compassion or respect.

To his surprise, his phone rang, and the display on his dash informed him he had an incoming call from Rusty Ramone. He pressed a button on the dashboard to connect the call through Bluetooth. "Hey, Russ."

"Hey, boss. Sorry to interrupt your date."

"It's fine. I left Noelle and Skyler at the festival. I'm on my way to Trudy's trailer to check on her."

"Everything all right?"

"I'm sure it will be. What's up?"

"I thought you might like to know an older man with a red Ford was spotted looking around Raina and Earl Miller's barn," Rusty said.

"Allen Conroy Senior?"

"Raina only got a partial of the plate, but it matches the license plate we have on file for him. On a hunch, I reached out to the Kirbys, and they said a man in a red truck pulled up along the road near their house and got out around the crack of dawn a couple of days ago. Mr. Kirby stepped outside with a shotgun when he realized the man intended to trespass, and the driver ran back to his truck and left."

He was visiting the arson scenes. Or . . . revisiting, if they were his handiwork. Some criminals enjoyed the thrill of revisiting their crimes.

"Anyone know where he is now?" Derek asked.

"He left before I got to Raina and Earl's. We're keeping an eye out for him at the site of the third fire. If he decides to drop by, we'll haul him in for questioning." Rusty paused before asking, "Why do you think he's visiting the crime scenes?"

"We'll add that to the list of questions we ask when we find him." Derek pulled into the driveway of Brian and Trudy's trailer. "Call me if someone picks him up tonight. I'd like to talk to him."

You made a promise, his conscience reminded him.

He told the girls he would come back and spend the rest of the evening with them once he was sure Trudy was okay. He needed to put them first, no matter how much his job demanded his attention.

"On second thought, Russ, if you pick him up tonight, go ahead and see what you can get from him. I'll follow up with any additional questions in the morning."

His deputies were competent enough to run an interrogation, and he needed to step back and let them handle it so he could prioritize Noelle and Skyler.

"Sure thing. Have a good night, boss."

"You too."

The call ended. Derek twisted the key from the ignition and climbed from his truck, confusion tugging at the corners of his mouth. There were no other vehicles in the driveway.

Trudy must've gotten a ride home from one of her customers because she was too upset to drive. She wouldn't risk baby Logan's safety by driving with her vision impaired by tears.

As he climbed the steps onto the small porch add-on, he heard the steady sound of water running. The shower.

He sifted through his keys for the spare to the trailer, but his fingers stilled when the flapping corner of a screen caught his eye. The window to the kitchen was open, and the screen had been cut on two sides, far enough to allow an intruder to fold it back and climb in.

Derek dropped his keys and drew his off-duty weapon. Someone was in his sister's trailer. He moved to look through the window, but pain pierced his back and thigh, and scalding pinpricks raced along his skin and through his insides.

His legs buckled, and he collapsed to the porch. He tried to hang on to his awareness, his thoughts, but the voltage coursing through his body scattered them.

Through the haze of pain, he was vaguely aware of boots approaching from the side. A cloaked figure leaned over him and pressed a cloth to his face.

The electric shock ceased, and he gasped involuntarily. Chemical sweetness from the rag filled his lungs and sent his mind spinning. Every breath drew it in deeper, and before he could do more than think about grabbing for the gun that had fallen from his fingers, his mind tumbled into darkness.

The festival was set up at the village park, and a cordoned-off road led to the cornfield owned by one of Noelle's fellow church members. Families streamed down the road, children's laughter and squeals filling the night with joy.

The church youth pastor, Lenny, stood by the entrance to the corn maze, greeting his students as they passed by. "Noelle, glad you could make it."

Skyler watched the other kids as they laughed and ran around in the maze. "Mom, can I go by myself?"

Noelle's maternal instincts recoiled from the idea, especially given the potential dangers. "I don't think that's a good idea, sweetheart."

"But kids even younger than me are going alone. I'm big enough."

Noelle folded her arms, uncertain. "I think we should stick together."

Skyler's face fell. "I want to try to make friends."

"We have adults scattered throughout, monitoring the event, and I was about to head on in myself," Lenny said. "Your lightning bug is safe."

"Firefly," Skyler corrected. "I even light up." She turned to show off the glow sticks down her back. "My grandma made it."

"Coolest costume ever." He gave her a high five.

"There's nothing scary in there, right? No . . . monsters?" Noelle asked. She didn't want Skyler to have nightmares.

Lenny shook his head. "We're not celebrating Halloween and all the scary stuff that goes with it. We're celebrating the seasonal change that God made awesome and beautiful. Right, Sky?"

Skyler bobbed her head once. "Right."

"All costumes are family appropriate, and thus far, all the kids have followed the rules—fun and lighthearted costumes only."

That was a relief.

Skyler turned her heart-melting blue eyes on Noelle. "Please, Mom, can I go by myself?"

"Okay," Noelle agreed. "But don't leave the maze for any reason."

She barely had a chance to finish speaking before Skyler darted into the maze, her youth group teacher not far behind.

I watched from among the cornstalks as costumed children bounced around with their baskets and buckets of sugar.

The little one I was looking for finally came into view in her firefly costume. She looked to be having such fun, and it was a shame to ruin it, but there was no other way.

I needed Noelle's undivided attention.

Taking her new "daughter" would guarantee it.

I adjusted the hat on my head as I waited. I had donned a scarecrow costume over my other disguise, a simple three-piece ensemble that took less than a minute to put on. The wheelbarrow portion of this disguise was more inconvenient. It had bumped and tilted down the row between cornstalks, catching every divot, but it was necessary for more than aesthetics.

I stood farther back, not quite in the maze but close enough to blend in with the other adults in the area. No one would think twice about my presence.

"Little Firefly," I called out. "Would you mind giving me a hand? My candy cart overturned, and it's stuck."

Her entire face brightened at the sight of me, and she started toward me, ducking under the red ribbon that marked the edge of the maze. "A scarecrow! One of my favorite people is a scarecrow. He's really old and grouchy, but I love him."

She must be talking about that infernal old man who rarely left the grounds.

"Come around here and help me set this upright."

She obeyed without question, crouching down behind the wheelbarrow and out of sight of any onlookers. I whipped the chloroform cloth out of my pocket and covered her face. She squeaked and kicked out, her foot striking the inside of the wheelbarrow several times before she finally went limp.

I shoved her into my "candy cart," covered her with a tarp, and wrestled it upright. My heart thundered in my ears, and I felt nauseous at the risk I had just taken. So many potential witnesses.

When I glanced back toward the maze, a boy no more than six stared at me with wide eyes. He'd seen something, and his miniature brain was trying to make sense of it.

I needed to keep him quiet.

I leaned forward and whispered, "If you tell anyone, I'll come back for you as soon as you go to sleep, and I'll drag you away by your toes. Your parents will never find you."

The boy gasped and then dashed away like evil was chasing him.

I released a breath and started toward the woods at the edge of the cornfield where my car was parked. It was a short drive to my destination, and I would have her locked away before anyone even noticed she was missing.

Fatigue left an ache in Brian's body as he scrubbed the grill, scraping away the remnants of a long day preparing meals.

He never realized how exhausting running a restaurant could be until life thrust him into his wife's shoes. Trudy had been worn out every night before the baby, and her tiredness used to frustrate him. Now he understood the desire to go home, take a shower, and crawl into bed.

He glanced into the dining room. Trudy hummed to herself as she swept the floor, her face—glowing from sweat—framed by the wisps of frizzy blond hair she'd been pushing back from her forehead all evening. But it was the peacefulness in her expression as she worked that struck him.

Despite her tiredness, she still radiated joy.

He was lucky to have her in his life. He should've realized that long before now, and shame flooded him as he thought about all the times his selfish actions had dulled that radiance.

Something outside must've caught her attention, because she walked toward the window. "Please tell me that's somebody burning their fall leaves or having a bonfire."

Brian joined her, searching the horizon until he found the smudge against the evening sky. "That's way too much smoke for a bonfire." He tugged his phone from his jeans pocket and called in the fire. "I'm at the diner in town, but given the direction, I would guess the fire is on Melbourne, past Hackette Road. The smoke is building fast."

Dispatch assured him emergency services was on the way, and he disconnected, but his gaze remained glued to the smoke.

Everything in Brian itched to climb in his car and respond to the scene as a volunteer fireman, but he wasn't on call today.

"Somebody's going to die in that fire, aren't they?" Trudy asked, rubbing at her arms.

Brian met his wife's innocent eyes, rounded with fear, and swallowed the answer that sprang to his tongue. If it was another barn fire set by the supposed Dragonfly, then there would be another victim, but that truth was too dark for his wife's tender heart. "There's a good chance the fire department will reach the scene in time."

There was *no* chance, but he wouldn't tell her that.

The telltale wail and honk of fire trucks broke through the quiet of the village, and two red engines blew past the diner in the direction of the smoke.

"Whoever's in that fire . . . they've probably eaten in my diner." Trudy pressed a hand to her chest. "It makes me sick to think . . ."

Brian wrapped an arm around her. "Don't think about that."

"I should call Derek. He's the head of this investigation, so I'm sure he knows what's happening." She pulled her phone from her apron and pressed the button on the side to wake the screen. When she called up Derek's contact information, she frowned. "It says I blocked his number. Why would it say that?"

Brian leaned in for a closer look. "It could've been an accident."

"How could I block somebody's number on accident? I don't even know how to do it on purpose."

"Has anyone else used your phone?"

"Of course not. I don't . . ." She trailed off, and realization crossed her face. "There was an Amish man in one of the booths this evening. He asked to use my phone, since he didn't have one of his own. He needed to text a family member to see if his nephew was out of surgery."

"And you said yes."

"How could I say no to that?"

Brian sighed. He would've said no, but as usual, Trudy's heart got the better of her. "Who would he have texted, Trudy? His family would be Amish, too, and they live by the same no-technology rule."

Trudy's hand went to her throat. "I . . . I don't know. I didn't think about that. Maybe he texted a friend of the family?"

"Maybe. But there's no way he blocked your brother's number by accident."

"Why would he not want me talking to my brother? I've never even seen the man before."

"What do you remember about him?"

"He had a scraggly beard, long gray hair that stuck out every which way, and one of those wide-brim black hats most of the older Amish men wear. I really couldn't see much of his face." Trudy paused in thought. "He was hoarse like he had really bad allergies or something."

"And that didn't seem suspicious to you?"

"Why would it?"

"Amish men take their hats off indoors." That, paired with the hoarse voice and request to text someone, Brian would've been instantly suspicious. "Did you see him call anyone?"

"No, but I did see him tapping on the screen like he was sending a text before I turned to wipe down a table." She opened her text messages. "There's nothing here. He must've deleted it when he was finished. Guess he likes his privacy."

Or he was covering his tracks.

Brian dialed Derek's number on his own phone, but it rang through to voice mail. "Come on, Derek." He sent the call through again. Voice mail. "When was the last time you spoke with or texted your brother?"

"Not since this morning. Why?"

Brian had a sick feeling in the pit of his stomach. He dialed Noelle's number and bypassed the usual greeting when she answered. "Is Derek with you?"

"No, he left a while ago," Noelle said.

"How long is a while?"

"Um . . . Skyler's been in the maze for about fifteen minutes, so . . . thirty-five minutes, maybe? Why?"

"Did he say where he was going?"

Silence stretched.

"Noelle," Brian prompted.

"He got a text message from Trudy. She said you relapsed in your gambling, and she left you to close down the diner so she could go home. She asked Derek to come over so they could talk."

Brian's heart thundered in his ears. Someone had used Trudy's phone to lure Derek to their trailer, which was isolated on a large piece of land. That *someone* was aware of Brian's addiction and how it affected his family.

"Brian, are you there?" Noelle asked.

"Yeah, um . . . I'll call you back later. Thanks for the information." He hung up. There was no sense in making her panic before he knew all the facts. He dialed Rusty's number next, and the older deputy answered immediately.

"Rusty Ramone."

"It's Brian Mason. I'm trying to get a hold of Derek, but he's not answering. I think he's in trouble."

"What sort of trouble are you thinking?"

"A man I believe was pretending to be Amish asked to use Trudy's phone, and he sent a text to Derek, luring him to our trailer alone. The man deleted the messages afterward and blocked Derek in her phone."

"I called him a while ago to update him on a person of interest. He said he was on his way to your trailer to check on Trudy."

"Trudy's here with me at the diner. She's been here all day." Brian looked at his wife, whose complexion had grown a few shades paler as she listened to the one-sided conversation. "Was the man wearing gloves when he used your phone?"

"No. I remember thinking that his hands didn't match his rugged beard. They looked like the hands of an office worker."

"Good. Hopefully we can get a print."

Trudy looked down at her phone. "When I took my phone back from him, my hands were full of dishes from the table I cleared. I asked if he could depress the pop socket and drop it into my apron." She showed him the round accessory stuck to the back of her phone case that helped prevent her from dropping her phone. "He pressed it in with his thumb."

Brian turned his attention back to the phone call. "Rusty, I need you to send the nearest deputy to the diner with materials to lift a print and an MFD."

"A what?" Trudy asked.

"Mobile fingerprinting device. It helps us run . . . helps *law enforcement* run fingerprints and facial searches in the field. Rusty, send me any pictures or sketches of the arsonist so I can show them to Trudy."

"Jimenez is in your area. She'll be at the diner soon. I'll head over to your trailer, see if I can piece together where the captain is."

Brian walked away from Trudy and lowered his voice. "Rusty, if the person who lured Derek out there is the arsonist . . ."

"I know. I saw the smoke." Rusty's voice held the same note of concern as Brian's. "I'll let you know what I find."

CHAPTER Thirty-five

Pain greeted Derek as he woke, radiating through his skull and down his neck. He searched his mind for an explanation, the fragments of memory difficult to pull through the fog surrounding his thoughts.

He remembered thinking there was an intruder inside his sister's trailer, followed by sharp pain, then darkness, and then being dragged out of a trunk. He'd fallen and cracked the side of his head against the ground before his abductor pressed another cloth to his face that sent his mind spinning back into darkness.

Groaning, he lifted his head and peeled open his heavy eyelids. He blinked at his hazy surroundings, trying to bring them into focus: a tractor, hay bales, stacks of animal feed.

He was in a barn, and the haze rolling through the air and stinging his lungs was smoke. It grew thicker by the second, making it harder to breathe, and the telltale glow of flames brightened every window.

Fire. He was in a barn, and it was on fire.

Instinctively, he tried to get to his feet, but he couldn't move. He looked down at himself. Rope coiled around his chest and arms, pinning him to a beam at his back, and his wrists were bound together.

Realization sent a shaft of fear through him.

This was how the Dragonfly's victims had died: chloroformed, bound, and left to burn.

Derek strained against his bindings.

He didn't fit with the previous victims, both of whom were violent criminals. Unless their criminal behavior had no bearing on why the killer chose them. It could've been any number of reasons, or no reason at all.

He would be the first to admit that he would never fully understand the motivations and desires of an evil mind. Serial killers didn't think like ordinary people.

As he twisted and stretched his wrists, a terrifying thought sliced through his mind: *What if Trudy is tied up in here too?*

She had sent Derek a text, begging him to come by the trailer, and that was where the killer had abducted him.

He turned his head to see as much of the barn as he could. "Tru!" He coughed and inhaled another gulp of hot, smoke-filled air. "Trudy!"

The only answer was the shattering of glass beneath the onslaught of flames.

She could be unconscious, but more than likely, the text message from his sister had been a setup. She was probably still at the diner.

God, please let her be at the diner. Let her be safe.

He could not lose his baby sister. Logan could not lose his mother.

A chunk of burning wood dropped through the shattered window, igniting the scattered bits of straw on the barn floor. Flames crawled hungrily toward Derek.

His eyes and lungs burned as the smoke grew thicker. He needed to get himself out of this, or he would die of smoke inhalation before the fire department ever arrived.

The remains of the last two victims—scorched beyond recognition—flashed through his mind. He couldn't die like this.

He gave up on his wrists. He could walk or crawl with bound wrists. What he needed to do was free himself from the beam at his back.

His upper arms were pinned to his rib cage by thick coils of rope, but if he could get his feet under him, he could stand. The ropes were moderately tight around his slumped form, but if he could straighten out his body, there would be enough slack for him to work with.

He dragged his feet toward him and lifted his hips.

Between the thinning air and the rough wooden beam snagging at the rope, standing took every ounce of strength he had. He gasped and coughed as he worked his way up. Finally straight, he shrugged and shimmied until the rope shifted up toward his collarbone. Arms mostly free now, he shoved the rope coils over his head.

That was the easy part.

Starving for oxygen with sweat dripping into his burning eyes, he staggered in a circle, surveying his options. Fire licked up the walls—rolling, splashing flames so hot his lungs would cook if he breathed in the surrounding air.

Distant sirens cut through the crackling and roaring of the flames, but the fire department wasn't going to arrive in time to save him. Judging by how light-headed he felt, he had a minute, maybe two, before he passed out from lack of oxygen.

He was going to die in here if he didn't find a way out now.

Lord, I need a way out.

Smoke drifting outward through an opening drew his attention. Was it a window? A door that hadn't closed all the way? There was too much smoke to be certain, but either way, it was an exit.

He staggered forward, but a wave of dizziness took him to his knees. The air was too hot and too thick with smoke.

Staying low to the ground, he crawled toward the opening. Searing pain bit at his skin as he dragged himself over hot debris. He had to get out, no matter how many burn scars this deadly inferno left him with.

He had to be getting close, but every inch forward felt like he was dragging a semitrailer behind him. His body was heavy, and he could no longer see.

His arms buckled, and he collapsed to the floor. His last thought before darkness pulled him under was somewhere between a hopeless statement and a desperate plea: *God, I can't leave my girls.*

Noelle checked the text log between her and Derek for the tenth time in the hope that her phone had glitched and forgotten to notify her of his responding message.

Still nothing.

She had asked him how Trudy was doing, but judging by the lack of response, consoling his sister required all his attention.

As she tucked her phone back into her purse, her gaze landed on a child leaving the maze with two buckets of candy. One was a glow-in-the-dark pumpkin with the letter *S* on the back. That was Skyler's candy bucket.

Why did he have Skyler's bucket?

Noelle approached the child and crouched in front of him. "Excuse me, where did you get that bucket?"

The boy's mother placed a protective hand on his shoulder, like she was about to tell Noelle to leave her child alone, but then she noticed the green pumpkin bucket too. "Where *did* you get that extra candy pail? Did you take another child's candy, Robbie?"

"No, I didn't!" His face pleaded with the two adults to understand. "I found it fair and square."

Robbie's mother took it from him and offered it to Noelle. "I'm sorry, does this belong to your child?"

"Yes." Noelle accepted it, unease growing in her gut. "Robbie, where did you find it?"

"All the way at the back of the maze. Outside the red ribbon. It was spilled over on the ground. I had to pick up all the candy, which means I should get to keep it."

Skyler would never have dropped her bucket and left the candy scattered on the ground. She was too excited about this event.

"Did you see a little girl nearby in a firefly costume?" Noelle asked, trying to keep the alarm from her voice. She didn't want to frighten him.

Robbie shook his head.

A set of twins dressed as Raggedy Ann and Andy brushed past Noelle. They had gone in about fifteen minutes after Skyler. She should've worked her way around the maze and back out by now.

Noelle rose and pushed past the other waiting parents and into the maze. Details blurred as she whipped her head left and right, searching for the black-and-green costume with lights on the back.

"Skyler?" she called out.

The concern in her voice drew attention from others, but she didn't care if she was disturbing their fun. She brushed aside cornstalks to look beyond the red ribbon that cordoned off the maze.

Skyler might've seen a baby deer or a rabbit and wandered off, despite instructions to stay inside. She was curious and amazed by everything.

"Sky!" Noelle called out again.

She dodged children and parents as she made her way to the back of the maze. Why wasn't her daughter answering? She must be able to hear Noelle calling. Unless something had frightened her and she had taken off in search of a place to hide. That would explain the dropped bucket.

Noelle's heart sledgehammered against her ribs with every passing second. And then she spotted it—a green glow stick about ten feet outside the red ribbon.

"Sky."

She dove under the ribbon, nearly tripping in her haste, and snatched up the glow stick. It still had the Velcro sticker on one side that kept it attached to the costume. It wouldn't have fallen off by itself.

She straightened, turning in a circle. There was no sign of her daughter.

"Skyler!!"

Her phone chimed, and she fumbled it from her pocket. It was a message from a number she didn't recognize. A picture loaded, and all the strength left Noelle's legs. She sank to her knees in the cornfield, struggling to draw in air.

Skyler's eyes shimmered with terror as she looked up at the camera, her mouth duct-taped. A text came across the screen:

> I have your little Firefly. Come to the asylum. Alone. Leave your phone in the car. If I see one cop or sheriff's deputy, she burns.

CHAPTER Thirty-six

Deputy Jimenez set the mobile fingerprinting device on the tabletop of the largest booth. "I need the phone the suspect touched."

Trudy handed it to her, her hand shaking from the anxiety of the situation. "Can I get you some cobbler and ice cream? I know you have a sweet tooth, and we have some left over."

"Could you sprinkle some cinnamon on the ice cream?"

Trudy forced cheer into her voice despite her worry. "Of course I can."

"You're a gem. Thank you." Jimenez pulled a container of fingerprint powder and a soft makeup brush from her bag, then a roll of clear tape and a square card.

"Do you have photos of the arson suspect that we can take a look at?" Brian asked.

Jimenez paused in her task long enough to pass her phone to him. "They're in the photo gallery."

Jimenez was one of the few deputies who didn't freeze him out after the shameful way he left the department. Rusty was the other. And he was grateful for that, because he needed both of them tonight.

Brian studied the images on Jimenez's phone. The first one was a sketch of a bearded man from the Copper Penny bar.

He scrolled to the next image. This one was a security camera snapshot of a bearded man in a baseball cap purchasing supplies at the local hardware store. The note at the bottom explained, "Unidentified man purchased the same brand and color of paint used to create the logo at the scene of the fire."

Something about the way the man was standing bothered Brian, but he couldn't quite pin down the reason.

He swiped his finger across the screen and found another sketch. This one depicted a man in an Amish hat with a beard. A note attached to the bottom of the sketch read, "Trespasser spotted around Miller barn a week before the fire."

Trudy came back with the cobbler and ice cream. "Here are your sweets, Ang . . ." She trailed off as her gaze locked on the phone screen. "That's him. That's the man who borrowed my phone."

"There are a couple of pictures here." Brian scrolled back through them, giving her a moment to study each one.

"That's the only one I recognize." Trudy set the plate of cobbler on the table.

Brian's phone rang, and he set Jimenez's cell on the table before walking away to answer his own. "Rusty, what did you find?"

"Derek's truck is parked in front of your trailer, phone in the cup holder, but he's not here. There are drag marks in the mud and another set of vehicle tracks."

Brian muttered a curse too soft for anyone else to hear. The arsonist had his brother-in-law. Brian's gaze trailed to the smoke stretching through the sky in the distance, and dread dropped into his stomach like a lead ball.

"We have a match," Jimenez called out.

"Call me if you learn anything more, Rusty," Brian said before disconnecting. He crowded around Jimenez and Trudy to see the ID that popped up on the screen of the MFD.

Brian frowned at the face on the screen. How had he missed the similarities? Jimenez raised an inquiring eyebrow at the result, and Brian nodded in confirmation.

"All right," Jimenez said. "I need to get this sent out to everyone. If we're lucky, tonight will be the last fire Cherry Creek has to worry about." She gathered up her supplies and headed out to her cruiser.

Trudy rubbed at her arms as though chilled. "What did Rusty say about Derek? Did he find him?"

Brian drew in a breath and let it out slowly. "His truck is at our trailer, but he's missing."

"No, he's not missing. I can track him with my phone. We have that app so we can find each other in case of an emergency. He won't mind if I use it."

"It'll tell you he's at the trailer, because that's where his phone is. Someone took him."

She paused, midreach for her phone on the table, tears in her eyes. "Why would someone do that? What are they going to do to him?"

"Rusty is going to let me know as soon as he has any more information."

"It's the arsonist, isn't it? It's because he led the town hall meeting. Something he said upset him and made the man come after him." Tears streamed down her face as she stared at the distant smoke. "He's in that fire, isn't he?"

Brian pocketed his phone and came up behind her, wrapping his arms around her and offering what comfort he could.

CHAPTER Thirty-seven

Anxiety wrapped around Noelle like a metal straitjacket, compressing her chest and making it hard to breathe. Every gulp of air scraped in and out of her lungs, leaving her light-headed and one step closer to a breakdown.

God, I can't lose another child.

She would come apart at the seams, and there would be no stitching her back together. She would end up like Walt— bitter, old, and unable to move on.

Lifting a hand from the steering wheel, she pushed the glasses from her nose to swipe at her tears. Navigating the unlit and winding back roads at night was difficult enough without tears blurring everything together.

She glanced at the dark screen of her cell phone in the holder on the dashboard, the warning the kidnapper sent still spinning and tumbling through her mind.

Come to the asylum. Alone. If I see one cop or sheriff's deputy, she burns.

Nausea churned in Noelle's stomach.

The kidnapper didn't simply intend to kill her little girl. He intended to burn her alive. There was only one person in this village cruel enough to do something like that—the Dragonfly.

Had Noelle stumbled across something in her research that she shouldn't have, something that brought her too close to discovering his location or identity?

But how would he know that without slipping into the house to look at the whiteboard in her writing room? Unless he let himself in while Walt was in a deep sleep.

Regardless of how the man knew whatever he knew, he had her daughter.

What was happening to her right now? Was he hurting her, or did he lock her in a room and leave her there? Would she be able to breathe through her tears with the duct tape over her mouth?

Noelle's fingers gripped the steering wheel so tightly she could barely feel them anymore. She needed to talk to someone. Derek always knew how to quiet her fears, but she couldn't reach him. Even if she could, he would pull together other members of law enforcement to storm the asylum.

And Skyler would die.

Using the voice activation on her phone, she said, "Call Dad."

Even though her dad lived on the other side of the country, the sound of his voice when he answered sent a wave of comfort through her. "Hey, pumpkin."

Noelle fought back her tears enough to squeeze out, "Dad, Skyler's been taken."

"What do you mean? By the state? I thought the adoption was final."

"No." Noelle's voice hitched. "Someone took her. She was in the cornfield maze, and he took her."

All the softness left his voice, like he'd switched gears from her father to the cop he used to be. "What do you know?"

"He took her to the old asylum. He sent me a text and said to come alone, no law enforcement."

"Under no circumstances do you go there alone."

"He said he would kill her if I don't."

Dad paused. "Did he demand a ransom?"

"No, nothing like that."

"Is this the man who attacked you at the book signing? The one you told me not to worry about?"

Noelle swallowed a sob. "I don't know. Whoever he is, I think he's responsible for the recent string of arson murders in Cherry Creek. I don't know what to do, Dad."

"Where are you now?"

"On my way to the asylum."

"Baby, listen to me. You cannot go on your own. If he didn't ask for ransom, it's because he wants you. If you walk in there by yourself—"

"I might not walk out. I know." The likelihood terrified her, but it was a risk she had to take. If he was open to negotiation, she would trade herself for her daughter without hesitation. Derek would take Skyler in, and his family would love her as their own. She wouldn't be alone.

"I can't convince you not to go, can I?"

"He said he's going to burn her to death if I don't follow his rules, Dad. I don't have a choice." She'd been trying to think of an alternative since she received the text message.

"You have your gun?"

"Yes."

"You need backup. Maybe you can't involve law enforcement without setting him off, but there must be someone. Someone who can sneak in under the kidnapper's radar."

Despite living in Cherry Creek for the past year, Noelle hadn't made that many friends. She struggled to connect with people, and she couldn't trust just anyone to help rescue her daughter.

"I'm booking a flight for your mother and me. We'll be there before morning."

"Dad—"

"You're not talking me out of it this time. If something goes wrong tonight, and my daughter and granddaughter both end up missing, I'm not going to be waiting for phone call updates in Seattle." A dresser drawer slid open and shut, and Dad shouted, "Abigail! Pack a bag and grab my gun from the safe!"

Dad hadn't touched his gun since shortly after the shooting that drove him to quit the force. Even holding it in his hand triggered a flood of traumatic memories.

"Your gun?" Mom asked, her voice growing louder as she came into the room. "What's going on?"

"Our daughter needs our help."

"What kind of help—"

"I'll explain later. Just please do as I asked. And quickly."

The asylum came into view, and fear sent Noelle's stomach rolling. "Dad, I have to go."

"I love you, pumpkin. Trust your instincts."

"I love you too." She ended the call and stared up the drive at the asylum.

God, please don't let this be a mistake.

She grabbed her phone and, fingers shaking with fear, she forwarded the picture of Skyler and the kidnapper's demands to the one person she thought might be able to help.

CHAPTER Thirty-eight

Noelle's unsteady legs threatened to buckle as she crunched through the dead leaves peppering the ground around the abandoned asylum.

The eerie building loomed in front of her, and every horror story she'd heard about such places whispered through her mind: patient neglect, abuse, torture, mysterious deaths and disappearances.

And her daughter was in there somewhere.

Steam left her mouth as she searched the unlit grounds for the monster who'd summoned her here. Her gaze passed over a No Trespassing sign in the grass and then snapped back to a figure standing by the building. Her heart skipped, and she instinctively stepped back.

The Dragonfly.

Steeling herself, Noelle said, "I came alone, like you said. No police, no phone." She waited for a response from the man, but he said nothing. "Take me to my daughter."

Without a word, the mysterious figure turned and dissolved into the shadows. No. She couldn't lose him. He was her only hope of finding Skyler.

Noelle sprinted across the grass to the building. Her brain registered the drop-off beneath her foot too late, and she gasped as she tumbled forward. Stone steps slammed into her body like cement fists as she rolled down them—punching her shoulders, her back, her hips. The final blow came from the stone block enclosure at the bottom, when the back of her head cracked against it.

She groaned, pain splintering from her toes to her skull.

Get up, she told herself. *Skyler needs you.*

Even if she had to drag her limp body through this twisted maze by her fingertips, she was going to rescue her daughter. Gritting her teeth against a cry, she pushed herself into a sitting position against the wall.

With gentle fingers, she probed the spot where her head had connected with the wall. The knot swelling there was almost big enough to be fitted for its own hat.

Bracing a hand against the wall, she struggled to her feet. She would be a walking bruise in the morning, but at least she could walk. A wave of dizziness sent her staggering sideways. Mostly. She could mostly walk.

A chain dangling from the door handle caught her eye. Someone had cut through it to gain access to the building.

Don't go in there. Whatever he wants from you, it isn't to give you your daughter back, her inner voice warned, and she knew that was true. Skyler was merely the bait to draw her here, but it didn't matter. She wouldn't leave her in this madman's hands.

She limped through the open door into the bowels of the asylum. Stale air and cobwebs greeted her, and she brushed aside the sticky strands grabbing at her hair.

The interior of the building was even eerier than the outside. The corridor before her stretched the length of the building, and the path forward was lit only by flickering oil lanterns. They provided enough light to soften the blackness into varying degrees of darkness.

It was bright enough that she could see the layers of graffiti trespassers had spray-painted on the wall, the most recent of which declared, "Evil lives here."

A shiver slithered down her aching spine.

It could be her imagination, but she could feel that evil pressing against her spirit as she stepped further inside.

A clang reverberated overhead, followed by a scraping sound, and she looked up at the ceiling. Someone was moving around above her.

Noelle drew her revolver from the holster at her back and held it at her side as she started forward.

"Where are you?" she shouted, and the vibration of her own voice in her head made her wince.

She passed what looked like a kitchen, and she squinted into the room to see if anyone was hiding below the counters. The last thing she needed was to get jumped from behind.

A door on her right, painted the same beige as the walls, became visible as she neared it. Skyler could be in any of the rooms. Of course, so could the Dragonfly.

She reached out to grab the knob, took a moment to gather her nerve, and then whipped it open. The muscles in her body tightened on reflex, anticipating the worst.

She released a breath.

It was a utility room with a furnace and water heater. She closed the door and checked the next two rooms she came across—a storage closet and laundry room.

Fear and frustration churned inside her. "I'm not interested in playing hide-and-seek! All I want is my daughter!"

The hallway seemed to breathe in response to her raised voice, the lantern flames flickering and the cobwebs above her head swaying.

It's only a draft, she told herself, fingers tightening on her gun, but she wasn't entirely sure she believed her internal voice this time.

She limped to the end of the hall to find a staircase leading up to a closed door. The Dragonfly must've gone through it, but she hadn't heard a single footstep or door latch.

Because he's not really here, her mind offered up, and her imagination leaped on board. *No one really knows what happened to Peter Ashton the night he set the fire. He mysteriously disappeared, but what if they covered up his death and his evil spirit has never left this place?*

"Don't be stupid," she muttered. "Whoever he is, he's just a man."

It wasn't like ghosts could send text messages.

Gripping the railing for support, she hobbled up the steps, her left hip protesting every movement. She opened the door at the top and found herself in another lantern-lit corridor, this one lined with doors inlaid with horizontal windows. Patient rooms, most likely.

She scooped up one of the lanterns and approached the nearest room to peer inside. A barred window, peeling paint, and a bed soldered to the wall.

Was Skyler being kept in one of these cells?

"Skyler?" she whispered.

She didn't expect a response, and her heart stuttered in her chest when another voice whispered back, "Hello? Is someone out there?"

The scraping sound she'd heard from below came again, along with a thump against one of the doors down the hall.

"Is someone there?" the feminine whisper called out. "If someone's there, please . . ." Her voice broke, and she pounded a hand against the door. "Please, you have to help me before he comes back."

Noelle followed the sound. She raised the lantern to drive back the shadows of the cell, and the light glinted off a pair of wide, frightened eyes. Familiar eyes.

"Oh, thank God," the woman cried.

"Hang on. Let me see if I can get you out of there." Noelle holstered her gun and tried the door, surprised to find it unlocked. Confusion rippled through her until she noticed the cuff around the woman's wrist. She was handcuffed to a metal bracket on the wall.

The woman twisted her wrist. "I've been trying to get out of it, but I can't fit my hand through it, and it won't budge from the wall. Please tell me you know how to pick a lock."

"I'd rather not lie to you."

Even if she had the right materials, she doubted she could outsmart the locking mechanism. Sure, she'd studied the method extensively for one of her books, but that didn't mean she knew how to implement it.

The woman hung her head forward with a whimper, blond curls falling over her face. "I'm going to die."

"You're not going to die. We'll figure this out." Figuring it out would be a lot easier if she had bolt cutters.

"You're . . . Nina, from the diner, right?"

Noelle looked up at her, studying her face. "Noelle. Have we met before?"

The woman rubbed tears from her face with a dirty shirt sleeve. "You brought me cobbler and ice cream. I was talking to that cute little girl."

Recognition dawned, and she realized why the woman looked familiar. "Sally, homeowners insurance."

Sally pressed her lips together and nodded. "I was going door to door, hoping the recent fires might inspire people to sign up for better homeowners insurance."

"Something went wrong, I take it."

Sally sniffled. "You could say that. I parked on the road so my tires wouldn't get stuck in the muddy driveway, and I was walking through the grass toward this really old house. I thought, *A place that old really needs insurance*. And then someone grabbed me from behind. He put something over my face and . . . then I woke up in my own trunk. He put that cloth over my face again, and then . . ." She gestured to her surroundings.

"Has he hurt you?"

"No. But he likes to drop by and remind me that I deserve to die. I guess . . ." She inhaled a quavering breath. "I guess I'm next. Unless you can get me out."

Noelle didn't know how to break the news to her that she couldn't remove this cuff. Not without a key, and more than likely, the Dragonfly had it. What if Skyler was chained up somewhere too? She needed that key.

"Do you know who took you?" she asked.

Sally shook her head. "I haven't seen his face. Every time he comes by to talk, he's wearing that creepy mask."

"How long have you been here?"

"Since yesterday afternoon. Are the police searching for me?"

Noelle pressed her lips together against a truth that would only dishearten her. Derek said no one had been reported missing yet, which meant no one was looking for her.

The arsonist had probably intended to kill her tonight before whatever drove him to snatch Skyler.

"He took my little girl tonight," Noelle said. "The one you spoke with at the diner. She's here somewhere. Have you seen her?"

Sally gasped. "Yes. I mean, not exactly, but he carried someone past the door. That must've been her."

"Where did he take her?"

Sally's mouth opened, closed, and then opened again. "I'm sorry. I wish I could tell you, but I can't see beyond what's right in front of me."

Noelle bit back the frustration that tried to sharpen her voice. "It's okay. She's here, and I'll find her."

A whisper slithered down the hall and up the back of Noelle's neck to her ears, making every muscle in her body tense. "Noelle."

Panic sparked in Sally's eyes. "He's back."

Noelle squeezed her fingers. "It'll be all right."

"Please don't leave me."

"I have to get the key from him, but I'll come back for you." Releasing the frightened woman, she stepped out into the corridor.

A tremor swept through her as she reached back and rested her hand on her gun, prepared to confront the haunting figure in the room at the end of the hall.

CHAPTER Thirty-nine

Noelle crossed the threshold into the room where the cloaked figure waited—a man who had murdered two people. More, if the mask he wore was any indication of his identity.

The mask was a dragonfly—iridescent wings splayed across his brow and cheekbones, with the thorax stretching up his forehead and down his chin. It left little more than his eyes visible, but they were shadowed by the hood he wore.

He tilted his head when she stopped with a good amount of space between them. "Do you know who I am?"

His voice tickled a memory—familiar but not distinct enough to stand out.

"I don't care who you are or what name you give yourself. All I want is my daughter. Where is she?" Her voice cracked on those last three words, betraying her desperation.

"Safe. For now."

She wanted to believe he was telling the truth, but the word of a murderer was worth nothing. "Where are you keeping her? Is she in one of those patient rooms?"

His head tipped ever so slightly. Was he indicating the upper floor, or was she reading too much into it?

"What do you want from us?" she asked.

He paused for a beat, then said, "Everything."

Noelle's heart thudded in her chest. What did that mean? What was he going to do with them? "If you let my daughter go, I'll do . . ."—she swallowed hard and squeezed out the rest of the words—"whatever you want. I just need her away from here and safe."

A soft thump came from behind Noelle, and she glanced over her shoulder toward Sally's cell. As much as she wanted to save Skyler, she couldn't forget about this monster's other innocent victim.

"Listen," he commanded, tipping his head to the side. "Do you hear the screams?"

Noelle listened, but all she could hear was the wind whistling past the building and rattling loose windowpanes.

"Every day there were screams," he said, his voice oddly flat despite the eerie words. "They locked me up in this place like I was one of those people with a broken mind, as if I didn't have a true purpose for the things I did."

"Your family pulled strings to have you committed instead of incarcerated."

He continued as if she hadn't spoken. "This is where we would sit most days, sedated, stewing in our own madness as life slipped away."

Something about his words tugged at a memory, and Noelle turned them over in her mind until the connection clicked. *Stewing in madness.* On the tape that AJ had played for her, Dr. Conroy had used that exact expression.

She studied the man in front of her—straight shoulders, about five foot eight, with no discernible crackle of age in his voice. Peter Ashton would be sixty-seven, on the edge of the age when that unsteadiness of voice usually began.

"Why are you doing all this?" she asked.

"Because I'm the Dragonfly, and I decide who lives and dies."

"You're murdering innocent people."

A pause before he said, "No one is innocent."

"My daughter is. She's eleven years old. She's a baby who's never done anything more wrong than argue about wearing shoes. Give her back to me."

Another maddening pause before he said, "I chose her. Like I chose the sex offender. The spouse abuser. And the sheriff's department captain who was getting too close."

His words punched Noelle between the ribs, stealing her breath. Derek. He hadn't answered her texts this evening, and that wasn't like him. And then the fire emergency services were responding to . . .

No, it's not true. It can't be.

"He tried to escape the flames, but he failed," the Dragonfly said.

Tears blurred Noelle's vision as grief sliced open her heart. He couldn't be dead. This was a lie. A way to mess with her mind. It had to be. "I don't believe you."

He stared at her for a long moment, and then he reached into his cloak, pulling something out. Light from the oil lanterns glinted off a knife.

Noelle jerked her revolver from the holster at her back and aimed it at him, hands shaking. "What are you doing?"

"Did you know dragonflies kill fireflies?"

Noelle's finger flexed on the trigger. "I won't let you hurt my daughter."

He stepped forward with the knife.

Noelle slid her feet back. "Stop."

"It has to happen. It's in a dragonfly's nature."

He took another step, and then another, the cloak giving him the appearance of floating above the floor. He was closing the gap between them, and she couldn't let him past her. Not without knowing where Skyler was being held.

She shifted her stance, the gun aimed at his chest. "I said stop!"

He continued forward, and fear burned through Noelle's body like acid as she squeezed the trigger.

The crack of the gunshot echoed in the empty room, piercing her aching head like bullet shrapnel. She bent forward, hand pressed to her temple, and tried to breathe through the pain.

She forced her gaze toward the masked man. He sprawled on his back, blood leaking across the cement floor around him.

Nausea roiled in Noelle's stomach. Whether it was a result of the concussion or the knowledge that she'd shot another human being, she had to fight to keep down what was left of her dinner.

"Noelle!" Sally cried out.

"I'm all right." Noelle straightened and forced her shaky legs to cross the room. She kicked the knife away from the man's slack fingers and jumped back.

She needed to search him for the handcuff key, but everything in her rebelled at the thought. What if he was pretending to be unconscious, waiting for her to bend over him so he could grab her?

You don't have a choice.

Despite the chill in the room, beads of sweat slid down the back of her neck as she crouched. She reached toward his cloak with trembling fingers.

He let out a groan, and she snatched her hand back with a gasp. She watched him, waiting for him to lunge, but he only breathed, his stomach rising and falling unsteadily.

Leaning over him once more, she patted down the cloak until she found a pocket. She pulled out a stack of cards and set them aside. She watched the rhythm of his breathing for any sign of an impending attack as she dug deeper with her hand.

Her fingers touched cool metal. She snatched the key and all but flung herself away from the man.

"I found it. I found the key." She limped to Sally's cell and worked the key into the cuff. "Help me find my daughter."

Sally hesitated as she rubbed at her wrist. "I . . . I know I should, but . . ."

But she wanted to escape this place as soon as possible. Noelle could understand that.

Sally swallowed and seemed to gather her nerve. "Okay, I'll help you look for her, but we have to hurry because I'm not sure he's the only person we need to worry about."

"What does that mean?"

"I always thought he was talking to himself because I never saw anyone else, but what if . . . what if he wasn't?"

Noelle tensed at the possibility.

The basement door opened behind them, and Noelle whirled toward the new threat with her revolver, keeping herself in front of Sally. Shock rippled through her, followed by relief, when she recognized Brian, and she lowered her gun. He'd received her desperate text for help.

He angled his gun toward the floor as he scanned the area, his attention snagging briefly on the masked figure at the end of the hall, before landing on Noelle.

He raised his gun and aimed it at her. "Step away from her."

Noelle staggered back a step in confusion. "What?"

"Step away from her now."

Noelle looked back at Sally, who seemed paralyzed by fear. "This is Sally. She's not a threat. He had her locked up, and he has Skyler here somewhere. I . . . I shot him, but I didn't have a choice."

Brian didn't lower his gun or pull his attention from the two of them. "I don't know who's under that mask, and I don't know what she's told you, but that woman"—he tipped his head toward Sally—"is the arsonist."

CHAPTER Forty

Noelle backed away from the woman who, until a moment ago, she believed to be another victim of the Dragonfly. "Derek said the arsonist is a man."

"She's a master of disguises. Men, women, it doesn't matter," Brian said.

Sally shook her head. "I don't know what he's talking about. I've been locked in here since yesterday." She held out her wrist to show the red marks from her struggles against the handcuff.

"She was at the diner this evening. Disguised as an Amish man. She manipulated Trudy into letting her use her phone, and she sent a text to lure Derek into a trap."

Noelle's head spun. "No, that . . ." *Doesn't make sense. None of this makes sense.* She rubbed at her throbbing head, and the urge to vomit returned.

"I don't understand what's happening. I don't even know anyone named Derek," Sally said, looking between the two of them.

Brian stepped closer, the aim of his gun never wavering. "I had your fingerprints lifted from my wife's phone. It takes minutes to run a set of prints nowadays.

Imagine my surprise when the person my wife described was a man, but the results kicked back a woman."

Sally shook her head again. "Obviously, there's been a mistake."

"There are multiple sketches of the arsonist from multiple witnesses, and they all have one thing in common," Brian continued. "Your eyes. They're further apart than most people's. You can disguise yourself with makeup and wigs, and you can whisper to disguise your gender, but there's nothing you can do to change the spacing between your eyes, is there, Ethel?"

The woman stiffened.

Ethel? Noelle studied the supposed arsonist. When she first found her in the cell, all she could see was the top half of her face, and she knew her eyes looked familiar. It wasn't only because she'd seen her at the diner. It was because she'd seen her somewhere else.

"You were at my book signing," Noelle realized. But she hadn't been wearing makeup, her brown hair had been cut to chin-length, and she'd been thinner around the middle. "I autographed your book."

She remembered thinking the name Ethel seemed too old for the forty-something woman in front of her table. It was a name better suited to a woman born eighty years ago.

"I'm sorry, but I've never been to a book signing," the woman replied. "I'm not much for reading."

"Ethel has a record for stalking and assault," Brian said. "Now she'll be adding murder, arson, and kidnapping to her rap sheet."

"This . . . all of this . . . was you," Noelle said, still struggling to wrap her mind around how this innocent-looking person could be a murderer.

The wrinkles of confusion on the woman's forehead flattened, and the glare she sent Brian's way was sharp enough to draw blood. "You've ruined everything. You're not even supposed to be here!"

"You took my little girl? Set those fires? You k . . ." Tears of grief nearly strangled Noelle's voice. "You killed . . . Derek?"

Ethel's expression softened when she looked at Noelle. "He wasn't right for you, and you couldn't see it. He put his job before you. Derek Dempsey was never meant to be a part of your story."

A part of your story. Those words echoed back in time to one of the worst days of Noelle's life. Barely able to stand beneath the onslaught of rain and grief as her son's casket was lowered into the ground, an unfamiliar woman shared her umbrella and said, "He'll always be a part of your story."

Realization slapped Noelle so hard she stumbled back a step. "No, that's not possible."

"Noelle?" Brian said. "What's wrong?"

Noelle stared at Sally . . . or Ethel. Whoever she was. "You were at my son's funeral?"

"I was trying to comfort you. You were in so much pain. All I wanted . . . all I've wanted since we connected was to do what's best for you."

Brian blinked. "Her son died almost two years ago. You've been stalking her ever since?"

Ethel's face reddened. "I'm not a stalker! I've been looking out for her."

"For how long?"

"That's none of your business."

Noelle studied the woman's face as she searched her memories for other places and times she might've seen her. "The flower delivery man. With the seasonal allergies."

Ethel smiled. "I wanted to speak to you, and I wanted to apologize for not protecting you in the parking lot at the bookstore. You deserve better than to be treated that way."

That was what she was sorry for? Not for stalking, murder, or kidnapping?

"What did you do with Skyler?" Brian asked.

"I'm not telling *you* anything," she hissed.

Rage and fear whirled through Noelle, and before she knew what she was doing, she flung herself at Ethel. "Where is my daughter you psychotic—"

Brian caught her around the waist before she could bludgeon answers out of the woman with her fists, her gun, or whatever else she could get her hands on. "Stop, Noelle. We'll find her."

He pushed her back before releasing her, keeping himself between her and the target of her rage. Noelle shoved one hand through her hair and backed away to regain control of herself.

Skyler had been adapting to this brand-new life after a lifetime of trauma, and this . . . lunatic abducted her and tied her up in an abandoned asylum.

"If you've hurt my little girl . . ." Noelle bit off the threat, even though everything in her wanted to strangle the life out of the woman.

"There's only three floors. Let me call for backup, and then we'll search room by room," Brian said. He grabbed Ethel's arm and dragged her back to the pair of handcuffs dangling from the metal anchor on the wall. "You're staying right here."

A pained groan came from down the hall.

Noelle turned toward the masked figure still lying on the floor. Her chest tightened. She'd been so focused on Ethel that she'd forgotten about him. She rushed toward him and holstered her gun as she dropped to his side.

Her gaze caught on the cards she'd pulled from his pocket while searching for the key, and she cocked her head to read the familiar handwriting: "Did you know dragonflies kill fireflies?"

What?

She picked them up and flipped to the second one: "They locked me up in this place like I was one of those people with a broken mind." She flipped to the next one: "He tried to escape the flames, but he failed."

Shock rippled through her. Their entire conversation had been scripted. That explained the odd pauses when she asked or said something unexpected, and why his tone didn't match the words. They weren't *his* words.

She dropped the cards and grabbed the mask on the man's face, pulling it back. She wasn't sure who to expect—AJ, his father, a stranger.

"Zac?"

Tears leaked from his eyes, and his chest shuddered, as he tried to speak. "So . . . s-s-sorry. Sh-she . . . made . . . me."

There were burns around his mouth. Noelle had seen these types of burns before when she was researching how chloroform affected victims. It left chemical burns on skin.

She checked his wrists, finding ligature marks, and her heart sank. Ethel's story about being held captive was true in a sense, only she wasn't the captive. Zac was. No wonder Derek and Brian couldn't find him after he posted bail.

Her throat tightened at the thought of Derek, but she didn't have time to grieve for him now. She wadded up the edge of the cloak and pressed it to the wound below Zac's rib cage.

He let out an anguished moan. "Never would've . . . hurt . . . you. Tried to . . . warn you."

Was that why he kept showing up and insisting they talk? Did he know Ethel's plan from the start?

He tipped his head toward the ceiling again, like he had when they were talking before. "Skyler . . . upstairs."

She looked up. Her baby girl was somewhere above her, afraid and alone. But if she released pressure on Zac's wound, he might bleed out.

Noelle choked back a sob, but tears dripped from her chin anyway. Shooting him was legally justified, but he was a victim in all of this, and he was dying because of her.

She called back over her shoulder. "Brian!"

He jogged toward her. "The police and ambulance are on the way, and Ethel's restrained. What's up?"

"Skyler's upstairs. I need to go get her. But without pressure on this wound, he might bleed out before the ambulance even gets here."

Brian dropped to his knees beside her. "I've got him. Go."

She lifted her hands, and Brian placed his over the wadded-up cloak staunching the blood flow. Noelle got to her feet and, ignoring the pain still throbbing in her hips and knees, she ran for the staircase at the other end of the hall.

She stumbled to the top and sagged against the metal door. It gave way, and she all but spilled into the second-floor corridor.

The lantern she brought with her was the only source of light, and she squinted against the shadows. "Skyler!"

A muffled thud came from somewhere to her left, and Noelle limped past the closed rooms lining the hall.

"Skyler!"

Another series of soft thumps. Were they coming from the closet up ahead? Noelle reached it and grabbed the knob, ripping it open.

Skyler lay on the floor, her ankles bound together and her arms cuffed behind her back. Ethel had wrapped layers of duct tape around her head, focusing on her mouth to stifle her cries.

"Sky," Noelle gasped.

She set down the lantern and helped Skyler into a sitting position. She peeled up the edge of the duct tape and unwound it, wincing every time it snagged a strand of Skyler's hair.

"I'm so sorry, baby." She peeled it gently from her daughter's face, and Skyler began to cry, her small body quivering from the trauma she'd been through.

"She said I had to be quiet, that if I cried . . . my nose would get all stuffy, and . . . I would . . . suffocate."

Noelle cupped her face and brushed away her tears with her thumbs. "I'm so sorry, sweetheart." She released her face and untied the cloth from around her ankles. "Are you okay? Does anything hurt?"

Skyler sniffled. "I have to pee really bad."

"We'll work on a bathroom in a second." She retrieved the handcuff key from her jeans. "Let's get these handcuffs off you."

"You found the key in the bad lady's shoe?"

Noelle froze. "Her shoe?"

"Yeah, it fell out of her pocket, so she put it in her shoe."

Noelle's pulse jumped, and she mentally kicked herself. When she researched handcuffs for one of her books, she made a note that almost every set of handcuffs she looked at came with two keys—in case one was misplaced. She had Zac's key, which meant Ethel had a key to the cuffs restraining her.

Noelle pulled Skyler to her feet and grabbed her hand, dragging her toward the door at the top of the steps. She yanked open the door and drew in a breath to shout a warning to Brian, but gasoline fumes filled her lungs.

Oh God, please no.

The first floor was dark, every lantern extinguished, but the sound of fuel splashing from a container told her Ethel was free of her handcuffs. She was priming the building for a fire.

"Ethel." Noelle's voice wavered with fear as she descended the steps, one hand gripping Skyler's as she kept her close behind.

Ethel appeared in the doorway to the basement with a canister of gasoline in her hands, barely visible in the glow of the moonlight coming through the windows. "It was all for you. Please believe that."

Noelle reached the bottom and, terrified of what she might see, slid her gaze toward Zac and Brian at the end of the hall. Her breath caught. Two bodies lay sprawled on the floor, neither of them moving.

"Uncle Brian!" Skyler tried to slip past Noelle to get to him, but Noelle caught her and pulled her back.

"What did you do?" Noelle demanded.

"What I had to," Ethel replied. "He'll live for now. I tased him while he was distracted and then chloroformed him. He'll be out for about five minutes. Ten, if we're lucky. Plenty of time for us to slip away."

Noelle's arms tightened around her daughter. "Us?"

"You and me, of course. We'll have to walk a ways to reach my car. I couldn't park out in the open and risk the police coming to investigate a trespasser. That would've made a mess of things."

Noelle shook her head. "I'm not going anywhere with you."

"No isn't an option." She held up a Zippo lighter, and Noelle stiffened.

With all the gas fumes in the room, one spark would ignite the air. They would all burn, including Ethel. But the madness glittering in her eyes suggested she wouldn't mind dying along with them.

"Your little firefly isn't fireproof. Neither is the former deputy. Killing us all isn't the ending I had hoped for, but you know how stories go. You plan everything out and then suddenly there's a twist," Ethel explained. "Now, set your gun on the floor and come with me."

"If I come with you, they don't get hurt."

"I won't touch them."

Noelle withdrew her revolver from the holster and set it on the bottom step. It was useless now anyway. If she fired it, it would ignite the gas fumes as surely as the lighter.

Skyler dug her fingers into the loose fabric of Noelle's sweatshirt. "No, you can't go."

Noelle's heart broke as she untangled the small fingers from her shirt. "I have to, sweetheart."

"No," Skyler wailed, grabbing for her. "She'll take you away, and you won't come back

"I'll be okay. And so will you. I need you to go see if you can wake up Brian, okay? Give him a good shake. Can you do that for me?"

Face glistening with tears, Skyler nodded.

Noelle kissed her forehead. "I love you, my sweet girl."

Ethel grabbed Noelle's arm and dragged her toward the basement doorway. Noelle strained to see her daughter's beautiful face one last time before the metal door slammed shut.

CHAPTER Forty-one

Ethel poured gasoline down the steps behind them as they descended into the basement—insurance, should Brian wake too soon and try to follow them.

Noelle jerked against the deranged woman's grip. "Stop that! You're going to ignite the lanterns!"

The flaming lanterns lined the basement hallway, lighting their way to the exit.

"There's plenty of room between the lanterns and the fumes. I planned for every contingency, even the possibility that you *wouldn't* come alone." Ethel frowned at Noelle like she was a child who failed to measure up to her standards.

"Fumes travel, Ethel."

"Only about twelve feet." She set the half-full canister down at the bottom of the steps, and Noelle caught sight of a gun in the back waistband of her jeans. Had she taken Brian's gun?

"If you thought I might bring someone with me, why did you accuse Brian of ruining everything?"

"Because you were supposed to save me and your daughter, and that was supposed to be the end of it. But he had to reveal my identity and ruin the ending."

"The ending?"

"Of the story." She looked at Noelle like she expected her to understand her meaning.

"What are you talking about?"

"You've had such a difficult time these past few years, and writing has been hard. When you asked us, your readers, for ideas about what to write, I knew you were struggling. It was . . . fate that I overheard the legend of the Dragonfly here in Cherry Creek. I thought if I could convince Peter Ashton to finish what he started in the 1970s, you would have an amazing story to write about."

Noelle stumbled around one of the lanterns. "This was all about a story?"

"It was all about helping you, and a story was what you needed. Of course, I couldn't find Peter Ashton, so I had to improvise."

"You were underneath all of those disguises. You pretended to be Peter Ashton, all the way down to the tremor in his hands and the birthmark on his face."

Her eyes lit with delight. "Everyone believed he disappeared all those years ago, so it wasn't *unbelievable* that he might come back. I even painted a birthmark on my cheek and lightly covered it with makeup to make people think Peter Ashton was trying to hide it."

It had unfortunately worked.

"My mother was an actress and a makeup artist before she became a drama professor at a prestigious university. I learned so much from her. She told me I was a perfect template, with features not too feminine and not too masculine. She could paint my face and dress me up to fill any background role the production needed. I could be anyone, anywhere." The pride in her voice dimmed with vulnerability. "It was myself I couldn't seem to figure out. I've never really known how to be me."

So she pretended to be anyone and everyone else instead, characters she could study and disappear into. Except for the book signing. She came as herself—an awkward woman who projected discomfort in her own skin.

"If my mother had loved me enough to stick around, maybe I could've figured out who to be," Ethel said, and hurt softened her voice. "But when I was twelve, she decided to give one last theatrical performance with a rope around her neck and a second-story banister. I had to move in with my uncle. He tried to have me committed. Said there was something wrong in my head that made me obsessed with people. He only wanted me committed so he could weasel his way into the trust my mother left for me."

"I'm guessing that didn't work out for him."

A disconcerting smile thinned Ethel's lips. "He had an accidental overdose on the painkillers he purchased from a street dealer to keep him happy and high."

Noelle swallowed. Either Ethel helped her uncle overdose, or she found pleasure in his death. Both possibilities were terrifying. "Are you going to kill me too?"

Ethel cut her a sharp look as they walked down the hall. "His death was ruled an accident, and I would never hurt you. You and I, we're forever connected. When

I read your second book, *The Unseen Girl*, it spoke to me. It was like you saw me and reminded me that I have a purpose."

"What purpose?"

"You, silly. *You* are my purpose."

The bout of nausea that swept over Noelle had nothing to do with the constant pounding in her head. Ethel was so dangerously attached to her that this situation could only end in tragedy.

"I always loved reading screenplays as a child. That love expanded to books. It was no coincidence that the day I went to the bookstore to find something new, you were there doing a book signing for your seventh book. It was like fate brought us together," Ethel explained.

Her seventh book? That was . . . five years ago. Ethel had been lurking in the shadows of her life for five years.

"You can imagine how upset I was when you moved while I was out of town. I panicked when I couldn't find you. I had to get your new address from your parents."

"My parents would never have given out my . . ." The pieces clicked together in Noelle's mind. "You took the book I sent them four months ago. The first copy of *Stolen*."

"I thought about just snapping a picture of the return address when I snuck on to their porch, but the package was so distinctly book-shaped, I knew it must be your latest book. I needed it more than I've ever needed anything in my life."

Noelle's heart beat faster in her chest. This murderous woman had walked right up to the front porch of her parents' house and taken what was meant for them. She'd been close enough to Noelle's mom and dad to fire a bullet or light a match.

"Did you have anything to do with my son's death?" Noelle asked, nearly choking on the question.

"Of course not. That dimwitted girl was texting and driving. I saw Tay's ball roll into the road, and he went after it."

The warmth drained from Noelle's body. "You were there? You could've done something?"

"I . . . I was afraid. I didn't know how you would react to me. I-I wasn't ready to be seen."

"You let my little boy die, and then you kidnap my daughter. What is wrong with you?"

Ethel's mouth opened, and she floundered for a response. "We shouldn't . . . dwell on the past. The present is what's important, and right now we should focus on getting you somewhere quiet so you can work on writing this book. You'll want to leave out everything after the climax. You unmasked the Dragonfly and rescued the child. The end. You'll find a way to make it perfect. You always do."

"I am not writing a book about this."

Confusion creased the older woman's face. "After all the work I put into it, why ever not?"

"You call this *work*?"

"I researched, I sent out emails to anyone connected to the Dragonfly so I could make everything as authentic as possible. I had to curate the right makeup, hairpieces, and clothing for each character I played. It was no easy task."

"People are dead, Ethel!"

"*Bad* people. Nick Nelson was a rapist, and he was going to hurt that girl. I saved her. And Bridget Morrison was abusive. It was only a matter of time before she killed her husband. Besides, you said it yourself in your interview: sometimes characters have to die to propel the story forward."

"Characters, not flesh-and-blood human beings!" Noelle shouted.

Ethel lifted her chin. "I'm not sorry. This book is going to be epic, and I got to be a part of it. I'll admit that some parts didn't go as smoothly as I hoped. I had to take Nelson sooner than I planned because of the girl at the bar, and I was afraid the police would come looking for him, so I tried to hide his car. And that first fire was, well, I've never set anything on fire before. It was good practice, but I did almost send myself up in flames with that barn. But the next two were perfect. Of course, there were some attributes of Ashton's crimes that were too gruesome even for me. The victims I chose were terrible people, but still . . . I couldn't stomach sewing their mouths and eyes shut. I did try with that rapist, but it made me sick."

"But you could murder them. That didn't make you sick?"

"I never wanted to kill anyone. I couldn't even stay and watch them burn. As soon as I lit the flames, I had to leave. But it was worth it for you."

Outrage flooded Noelle. "I never would've asked you to hurt people."

"But you did ask. You asked your readers for help, but none of the ideas we offered up helped. You needed it to be personal, something you could feel and connect to. That's why I took your girl. That's why I dressed up in that ridiculous costume and appeared outside your house and outside your daughter's window. To inspire you."

Noelle tried to jerk her arm free. "You're insane."

Ethel jerked back, her fingers tightening. "Don't say that. I don't like that."

"You murdered the man I love," Noelle choked out.

They were almost to the exit Noelle had stumbled through earlier, when the metal door at the top of the steps squeaked open.

"Noelle?!" Brian shouted.

Ethel stopped and threw a furious glance over her shoulder. "Why couldn't he stay unconscious a little bit longer?"

She flicked the lighter in her hand, sparking the flame, and drew back her arm to toss it toward the gasoline canister.

"No!" Noelle lunged for the lighter and knocked it from her hand. It clanked on the floor and skidded across the tile.

Ethel reached for it, but Noelle slammed into her, sending her crashing face-first into the wall. Ethel cried out and clutched at her face, blood seeping between her fingers. Noelle snatched up the lighter and closed it, but it wasn't enough.

Ethel hurled one of the lanterns back toward the staircase, and the gas fumes in the air exploded into flames. They roared backward toward the gas canister and up the steps toward the first floor.

No . . .

Noelle threw herself toward the flames, determined to get to her daughter even though there was no safe way through. She had to save her.

Ethel dragged her away. "There was no other choice."

The gas canister exploded, sending liquid fire in every direction. Noelle staggered back, her ears ringing from the boom of the can exploding like a miniature bomb.

"You don't need them," Ethel was saying, her words muffled by the pounding in Noelle's head. "You have me, and we can—"

Noelle punched Ethel in the throat with every ounce of strength she had, cutting off the rest of her sentence.

Ethel's eyes widened, and she released Noelle's arm to clutch at her throat as she dropped to her knees, trying to breathe through her spasming windpipe.

Noelle staggered out of the exit doors and up the steps onto the grass. She collapsed to her hands and knees and heaved up her stomach.

The distant wail of an ambulance and honk of a fire truck brought her head up. Help was coming.

She wiped her mouth on her sleeve and wobbled to her feet. There had to be another way into the building. Another way to get her daughter out. She stumbled through the dense blackness to the front of the building.

She collided with the double doors, and a chain rattled. She found it with her fingers, following it through the door handles to a padlock.

"No," she whimpered.

She wrenched one of the handles anyway, to see how much slack the chain would offer, but the door was locked.

"God, please . . ."

"Mommy!"

Noelle followed the voice to a window high off the ground. Skyler stood on the inside, light from the creeping fire brightening the room around her.

Skyler pounded her hands against a wire mesh on the inside of the window, huge tears rolling down her smoke-stained cheeks. "Mommy!"

Noelle's heart squeezed in her chest. She pressed her hands to the window as she tried to find a latch or a way to lift it. There wasn't one. Even if there were, she wouldn't be able to get through the wire mesh.

Skyler drew her arm up to her face and coughed as smoke curled through the room.

Brian's voice called from inside, "On the floor, Sky. Stay . . . below the . . . smoke." His instructions were interspersed with coughs. Something slammed against the interior of the locked doors—once, twice, three times without success—and Brian let out a curse.

Skyler coughed again, and Noelle said, "I need you to do what Brian says, sweetie. On your belly. I will find a way to get you out."

"Okay." Skyler ducked out of view.

Brian appeared a second later. "The doors won't budge. I can't . . ." His gaze fixed on something over her shoulder, and his eyes widened.

A gunshot sent a jolt of panic through Noelle, and a bullet missed her by inches as it blew a hole through the window without shattering the glass. Brian dropped, and Noelle swallowed a scream. Was he hit?

"You were supposed to understand," Ethel said, her voice shaking.

Noelle turned to face the insane woman, pressing her back up against the building. "Ethel, I know you're upset, but—"

"You were supposed to see everything I did for you and understand." Ethel's breath hitched under the weight of her devastation. "My mother chose death over me. My uncle wanted money, not me. My dad left when I was a baby because he didn't want me. You . . . you were supposed to accept me. To love me. We're connected."

Twin beams of light appeared at the top of the hill near Noelle's car, the glow splashing over the building. Ethel turned, raising an arm to shield her eyes.

A silhouette stepped in front of the lights. "Police! Put down the gun."

Ethel let out a growling scream of fury. "Why is everyone ruining everything?!"

The silhouette stepped closer. "Ma'am, put the gun on the ground. I will not ask you again."

Ethel swung the gun away from Noelle and toward the officer. Gunshots erupted, and Noelle dropped to a crouch behind a bush, praying she wouldn't get hit by a stray bullet. Ethel's legs buckled, and she hit the ground.

The officer moved in. He kicked the gun beyond Ethel's reach and bent down to secure her with handcuffs. His gaze landed on Noelle, and he asked a question, but her mind was still reeling from watching a woman get shot.

"Ma'am," the officer said, his tone impatient. "Are you hurt?"

"Um . . . no, I'm . . . I'm okay. But my friend and daughter are in the building. I don't know how to get them out. She set the first floor on fire and the entrances are sealed."

"Fire department's already been alerted. They're on the way. Step back from the building and make room for them to do their work."

Reluctantly, Noelle backed away from the building. A fire truck arrived within the next two minutes, and they rushed the scene.

Noelle hugged herself as the firemen worked to rescue her loved ones. They seemed to move in slow motion, taking too long to breach the building and put out the growing flames.

Hurry. Please hurry, she wanted to shout.

She'd already lost Derek tonight. She wouldn't survive losing Skyler and Brian too.

When the firemen began pulling people from inside, her heart leaped with hope. Skyler jerked away from the fireman holding her and raced across the grass, coughing and crying with every breath.

"Mom." Skyler flung herself into Noelle's arms.

Noelle squeezed her tight and buried her face in her daughter's smoke-scented, corn-silk hair, breathing deep. She was all right.

Brian walked over to join them a few minutes later, his skin smeared with soot and his eyes watering.

Noelle reached up to grab his hand. "Are you all right?"

He nodded as he crouched. "Just a little smoke damage. Nothing permanent." He ran a loving hand over Skyler's hair before adding, "Our fire truck was one of the two engines at the barn fire. They broke away to come here."

Noelle couldn't fight back the fresh flood of tears. She was weary to her bones, and her heart couldn't withstand another assault. "Don't tell me. Please, I don't want to hear it from you too."

"Someone pulled Derek out of the burning barn before the engine arrived."

Noelle stared at him as she struggled to make sense of his statement. "S . . . so you're saying he's . . ."

"Alive. Derek is alive."

CHAPTER Forty-two

Noelle bent forward in the waiting room chair, the hospital tile blurring through her tears, and shoved her fingers into her hair.

Critical condition, the nurse had said.

Derek was clinging to life by a thread that could snap at any moment. Smoke inhalation, burns, chloroform toxicity—it was a miracle he had survived the trip to the hospital, let alone the past several hours of treatment.

If not for the courage of a stranger, he would've never made it out of the barn. The homeowners had gone out for their usual Friday night date, but the husband had forgotten his wallet. He saw the smoke when he turned back onto their road. He'd heard the news about the arsonist killing his victims in barns, and he knew that if he waited for the fire department to respond, it would be too late to save the victim inside his barn.

The homeowner saw a figure lying on the ground just inside the open barn door, and he put himself at risk to charge in and drag him out.

Now Derek's life was in God's hands.

Noelle squeezed her eyes shut and sent a desperate plea heavenward: *God, I know he's yours. I know he belongs to you, but please . . . let me borrow him for another seventy years. Please. Don't take him from me.*

Derek was the most amazing man she had ever met, and if she could have her way, they would spend the rest of their lives together—fixing their perpetually falling apart house, raising their daughter, giving her a brother or a sister, growing old together.

A small hand pressed between her shoulder blades, and Skyler's trembling voice asked, "Is Derek going to die?"

Noelle lifted her head and wiped at the tears saturating her face. *I don't know*, was the answer that hovered on her lips, but she couldn't say that. Not to her little girl.

"He can't die," Skyler said with a sniffle. "He's supposed to be my daddy. I prayed and everything."

Noelle pulled her into a hug. Through the lump of grief in her throat, she managed, "We have to have faith that he'll be okay. The doctors here are really good at what they do."

As she consoled her daughter, she took in the people around the room.

Trudy cradled her son in one arm as she spoke into her cell phone, no doubt filling her mother in on what was happening. Brian paced in front of the wall, tearing bites off a Snickers bar he didn't seem to be enjoying.

Deputies milled around the room, every face drawn with concern. Derek was their captain, a man who treated each and every one of them with respect and compassion.

Kara Grisham was on the verge of tears as she methodically chewed off her fingernails, and Angel Jimenez bounced her leg, fists clenched at her sides, like she was a rocket on the verge of launching into the air.

"Can I go outside so I can pray really loud without bothering everybody?" Skyler asked. "I want to make sure God hears me."

Noelle released her and leaned back, brushing the sticky strands of hair from her daughter's tear-stained face. "God will hear you, honey, even if you only pray in your heart. You don't have to shout."

"I like my way better."

The last thing Noelle wanted to do was let Skyler out of her sight, but the danger had passed, and she couldn't deny this request. "Okay, but I'll be watching from inside the doors."

Skyler reached out and took Noelle's hand as they left the waiting room and turned toward the emergency room entrance. Noelle walked Skyler through the first set of doors and let her pass through the second set into the night on her own.

Before the double doors closed, Skyler looked up at the sky and shouted, "God? It's Skyler again!"

Noelle hugged herself and leaned against the wall while Skyler gestured with her hands and prayed, putting more passion into her conversation with God than most adults ever did. She was talking to the air in front of her like God was standing right there.

More familiar faces flowed through the first set of doors into the room where Noelle stood—church members.

Pastor Jim, a gentle man with thinning hair, approached her. "How are you holding up?"

Her voice cracked as she admitted, "It's been a really rough day."

"What can I do?"

She shrugged. What could any of them do?

He touched her arm to offer comfort. "We're going to find a quiet room to pray as a congregation." He continued into the hospital, and other members of the church followed after him.

She watched the last of them disappear before turning her attention back to the darkness outside. She wished her parents were here, but it would be hours before their flight even landed. She wanted her mom to tell her everything would be all right, for her dad to wrap her up in his arms like he did when she was a child.

The doors slid open, and Skyler came back inside. "Derek's going to be okay."

Noelle touched the top of her head. "I hope so too, honey."

"I don't *hope* he'll be okay. I *know* he will. God told me so."

Her daughter's explanation surprised her. "God told you Derek will be okay?"

Skyler nodded and pointed to the spot on the sidewalk where she'd focused her prayer. "I was talking to Him right there. You didn't see Him?"

Noelle stared at the empty patch of sidewalk. She hadn't seen anyone standing there but Skyler.

"I'm hungry. Can I have quarters for the snack machine?" Skyler held out her hand. "It has cheese crackers."

"Sure." Noelle rummaged through her purse for change and placed what she could find in Skyler's hand. "Go ahead. I'll be right there."

She stared at the sidewalk where God had supposedly stood and had a conversation with her daughter while she looked on. Skyler had a wonderful imagination, but she had never spoken to imaginary people. For that habit to start at the age of eleven would be unprecedented.

Derek's going to be okay. God told me so.

Skyler had spoken those words with absolute confidence, and as Noelle reflected on them, she felt a sense of certainty and calm this crisis didn't warrant.

This wasn't a case of a child's imagination. This was God communicating with one of His little ones who had more faith than a roomful of adult Christians.

Noelle closed her eyes in relief.

Derek was going to be all right.

Chapter Forty-three

Noelle watched the steady zigzag of Derek's heartbeat on the monitor as she sat in the uncomfortable hospital chair.

He had drifted in and out of consciousness the past two days, but the doctors were confident he would recover with little more than a handful of burn scars to serve as conversation starters.

She could've lost him. All because some disturbed woman thought she knew what was best for Noelle's life.

Ethel Thatcher had a history worthy of a crime documentary—insecurities and imbalances that evolved into identity issues and mental illness, which spiraled into stalking and acts of violence. Her uncle may not have had altruistic intentions when he tried to have her committed, but he had reason to be concerned.

As awful as it was to admit, Noelle was grateful the woman was dead. She tried to kill three people Noelle cared about. Knowing that she was no longer a threat to her loved ones offered Noelle a small measure of peace.

Derek groaned and peeled open his eyes. He blinked at her beneath heavy eyelids. "Hey."

She shifted in the chair to angle her body toward the bed. "Hey, handsome."

"Have you been here all night?"

"I didn't want to go home and risk you flirting with other women while you're doped up and irresistibly adorable."

He gave her a groggy smile. "I'm not doped up enough to do something like that."

"My mother would disagree with you."

Her words took a moment to connect, and an expression of concerned horror crossed his face. "Are you saying I hit on your mother?"

"Mm hmm, but in a very sweet way. It's been a long time since a man told her she's the most beautiful woman he's ever seen. She was flattered. Dad . . . not so much."

He groaned and pushed his head back into the pillow. "That's mortifying." He squinted, like he wasn't sure that was actually a word.

Noelle patted his shoulder. "It was an easy mistake. You were stoned on morphine, and she and I look a lot alike."

"Well, if you were ever worried whether or not I'll still think you're gorgeous in twenty-five years, now you know."

"You think my father will let you live another twenty-five years after you hit on his wife?" she teased.

He laughed, but it deteriorated into a coughing fit, and he struggled to recapture his breath. "I at least . . . deserve a chance . . . to redeem myself."

"The first impression has been made. You'll just have to own it, because no one will ever forget it. But you can try to reintroduce yourself this evening when they bring Skyler by to visit."

Knuckles tapped on the hospital room door, and Noelle twisted in her chair to see Brian and a vaguely familiar deputy with salt-and-pepper hair.

Brian sauntered over to Derek's hospital bed. "Wow, brother, you look like crap."

"We finally have something in common," Derek rasped.

"Half dead and still cracking jokes. Well done."

"Like me."

Brian snorted, and Derek let out a wheeze of laughter that turned into another coughing fit. Noelle rolled her eyes at their fire victim humor and turned her gaze to the deputy. "You're . . . Rusty?"

He removed his hat and dipped his head in greeting. "Yes, ma'am. I'm one of a handful of deputies working this case." He held out a container of chocolate muffins. "Carol asked me to pass these along to you and Captain Dempsey."

Noelle accepted the muffins, though she had no idea who Carol was. "Please tell her thank you for us."

"I'll tell her when I see her this evening."

Brian grinned. "About time you two got together."

Rusty cleared his throat, uncomfortable with the commentary on his love life. "I wanted to come by and fill you both in on my interview with Zac Inman."

Noelle tensed at the name, and Derek moved his bandaged hand closer to hers on the mattress. What she wouldn't give to be able to hold that hand right now. "I haven't heard much on his condition."

The man unsettled her, but the last thing she needed was his death weighing on her conscience.

"Doctors said he'll pull through, but he'll be in the hospital for a while," Rusty explained. "He's handcuffed to the bed railing, so you don't need to worry about him wandering down the hall to bother either of you."

"Did he ask for a lawyer?" Derek asked.

"Strangely no," Rusty said. "The only person he asked for was Noelle. He only wanted to speak with her."

"I told him that wasn't an option," Brian added.

Derek tried to blink away the drug-induced tiredness pulling at his eyelids. "You were there for the interview?"

"I caught him in the hallway on the way to Zac's room and asked to stand in on the interview. I hung back to observe for most of it."

Rusty cast Derek an uncertain look. "I know Brian's not formally with the department anymore, but I thought he might have some insight."

"It's fine, Russ. I trust Brian to keep any information in-house. How much of this mess was Zac involved in?"

"He claims he wasn't involved until after he was released from jail. He received an email he believed was from Noelle, requesting to meet somewhere private to talk."

Noelle's eyebrows pinched. "I didn't send him an email."

"Ethel Thatcher did, and when he arrived at the secluded meeting place, she tased and chloroformed him. He's got the physical marks from the taser barbs and the burns on his face from the chloroform to back up his story. He woke up bound and gagged in a trunk."

"Ethel originally planned to make him one of the fire victims," Brian said. "Even though he doesn't have any documented crimes like the first two victims, she witnessed the book signing incident, and she was present when the police arrived at the diner after the parking lot incident."

"He wronged Noelle," Derek said.

"But then she realized, in order to bring this story she was building full circle, the villain needed to die," Noelle said. "So she forced him to take her place in the mask and cloak."

"How did she ensure his cooperation?" Derek asked.

"She threatened to kill his mother," Brian said. "After meeting that woman, I'm surprised he didn't thank Ethel for her generous offer and walk away."

Regardless of how the woman treated her son, the parent-child connection was a strong one. Zac would've grown up thinking however she treated him was normal.

Rusty bobbed his head in confirmation. "She also threatened *his* life. She used those threats to force him to abduct and transport Captain Dempsey to the next barn."

Derek grunted. "Not surprising. I doubt Ethel could move me if she tried. I'm a lot bigger than the first two victims."

"He admits to tying you up and setting the fire, but he left some slack in the ropes and opened the barn door. He hoped that by doing so, you would be able to save yourself while he still followed Ethel's instructions," Rusty explained.

He would've had every reason to believe Ethel would kill his mother if he refused to obey. She had already murdered two people.

"And then he came back to the asylum to greet me," Noelle said. By that time, Ethel was inside the building, where she slipped into her role as Sally the victim. "I know that Zac was trying to warn me about Ethel's plans when he approached me outside the bookstore and in the diner parking lot, but if he wasn't involved until after he was abducted, how did he even know about her plan?"

"Chatbee," Brian said. "Some of your readers set up a chatroom on the platform, discussing possible ideas they would like to see you write about in future books. One reader, who went by the username Forever Mine NE, made some disconcerting suggestions, and the administrator of the group removed her. Zac thought the ideas were interesting, so he reached out in a private message, but when Forever Mine's hypothetical scenarios began to sound like literal plans, plans that involved murder and kidnapping, that's when Zac realized he needed to warn you."

"Why not send me an email warning me of the danger instead of stalking me?" Noelle asked. "Or better yet, contact the police about a possible threat?"

"After talking with the man, it's clear his brain is not on the same wavelength as everyone else's," Rusty replied. "He was trying to do what he believed to be the right thing by warning you at the book signing, but things didn't go the way he expected."

Noelle rubbed at her right temple. "The message I received after he was released from jail, the one telling me bad things were going to happen because I didn't listen to him, was that him or Ethel?"

"That was Zac. He was upset that you had him arrested," Brian said. "Shortly after that, he received the email from Ethel. She used bits of the conversation you had with him in the bookstore parking lot to convince him she was you. He was all too happy to meet you somewhere alone to talk."

Noelle shuddered inwardly. "What's going to happen with him? I understand that he's technically another one of Ethel's victims, but I'm not comfortable with him being free."

"What happens to him is up to the justice system," Rusty said. "But I think he needs to be evaluated by a psychiatrist. He's socially awkward to the point that it's dysfunctional, he tends to fixate on people and things, he has a structured daily routine with very little variation, and he doesn't express himself well."

Noelle frowned. "What does that mean?"

"I'm not a doctor, but I have a grandson who's at the higher end of the autism spectrum, and I've seen a lot of those things in him. He even fixates on certain subjects. He could tell you the names, locations, and characteristics of every breed of deer on the planet. Zac fixates on authors, and he admits that he keeps a 'log of information' on his favorites."

Noelle shifted uncomfortably in her chair at the thought of him piecing together all that personal information.

"I know it's disturbing, but I didn't get the impression that his motivation was sexual or possessive in nature. He's simply fascinated by authors, and the binders he keeps are his way of trying to understand, categorize, and connect, which is something autism makes difficult," Rusty said.

"So he's not stalking me."

Brian shook his head. "His mother said he almost never leaves the house. Coming to see you was a break from his usual routine, and it was because he realized people were going to die if he didn't."

"The deputy monitoring the jail said Zac spent the entire night rocking in the corner of the cell," Rusty said. "I suspect he's never been away from his own bed at night."

Noelle felt a twinge of regret at the fear and anxiety the man must've felt. Autism would explain a lot of Zac's abnormal behaviors. He genuinely had no idea how to interact appropriately, and he missed every social cue.

"If he was that traumatized, who bailed him out of jail?" Noelle asked. "I doubt he would've had the presence of mind."

Rusty and Brian exchanged a glance before Rusty said, "Ethel Thatcher. She arranged for his release. She pieced together who he was from their private conversation on Chatbee, and Zac said she was concerned he would tell everyone her plans. She needed to keep him quiet."

"So she abducted him and threatened him into compliance." Noelle wrapped her fingers around the pendant at her chest. "So what happens with him now?"

"Depending on the judge, he may take your opinion into account. I don't want to pressure you one way or the other, but I know if it were my grandson, I would want someone to show him mercy," Rusty said. "I think Zac Inman can be helped, especially if he's removed from the emotionally abusive environment he's in."

Noelle would need to have a deeper discussion with Derek, but she suspected he would want to help this abused and confused man in spite of everything he had done.

"Ethel's dead, Zac is in custody. Hopefully that means the village can finish out the year in peace," Rusty said.

"I don't know about peace. That woman dredged up stories about the Dragonfly, and since no one knows what happened to him, I expect there will be a lot of questions and anxiety for a while," Brian added.

Noelle glanced at Derek, who had slipped back into his medicated sleep sometime during the conversation, then said, "Actually, I might know what happened to the Dragonfly."

Epilogue

SIX WEEKS LATER

Noelle peeled the pictures from the whiteboard in her writing room and scrubbed away the dry erase notes that had sat there so long they stained the board.

Ethel was right about one thing—the mystery of the Dragonfly was a story worth telling. The son of a pastor who became a serial killer, only to disappear and fade into legend.

Except he didn't truly disappear.

Peter Ashton was murdered.

Allen Conroy Senior was obsessed with tracking down the man who murdered his father, so much so that he neglected his son to follow leads. It took him twenty years to find his father's killer. How he managed to track down a man living like a ghost would be an interesting mystery to unravel. She intended to interview Conroy for those details.

Distrustful of the legal system that had twice failed to dispense justice, Conroy dragged Peter Ashton back to

Cherry Creek in secret. He buried him beneath the shed in the side yard of his family home, where his body would never be discovered.

After murdering his father's killer, Conroy left Cherry Creek and his life behind. Noelle could only imagine how adrift the man felt once he achieved the goal he spent over half his life pursuing. And he no doubt felt haunted by the fact that he had taken a human life.

When Conroy learned that barn fires and murders had started up in Cherry Creek again, he dropped everything to come home. His comment in the diner about making a mistake he couldn't undo stemmed from the fear that he might've murdered the wrong man twenty five years earlier—an *innocent* man.

He asked for details about the ongoing investigation, hoping for peace of mind. When he didn't get it, he visited the crime scenes with the goal of piecing the information together on his own. He was arrested for trespassing on the third crime scene and taken in for questioning. Twenty-five years of guilt, and the fear that he'd killed an innocent man, loosened Conroy's tongue in the interview room.

Deputies unearthed the body and, after examination, confirmed the remains to be those of Peter Ashton.

AJ had at least suspected his father killed Peter Ashton, because he tried way too hard to deflect attention from it by spreading rumors about the Dragonfly still being alive. He told everyone he could, sparking panic in the village.

Those rumors got a teenage boy killed. Unfortunately, there was no legal recourse for AJ's actions.

With the whiteboard cleared, Noelle could start her investigation into the original Dragonfly murders—a story devoid of Ethel and her copycat crimes. Excitement zipped through her at the prospect of digging into a new book.

"Anyone home?" Derek called out, his voice rising up from the first floor.

Noelle set aside the stack of papers in her hands and padded downstairs in her flamingo slippers to find him standing in the foyer. "Hey, handsome."

"I'm not sure you can still call me that."

She kissed his cheek. "It's still a true statement."

She didn't mind the burn scars that spider-webbed bits of his hands and forearms, and even the side of his neck. He survived the fire, and that was what mattered to her.

"It did kind of throw me off when you only had one eyebrow, though. I'm glad that grew back. And your beard's not singed crooked anymore," she teased.

"Not to be argumentative, but I had one and a half eyebrows. That half counts."

"Okay, I'll give you that."

He smiled. "You seem extra happy today."

"I suppose I am. There's a certain exhilaration and relief that comes with knowing what you're going to write about. Like a weight lifted."

"Well, I'm afraid I have some weight to replace that with."

Concern crept in. "Is everything okay?"

"I think Skyler should be here for this."

Noelle searched his face for any indication as to what this might be about, but expression gave away nothing. "It's not bad news, is it?"

"No, it's not bad news, but it is important."

"Okay. I'll go get her."

Noelle strode through the house to the kitchen and opened the back door. December had transformed her backyard into a winter wonderland of snowdrifts and icicles ornaments.

Skyler was bundled up against the cold, but the pink flush in her cheeks was visible from the kitchen doorway. She patted a clump of snow into the bottom of what would soon be a snowman and then looked to Walt for his opinion.

"Should've put that on the other side. Now his butt's crooked," he informed her.

"Sky, honey," Noelle called out. "Derek's here."

Skyler sucked in such a deep breath that she probably inhaled half-a-dozen snowflakes. "Is it time?"

Noelle cocked her head curiously. "Time for what?"

Skyler slapped two mitten-clad hands over her mouth, her eyes wide. Slowly, she lowered her hands and said, "Uh . . . I can't tell you. I made a promise. Pinky and everything."

Now she was *really* curious.

Skyler hopped through the snow toward the house. Her boots left clumps of mushy wetness across the porch, and she kicked them off before coming inside. She rushed up to Derek and whispered too loudly, "I almost spilled the peas."

"I think you mean 'beans'," Derek corrected.

Skyler scrunched her face in disgust. "I hate beans. I would be happy if I spilled those. But I would be a little sad if I spilled the peas."

"I can't argue with that logic."

"Someone going to tell me what's going on?" Noelle asked, looking between the two of them.

Derek reached into his pocket, and Noelle's heart skipped when he pulled out a black velvet box. Was that . . . what she thought it was? He dropped to one knee, answering her unspoken question.

But they hadn't even talked about marriage.

"Noelle McKenzie, you are one of the most interesting, intelligent, and beautiful women I have ever met," Derek said. "You make me laugh with your bizarre author antics, and you never cease to amaze me with your heart. The way you open it to people around you and make them a part of your family."

"Like me," Skyler chimed in. "And Mr. Walt. We can't forget Mr. Walt."

"Don't drag me into this embarrassing ritual," Walt muttered from the kitchen doorway.

Noelle rolled her lips between her teeth, torn between laughter and tears.

"Every day, I wake up and thank God that He brought you across the country to this little village," Derek continued. "I'm grateful that you purchased this house on a whim, because it's what connected us. I knew the very night we met that you were someone special. I didn't know how yet, but I knew you were." He swallowed at the emotion rising in his voice. "Six weeks ago, I thought I would never see you again, and I am . . . eternally grateful that God gave me this opportunity to do what I should've done months ago."

Noelle reminded herself to breathe as anticipation swelled in her chest.

"I would love to come home to you every day for the rest of my life. I would love to help you fix up this perpetual project of a shack until I'm too old to hold a hammer." Derek opened the velvet box and held it up. "Noelle McKenzie, will you be my wife?"

Tears of joy spilled onto her cheeks, and she wiped them away. "What could a girl possibly say after such a heartfelt proposal?"

"I'm hoping for a yes, though I'm willing to accept less enthusiastic responses like *sure* and *maybe*."

Noelle wiped away another tear as she laughed. "I told you I wouldn't do that." She held out her hand. "Yes, I will be your wife."

Derek released a trembling breath, as if he'd been holding onto the fear that she might say no. He slipped the ring onto her finger and kissed her knuckles.

"Wow," Skyler breathed, mesmerized by the way the stones sparkled in the light. "It's so pretty."

The inset pink stones were perfect, and Noelle couldn't have chosen a more beautiful piece.

She expected Derek to rise so she could kiss him, but he smiled and pulled a plastic-wrapped, blue ring pop from his pocket.

He held it up and cleared his throat. "Skyler Jones McKenzie."

Skyler pulled her eyes away from Noelle's engagement ring and gasped when she saw the ring pop.

"Will you be my daughter?"

She nodded, mouth still hanging open in awe, and held out her hand the same way she'd seen Noelle offer hers.

Derek unwrapped the ring and slipped it onto her pinky.

Skyler stared at her candy ring, uncharacteristically still and quiet. And then she whispered, "I have a daddy." When she looked up, tears shimmered in her eyes. "I . . . have a daddy." As the reality of that statement sank in, she leaped into Derek's arms and cried with joy, "I have a daddy!"

Noelle's heart melted into a puddle in her chest, and she sank to her knees beside them. She hadn't realized she could love Derek more than she had when he walked through the door, but this moment proved her wrong. This beautiful, unforgettable moment . . . with her family.

AUTHOR NOTE

The Cherry Creek Mysteries are set in Ohio. Cherry Creek is modeled after the village where I spent most of my childhood. I had a great deal of fun changing the names of surrounding cities and towns, tweaking them just enough that locals would still recognize them and laugh at the difference.

Since Cherry Creek was inspired by my hometown, there are quite a few similarities. I have a vague recollection of a dine-in restaurant that went out of business in the center of town. That was the inspiration for Trudy's Diner. Of course, Trudy brings her own style and warmth.

We did have a Developmental Center at the edge of town, which some people simply called the "asylum." To my knowledge, it was a pleasant facility. The occasional rumor about hauntings came after it closed down. A few people even tried to break in to look for ghosts. The asylum in Dragonfly Ashes, however, is both spooky and alive with mystery.

The park, local store, and the bar are also inspired by my hometown, though the bar and store are no longer there. My hometown has gone through many changes over the years, but I preserved little pieces here and there in the Cherry Creek Mysteries.

Noelle lives in a house no more than five minutes down the road from the man she eventually falls in love with. While that detail is convenient for the story, that's not the reason I chose to place them so close together. My husband and I grew up on the same road in our real-life version of Cherry Creek, less than a mile apart. On several occasions, he drove past me when I was out walking. We never paid much attention to each other until God brought us together in our twenties. That's an interesting story, but I'll save it for another time.

Our hometown was a relatively peaceful place. I only remember a few times when crime touched our small community. One of those times was a string of suspicious barn fires later identified as arson. That was the inspiration for the crime in Dragonfly Ashes. From there, the story grew and twisted to become something new.

I'm fascinated by the idea of myths and legends—curious things we're taught to believe that have little to no foundation in reality. Such as dragonflies weighing souls and stitching up eyes. Peter Ashton was mad enough to not just believe those myths, but to bring them to life. It would've been interesting to write a story solely focused on his crimes and capture, but he was only the origin of this story.

One of my favorite moments in this book is when the characters realize Zac is living with undiagnosed autism. I have three family members with autism, so it's an issue that's close to my heart. It's such a broad spectrum that not everyone exhibits the same behaviors or degree of behaviors, and I've seen this lead to incorrect assumptions, social discomfort, and misunderstandings—all things that happen with Zac in this story. In the end, the characters realize he was never a villain; he was simply responding to the world in a way that was normal for him, and he deserved grace.

Dragonfly Ashes was a complicated story to weave, and there was no shortage of stress-eating involved—seriously, someone hide the boxes of crackers next time—but it all came together in the end.

I hope you all enjoyed revisiting Cherry Creek and the wonderful people who live there! And as always, thank you for plucking my novel out of an ocean of options and taking the time to read it. I appreciate each and every one of you!

ABOUT THE AUTHOR

C.C. Warrens lives in a small town in Ohio. She enjoys painting, sketching, and writing, with the occasional foray into baking. Writing has always been a heartfelt passion, and she has learned that the best way to write a book is to go for a walk with her husband. That is where the characters—from their odd personalities to the things that make them bubble over with anger—come to life.

HOW TO CONNECT

Facebook: facebook.com/ccwarrens/
Instagram: @c.c._warrens
Website: ccwarrens.com
Email: cc@ccwarrensbooks.com

www.ingramcontent.com/pod-product-compliance
Lightning Source LLC
LaVergne TN
LVHW041307220425
809289LV00007B/152

9781959349044